THE
ONE TO
BLAME

BOOKS BY S.E. LYNES

Mother
The Pact
The Proposal
Valentina
The Women
The Lies We Hide
Can You See Her?
The Housewarming

THE
ONE TO
BLAME

S. E. LYNES

bookouture

Published by Bookouture in 2021

An imprint of Storyfire Ltd.
Carmelite House
50 Victoria Embankment
London EC4Y 0DZ

www.bookouture.com

ISBN: 978-1-80019-521-9
eBook ISBN: 978-1-80019-520-2

For Dr Sara Bailey, aka Sally Miller – my first ever writing tutor, mentor and friend

PART ONE

CHAPTER 1

Isla

January 2005

In my hands is a black-and-white photograph of my sister and me as kids. I remember this picture being taken so vividly. We were in the back garden of our parents' wee white house in our wee white town on the edge of Loch Fyne. Inveraray. West coast of Scotland. Our dresses are home-made, floral, real *Sound of Music* curtain jobs. My mother didn't make them out of actual curtains, I don't think. She probably made them from one of her old dresses, some sixties creation – she was always making new clothes from old, making repairs, making do. This will have been '73, '74. Annie was about eight, myself about three. I was still a younger sister then. I was still a sister.

I look out over her garden, cleared now of the black wreckage beyond the apple tree. The last time I saw my sister was here, almost two years ago now. The apples were still hard and small, the wasps still feisty, the days long and warm. I always loved coming to her cottage – the change of pace, the air, the sea. Four months have passed since I got that terrible call, and part of me still finds it impossible to believe I will never see her again. The fire, what came after the fire, the reality of my sister's life, her death – the truth has fallen in slow rain. Even now, I know I have yet to turn my face to its last acid drops.

My eyes return, can't help but return, to the photograph. It's our chubby knees that make my eyes prick – legs locked with the effort of standing nicely for my dad's Kodak Brownie. Photos were a rare thing, to be stuck into the album with tiny white adhesive corners that would yellow over time, lose their glue and fall off. Our entire family history contained in one battered cardboard book.

We will have had to brush our hair. Will have put on those dresses especially for this moment. Come out into the garden where it's light. It was probably someone's birthday.

'Stand nicely,' Dad will have said, arranging us in front of the best flower bed, heels sinking into the damp grass as he backed away. 'That's it.' Raising the camera to his face, remembering his glasses, pushing them onto his head before pressing his eye to the viewfinder once again. 'After three,' he'll have said. 'And one, two, three… say cheese.'

'Cheeeeeese.'

One shot. Don't want to waste the film. We wouldn't have thought for one second about what we looked like. Wouldn't have seen the image for another year, maybe two, once the film was full and had been taken to Boots to be developed.

The dog-eared photo quivers in my hand. How short, how uneven, how adorable are the fringes of our practical bobs, chopped by my mother with the kitchen scissors. Saying cheese, holding hands, we are thrilled with ourselves. We are marvellous, we are smart. My sister's knuckles are white – a tight grip. Five years older, she was proud, overprotective. She was also bonkers. I say it with love, but Lord, she was a case right enough.

Back then, Annie was the boss of me. If she'd told me to put my hand in the fire, I would have, no bother. It would be another eight years before our roles began to switch, before I became the elder, in a sense; not that I knew it was happening, not then. The change was slow, but I think now it began the night she crept down the creaking wooden steps of our bunk bed, shook me by the shoulder and whispered my name.

'Isla.'

I blinked awake, startled at the white-nightdress ghost, calmed when I realised it was her: solid, alive, bent almost double. She was crying.

'Annie?' I whispered, nerves rising. 'What's the matter?'

'I think I'm pregnant.'

'Pregnant? Like with a baby? How?'

'I got carried away,' she wept into her hands.

Carried away. In my mind bloomed the image of her netted inside a drawstring sack slung over the shoulder of a bony hunch-backed thief who looked exactly like the Child Catcher from *Chitty Chitty Bang Bang*. I didn't say any of this of course. I was rising to the gravity of the occasion.

'Who with?' It was the most grown-up question I could think of.

She let out a quiet howl, like our dog when Mum played hymns on the piano. 'His name was Malcolm.'

'Malcolm what?'

'I don't know.' She burst into fresh tears. 'He was through from Glasgow. What am I going to do? I'm still at school.'

She was not quite sixteen. That means she was fifteen obviously. To protect ourselves, I suppose, we never said it like that, even years later. The shock of it is stronger now in retrospect, with hindsight's understanding of the implications. Getting pregnant at that age in that place with those parents would define her whole life and, I can't help but think – today of all days – her death. But I was ten and she was fifteen, both of us far too young to grasp all that, though the enormity of what she was telling me is something I am still able to feel bodily – that strange heat: part dread, part exhilaration.

'It'll be all right,' I said, solemn as a judge. 'I'll help you.'

But neither of us knew what help meant. Even when I made my trip to the mobile library that week and scanned a book on reproduction hidden behind the pages of the world atlas – arms shaking with the effort of holding the weight of both because I could not take a book about sex home, could not even think about our parents finding it hidden in our shared room – still I could not figure out the information I needed to help her. I thought I'd heard something about hot baths, but I had no idea where or who from. Weeks later, desperate, Annie asked me to steal vodka from my best friend Rhona's house (our parents didn't keep alcohol at home). I did it. Shaking with the sin, I did it, for my big sister. I was the hero of the story, the angel, the avenger – me, Isla Andrews: hold my coat, I'm going in. Only I had to tell Rhona the secret because I needed her help. Together we emptied the vodka into a soup flask I'd brought from home. We had to top up the bottle with mineral water because the tap water in our town was a wee bit brown owing to it coming from the hills.

The next night, our parents asleep, I sat on the bathroom floor while my sister climbed weeping into a scalding bath, neat vodka in a mug with her name in pink calligraphy on the side –the words *gracious* and *merciful* beneath, which is what all lassies called Annie are supposed be, according to that mug.

She raised it to her lips but lowered it almost immediately.

'I can't,' she wept. 'I just can't do it.'

She was so distraught, I had to help her up to her bunk and stroke her hair while she fell asleep. In the morning, she still didn't feel well. I think she'd upset herself so badly she'd given herself a poorly tummy and a headache. With the solemnity I was still trying on like a cape, I told my parents she had a stomach bug. They were busy with a stocktake and didn't pay much attention. They never fussed us when we were ill – a glass of water by the bedside, a day-long fast, a boiled egg and soldiers in the evening if you were up to it. Temperatures were taken with a hand against a forehead. To this day, I've never had an antibiotic.

And so the bump got bigger. Annie wore loose clothes – big sweatshirts, jeans unbuttoned at the waist. Rhona had crossed her heart and hoped to die, but she must've told just one other person, who promised to take it to their grave, and that one person told maybe two others in absolute confidence, who in turn swore they were tombs, absolute tombs, but who told maybe four more, but it didn't come from them, all right? That's how it is with secrets: they dilute. Your own is the strongest possible concentration, someone else's already weaker, and so on until the secret is water running as freely through the village as from a burst main. And then everyone knew, and someone told my mother – low whispers over the counter of our gift shop, dark clouds gathering overhead.

Growing up, there'd always been terrible scenes between my sister and my parents. She was always disappointing them or cheeking them or doing too much on a Sunday or giggling in church or staying out later than she was allowed or being seen with a boy at the one dismal bus shelter or, later, giddy on one too many ciders down at The George. It doesn't take a psychologist to see that I grew up to be cautious because Annie was always so bloody reckless. It was me quaking on the pew every Sunday – for her sins, not mine; her who took no notice of the fire or the brimstone; me who was 'a good wee girl'; her who was 'trouble'. That cape I had been trying on for years fitted, became comfortable, impossible to take off. I was the counterbalance for my beautiful, wild, impetuous sister, whose refusal to be contained turned out to be the very sealing of her containment.

But the night she told our parents, there was no terrible scene. No raised voices, no slammed doors, no cries of:

I hate you!
Mind your tone, young lady!
I can't wait to leave this place!

Well, we'll be putting you out in the morning, so off you go and pack a bag…

From the hallway, the only sound, beneath the high intermittent sobs from our mother, in tones so low and calm I could only just hear with one ear pressed against the living-room door, was my father's voice: 'You've made your bed now, right enough. You're going to have to lie in it.'

They didn't send her away like that other lassie whose name I forget but who we never saw again. Instead, over the weeks and months that followed, Dad cleared out the storage space above the shop and had a bathroom and a small kitchen put in. This astonished me, because from the way we lived, I'd always assumed we were poor. And in all of this, my sister: walking down High Street with people staring at her as if she'd been stripped naked and paraded before the eyes of the entire town. *Shame. Shame on you. We know what you've been doing. Slut. Slattern.* It's hard to believe people still thought like that in 1981, but they did – some still do. Meanwhile, Malcolm, whoever and wherever he was, continued his life exactly as before. Even now, especially now, when I think of what she went through so young, I feel the burn of injustice on her behalf. But she bore it in silence, head tipped ever so slightly back, refusing absolutely to bow in any kind of gesture of penance. She toughed it out.

And then came my nephew, my tiny, raven-haired, pale-skinned Callum, lilac thumbprints under his eyes, mouth like a miniature rose. He looked, apparently, just like his father.

'I want you to be his guardian,' Annie said to me the day he was born. We were in the cottage hospital after a labour so quick he almost landed on the floor of the shop. In the bed, Annie looked peely-wally. I stood guard between her and the wooden crib where her brand-new boy slept with his fists raised above his head. Our parents had softened by then. Callum had thawed them simply by turning up.

'I've told Mum and Dad I'm an atheist,' Annie said – I can still remember the scandalised thrill that coursed through me. 'They'll have him christened all the same, you can bet on that. They'll make me go for the sake of their reputation, and sure enough, I'll go. But they don't get to say what goes on in here.' She jabbed her forehead hard with her forefinger, her nose and eyes wrinkled up tight. 'So this arrangement would be between us. You would be Callum's official guardian. I'll write it down on a piece of paper and we can both sign it and then it will be a legal document, OK?'

On the woollen blanket, her warm, dry hands wrapped themselves around mine. Filled with the kind of seriousness that follows a huge bestowing of faith, I gave a grave nod. I had no idea what she was asking of me, only that it was big and that I was the only person in the world who could do it.

'Yes,' I said, but then blew it by asking her what a guardian was.

'It's the person who'll look after Callum if anything ever happens to me.'

Heart quickening, I searched her face. 'Why? Is something going to happen to you?'

She laughed; her near-white blonde hair fell across her face. 'Of course not, you wee daftie! Nothing's going to happen to me. It's just… in *case*. If I, y'know, die or something.'

'You're not going to die, are you?'

'No! No, no, no! It's for, you know, when we're grown up. If I died, you'd be Callum's mummy. But I won't die obviously. Promise.'

What promises we made. Promises we couldn't keep, as it turned out.

Annie was devoted to Callum. But I soon saw how she'd changed. How she *was* changed. She was… diminished. I wish I'd been older. I wish I could've protected her from the judgemental stares, the whispers and the lack of support I didn't have the experience to perceive as such. My parents were scared, I see that now. Naïve themselves, they believed absolutely they were doing what was right, teaching her to be responsible and to take the consequences of her actions. They were ignorant of how she might have continued to educate herself with a small child in tow. She did educate herself, in a way, continuing to read voraciously, and to paint the landscape of our homeland as a way of surviving, particularly once Callum started school. But in those early years, I would go to her flat after I'd finished my homework and hang out with her and my shiny new nephew. I'd take Cal for walks and show him off to those who had been so damning but who had knitted cardigans and blankets for him and dropped them off at the shop. I would see their cold eyes warm at the sight of my nephew, with his shock of black hair, his green eyes, his wee rosebud mouth.

'We'll bring him up together,' I promised her, all through my teenage years. 'We'll run the shop when Ma and Pa retire and we'll live next door to one another. I'll have children too and we'll be Auntie Annie and Auntie Isla.'

More promises broken.

But this photograph was taken before all that, at a time when we saw the world only as a place to stand in frocks made from old bits of fabric, a simple place, a safe place, in shades of black and white. I slide it into our father's old wallet, which I kept back from our parents' things. Their funeral was the second-to-last time I saw Annie. I took her pallor for grief, her weight loss for a life running a business and running round after Cal. I know differently now. I know I failed her. I know I should have been more vigilant. I know I should have watched over her better.

I know I should get a move on and get dressed – I can't afford to be late.

Callum goes on trial today.

CHAPTER 2

Isla

Four months earlier: September 2004

I'm drunk when I get the call. Later, I'll feel guilty about this as well as all the rest. There's a world of guilt waiting for me, but I don't know that yet. I'm living another life entirely right now: my own. And, cautious as I am, even *I* don't live my life as a constant precaution against disaster. Even *I* don't say, *Actually, I won't have another drink in case I get a call that will put an end to everything I know.*

And later, in my darker moments, I will remind myself that Annie wouldn't have wanted me to live that way. No matter how little I saw of her these last few years, we always wanted the absolute best for one another, would have hated the idea of the other one suffering.

As for me, there I am: the quintessential single thirty-something. My life in London is… good. Area manager for Habitat – I love design, love my staff, love my job. A house in Clapham, which I bought using my savings plus my share of our inheritance. And Patrick is a great tenant – kind, tidy and a lot of fun. And if I'm drunk on a Wednesday night, it's only because, in retail, Saturday is whatever day you've taken off in lieu of the Saturday you worked. This week it happens to be a Thursday, which makes Wednesday my Friday night, if you follow. Patrick and I have been at the Edge in Soho for a post-work just-the-one that has turned into a just-the-five, as it often does. My lips have gone numb, and when I move my head, I have to close my eyes and wait for my brain to catch up. So yes, drunk. Drunk is what I am.

The cab drops us outside my house in Englewood Road, just off Clapham Common. We stagger in, giggling. It's one in the morning. In the living room, the phone is ringing.

'Phone's ringing,' I say. Like that. *Phone's ringing.* Like it's nothing.

But the moment I hear Cal's voice, I sober right up.

'Auntie Isla? Is that you?'

'Cal? Is everything all right?'

Patrick is staring at me – *What?* I shrug and shake my head – *I don't know.*

'There's been...' He breaks into sobs.

'Cal? Cal, hon, can you talk? It's OK, love. Just... just take a breath. Where are you?'

'I'm at Mum's...' Another gut-wrenching sob. 'Oh God.' A gasp. Silence.

'Cal.' I slide down the wall; my bottom hits the hall carpet. 'It's OK. It's OK, darlin'. I'm right here. Just... take your time. Take your time, OK?' My heart has started to thud. I close my eyes, desperate for him to recover himself and tell me what the hell is going on. I don't ask if it's Annie. It doesn't occur to me that anything could have happened to Annie.

'It's... I'm... It's... There's been a fire.'

'A fire? Oh my God. Where? In the house? Are you OK? Is everyone OK?' Still I don't think of Annie.

'Not in the house.'

'Oh, thank God.'

'No! No. They're... they're dead.'

'Dead? Who's dead?' I glance up, but Patrick is no longer there. From the kitchen, I hear a tap running. I feel sick. I'm going to be sick.

'There was a fire. I... I tried to... but...'

'Cal? Just stop a second. You're not making sense. There's been a fire? In the house? Can you put your mum on?'

'The fire wasn't... Mum and Dominic were in the... Mum's... She's dead, oh God, oh my God.' A terrible wail; my throat blocks.

Patrick is standing over me, holding out a glass of water. I take it from him and drink. Cold water runs down my gullet. The woodchip on the wall blurs.

'That can't be...' My body fills with heat; a strange prickling sensation covers my skin. 'She can't be... She... Are you sure? Have you called 999?'

'I tried to get to her, but... I called the fire brigade, but I couldn't get to them. I couldn't get to them.'

'Get to them? Get where? Where, love? Can you tell me?'

'Her studio. They were in her studio. It just went up. They've put it out now. There's an ambulance. I tried to... but I...'

I am constructing what has happened from pieces. Down the line, sirens grow louder.

'I think that's the police,' he says.

'Cal? I'm coming, OK? Just... hold on. I'm on my way.'

The sirens stop. Another second, and I realise they haven't stopped. Cal has ended the call.

'Cal?'

'Babe?' Patrick is staring at me. 'What's happened?'

'That was my nephew. He's saying there's been a fire. He's saying my sister's... He's saying he thinks she's dead. He's saying she and Dominic are dead.'

CHAPTER 3

Isla

Sitting on my living-room floor, half a glass of water in my hand, do I get anywhere near believing my sister might be dead? That Dominic has died too? Am I even remembering right? Did Cal say it like that or have I forced the jigsaw pieces together and got the wrong picture? Bewildered and sobering up fast, do I know Dominic and Annie were in her studio and that somehow it caught fire?

It's possible I get that far. Just as it's possible it's no more than a cloudy feeling held at bay, the knowledge and what it means not yet solid.

Later, I lie in bed, my body held in tension from head to toe. Night trails shadows across my bedroom ceiling. Patrick has come into my room. He spoons against me while I wait wide-eyed until a coral dawn creeps up the bedroom window. It won't be as bad as Cal said. He was hysterical. They wouldn't send an ambulance if Annie and Dominic were already dead. The fire had been put out when he called, so it can't have been too major. The police were on their way. I'll get the earliest train. We'll go to the hospital – Southampton, I should imagine that's where they'll have taken her and Dom. Cal needs me. He needs support.

Eight a.m. at Waterloo. I flip open my Motorola. Seven missed calls from the cottage – four from last night, three from early this morning when I must have been on the Northern Line. Flushing hot, I return the phone to my bag. Best to board the train before calling back. I don't have a mobile number for Cal, and Annie doesn't have one at all.

I hate the idea of folk being able to get hold of me every minute, I hear her say. *It's so oppressive.*

My belly aches. The slick sheen of a hangover coats my skin. Last night, he must have been desperate, and where was I? And when he finally got through to me, I told him it would be OK. It isn't, of course it isn't. That was a reflex, the instinct to protect him. I still think of him as a child, even though he is twenty-two, maybe because he was only twelve when he and Annie left Inveraray, maybe because the heart-wrenching sight of him crying and waving out of the back window of Dominic's big posh car is forever branded in my memory. Or maybe because he's always had a childlike sensitivity that put him at odds with a world so much harder than him – just like his mother, my sister. My Annie.

On the train, I find an empty seat, throw my coat on the overhead rack and sit down. I take out my phone and place it on the table.

There's been a fire. They're...

Please, God, let Cal have spoken in panic. Please, God, let them have survived. God, if you're listening, I will trade everything, everything I own – I will shave my hair, I will cut off a limb. Just let Annie be alive.

Last summer, Cal came to stay with me after finishing uni. His mop of black hair was bigger, floppier than ever; that hint of lilac still smudged beneath his eyes, his skin still pale as a vampire's. A young man figuring himself out. I took a week off, took him to all the galleries, the museums, knowing that was what Annie would want me to do. He'd grown up a lot. We talked about art, about literature, films, television, favourite actors, his plans to move to London once he'd saved some money. He was trying on a smoking habit – Marlboro Lights. I didn't remark on it, keen to let him have his youthful rebellion in peace. But I did laugh at him when I took him for a picnic on Clapham Common and he asked if I wanted to share a joint.

Oh God, I hope he was jumping to conclusions last night. I hope Annie hasn't been scarred. And God? If one of them has to be dead, please let it be Dominic.

My face burns. What a dreadful thought. I am a terrible, terrible person.

A stunning black woman with her hair tied in a turquoise and pink scarf sits down opposite me and smiles. I try to smile back but have to look away. An image of Annie bandaged up in a hospital bed flashes, her beautiful face disfigured. I close my eyes. My head falls back against the strange upholstery of the headrest. A memory: Cal, aged no more than seven, standing on a chair; me teaching him how to use the pricing gun in our parents' gift shop. Last night he called me as a child calls a grown-up – in the desperate hope they can put everything right. There's been a fire. My nephew is alive. My sister and her husband are feared dead. I am the only person who would drop everything and run to him.

I call the cottage. At the sound of the ringtone, I straighten in my seat. When Annie answers, I almost shout for joy until, with a pressing feeling on my chest, I realise it is the answering machine:

'*Hi, you've reached Annie Rawles at Purbeck Cottage Holiday Rentals. I'm not here at the moment, but please leave your name and number…*'

I end the call and grip my knees. Tears drop onto the backs of my hands. I have no tissues. I am not prepared. I am not prepared for any of this. 'Oh God. Oh God, oh God.'

'Are you OK?' My fellow passenger is looking at me with concern.

'Sorry. Just some bad news.'

She searches in her bag and pulls out a packet of Kleenex. 'Here,' she says. 'Take the pack.'

'Thank you.' I meet her eyes, see kindness. 'Thank you so much.'

I head for the corridor, unsteady in the swaying motion of the train. The window is open. A cool rush of air chills my wet face. On the outskirts of the station, pollution coats the bricks black. I dial again. Brace myself for my sister's voice. I want to listen to her over and over. I cannot bear to hear her speak.

'... *please leave your name and number after the beep and I'll call you back as soon as I can.*'

'It's me. If you get this, I get into Wareham at one fifteen. If you're not there, I'll jump on a bus. Don't worry about me; I can find my own way. Just hang on, OK? I'll see you at the cottage. I'll be there as soon as I can.'

At Wareham station, I spot Cal immediately. He is standing with a short blonde woman in loose dungarees who, when I wave, grips him by the elbow and points at me.

Together they walk towards me, their faces grim. Dread fills me. There are no fragile smiles, no sign that the situation is not as bad as I think. Cal is taller, thinner too, and as he gets nearer, I see that his eyes are hooded, the lilac smudges almost purple, his hair longer, pushed back off his face. He looks like Annie.

'You came,' I manage.

He pulls me into a hug. It is the embrace of a man, with a man's breadth and strength. His neck smells of Imperial Leather soap. Annie always bought it, told me once it reminded her of our parents' home, to which I replied that that made no sense, since she'd always been so desperate to get out of there.

We break apart. I smile a watery apology to the woman. Her hair is quiffed up, shaved at the sides, her skin etched with fine wrinkles.

'This is Daisy,' Cal says. 'Mum's best friend.'

'Hi.' I raise my hand and we lock eyes, hers large and pale blue, framed by eyelashes clumped into wet spikes. Brightly coloured feather earrings dangle from her lobes. She's a Spanish teacher at Swanage Comprehensive – that's all I know. *You'd love her,* Annie told me once. *She did modern languages too! You guys can speak Spanish together!*

Not today.

'I'm so sorry.' She wipes at her face with blunt square fingers. 'We're all devastated. It's terrible, just unbelievable.'

'So…' I search their eyes. Annie has regained consciousness. She inhaled a lot of smoke, but she's alive. She and Dominic are recuperating in hospital; that's where we're going to go now, to visit. They'll have to have skin grafts, but…

Cal is shaking his head too. He is crying.

'So she's definitely… they're definitely…'

We stare at each other, mute and frozen in our triangle of shock.

Cal digs a handkerchief from his jeans pocket and wipes his eyes and nose. 'We've just come from the morgue.'

I gulp down this bitter information. My sister lies white and cold in a metal drawer, her beautiful hair a golden halo. Would they have tied it up, I wonder, or let it loose around her shoulders? Dominic – short but handsome, his expressive hands, his crisply laundered polo shirts, his hoarse, high-pitched chuckle – still and silent on a slab.

Yesterday they were alive. Now they are not.

'Can I see her?'

Callum pinches the bridge of his nose. A moment passes before I realise what I've said, how stupid I've been to say it. There's been a fire. My sister is not laid out like a princess under glass. Her hair is not a golden halo, her beautiful face…

'It was just personal effects,' he manages.

'Oh, Cal. Oh, darling.'

Another burst of grief shakes through him. I take him into my arms.

'My poor lamb,' I whisper. 'My poor wee lamb.'

I have no idea how I am able to do this. I am older than him, that is all. Protecting him is all that's protecting me.

'I can't believe it,' he sobs into my shoulder. 'I can't believe this has happened. It's a nightmare, an absolute nightmare.'

'Let's get you home.'

'We're in my car,' Daisy says quietly, turning away. 'Come on.'

On Daisy's insistence, Cal and I sit in the back. I hold his hand. Perhaps to save us from the silence of our shock, Daisy talks. A cop called her late last night; she came over to the cottage and sat with Cal while the police combed the scene. Jan, a family friend, came at first light. They've been awake all night.

I don't ask Daisy if she's had to leave her own kids or her husband at home. I don't ask her anything at all about herself. Mainly I have questions for Cal, but I don't know what they are. Flames rise and lick at my sister's cabin, filled with tubes of paint, with brushes stacked in handle-less mugs, in jars half filled with turps, sometimes with vegetable oil, her easel displaying her latest landscape, seascape, sunset, sunrise, storm, blue sky, mist over a hamlet, over a cliffside, the iconic silhouette of Corfe Castle. Steam rises from the blackened ruins of her beloved workspace. Red fruit dots the apple tree. Fields roll away beyond the garden fence, to the horizon, the sea. So many times I have stood at that fence with Annie, both of us warming our hands on coffee mugs, standing there to get a moment's peace, though it's a few years since we've done that. I see a half-collapsed black shack, two sets of feet poking neatly from the wreckage. That is how my mind censors my horror: a childish image, stolen from *The Wizard of Oz*.

Daisy pulls onto the gravel drive. The thatch is cut at right angles around the leaded windows, a thick, heavy fringe above the Purbeck stone. *Rainbow Cottage*, reads the oval sign beside the red front door. A police car and van are parked on the driveway. A policewoman is standing on the front step. She is watching us, pretending not to. On either side of the drive, green rose bushes, red roses. Annie loved roses. She loved anything that grew.

We approach the cottage. I put my arm around Cal's waist, but a couple of metres shy of the door, he stops, making me stop too. Daisy is further on, saying hello to the cop, now stepping inside.

'They were fighting,' he says in a voice so low I barely hear him. 'Do you know what about?'

'No, I…' He stares at the ground. 'It's not that. I… They were *fighting* fighting. Physical fighting, I mean. Dominic was… You don't know what he was like. Mum didn't want you to know. But… he hit her. He used to hit her.'

CHAPTER 4

Annie

May 1991

'Come on, slowcoach.' Annie waits, hands on hips, for her wee sister to catch up.

They have been climbing since a little after 8.30 a.m. Finally, Isla reaches her and claps her on the shoulder, gasping for breath and swearing like a navvy.

'Look,' Annie says, gesturing towards the South Glen Shiel ridge behind them.

Isla consults the map. 'This is Bealach am Lapain,' she says. 'The next climb is Sgurr nan Spainteach; that's the first of the peaks.'

They sip water, still full from the bacon rolls at the hotel, and continue on. The sky is almost black, yet a sticky heat soaks their T-shirts, slicks their hair to their heads. Scottish weather: if you don't like it, wait five minutes.

They pass the hours chattering in the long, breathless flow that has been their soundtrack since Isla was old enough to speak. Annie hangs on Isla's stories of her year abroad in Seville, her funny anecdotes of teaching English in a sixth-form college, the spectacle of the street in Semana Santa.

'Semana Santa,' Annie says. 'That's... week something. Saint week?'

'Holy Week, yeah, right, so next thing there's all these folk in the street in cone-shaped headdresses carrying flaming torches. I nearly freaked. I thought they were the bloody Ku Klux Klan!' Isla laughs, though she barely has breath enough on the steep rise, her silly student smoking habit catching up with her.

'That sounds *amazing*.' Annie's awe is tainted with an envy she hates herself for feeling. How she would've loved to have seen it, smelt the garlic on the air, eaten tapas sitting on a high stool in some bar with sawdust on the floor, drunk *vino tinto*, walked through narrow streets filled with the unintelligible bubbling of a language in which Isla is now fluent enough to tell jokes while she, Annie, is stuck at home with her stupid *Spanish for Beginners* tapes. Every time Isla returns, she brings bigger tales to tell with her new-found articulacy – bilingual now – and, of course, her increasingly sophisticated opinions.

'Are you still doing the Linguaphone thing?' she asks now, as if she has picked up on Annie's thoughts, which no doubt she has.

'*Mi tia es muy ricca y me gustan los perros.*'

'Your auntie is very rich and you like dogs? You should get by on that no bother.'

They take frequent breaks – all for Isla, who insists she's quit smoking – drink water and nibble at oatcakes and dried fruit, and admire the vast expanse of a landscape they've been meaning to lay eyes on for most of their conscious lives: the Five Sisters of Kintail.

According to the old story told to them at bedtime by their father, the five human sisters were originally seven. The youngest two fell in love with two Irish princes who were washed ashore one night during a terrible storm. But the girls' father would only allow them to marry once their older sisters had also been married, and so the princes agreed to send their remaining five brothers back to Scotland once they had returned to Ireland with their new wives. When the promised princes failed to appear, the five sisters continued to wait.

'They waited and they waited and they waited,' their father would finish, Annie and Isla by now breathing slowly, deeply. 'And eventually they turned… into mountains.'

After their dad returned downstairs, Isla would often creep up the creaky ladder into Annie's bunk, and they'd lie awake, huddled close, scared of the wind that whistled across Loch Fyne, made the sashes shudder in their ancient frames. They would imagine themselves to be those two younger sisters, carried away by Irish princes.

'One day we will return to the mountains,' a solemn ten-year-old Annie would tell her wee sister, then but five or six. 'And when they realise we're their long-lost sisters, they'll come back to life and we'll have a party and live happily ever after.'

'Do you really think that?'

'I know it.' Annie would squeeze her sister tight, feeling important and old.

'But how will they know it's us?' Isla never stopped asking questions, which could be tedious at times.

'Look, I know things. Like I know that a white feather means an angel has visited you, and I know there's a lady living under the loch, and I know that when we get to the top of the Five Sisters, the hills will know us.'

Twenty-one and not so gullible these days, Isla is on a reading break from uni. Annie is twenty-six, mother to a ten-year-old son and still working in their parents' gift shop. Both too old for fairy tales, but here they are, finally fulfilling a childhood promise. Seven hours in, the weather has held all day, but now Annie can feel oncoming rain – in the closing of the air, the switch from May's hazy warmth to a distinctly autumnal chill.

'My legs are jelly,' Isla moans from further down the slope. 'I literally can't walk another step.'

'Well, I'll no' be carrying you, so you're going to have to.' Annie waits, holding out her hand.

'This is Sgurr nan Saighead.' Isla pretends to consult the map, panting. 'After this, it's downhill all the way to Shiel Bridge.'

'There you go. You'll soon be tucking into your venison with a blackcurrant coulis.'

Last night, they studied the menu before they studied the map, which Isla had brought, announcing smugly that she'd known Annie would forget, before insisting on going through every single peak until Annie was ready to scratch off her skin with the boredom – Isla went into such *detail* about everything.

Not so high and mighty now, her kid sister looks shattered. Annie is glad of her regular sketching trips around the loch, up into the hillsides around Inveraray. Trapped she may be, but she has learnt to take her freedom where she can find it.

They are just shy of the summit when Annie's feeling is confirmed by a sudden sheeting downpour. Shrieking, they dig out their jackets, all but run the last ten metres to the top, holding their hoods down over their faces, giggling with relief and exhilaration at reaching the final peak. After a minute or two, the rain softens a little.

Annie cups her hands around her mouth.

'Hello, sisters,' she calls into the air. 'We're here.'

Isla looks about, throws out her hands in mock indignation. 'Nothing. After all that. It's because we didn't bring the princes.'

'Well, we'll have to see if we can find some on the way down.' Annie grins, expecting Isla to shoot something back, but instead Isla's eyes widen, tendrils of chestnut hair waving over her pink face.

Annie follows her gaze. On the right of the ridge, forty or so deer are sheltering from the rain. A little apart from the herd and only a few metres away, a huge stag eyes them with disconcerting frankness.

'Wow.' Annie meets his bald, unblinking stare, feeling a connection she knows she cannot voice to Isla, who would tell her she's nuts. What a shame it's too wet to take out her camera. She'd love to sketch this guy, if only from a photo.

'That stag's giving me evils,' Isla says.

'Och, he won't do anything. It's the mothers you have to watch. Come on, we're getting soaked.'

In the dogged rain, they pick a path down through the bracken until, as if to reward them, the land opens itself around flat blue water.

'Ah, would you look at that,' says Isla, her mood visibly lifting. 'That'll be Loch Duich. We're not far at all now. If we keep going, we'll easy catch the shuttle bus.'

All tiredness in her limbs forgotten, Annie sets off running down the steep rise but almost immediately loses her footing on a slippery wet rock.

A moment later, Isla is crouching in front of her giving her a look. 'What the hell were you thinking? It's bloody treacherous underfoot; you could've really hurt yourself and we're miles from anywhere.' She closes her eyes a second, appears to compose herself. 'Are you all right?'

'I'm fine.' Annie tries to stand, her pride dependent now on getting back on two feet, though from the pain in her ankle, she... 'Ouch! Bugger!' She meets her sister's eye, expecting her to be furious, but instead Isla's gaze is soft, and she half stands, lowering her shoulder.

'Here,' she says. 'Put your arm around me.'

At the bottom, near the snack shack, fellow walkers sit around on cagoules, waiting for the shuttle bus: six teenage boys, four older women, and three men she estimates to be in their early thirties. The men are wearing all the labels – expensive hiking boots, gaiters. A pile of sliced fruit loaf in foil at their feet, they pass a silver flask between them, steam curling from the top. They are chatting and laughing with the easy intimacy that comes after a long and arduous day in the hills. As Annie limps past, one of the men, whose dark hair is pushed back with Ray-Ban sunglasses, looks up and meets her gaze as boldly as the stag.

'Have you hurt yourself?' he asks – his accent is English.

'Just a wee sprain.'

'Sit down.' One of the others is already on his feet. 'Let's have a look.'

Annie glances at Isla, who nods and says she'll grab some snacks.

'It's OK. Gavin's a GP.' It is the first one, the English one, who has spoken.

Annie throws her jacket onto the grass and sits. The GP chap – Gavin – helps her off with her boot and takes her foot in his hand.

'It's probably smelly, sorry,' Annie says.

He doesn't laugh. He is concentrating, hasn't heard her. After a few questions – his accent is soft, East Coast – and a gentle waggle of her foot, he takes a bandage from his rucksack.

'Och, there's no need for that,' she says, embarrassed.

'It's not a sprain, but you've strained it,' he replies, already binding her ankle. 'I'll put this on for now, but you should keep it up high once you get home, or to wherever you're staying.'

'Where *are* you staying?' the English one says, eyebrows raised.

'The Cluanie Inn.'

'What a coincidence, so are we. In which case, we should introduce ourselves properly.' He grins, claps his pal on the shoulder. 'This handsome brute with the first aid kit is Dr Gavin Stark, an old Edinburgh Uni friend and today's expert Munro guide. The other chap over there, looking sheepish and snaffling the rest of our cake, is my friend from home, Thomas Bartlett.' He places his hand flat to his chest; his ring finger is bare, she tries not to notice. 'And I'm Dominic. Dominic Rawles.'

CHAPTER 5

Isla

September 2004

Cal's hand is warm against my back. My own hands push against my knees. The gravel driveway comes in and out of focus. I should stand up straight. I should be the one comforting him. He's lost his mother and stepfather and I'm all the family he has. But the information he's just given me is only seconds old and my body cannot yet find anywhere to put it. My Annie. Married to a man who hit her. It's not possible.

'Bastard,' I whisper. 'Bastard.'

'I'm sorry. Let's go inside.'

He leads me to the cottage as if I am lame: arm around my shoulders, gripping me tight.

The policewoman nods a sombre hello as we step inside. Immediately, I see the tape across the stairwell. I wonder what I am stepping into. What is solid is no longer solid; the air has the quality of a dream. I have come here without thinking further than this moment, my mind blank to all but Cal's call, to my sister and her husband, flames, the visceral pull to just get here, to find that she is still alive. Half an hour ago, the worst had happened, but now it's *worse* than the worst and I must absorb it. Annie is the person I have loved since I was able to feel. She and Cal are my only blood. But even in my denial, I did not consider what lay beneath. I did not consider abuse.

I have no idea what happens next. Questions are fog; I can't form them.

More tape blocks off the hall where it leads down to the back door. We step into the living room, where yet more tape flickers on the other side of the French windows. There are two people in hooded papery jumpsuits in the back garden. An older, hippy-ish looking woman I don't recognise is sitting on the sofa. She looks up and says hello, her sleek silver bob catching a shaft of sunlight. Dust motes drift, glitter.

'You must be Isla,' she says, her eyes pale grey but warm. She is near seventy, I think.

'Hi,' I say.

'I'm Jan. I'm so very sorry for your loss.' She presses a screwed-up tissue to her eyes and sniffs deeply.

'Thank you.' I try and fail to prevent my gaze from straying out to the garden. The apples are ripe. The thought strikes me as bizarre even in the moment. Beyond the tree, what remains of my sister's studio – once a charming chalet painted duck-egg blue, now a charred black wreck. Part of the back wall is still standing. Among the fallen fruit, glass glints in the green grass. On the floor of the cabin, the hint of black debris: tins, boxes, what looks like a wine bottle, the whole surrounded by more police tape, which extends towards the back door to the right by the garage. Small plastic flags flicker in the ground. The chemical smell hits me. The living-room window is open an inch, its leaded catch a black curlicue against the white frame. We should close it. I can't bear this smell. But it would be stuffy in here with so many of us; the fact that it is warm and sunny only occurs to me then.

'We're not allowed to go through that door for the moment,' Jan says. 'We're not allowed upstairs or anywhere they've taped.

They've dusted everywhere for prints but we have to let them do their job.'

'How do you...' I begin, returning my gaze to Jan. 'How did you know my...'

'Used to look after Cal before he grew up. I suppose you'd call me a close family friend.'

It occurs to me that Jan knows my nephew better than I do. It's possible she knows my sister better than I do. Knew.

I lower myself onto the sofa beside her. 'I meant to come this summer. But I was in New York with my flatmate. Then last Christmas I was working all the hours, you know? We were trying to get a date in...'

I edge further back onto the cushion. Dimly, I am aware of Cal stalking about, the creak of the armchair as he sits down, the heavy huff of his breath.

Daisy enters the small crimson room carrying a tray loaded with a china teapot, mismatched cups and saucers. Everything, every detail, is Annie. Every colour, every cup and saucer, this worn-thin Persian rug, these second-hand gold shot-silk curtains twitching in the breeze, the dresser she won at a house clearance auction and stripped, stained and varnished single-handedly, this gloriously dilapidated, ridiculously comfortable bottle-green velvet sofa, and of course, her paintings on the walls – Chapman's Pool, the castle, sunset over Swanage Bay.

'We're allowed in the kitchen now.' Daisy puts the tray down on the coffee table. The crockery shivers and clinks. 'They said they'll soon be finished in the house.'

'Where's Dom?' I almost say, my sister's impossible absence making me forget momentarily that my brother-in-law too is dead. With a jolt of rage, I remember. Dominic hit her. Bastard. If he weren't dead, I'd kill him myself.

But he has killed her is the thought that lands, that should have landed minutes ago. Of course. He hit her; she tried to defend herself, something got knocked over, caught light. The flames rose, smoke overcame them. Is that what happened?

Too much, too much. It's not possible. If he'd ever hit her, I would know. She would have told me. But then, in less than twenty-four hours, what is impossible has become possible. It's possible my brother-in-law hit my sister, and it's possible he's responsible for both their deaths; that by the time the fire took hold, they were unable to crawl to safety. And here I am expecting him to come in, dressed in a crisp pastel polo shirt, tragic stone-wash jeans and poncey wee boating shoes, to clap his hands and rub them together and ask in his slightly husky, mischievous voice how we're all doing and who's having a drink *'cause I know I am!*

Daisy pours the tea, the trickle as loud as a bath running. Cal's hands press against his face. His nails are bitten to the quick. Daisy hands out biscuits, tells us we should get some sugar down us, Dorset soft in her vowels. She is the last to sit down, on the other armchair, eyeing us all with an expression I can't fathom. Caution, perhaps. This is not her tragedy, not her family. But she is my sister's best friend – in this moment she is more family than I am. To my growing shame, I am the outsider here.

'Were the police here all night?' I ask.

Cal nods.

'We stayed in here,' Daisy said. 'You have to let them do their work, don't you? Jan came over this morning, and then I went with Cal and Ross to the morgue.' She falters. 'They said we should get the house back by this evening. Sorry, I said that, didn't I? I suppose the main... the... is the garden obviously.'

Crime scene is what she can't say.

The air fills with the chink of cups against saucers. The bitter smell of burning lines my nostrils, catches in my throat. I want it out.

There's a knock on the living-room door. A man of about fifty, in a suit and tie, is leaning in. He is tall, his chin dark with stubble, his hair a greying brown cuff around the bottom half of his head.

'Ross.' Daisy gestures towards me. 'This is Isla, Annie's sister. She's come from London this morning. Cal called her last night.'

He gives a perfunctory nod. 'Detective Inspector York,' he says, as if to assert his professional capacity. 'I'm sorry for your loss, ma'am.' He turns towards Cal, tips his head towards the dining room, his expression so uncomfortable my insides fold. 'Can I have a quick word?'

Cal's eyes widen. His nostrils flare. He glances at Daisy, who returns his gaze. Something flashes between them. It is a split second before he looks away, glances at me, looks away again. He appears… edgy. Wired. For the first time, it occurs to me that Cal lives here now, that he must have been living here since he finished uni last year. I know he didn't get on so well with Dominic; moving home might well have caused some tension.

How much tension?

They were fighting, he said. Physical fighting. Over him?

'No one else inside the cottage, all right?' DI York says, to all of us. 'We'll be as quick as we can.' His attention returns to Cal. 'Callum?'

Cal rises from the armchair like an old man. Slides his cup back onto the tray so carefully it makes no sound.

'I'll come with you,' I say, also rising.

DI York considers me briefly before giving a brisk nod. 'All right.'

I follow Cal, who follows DI York, into the dining room. Here, too, Annie is everywhere. A stuffed bird casts its beady eye from under a glass bell; old, mismatched chairs sit around a teak table with a fluted edge; the walls, dark bluey green, are filled with photographs of family and friends; floral curtains somehow stop short of chintz. It's stuffy in here, but the smell of burning is less acrid.

We sit. Callum folds his arms, unfolds them, pinches the end of his nose between his thumb and forefinger before folding his arms once again. I want to tell him to stop fidgeting, but I don't, for obvious reasons, but also because he is on the edge of tears.

'Nothing formal at this stage.' The detective takes a notepad from his inside breast pocket. 'We're still building a picture, but I will need you to come to the station this afternoon and give us a formal recorded statement. OK?' He pauses. 'I know you told my colleague DS Lewis what happened last night, and we have the report from the first responders, but I'm going to ask you to tell me again, in as much detail as you can, in your own words. Do you think you can do that?'

Outside, pebble grey shades the white fluffy clouds. My nephew's eye sockets blacken, as if he too is changing weather. From under swollen lids, his eyes dance before he looks down, as if to hide them. Perspiration beads on his forehead. His bottom lip trembles.

'I woke up to them shouting,' he begins after a long moment.

'OK.' York is jotting everything down. 'You were in bed?'

'Yes.'

'And this was?'

'It was... around half twelve, one.' Again Callum glances up, as if to check I'm here with him – a hesitant smile that is almost an apology, almost a... plea?

'You've been working at the pub since you've been back,' DI York says. 'Is that right?'

Cal nods slowly. 'And at Santori's.'

'And were you there last night?'

'No. I was on the day shift at Santori's. Dominic went to the Square. There was a gig, he said. I was really tired, otherwise I might have heard them sooner.' Again his eyes flick to mine, the same faint smile.

'Had you been drinking?' York asks.

'No.'

'Is that your vodka in your room?'

'Yes, but I hadn't drunk any. I'd smoked a bit.' He glances up at York. 'Sorry.'

'No, it's better to be truthful,' the detective mutters as he scribbles a note before looking up. 'And you went downstairs?'

Cal chews his cheek. 'Yes. But by the time I reached the back door, the whole thing had gone up in flames. It just… went up.' He mimes an explosion with his hands. 'Poof, you know? I mean, I suppose my mum keeps a lot of flammable stuff in there. White spirit catches, doesn't it? I think it was probably that. And Dominic… he smoked in there. And candles and stuff…' He falters. 'Dominic. I mean my stepdad.'

DI York shifts in his chair. 'You know I know who you mean, but I can imagine it's a bit strange for you, talking to me like this.'

Cal uncrosses his arms and lays his hands on the tabletop as if preparing to play the piano. Softly he bounces his fingertips on the dark wood. 'Mum didn't like him smoking in the house, so he went in the cabin. He was always nicking my gear. Always nicking my stuff, to be honest, even cash. Mum hated him going in the cabin. It was her space, you know? It was hers, not his.'

At the hardening in his tone, goosebumps rise on my arms. In London last year, when Cal rolled a joint, it felt like a test. I was his mother's younger sister, the groovy aunt who lived in the city – was I cool enough to smoke a doobie? I wasn't. Now, I doubt it was a test at all. It's possible he needed the ritual – or maybe the lull of the drug – to build up the courage to tell me about Dominic. Courage he never found. Maybe if I'd smoked that joint with him, he would've felt able to confide.

And my sister would still be alive.

His fingertips bounce faster, harder on the tabletop. Sweat trickles down the sides of his brow. 'It was her professional space and he didn't… he never respected it. Didn't respect her. But you know that.'

York raises his eyebrows. But it is not surprise I see there – it is acknowledgement. Daisy introduced him as Ross, not DI York. I wonder how close he is to the family.

'So,' he says. 'You called the fire brigade?'

'I was going to get the hose, but the flames were too high, so yeah, I ran back inside and I called 999. I thought I should do that first, then try again with the hose.'

'And this was, what, around one?'

'I suppose so. A bit earlier, maybe. It'll be on the call records, won't it?'

'And did you go to your mother's studio then?'

Cal screws up his face, as if to think.

'I went back into the garden. I tried to hose it down but it didn't seem to be doing anything. I mean, no, I couldn't get near, it was so hot, and then… then the fire guys turned up and I… I can't really remember, but then they put it out and… and then I called my auntie.'

'So you're sure you didn't get near the studio?'

'I don't think so, no.'

'What time was that?'

He glances at me. 'About one?'

I nod. 'I'd been out. I was just getting home. London, it takes ages, you know?' I press my mouth closed. I am not here to justify myself.

'And then the ambulance arrived,' Cal is saying. 'And the next thing, Mum was… they were putting her and my stepdad onto the stretchers and then they… they covered their faces.' He gasps, pushes his hands flat to his cheeks. 'They covered their faces.'

The carriage clock chimes 2.30 p.m. I shift my chair nearer to Cal and put my arm around his shoulders. He is crying fully now; I am blinking hard. When I look up at DI York, there is something in his eyes I don't like. Sadness is what it looks like.

Pity, perhaps. But I don't like the way he bites his bottom lip. I don't like the way he scratches the back of his balding head. For what seems like minutes, he and I sit listening to Callum sobbing.

'Have you got what you need?' I ask.

'It's just procedure,' he replies.

Cal wipes his eyes with the heels of his hands. 'I'm fine.'

'Just a couple more questions, all right?'

Cal nods. I reach for his hand and squeeze it, but he doesn't look at me.

'You've given us a positive ID from the personal effects,' York says. 'But given the nature of the injuries, we might need to send for a DNA check.'

My hair follicles lift. Nature of the injuries. Does he mean burns?

'They said like a hairbrush or something?' Cal almost whispers.

'That'll do. Can you tell me where we might find it?'

'I can get it.'

York shakes his head. 'It's better if one of our officers gets it.'

My stomach hurts. He isn't letting Cal get it. He doesn't trust him.

'It should be on her dressing table,' Cal says. 'My stepdad keeps his comb on there, but if it's not there, it'll be in the bathroom on the window ledge, or there's his razor in the little seahorse pot thing on the sink.'

York stands and walks out. Cal and I sit in hanging silence. *Hairbrush* we hear from the other side of the door, and *dressing table* and *bathroom*. After a moment, York returns and sits, every movement loaded with a kind of heavy-hearted calm.

'I know this is difficult,' he says. 'I have to ask you about the injuries not relating to the fire.'

Bruising, I think, surprised they could have spotted that – they can't have run forensics yet, surely? But what do I know?

'According to the initial examination post-mortem' – York's eyes bore a hole in the top of Cal's head; Cal, who will not look up – 'your stepfather had sustained a deep stab wound to the stomach.'

Cal's knuckles whiten but his head stays low. I can hear him breathing. I can hear myself breathing. A stab wound. A deep stab wound.

DI York clears his throat. 'And your mother,' he says, his voice grave. It appears to be costing him to speak. 'Your mother suffered a… a trauma to the head, which we believe to have been fatal. Can you tell us anything about that?'

A whimper leaves me. My hand is damp over my mouth, the air electric on my skin. Stab wound. A blow to the head. What on God's earth has happened here?

York has switched his attention to me. I realise I've said the words out loud. Cal did not mention a knife. He did not mention any kind of weapon. Their deaths were caused by the fire, was what he said. Did he say that? Whatever, it's what I've believed since… whenever I started to believe my sister was dead.

'You think the wounds were fatal?' This time I'm aware of speaking aloud. 'As in before the fire?'

York doesn't reply. Silence presses in.

'I…' Callum begins after a moment. 'They were fighting. I could hear stuff getting broken – bangs and crashes and stuff. I mean, I can't remember if I heard banging and stuff before I woke up properly, or whether I heard it once I was awake. But when I looked out of my bedroom window, I think I saw Dominic with a hammer. Sort of holding it up. Like this.' He raises his arm above his head, his fist clenched.

Nausea rises; I suppress a heave. He made no mention of a hammer earlier, on the driveway. He made no mention of it just now. He would have mentioned a hammer. Had he seen one, he would have mentioned it.

York considers him for a second, two, before dipping his head. The pencil whispers across the page. From outside comes the offended screech of gulls. All I can think about now is a hammer, Dominic's face contorted with anger, his arm raised ready to strike.

I close my eyes, but we cannot close our physical senses to what our mind conjures for us: what images, what sounds.

'You *think* you saw your stepdad with a hammer,' York says, 'or you saw him?'

I open my eyes to see him fixing Cal with his sad brown gaze.

Cal's fingers have started to bounce again, faster and faster, on the tabletop. Bitten nails, red cuticles. 'I mean, it all happened so fast. I think I saw him, but then I was running down the stairs. I was panicking.'

'Was it possible the studio was already on fire before you woke up?'

'It's possible. Yeah. I mean, it must have been.'

'And they were fighting when you woke?'

'Yeah. That's what woke me.'

A moment ago, he wasn't sure.

'So, let me understand… You couldn't see the flames when you looked out of your bedroom window, but you could see your stepfather wielding a hammer through the studio window. And the flames rose to an impossible height in the time it took you to get downstairs?'

'They must have done. That's why I think they must have hit some white spirit or something. There were candles in there. It was an absolute tinderbox.' Cal presses his lips together tight. His eyes brim. Under the table, I can feel his leg jiggling. Heat fills me; I want desperately for this to stop. More, I want it to rewind.

'And that's how you think the fire started?' York asks.

'I mean, I'm guessing it was a candle or a joint or a cigarette. Dominic brought musicians back from the pub all the time. He didn't care what he did.'

'And was there anyone else here last night?'

'Not last night, no. Maybe that's why they ended up fighting, while there was no one there for a change.'

'And you didn't go into the studio or try and pull them out?' The detective's eyes search Cal's face; my own search the detective's.

He has asked this question numerous times, as if in pursuit of a different answer. It feels like he's trying to implicate Cal or to throw him a lifeline, I'm not sure which.

'Like I said, the flames were too high,' Cal says. 'I did want to pull her out. Pull them both out, I mean, but I couldn't get near. I couldn't get to her. I couldn't...' He breaks down.

'I think that's enough, don't you?' I meet York's eye, try to read him, but he is inscrutable. After a long moment, he folds the notepad closed and, with that same mix of sadness and disappointment, leans back in his chair. Another beat and he is getting up and heading for the door, where he pauses, one hand on the handle, before opening it and calling to the other cop, who hands him two transparent plastic bags.

'Are these your mother's and Dominic's?' He holds up the bags. One contains a blue disposable razor, the other a large black hairbrush with a tangle of blonde hair, the sight of which brings an ache to my throat. My sister's beautiful hair. I used to think she was a princess. She was *my* princess. My beautiful, crazy, flibbertigibbet princess. My Annie.

Cal must have nodded yes, because York appears to be leaving. But at the door, he stops and turns, as if to add an afterthought.

'Cal,' he says, 'I need to ask you to come into the station this afternoon, OK? And before you do, I want you to think about something.'

It occurs to me that this was no more an afterthought than a military strategy. My chest begins to hurt. I glance at Cal, whose eyes are bloodshot.

'If you can jog your memory a bit,' York goes on. As he speaks, I watch my nephew closely – watch him lower his eyes to his hands clenched on the tabletop. 'See, we've got several recent sets of your footprints going right up to the remains of the studio and back to the house, so I want you to try and remember how they got there, OK? Good lad.'

The door closes. My nephew's head falls into his hands.

'Cal?' I say, without knowing what comes next.

He gives a kind of half-sob, half-groan.

'Cal?' I try again. 'You can tell me the truth, you know.' But even as I say the words, I'm not sure the truth is what I want. If, as I now suspect, the truth is darker still, I doubt I can handle it. We are already too close to absolute black.

'I didn't kill her,' he says, head still cradled in his raw hands, before raising his forehead an inch and letting it fall on the tabletop with a thud. Another beat – he lifts and lets it fall once again. And again. I want to tell him to stop, but then he raises his head, looks right into my eyes and whispers: 'I didn't kill her.'

'Of course you didn't,' I reply. 'Why would you say that?' Again, the words are out before their meaning catches up with me. *Of course you didn't…* Already I'm no longer as sure as I sounded even a moment ago. Another second, and another degree of certainty falls away. *I didn't kill her.*

No one is saying he did, so why would he say it? And why didn't he say *him*?

CHAPTER 6

Annie

May 1991

Back at the hotel, Annie throws herself onto the bed while Isla sets a bubble bath to run before taking their wet jackets to the drying room. When she returns, she teases Annie for lying about like a lazy besom, then fills the kettle and sets out the hospitality kit – teabags on string, cartons of UHT milk and some weird little brown biscuits that wouldn't feed a bug.

'You get in your bath,' Annie says, feeling guilty. 'I'll bring you your tea in.'

Moments later, Annie takes their tea into the bathroom, where Isla is stripping off. She is taller and longer-limbed than Annie, with a broad back, like their dad. The pale, prone-to-freckles skin they both share with their mother.

'There's a half-bottle of champagne in the minibar,' Annie says, sitting on the loo and blowing on her tea. 'We should be drinking that, out of coupes.'

Isla, who has clambered into the bath, looks appalled – with a ruff of white foam around her neck, she resembles an outraged Elizabethan.

'Not on my grant,' she says. 'Let's just get dressed, eh, and grab a drink in the bar.'

'Yes, boss.' Annie reaches into the bath and flicks water in her sister's face. On the bus from Shiel Bridge, she eavesdropped on Dominic and his friends, sitting on the back row. They mentioned going for dinner at eight, information she has stored as a squirrel stores a nut. But Isla knows she rarely has her tea after six, so if she suggests going at that time, her wee sister'll see right through her. Instead, Annie sips her tea and watches Isla's head disappear under the bubbles, steam rising like mist off the loch in the early morning, the bathwater sloshing. After a perfunctory wash, she stands, suds sliding and winking down her long white legs.

'Leave the water,' Annie says, pulling off her clothes.

'You can have a fresh bath, you know. It's a hotel.'

'God, no. The guilt'd kill me.' She steps in as Isla steps out. The water is just right, just enough bubbles still.

'How's your foot?'

'Fine. I can barely feel it.'

'Good.' One white towel a turban around her head, Isla is wrapping an enormous bath sheet around her. 'Shall we aim to eat about eight?'

'Great. The guys said they...' Bugger. The words are away, dancing down the road, too late, no way of catching them now.

Isla's eyes round; her cheeks redden from fresh air, fresh disapproval and the stifling central heating of the hotel. 'For God's sake, Annie, this is *our* weekend.'

'It's all right for you,' Annie snaps. 'Plenty of men at uni, plenty of *single* men. I can't remember the last time I saw a decent-looking bloke with all his own teeth. I heard them talking on the bus, that's all.'

Isla fixes her with a stare. It has been like this for as long as Annie can remember – a blanket of love edged with a fine lace of disapproval. She knows that look; Isla knows she does, and so when she speaks, all she needs is one word:

'Don't.'

*

In the bar, Annie begins to question the wisdom of letting Isla do her make-up: black eyeliner and red lipstick – far more than she usually wears.

'My lips look like a baboon's arse,' she complains, frowning at herself in the mirror behind the optics. 'I look like Mick Jagger.'

'No you don't. You look hip. You look young.' Isla is trendier than ever in loose ripped jeans, huge Teddy boy shoes, and a bright blue silk scarf tied around her back-combed hair.

'Young? For God's sake, you'd think I was thirty.' Annie knocks back a third of her Chardonnay. Dominic and his friends are older than thirty, she thinks. But she doubts any of them feel as old as she does, doubts they even have babies at home, let alone a ten-year-old child.

She sighs dramatically, but Isla doesn't take her on; Isla who has barely sipped her gin and tonic. 'I don't know how much longer I can work in the shop,' Annie tries. When there is no response, she continues anyway. 'I work all day, cook Cal's tea, help with his homework, tidy up, watch some TV or read a book and then I go to bed. I haven't been out for a drink in months. I haven't had sex for four years.' She thinks of her flat above the shop. She is grateful for it, she is, but it makes her feel sad.

'At least you've *had* sex.' Isla looks away, her cheeks flushing. But before Annie can press her on it, Isla must sense she's derailed herself, because she promptly hoists her wheels back on track and chugs resolutely on. 'Four years? Do I know about that one?'

'That guy Kelvin. Kelvin from Kilmartin?'

'You kept that quiet.'

'It was only a couple of times and he never came to the flat. But that's not the point; the point is, what if that's *it*? What if when Mum and Dad die and you're off having an amazing career in Glasgow or Madrid or wherever, I'm… I'm stuck, you know? And past it. All I know how to do is run a shop.'

'It's a transferable skill. As is juggling motherhood and work.'

'Transferable to where?' To her annoyance, her eyes fill – this was meant to be a rant, not a sob story. 'I wanted to take my sketchbook around Europe.'

'You're still painting.'

'Yes, but it's not real education, is it? It's not a degree.'

'Why not do OU?'

'I'm not after solutions,' Annie says, failing to curb the irritation in her tone. 'I'm just… I mean, you won't be coming back, will you? You'll have a life*style*, not just a life. I'm going to die where I was born.'

'No you're not.' Isla's forehead wrinkles; she reaches for Annie's hand, but Annie picks up her drink and slugs it. 'Look, Cal will be grown up soon and you'll still be really young and you'll be able to travel then. I know it doesn't feel possible right now, but hey, we never thought we'd get to do this, did we? But we did. And Cal's already ten; just think how independent he'll be in five, six years. Haven't I said this a thousand times? When I'm up to my oxters in nappies, you'll be the one out there having a ball.'

'Maybe.'

'Not maybe, definitely. We'll do a tour of Spain – Gaudí in Barcelona, the Prado in Madrid, wine in Rioja. You can bring your camera and your sketchbook. And when Mum and Dad… you know, pass on, we can sell the shop and you can come and live near me.'

'I have been painting a lot actually,' Annie admits, momentarily buoyed.

'That's brilliant.' Isla thumps her softly on the arm. 'Why didn't you tell me?'

'Sold a landscape the other month. In the shop.' She feels herself blush.

Isla hits her again, this time on the leg. 'You sold a painting? As in, someone paid money and took it away to hang in their home?'

'Aye. A tourist.'

'Someone you didn't even *know*? That's amazing! Why didn't you tell me? You see? You're so talented. And there's loads of galleries in Inverness and even Glasgow. You need to put yourself out there – you'd sell tons.'

'Let's not get ahead of ourselves.'

'Don't. There's nothing stopping you. It's not the stuff of fantasy; it's perfectly possible.'

'There's the small matter of no art degree.' Annie slides off her stool. 'A handful of crap O grades. Come on. Bring your drink; you've hardly touched it. What kind of student are you anyway?'

The three men are sitting at a table for six in the bay window. But Isla has already settled at the table furthest away. She shoots Annie a warning look. Heat blooms in Annie's cheeks, creeps down her neck. Reluctantly she follows her sister and sits down.

'You'll be having the chicken, won't you?' Isla asks.

'Excuse me,' a man's voice interrupts.

It's him. The dark-haired one. Dominic. He smiles. He really is quite wee, though not skinny. He's holding on to the back of the spare chair, and Annie hates herself for noticing that he has still not put on a wedding ring now that he is down off the hill. Not that that means anything anymore. He's wearing a soft white shirt and he smells lovely – like aftershave but not cheap aftershave – eau de cologne maybe.

'We were taking bets…' He grimaces and spreads his hands. 'Sorry, that came out wrong. We *wondered*…' He gestures towards his friends. 'We were wondering, since we all did the big walk today and are sick to death of one another's conversation, we were *wondering* if you'd care to join us. We haven't ordered food yet.

We thought we could compare notes on the highs and lows, so to speak. The peaks and troughs. The hills and valleys?' His eyelids lower a fraction. 'Oh, shut up, Dom.'

'We'd love to.' Ignoring the gamma rays of her wee sister's furious gaze, Annie tips up her chin and smiles.

'That's great.' Dominic – *Dom* – rubs his hands together. 'Come on over!'

A moment later, Annie is lifting her bag from the chair back and following Dom to the other table. She has the impression of floating, of a not unpleasant detachment from both the shimmering vibrations of Isla's exasperation and the delicious, rolling inexorability of it all.

At dinner, the men make them laugh with tales from their friendship, sustained over the decades by this, their annual walking trip. Last year, they climbed Kilimanjaro, or 'Kili' as they call it. Next year they are planning to walk the Purbeck Ridge, an event Dominic will host at his cottage in a village in Dorset. He runs a little holiday let business, he tells them, the 'little' making it sound big, for some reason Annie cannot fathom. Thomas is a barrister in London. Doctor, businessman, lawyer: it's all a bit intimidating. But they are friendly without being creepy, and out of the corner of her eye, Annie sees Isla's smile becoming quicker, her shoulders lowering as the minutes pass into hours. She knows her sister treasures their time alone together, but Isla is having the time of her life at uni, whereas for Annie, this is the most fun she's likely to get until she sees Isla again at Christmas.

The bottles of red keep coming. Annie feels the menthol tingle of her cheeks where the elements have whipped them. She is a bit drunk, but it's the youngest she's felt in years, and when Isla steps outside with Thomas – Tom, now – for a cigarette and Gavin excuses himself to head up to bed, Annie finds herself alone with

Dominic, whose dark colouring, straight nose and thin, almost mean mouth have become utterly his own.

'So, Annie Andrews,' he says, pouring the last dregs of the wine. 'What's your story?'

She has the impression he has waited until the others are not there, as if it is something he alone would like to hear, or as if he has sensed that she wouldn't be comfortable talking about herself in front of the group.

'Och, there's not much to tell,' she says.

'Oh, come on. I bet there is.'

'I have a ten-year-old son.' If he has a problem with that, well, she has a problem with him.

'Ten? You don't look old enough. You're what? Twenty-five?'

'Twenty-six.' She laughs, but Dominic does not, unsure perhaps whether he should. 'His name is Callum. He's a great kid. I had him when I was sixteen. Quite the scandal.'

He grins. 'I love a bit of scandal. And are you still with the father?'

'I was never really with him, you know? His name was Malcolm, and… No, he's not on the scene. I never knew his last name, or if I did, I've forgotten it.'

'I'm sorry.'

'Don't be. I'm fine, honestly.'

She expects him to tactfully draw the conversation to a close, like a curtain over a mouldy wall, like most people do, but instead he continues to ask her all about herself, her life. She ends up telling him that she overheard them on the bus talking about television, and that she too enjoys *Twin Peaks*, which she watches once Cal is in bed. And somehow from there, they get onto books, then, through her parents' Presbyterianism, to religion.

'We weren't allowed to do anything on a Sunday,' she tells him, hiding her delight at his apparent fascination. 'Anything beyond knitting was *forbidden*.'

'Really?' he says. And, 'Wow.' And, 'I bet that was—'

'God, make me stop,' she says, realising she's been blethering on. 'I talk too much. This is the most civilised company I've had in—'

'Don't apologise. You left school at sixteen and you're more articulate than most of my overeducated friends.'

'Get away.' Heat creeps up her neck, her face. They are both ridiculous. He is pretending to be interested; she is pretending to be a grown-up.

'I mean it. You have a way of analysing the world… I wonder if that's the autodidact thing. Self-taught, you know?'

'I know what autodidact means.'

'God, sorry, that was patronising.'

She laughs it off, though she is pleased he apologised. 'Don't worry about it. *Educating Rita*, that's me, if Rita hadn't been taking the pill in secret.'

'Amazing,' he whispers, shaking his head. 'I don't get to meet many *true* creatives. I guess I *aspire*, but you… you're the real deal. Maybe we're both out of time. Maybe we're both Renaissance people. Freethinkers.'

'I'm not a freethinker,' she scoffs. 'I never think, that's my trouble. Go in feet first.' She holds up her hand. 'Don't argue. I know what I am. Serial sufferer of crushes, hopeless romantic, lost cause. Isla says I'm a nightmare.'

He glances over at Isla, who has come in from the courtyard, before returning his attention to Annie. 'She's delightful, of course. But she doesn't have your spirit. She's *afraid*.'

'Don't say that. Isla's studying Spanish and business. She's been to Seville.'

'And I'm sure she's very enterprising, but you… I think you'd have been a bluestocking or a bohemian or something in another life. You might get yourself into the odd muddle, but at least you're living an authentic life. And I absolutely get the crushes thing. I fall hard too. I fall hard.' He fixes on her for so long she laughs, flustered.

'Authentic, my eye. The most excitement I ever get is when there's something good on the telly. Anyway, it's your turn. Do you have a teensy bit of an American accent, or am I imagining it?'

'Oh God, really?' He laughs before sliding into an American drawl. 'I did an MBA over there, so yeah, sure, I guess.'

He tells her he worked in investment banking in London before moving back to Dorset to take over his parents' business last year. He lives in a beautiful cottage overlooking the sea. He loves the Isle of Purbeck, he tells her, and she tells him she's never been to England, or anywhere really, apart from Glasgow, and once to Edinburgh for the festival. He lists places for her: Winspit, Seacombe Cliffs, Church Knowle, Old Harry Rocks, Chapman's Pool, Studland Bay, Shell Bay. They sound magical, like he's made them up.

'You should come.' He half smiles in a way that makes her unsure if he's serious. 'It's not majestic, like here, but it's pretty and wild, if you know what I mean. Did you ever read the Famous Five?'

'Everyone read the Famous Five. And the Secret Seven and the... there was a Four, wasn't there?'

'You've out-Blytoned me, sorry, but it's definitely got castles, cliffs and inlets perfect for smugglers from Kirrin Island.'

'Is that a real place?'

'No.' He gives an ironic frown. 'Sorry. Is that a deal-breaker?'

'Not at all, I...' She what? She is old and she is a child. He has told her she is a freethinker, amazing, articulate. She has told him she jumps in with both feet. He has told her he does too. What have they really told each other? Where are their feet?

He takes her hand. 'Will you come?'

She laughs, almost panicking at his touch. He is so obviously trying to get her into bed. Isla has gone; she wonders if she's with Tom. She hopes so. 'I wasn't born yesterday.'

She can feel his breath against her knuckles. Her own is held in her chest. If he kisses her hand, she'll laugh, she will, she'll throw back her head and…

'You were born centuries ago, I think.' He lowers her hand and peers at her as if through weak lenses. 'Yes, Annie Andrews, you've been here before.'

'Aye, well,' she says. 'Some of us need a few goes before we get it right.'

CHAPTER 7

Isla

September 2004

Cal rushes from the room. Torn between chasing after him and letting him go, I do nothing but watch him through the open door. He reaches the bottom of the stairs, turns away at the police tape. His hands clench into fists. He gives a kind of suppressed growl before opening the front door and storming out of the house.

I sit for a moment, anxious and bewildered. It feels like barely seconds have passed since Cal stopped me on the driveway and told me Dominic was abusive towards my sister, leaving the world and everything in it on a kind of strange slant, as if someone had taken the very foundations of my sister's beautiful cottage and tipped it at an angle. Now, everything has been thrown off-kilter yet again – crockery slides off tabletops, pictures drop from their hooks, the walls begin to crumble. My sister and her husband may have died *before* the fire from violent, intentional injuries.

I'm pretty sure DI York shouldn't have been asking Cal those questions without another officer present. And he gave him quite a bit of information about the injuries. Was he trying to trap him into a confession? Or was he warning him – *we know they died before the fire; we have footprints* – trying to help him get his story straight before he gives a formal statement? But he's police. Why would he do that?

Dominic and Annie were fighting, Cal said. He did say that, maybe even on the phone. He wouldn't have known about the injuries. He told York he saw the hammer in Dom's hand. But he didn't mention a hammer to me or to the first police officer on the scene or even to York, actually, until prompted. He said he couldn't get near the studio. So why would his footprints suggest otherwise? Could they have been from earlier? Yes, yes, they must be. He will have gone in there to chat to Annie, take her a cup of tea. The rest... well, the rest is confusion. Post-traumatic stress. Whatever. Not guilt. Absolutely not guilt.

I press my palms to my cheeks and force myself to exhale. Calm down, Isla. Get a grip. What's obvious is that DI York knew my sister and Dominic well enough to know there were issues in their relationship. Which is more than I did. *He never respected it*, Cal said of her studio. *Didn't respect her. But you know that.* Yes, he said that – not to me, but to York.

Daisy, Jan and now York. All of them knew my sister better than I did.

But what on earth happened last night? What was the glance between Daisy and Cal, and why is Jan in the house? What's any of this got to do with her?

I'm spiralling. Stop, Isla. Cal is Annie's boy, my wee nephew. He wouldn't hurt the proverbial fly, let alone drive a blade into his stepdad's belly. The only thing that makes sense here is that Dominic was not the charming if chauvinistic prat I thought he was. He was not a nice man at all, and Annie hid this from me. Was she ashamed? Embarrassed? I hid my opinion of him from her, I suppose, although was that even possible when she could read me from the room next door, could tell by a pause or a sniff down a phone line that things weren't great with me? As I could her. Or so I thought. But I never criticised Dominic. He was her choice, and as long as he made her happy, that was all I cared about. I may have raised an eyebrow at him sitting there while she waited on him – I never once saw him make so much as a cup of tea. But if I cast my mind right back to when they first got together… I was scathing, yes – yes I was. I can vaguely remember saying something sarcastic about women who wait for knights on their white chargers.

'Shit,' I whisper to myself.

If there is one thing I would never have wanted to make her feel, it is shame. God knows she had enough of that growing up. But perhaps that's exactly what I did. Perhaps she withheld from me out of fear that I would say *I told you so*. That I would criticise her as I have done in the past – *Oh, Annie, for God's sake, there you go again.* Or was she protecting me, knowing that one whiff of harm to her would bring me running, running with my fists up and a roar in my throat?

'Oh, Annie.'

I look out onto the wreckage, black against the blue sky now wisped with thin pale cloud. The last time I saw Dominic, he was standing right there, just beyond the apple tree, drink as ever in hand. I see him: pale pink Ralph Lauren polo shirt, fine-knit navy jumper tied over his shoulders. As he talks, he looks out over the fields towards Winspit. Annie is not there. She must be inside preparing dinner. Dominic's laugh is husky, almost girlishly high, like a fifth former with a twenty-a-day habit. He is asking me, *So, Isla, how's life in the Big Smoke?* He waits for an answer with more than politeness, as if his own life leaves him hungry for tales of the city. Yet the moment I begin to reply, his gaze returns to the sea, and before long, he interrupts to ask me if I've seen any gigs recently.

'Not recently,' I say. 'I'm not really—'

'The Beastie Boys at Brixton Academy, now there was a gig. And… and this is going back… I saw the Sex Pistols at the 100 Club.' He shakes his head. 'God, I was only a kid! I don't know if I was even twenty.'

He never looked like someone who attended gigs. His clothes were too clean, too pressed, his hair parted and combed in a way that would have made Patrick throw up his hands in despair before reaching for the wax. But all I had to do was like him well enough to get along with him. I didn't love him, I realise.

'I've been handling the bookings at the pub actually,' he said, that last time, before going on about how he'd been doing this for the last few years. 'Just for the love of it, you know? They don't pay me.'

I'm picking over things, I know, but it occurs to me now that every time I suggested we should help my sister set the table or see if she needed anything, he would wave his hand.

'Annie's got it all under control,' I hear him say. 'She's a trouper.'

A bit of a pig then. But that's not a fist, is it? It's not a hammer. Think, Isla.

Annie was happy, wasn't she? The day she left in Dominic's shiny jeep, Callum so small and pale in the back seat, their entire worldly possessions in two suitcases and a couple of boxes, she was happier than I'd seen her in years. He'd driven all that way to come and get her, even made my parents laugh in our dark and frugal kitchen before whisking their daughter and grandchild from under their noses, an event I believe kick-started their decline.

He stole my sister is what part of me still thinks, deep down. But I couldn't complain; that wouldn't have been fair. I no longer lived in Inveraray; I couldn't promise her anything. Loving her meant letting her leave. Of course it did; we weren't kids anymore. And I wanted it for her, no matter how much sadness that caused me. I can't remember much about him that day beyond noticing a few white hairs among the brown and feeling shocked that this man, this *grown-up*, was taking my sister away. I wanted her to go, just go. The anticipation of separation was worse than the moment itself.

No, not worse. My God, when they disappeared out of sight, that was the first time I'd felt loss as a physical pain, as if my ribcage wasn't big enough for my bruised and swollen heart. I cried on and off for days; grief that took me unawares – a song on the radio, the splash of low sun on the loch, the bubble of the stream on the hill. Even months later, the first chill breath of autumn hit me like a rock because I thought of her and how she would sniff the air.

'Isla,' she would say, 'can you smell the change of season?'

Memories. A smaller grief wrapped in this larger one. Annie is dead. And all I want is to call her and have her tell me not to worry. I want to tell her I miss her, that I've missed her since the day she left Scotland, and that I remember absolutely all our night-time chats in our bunk beds, all our times spent together.

Think, Isla. Were there signs? I never saw her alone, never away from here. I'd come to the cottage for a week in the summer, a few days at Christmas, then back I'd go for my metropolitan New Year.

'I absolutely have to get to London one of these weekends,' she would say when we said goodbye, but I took it as just something she said.

'Let's get a date in,' I would reply, squeezing her tight. 'You'll love it.'

We never did. She would say she had plenty of free time, just no actual days off. I know she did the lion's share of everything, but she didn't complain. She had time to paint. She was selling work and she seemed OK. Tired but OK. And I loved coming here. Dom was often out and about, so I had plenty of time with her and Cal. But I was always so keen to get back to my life. I always left.

It strikes me now that she had become older than me once again. Like raindrops on a window, our respective ages raced ahead or fell behind according to whatever obstacles our lives were throwing at us. I think about that now. And I think about how saying goodbye to her always felt as if I were betraying her somehow, even though she was living the life she'd chosen and to which she seemed so suited: wide-open spaces, painting the sun on the water or the wind on the sea, charming the cottage clients with her warm and easy way.

She never said she was unhappy, not once, not in words.

But she was my sister; I should have trained my hearing to her pitch, the silent notes that once only we could hear but which over time became lost in the noise of our lives.

Think.

In all this, what about Cal? Cal, whose translucent skin gave away his every emotion, pink as red paint dropped into water whenever he was embarrassed, which was constantly; whose eyes would blacken when he was angry. When he came to visit me last year, yes, he was subdued – I can see that now. He'd never come to see me before – I thought it was because he finally felt old enough. I'm sure now he came to tell me about Dominic's treatment of my sister but never found the words. Or something else? I don't know, I don't *know*.

And now my sister is dead.

It's possible she was murdered.

Why didn't I pay attention?

A sob leaves me. I cover my face with my hands, feel the tears wet against my fingers. I am hiding my face as if ashamed, and actually, that's in there too. I have relied too heavily on what Annie and I were to one another when we were young. I have relied on blood. I have relied on time being plentiful when in fact it was disastrously short. Now my sister is gone and my recent memory of her is of a close friend I used to know. And Dominic is dead too, and I'm pretty sure my nephew is not telling the whole truth about how that happened.

CHAPTER 8

Isla

When I come out of the dining room, Jan is creeping up the hall like a thief.

'Sorry,' I say.

She startles slightly and turns, her brow furrowing. 'What on earth for?'

'I'm not much of a… I mean, it's all so… Where's Daisy?'

'Popped into Swanage. To the Co-op.'

'Right.'

Neither of us moves. I have no idea what to do or say.

'I'll get out of your hair,' Jan says finally, her head leaning to one side. 'You'll be wanting to talk to Cal.'

'He left.'

Her mouth falls open; she clamps it shut.

'I don't know where he's gone,' I add. 'They need him to give a statement.'

But she is backing towards the door, opening it, stepping outside. The policewoman from earlier is talking into her radio. Seeing us, she wanders towards the end of the driveway, giving us space. I remain just inside, on the welcome mat. It is so light outside. Oceans of time have passed and yet, impossibly, it is still only 3 p.m. Dominic's new jeep is parked in front of the garage, but Annie's sky-blue soft-top Mini he bought her when she passed her test is gone. It has been stolen, I think, before remembering Cal is not a teenager anymore.

'Looks like he took Annie's car,' I say. 'Maybe he's gone to give his statement, get it over with.'

When I look at Jan, she is peering at me as if she's about to ask me a question. Instead, I ask one of her: 'Did you look after Cal a lot?'

'When he was much younger, yes, but more recently, we just hung out, you know? He'd drum for me while I played or we'd watch an old movie together, nothing too wild.' She leans into the doorway, pulling her oversized cardigan around her. 'He stayed with me plenty of times, obviously, when…' She shakes her head a fraction and looks away, towards the roses, the lane.

'When what?'

She shakes her head again, as if to clear water from her ears, and half closes her eyes. 'Oh, just the odd time when things were… difficult.'

'Difficult how?'

'Just… you know how they were.'

I don't, I think, blushing. I don't want to betray my sister's private life by sharing what Cal has told me, but there is no time now for dancing around.

'Cal said Dominic used to hit her,' I half whisper, leaning out now so that our foreheads are almost touching. 'Did you know anything about that?'

A barely perceptible nod, her mouth a tight, grim line. 'Occasionally.'

'And Cal would come and stay with you? With Annie?'

'Annie stayed with Daisy. I took Cal to give Annie the chance to talk without wagging teenage ears. He always liked hanging out with me. As I say, we'd jam, cook, whatever.'

'So it's been… it was a long-term thing?'

'The hitting less so. Dominic took… liberties.' She blinks, evidently a little flustered. 'Look, I'll let you go.'

Funny how people say that when what they mean is *I need to go*.

I meet her grey eyes. 'Did things get worse when Cal finished uni, do you think?'

She wrinkles her nose, opens her mouth to speak, but the policewoman has returned and smiles at us awkwardly.

Jan gives a kind of shiver, though the sun is warm. 'My number's on the fridge under the ladybird magnet,' she says with a brief glance at the cop. 'If it's not there, Cal will have it. Or Daisy. Call me if you need anything, OK? I mean it. I'm just down from the pub.'

And away she goes, calling goodbye to the policewoman, who, I realise, she must know. Her voice is lilting and light, the kind of sing-song that almost masks extreme stress. The stress of this horrible situation. The stress of shock. The stress of knowing more than she wishes to tell me.

I return inside. The cottage swallows me whole. In the hallway, I stall, unsure what to do, where to stand, how to be. But moments later, as if on a shift rotation with Jan, Daisy lets herself in with a key.

'Hi,' she says and plonks two bright blue carrier bags on the kitchen table. 'Just got some bits. I hope you're not veggie.'

'No. I mean, we only had fish growing up, but I've lapsed since. So, no. Sorry. Thanks.' I push my hand into my pocket, touch what I think is a tenner but am unsure if I should offer it. Or more. 'Thank you so much,' I say again. 'What do I owe you?'

She bats me away. 'Don't worry. It'll all come out in the wash.'

'Well, thank you.'

I make tea, glad of something to do with my hands, and we go and sit in the living room. Another policewoman stands guard at the back door. The French windows to the garden are shut against a strong sea breeze. I avert my eyes from the sight of the black wreckage.

'Cal's away out,' I say. 'He's insured for Annie's car, isn't he?'

'I think so.' She sips her tea, pensive. 'Actually, he was saving for his own car, I think. He'd been saving his tips since he was fifteen, maybe even fourteen. I think he was planning on buying a second-hand one to fix up. He can turn his hand to anything, that boy.'

'Like his mum.'

'Yes.' Her smile is so sad I have to look away.

'He keeps his cash rolled up under his mattress,' she says after a moment, her eyes filling. 'He's like her that way too. Eccentric, you know? He likes the idea of it being hidden away, I think.'

'I suppose he won't need to buy one now, will he?'

Her eyes spill over, as do mine. And then the tears come fast and I plunge my face into my hands.

I feel Daisy sit beside me, hear her rootling in her bag. A moment later, she hands me a tissue and takes one for herself. We sit with them pressed to our eyes, both completely failing to stop crying.

I shake my head, attempt to compose myself. 'I'm sorry, I don't even know you.'

'I don't know you either. But I guess we'll have to bypass the small talk.'

'I just wish I'd seen her, you know? I wish I'd come more often. I wish… so many things. How can my big sister have been murdered?'

'Murdered?' Daisy blinks in shock, her eyes red.

'Sorry. When York spoke to Cal, he said Dominic had been – he'd been stabbed.' I can only bear to whisper it. 'And Annie—'

'Annie what?' Her voice is urgent. 'Annie what, Isla?'

'An injury of some kind.' I can't say *hammer*, I just can't. 'To her head.'

Daisy gasps. It is a horrible sound. It is a long time before either of us can speak. Waves are coming at us, one after another. It is all impossible to think about, impossible to voice.

'So,' she almost whispers, wiping her nose, 'they killed each other in the end.'

'Did you know? About him hitting her?'

'Oh, they hit *each other*. It was a very… stormy marriage. She used to say she'd made her bed, but I told her that was nonsense. People change beds all the time. She had some funny ideas. Hard notions. Hard on herself.'

'Aye, well.' I don't say any more. Don't mention our upbringing, though resentment flashes through me now at the thought of it. Besides, Daisy probably knows all about it.

'I just wanted her to choose someone who'd love her properly, you know?'

'I should have come more often, but I didn't. I… didn't.'

'Annie knew you were busy. She wanted you to be off living your life. Honestly.'

'Did she?'

'Yes! She was happy you were loosening up. Sorry. No offence. I'm only saying what she said. She loved you very much.'

'Don't.' I shake my head; she passes me another tissue.

'Let's not say anything sad.'

I blow my nose; it hoots. 'Christ, I'll get a tune out of it at this rate.'

We share a sad half-laugh.

'Listen,' she says after a moment. 'Let's get you out for a walk, eh? I'll take you down to Seacombe and we can sit on the rocks and watch the sea for a bit. It's very calming. I could do with some air myself.'

'But what if Cal comes back? What if the police need me? I feel like I should be doing something. Helping.'

'Cal's got my mobile number. You can't help him give a statement, and you can't go with him if he's chosen to go on his own. The police won't get any forensics for a day or two. Have I missed anything?' Her smile is shaky and kind. She is holding out her hand. I want to trust her, I realise, even if I shouldn't.

CHAPTER 9

Isla

Despite her short legs, Daisy is nimble and swift. Opposite the duck pond, she points out Jan's tiny terraced house, which looks empty, tells me the one next door belongs to Dominic and Annie's business, which I already knew. Leaving the wee village centre behind us, we carry on up the hill to where the road forks around the raised triangle of The Square and Compass pub garden. In one direction lies Kingston and Corfe; in the other, the village of Langton Matravers and, further on, Swanage, with its wide curve of yellow sands. To think of Swanage is to think of Annie, Cal and me sitting on the old harbour wall eating fish and chips, our legs dangling, seagulls screeching and dive-bombing overhead. It is to think of happiness utterly gone.

One hand to my chest, I lean against the wall for support. The pub garden is as full as it always is. Late summer holidaymakers, many in walking or biking gear, drink pints of beer and cider at tables made from great stone slabs. It occurs to me as I compose myself that it is a warm September afternoon and the sun is shining and the people in this garden are happy. Their happiness is absurd. How can they be happy? How can anyone? Anger rises in my chest, but Daisy must have retraced her steps, because now she is taking my elbow and guiding me away over the road.

'Let's get to the sea,' she says. 'It'll make you feel better.'

We take the footpath down to where Friesians graze, their bovine stares blank amid brown pats crusted on tufted grass.

We walk without talking. I have come this way before, a few times, with Annie. Now, Daisy and I concentrate on our feet, positioning them with care on the steep rocky steps, the erratic rise and fall of the land. It helps. In the vast blue air, I am aware of Daisy's grief as if it were floating over me in particles. My own is sticky on my face; it pushes up my neck to the back of my head. I square out my shoulders, consciously, and follow Daisy down the rock staircase. It is years since I came here with my sister, years. The last time, the two of us brought a bottle of red wine and a picnic of pasties and Dorset apple cake. That must be five or more years ago now. My heart constricts. It was nothing. It was everything. And I would give up all I own to be able to do that again, just once.

The land spits us out onto a natural amphitheatre of rock flats. Directly in front, a teal sea roils, shoots white spray fireworks up and out over the grey. Daisy makes her way to the right, sits on the level stone ledge. I follow suit. For a while, neither of us says a word, eyes on the flashing foam, the angry water, both lost in thoughts of Annie, of Dominic, of fire, blackness and the smell of burnt wood.

'What do you think happened?' It is easier to ask her now that we have somewhere else to look besides each other. Perhaps it will be easier for her too. Easier to talk but also, I realise, to lie.

She brushes the leg of her jeans and sighs. When she speaks, it is as if to the sea. 'Looks to me like they had a fight that got out of control. I don't know who struck who first, but they must have tumbled and knocked stuff over. Dominic used to smoke in there. They had candles and all sorts, and of course she had turps, oils and such. An absolute tinderbox.'

Cal mentioned Dom's smoking, the candles and the turps. Both of them used the word tinderbox. It's as if they've compared notes.

'Annie had put beanbags and stuff at the back,' Daisy goes on. 'Typical her that she'd make it welcoming for her friends. She never made you feel like you were disturbing her. But after the miscarriage, Dom used to go in there. Not sure what was going on, some sort of midlife crisis if you ask me, but…' She must see the shock on my face, because she falters.

'Annie had a miscarriage?'

She reddens. 'I'm sorry. I assumed she'd… Sorry. I was just trying to say there was a lot of tension.'

'Between Annie and Dominic?'

'As I say, after… she lost the baby.' She glances at me, only briefly. 'I… I was with her. She was at my house. Anyway, yes, things got grimmer after that.'

'Jan said Dominic took liberties.'

'Annie was resigned to what Dom was like,' Daisy replies with a flick of her hand. 'She'd made her own life. But when Cal moved back… well, things weren't great between him and Dominic. Not great at all.'

'In what way?'

'Oh, you know, clashing antlers. Boy becomes man. Too many stags. Dom was my friend, but he was an arsehole. I'm sorry, I know he was your brother-in-law, but…'

'But what?' I manage, struggling to choose where to push for information.

She shrugs. 'It's not for me to say.'

'Oh, come on.' I almost laugh. 'You can't hint at something then clam up.'

Her head falls back and she blows a long breath of air, her lips puffed out. 'Annie and Callum were close.'

'Of course they were. For the first ten years of his life, there was only the two of them; you know that, don't you? They're only sixteen years apart.'

She nods, her lips press tight. 'Yeah. I mean, I know. And I only teach kids, I don't have any of my own, and I know it's different bringing them up. It's just that Cal's sensitive. Artistic, like his mother. And the combination of that and the fact that Dom was the way he was…'

'Abusive.'

Her shoulders rise to her ears, drop heavily. 'Sometimes I'd catch Cal looking at her and it was very… intense. Yeah, intense. His eyes would be… they were black, you know? Boiling.'

'So… what? Do you think he…' I can't ask the question. *Do you think Cal is involved?* is the question. And yet, no, that's not quite it. The question actually is: *Do you think Cal killed Dominic?*

And I'm afraid the answer she'll give me, the answer that maybe she's trying to give me, is: *Yes.*

A huge wave crashes, reaches a great white hand of water over the square rock, almost drenching us. The long frothy fingers slide inexorably back, slipping over the edge and away, as if they can't hold on.

Back at the cottage, the tape across the stairs is gone. The police-woman at the front door tells us that only the studio is out of bounds now. As we step inside, it occurs to me that Daisy should be at work, and when I ask her about it, she tells me she's taken time off on compassionate grounds.

'I can barely speak English,' she says. 'There's no way I can face thirty kids mangling their reflexive verbs.'

Shock and grief have made her too ill to work. She must have loved my sister so much. I watch her a moment, busying herself, tidying, making sandwiches, calm and practical in the midst of this storm. Is there a disconnection? Is she too calm? Too practical? Or is she simply finding something, anything, to do to keep herself from falling apart? I try and block from my mind what she said about Cal at the cliffs – a sure-fire way if ever there was one of thinking about nothing else. His eyes – black and boiling. That's hate, pure hate. He didn't just not get on with Dominic, he *hated* him. Was Daisy trying to implicate him? Earlier, when I told her the police suspected murder, I wasn't looking at her like a cop would, to gauge her reaction. Was she shocked? I check myself. Stop. It isn't Daisy who has set me on edge; it's my own nephew, who, after being told to stick around, has apparently disappeared, unless he's gone to give his statement – in which case, why didn't he tell me that? Why not just say where he was going? Surely he would want me with him, for support? Surely he would want to hurry back and sit with me, his auntie, while we both figure out how to even begin to grieve?

'It's handover day tomorrow,' Daisy says, breaking into my spiralling thoughts. 'The cottages, you know? I'll help you with it. I've done it the odd time when Dominic and Annie were away skiing.'

'She *skied*?'

'Dom did. Annie used to let him go up to the black runs, then she'd stash her skis, order a hot chocolate and spend the day reading. He never knew.' She gives a sad laugh, shakes her head before returning to her task: granary bread is slathered in butter, piled with tuna mayo, cucumber.

'I hadn't even thought of the cottages,' I say after a moment.

'It's not too onerous, don't worry. You'll only get a call if something is broken or damaged or a guest hasn't checked out on time, but that's rare.'

It is almost six by the time we take our sandwiches into the living room to eat off our knees. For the first time since Cal called me – and it feels like a week ago – I'm hungry. But when I raise the sandwich to my lips, my throat blocks and I feel sick.

Daisy lifts the plate from my hands. 'I'll pop cling film over it. It'll be in the fridge if you or Cal fancy it later.'

When she returns from the kitchen, she is carrying two shot glasses and hands one to me.

'Brandy,' she says. 'You're still in shock.'

'So are you.'

'Which is why I poured one for myself.' She smiles that sad smile again and downs hers in one go. The pink in her cheeks deepens. Like Cal, any change in her shows on her skin. I want to trust her so badly it gives me a pain in my chest.

I sip the brandy, feel it run hot down my throat. Outside, what's left of the workshop is still taped off. At the back door, a policewoman stands with her arms folded at her chest. It is getting chillier now the sun is low, and I feel sorry for her. She must be bored too. In the lawn, the little flags flicker in the wind. I wonder if the police can tell when the footprints were made. I hope not, then check myself for hoping not. I hope they *can* tell. That way they will know they were made days ago. Or someone could have borrowed Cal's shoes. It's easy enough to get small feet inside size-eleven trainers.

'We all loved her,' Daisy says into the silence. 'We'll miss her every single day.'

I try not to notice her tiny feet.

Before she goes, Daisy puts hers, Jan's and Cal's numbers into my Motorola and leaves her address on a map scribbled onto a scrap of card, with arrows pointing to her house and to Jan's. I know the village well from countless visits and can picture where Daisy lives, on the edge, towards Langton Matravers. I wave her off and close the thick front door of the cottage. And it is only once she's gone that I realise neither she nor Jan has expressed any sadness over Dominic. It is as if only Annie has died, or at least as if only her death is the tragedy here. Did they love my brother-in-law as they loved my sister? Will they miss him every day? From what I've gleaned, it appears the answer is no.

I think about calling Jan to arrange a coffee. She knows more than she's told me, I'm pretty sure, although I don't want to start down the road of conspiracy theories. I'll leave it for now, I decide. If I push too hard, she might close up altogether. Thankfully, at that moment I am distracted by a text from Patrick.

How's it going, babe? Xx

Grim. Just getting on with it. Thanks. Xx

Call me if you need to. Any time, day or night. Love you.

Thanks. Love you too.

I won't call. I haven't the energy to talk about it. I have support, I know that, but I really am the only person for the job of my own grief; no one can possibly understand what I'm facing, no one else can carry it. And whatever my needs are, other needs come first. Cal will need support, emotional and practical. The business will need attending to. Rainbow Cottage will need to be kept and run as the family home it is. The estate will need to be sorted – it will all go to Cal, I imagine. He won't need his roll of cash under the mattress after all. He has become a very wealthy young man.

And at that thought, another follows: in all likelihood, my life in London is over, at least for the foreseeable future. Cal has no other family and Annie would never forgive me if I wasn't here for him now. God knows, I'd never forgive myself.

Too much. I must only think about what happens now, today, at least for the moment.

I climb the stairs. In my sister and Dominic's room, I sit on the bed, restless and numb and suddenly incredibly tired. The drawers are open, their contents spilling out. The wardrobe door gapes; at the base, two shoeboxes have been searched. For what? I wonder. What on earth were they looking for?

I open a bedside drawer and find it to be full of men's black socks. Dominic's side of the bed then. In with the socks, a black box with *Tag Heuer* written on it – a watch that I presume will now be somewhere in the police station, along with wedding rings, my sister's watch. I wonder if the bracelet I gave her when she left Inveraray is there too, with its white gold charm of half a heart, the other half a pendant around my own neck. A cheesy parting gift and one I couldn't really afford at the time, but she loved it. Ironic that I will claim her half of the heart now that my own is broken.

I flop onto my back, half roll across the bed. I tell myself I'm tidying up after the police search, but whatever excuses I make to myself, I don't get that far. Instead, I am caught off guard by the smell of her. A second later, I have pressed my face into her pillow and am breathing her in, down into my lungs, my legs, my feet.

Too much, it is too much.

I sit up, snivelling, a blunt pain in my chest. I cannot go near that pillow, I cannot.

I lie down, press my nose to it again and close my eyes.

I wake up a little stunned. It is dark in the house; the sky is deep blue. Once I've got my bearings, I creep along the landing to Cal's room. There's no need to be furtive; the silence tells me he's still not back. On his bed, his red and white Southampton FC duvet is a jumble, his room an explosion of clothes, the units cheap pine, suitable for a teenager, a boy. I'm not sure if the mess is from him or from the police search.

I hover at the door. There are band posters on the wall – the Prodigy, KLF, others I don't recognise. Photographs are stuck up with torn strips of masking tape; a plant wilts on the window ledge. The room smells stale, stuffy. The police will have taken anything of note, I suppose, though I can't think what that might be. And if they've missed anything, I don't want to be the one to find it. I do not want to find evidence to support the dark feeling in my gut. It worries me that my nephew is still not home. But the thought of him returning worries me more.

CHAPTER 10

Isla

On the bookshelf, Annie's entire Almodóvar collection is lined up in chronological order: *Pepi, Luci, Bom* all the way to *Talk to Her*. I can't watch any of them, not without her, so I peruse her book collection instead. I'm in the living room, trying to read *The Blind Assassin* by Margaret Atwood, when I hear the rattle of the key in the front door. And there he is: my sister's boy, my closest kin on this earth, my wee pal of old. Cal.

He stretches up, rests both hands against the living-room door jamb, and I have to fight not to draw breath too sharply. He is so pale, his skin almost transparent. He looks like a ghost, or like he's seen one. His eyes are bruised hollows.

'Are you all right?' I ask.

He shakes his head but says nothing. A kind of haunted weariness comes off him in waves.

'Did you… did you have a think about your footprints?' What the hell did I say that for?

He glares at me, his eyes small, his mouth a black line. 'What?'

I lean away from him, though he is nowhere near me. 'Nothing, just… you know, the detective said to have a think. Sorry, I thought that's what you might be doing. Thinking.' Shut up, Isla. Shut. Up.

'So, what… you're suspicious of me too?'

'No, not at all. I…' I feel myself shrink into the corner of the sofa. He is taller than me, a lot taller than Dominic was. Younger, with a youth's unconscious strength.

'I… I was just asking.'

'Do you *actually* think I've got something to do with this?'

Do I?

'Of course not,' I say. 'I'm only asking if you remembered about the footprints, that's all. Sorry, that was tactless. I'm so tired. I'm not myself.'

He slackens but stays at a distance. 'I gave my statement.'

'Did it go OK?'

He sighs. 'The problem is, they want you to give them all the details as if you were taking notes. It's a blur. I must've got nearer to the studio than I thought. Or I went up there earlier or the day before or something. How should I know?'

Because it was you, your feet? I think but don't say.

'There's a sandwich in the fridge,' is what I do say. 'Daisy made it.'

'Is she here?' He glances towards the kitchen, back to me.

'No, she was away around seven.' I get up slowly, approach the door, aware of him filling the frame. For a moment it seems as if he isn't going to let me through, but at the last second, he shifts and I edge past into the hallway.

He doesn't follow me. It's nothing, less than nothing, but he would usually. Usually, he would shadow me, chatting all the while like he did when he was wee. But he doesn't. I wonder where he's been. I wonder what he's been doing all these hours. I wonder who he is.

The sandwich is cold. I add some crisps I find in the store cupboard. Thinking he needs something hot, I make him a cup of tea. It's not a proper dinner. Annie would have made him something proper – the kind of hot meal grown-ups provide for their children.

Despite being a kid herself, she always looked after him so well, always had him turned out so clean and tidy: clothes second-hand or run up by our mother on the sewing machine, all laundered and pressed. When he was two, he had this wee hand-knitted Aran jumper that Annie put him in together with the Campbell tartan kilt I bought him for his birthday, and oh, he looked so bloody cute in that outfit it was all I could do not to squeeze the breath out of him. But today he has a cold sandwich and a mug of tea and he looks like he's wearing yesterday's clothes. My last evening meal was hummus, tortilla chips and a bottle of white wine with Patrick, watching TV, feet on the coffee table, not a care. Annie never got to do that: drink cheap wine with a pal with her feet on the coffee table. She never got to eat crisps for tea with no thought but for herself.

Cal is not in the living room. A movement outside catches my eye and I see him walking down the garden, beyond the studio. Still with the plate in one hand and the tea in the other, I stand at the French windows and watch. He stops, stares out to the sea, pushes his hands deep into his jeans pockets. His shoulders rise, fall. His head dips and shakes slowly from side to side. A moment later, his left hand leaves its pocket and covers his eyes. I should go to him, I should. But instead, I watch.

A minute or so later, he turns back. I hide behind the curtain, spying on him as if he were a criminal. I am appalled at myself, but still I keep my eyes fixed on him. He walks slowly, studies the ground, his steps slow. He could come back through the open French window, but he doesn't, instead continuing past to the back door, which he appears to study before re-entering the cottage. I hear a loud sniff. A sigh. And then he's there again and I am handing him a sandwich and a cuppa and he is taking these offerings as if from a stranger and turning away and going up the stairs, and I know I should follow him and sit with him and comfort him and try to get inside his mind. But I don't. I can't find the strength. I can't find the courage.

*

It is hours later, unable to bear the quietness in the house, that I climb the stairs to his room. Outside his door, I listen, breathless, taut, but I can't hear any human noise above some tinny, frantic music. I knock, gently, then again, harder.

'Yeah?'

I push the door, trying not to notice the thumping of my heart. Impossibly, everything is bleaker, more unfathomable than before.

Cal is sitting on the deep window ledge, smoking a roll-up out of the leaded window. The sweet smell drifts inside. From his CD player, 'Roses' by Outkast plays. Normally, I would comment on this, out of a desire to prove that, hey, I might be in my thirties, but I'm still hip. But this isn't normally. Nor do I ask him what's in the cigarette. I know what's in the cigarette.

'Hi,' I say instead.

'Hey.' He blows smoke out across the back garden. I think of him hearing my sister and her husband screaming at each other, jumping out of bed, seeing them through this window. The hammer.

Is that what happened? Was he asleep, or did he watch the whole thing unfold while sitting here smoking? Did he run to the cabin and see something so horrific he can't talk about it? Did he intervene?

'Would you like something hot?' I say. 'You haven't really eaten.'

He shakes his head. 'Not hungry.'

'OK. I'll maybe make some pasta or something, then you can heat it up in the microwave later if you want, eh? You might get the munchies.' I'm lowering rope down a deep, dark well… *Here, grab hold. Let me help you climb out.* But he won't grab hold. He won't grab hold of the rope. 'I'll be downstairs if you need anything.'

On the landing, I press my forehead to the wall. I was the first person he called. He needed me, but now that I'm here, he has no idea how to ask me to help. It is me who needs help. I need him to help me understand what the hell happened last night.

Just before midnight, I text him from the living room and ask if he's OK.

Fine. Just tired, he replies.

Me too. We should try and sleep.

Sure. Night.

Night.

I haven't asked him where he went today besides the police station, not even by text. He hasn't volunteered this information.

I head upstairs, pausing outside his room before continuing into the spare room. There are no towels on the bed, no posy of flowers in a wee half-pint milk bottle. My sister always made this room lovely for me, as if I were a royal guest. If I'd come more often, maybe she would have treated me with the benign disregard I realise comes only with our closest relationships and which I have only ever known with her. I wonder whether what we lost over distance and time she found with Dominic. My own romantic relationships have been short-lived, courteous, ultimately unaffecting, but Annie isn't me. Wasn't.

As I clean my teeth, I remember how she used to climb into bed with me when she brought me my morning tea and we would chat through the day's plans; I guess you don't do that with a stranger, which means we were still us. Sometimes she would have to see to an issue in one of the cottages and I would take Cal out to a café or to the beach. We would ride the steam train to Corfe, sometimes take him for a pasty at the pub while we drank a cheeky pint of copper ale. Cal was happy, a happy kid.

I climb into bed like an arthritic ninety-year-old. I must fall asleep within moments, because when I stir, I have no memory of anything beyond the cold press of the sheet against my shoulders.

It takes me a second to remember where I am, reality a punch in the chest. Guilt then. I should have checked in with Cal one last time before turning in.

Another second, and I sense the presence of someone in the room. Yes. There is someone. There is a man sitting on the end of my bed.

'Cal?' My heart is thudding even as I realise that, yes, it is him.

'Sorry,' he whispers.

'What are you doing in my room?'

'I… I was just checking you were here. You were breathing so quietly I couldn't tell if you were in the bed.'

'Of course I'm here. Where else would I be?'

'I don't know.' His voice trembles.

'OK,' I say carefully. 'Sorry I didn't say goodnight. I was shattered.'

His silhouette clarifies by the second. Wan moonlight leaks through the gap between the curtains. It catches his eyes, makes them glint.

'Did you want to talk to me?' I ask.

He sniffs, wipes the base of his nose with the back of his hand. 'No, I… I was just checking you were OK.'

'Well, we're none of us OK, are we?'

He pushes his face into his hands. Another sniff. I pull myself out from under the covers and kneel beside him. Tentatively I place my hand on his shoulder. But still my heart bangs against my ribs, still I want to ask what he was doing watching me in the dead of night, where he has been all day, what he is hiding. I have known him all his life but I have not noticed his strangeness until now… Maybe a bit when he came to see me last year, maybe then, but not consciously. Daisy said he was close to Annie – intense, she said, hinted at darkness boiling within, at trouble.

'Is there anything you want to tell me?'

No reply.

'Is there something you're not telling the police? I... I can't help you if you don't trust me.'

I shift position so that I'm sitting beside him. He is so much bigger than me now. He could overpower me easily, pin me down, press a pillow to my face if he wanted to. In the silence, the violence of last night grows into something almost alive. Fire, a knife, a hammer. The frantic phone call. Sirens. For a moment I see Annie with the knife before I dismiss the idea. It is not her, not my Annie. Dominic with the knife. Dominic with the hammer.

Cal with the knife...

'I can't tell you,' he says, the words muffled behind his fingers.

I swallow shock. In telling me nothing, he has told me there is more. A core of heat travels the length of me.

'Was there... was there an accident?' It is less, much less than I want to ask, but it is as far as I can get.

But he shakes his head, his face still pressed into the flat of his hands.

'Where did you go today?'

He twists towards me, grabs my wrist, tight. Weak light catches the slick wet rectangle of his mouth, and for the first time in his life, I am aware of some dark force coiled within him. 'Don't ask me anything, OK? Whatever happens, don't ask me again.'

I shrink from him. Heat burns in my face, my chest. I don't want to be afraid of him, but I am – I am afraid.

'All right,' I whisper. 'It's OK. I won't, I promise. It's OK. It's OK, Cal. Promise.'

'And don't tell anyone we even had this conversation, will you?'

'I won't.'

'Promise?'

'I promise.'

He releases me and runs from the room. My own fingers circle where his were. My wrist stings.

And then I'm weeping into my hands, scared and powerless as a child.

'Annie,' I sob. 'Come back. Please come back to me.'

It is a long while before I'm able to lie down, by which time I'm shivering with cold. I lie awake, rigid. Cal shuffles around – I hear him in the kitchen, hear him climb the stairs, the shush and click of his bedroom door. He is awake. I can feel it, feel the loneliness of the two of us trapped in our cells.

It is almost dawn before I fall finally into deep sleep, and in those few snatched hours, I dream of my sister. We are at the loch and the sun is shining. I am back from uni and I have a picnic laid out on the shore, and in my dream there are no midges. Annie is walking along the shoreline. She is wearing a thin denim dress she used to have and her feet are bare. She sees me and waves and walks towards me. In her other hand are her sandals. She is smiling, but then, as she nears, her face collapses and she starts to cry. When she reaches me, she falls to her knees and throws herself forward as if to beg me for mercy.

'I'm sorry,' she says. 'I'm so, so sorry.'

A shadow falls over us. Cal, his eyes black. 'I didn't kill her.'

I wake up with a start, doubled over, my heart thudding.

I didn't kill her, I didn't kill her, I didn't kill her...

I sit up, breath shallow and quick. I know what Cal was trying to tell me. *I didn't kill her* doesn't mean *I didn't kill anyone*. It means *I killed someone*. It means *I killed him*. Dominic. I am as sure of this as I am of my own fathomless grief, and no sooner has this knowledge hit me than something else, something darker, forms, crouches, unfurls: if Cal killed Dominic, I can forgive him. I can.

CHAPTER 11

Annie

June 1991

Annie opens the envelope on her way back to the kitchen, where she was making a cup of coffee when the post dropped onto the mat. The letter is handwritten on stationery headed *Purbeck Cottage Holiday Rentals*.

There's an address below: Rainbow Cottage, then one of those funny-sounding place names like the ones Dominic listed for her when they met. Is this…? There's a phone number. As she reads further, her body fills with so much heat she has to open the front window of her flat and put her head out into the cool air.

Dear Annie,

I'm just going to come out and say it. Meeting you is the best thing that's happened to me in since – well, there, you see, I was going to put 'in years' but that wasn't right. And then I thought I'd try 'since I reached the top of Kili', but the fact is, meeting you is the best thing that's happened to me full stop. I can't explain it very well and I'm horribly aware of coming on too strong, but I had to write to you and ask you a very simple question:

Do you feel it too?

I can be brave by post. If I don't hear from you, I'll know that you don't feel the same and we can both be spared our blushes. I know I'm a little older, and a bit on the short side, but, literally, I would wear a Cuban heel for you and that's not something I'd do for just anyone.

She laughs out loud, pressing the letter momentarily to her chest before holding it up once more.

I'm being flippant, but to be serious for a second, I can't stop thinking about everything we talked about. I can't stop thinking about you. You are a butterfly, that's what I think, with a butterfly's deep need to be free. I know you feel trapped and I want to tell you that I believe you're only trapped because of that very need – because you are that butterfly! You see, when a butterfly flies into a net it does so because it's not thinking about the net; it's thinking about the sky. You think about the sky, Annie – that's what connects us.

Like you, I had dreams, which I didn't really go into the night we talked. I wanted to stay in London and start my own business – something cool, maybe something to do with the environment, but I'm an only child and my parents wanted to retire and I knew if I didn't continue the business and keep Rainbow Cottage in the family, it would kill them. I swore I'd never waste my MBA on the holiday lets, but they needed me, and the fact is, it's beautiful here, Annie. I know we talked so much about beauty and meaning and life and… Well, we talked about everything, didn't we? And the thing is, I think I can give you the freedom you need. That's what I want to offer. I believe I could make you happy here, and before you think this is chivalry, it isn't. I know how suspicious you are about that! This is a completely equal proposition, because if you were here, I'd be happy too. I strongly suspect that you alone can give me the freedom I need, do you see? I too am aiming for the sky, and the women I've met in the past, to stretch this metaphor to breaking point, have all been nets. Until you, I'd never met anyone else who I knew could fly with me. You are the free spirit I have been looking for and, typically, the moment I stopped looking, there you were: a butterfly who is not afraid of the sky.

Does that make sense?

I'm not saying move here immediately, don't panic! (Although wouldn't that be the most free-spirited, amazing thing in the world?) All I'm saying is, I'd like to write to you and I'd like to call you and hear your voice and talk to you sometimes. I'd like us to have the chance to find out if what I think we have is what we really do have. And then, only if you feel it too, perhaps I could come and visit or perhaps you would consider visiting me here at the cottage and I could show you all the places I told you about: the waves crashing at Seacombe Cliffs, the acres of yellow sand at Shell Bay, a pint of cider at The Square and Compass — it'll put hairs on your chest, I guarantee it! You'd love it here, Annie, I promise.

Am I wasting my time?

Say no.

Can I call you?

Say yes. Please, say yes.

My address and phone number are in the header, just in case you lost the classy eye-pencil-on-receipt version. Write to me and let me know what you think. Or call me. I'm here. I'm waiting. I think I've been waiting for you for a long time, maybe my whole life, maybe even since a previous lifetime.

With love
Dom x

Hand shaking over her mouth, she lowers herself onto the couch. She has never received such a letter. She has never seen one. Didn't know people even wrote letters like this in real life. Has never known anyone who would dare. It is an almost love letter, she thinks. Perhaps even an actual love letter.

'Dom,' she whispers, tracing her finger over his name.

She stands and waits while the strength returns to her legs, then she crosses the wee sitting room and heads into her bedroom. From the front centre drawer of her childhood dressing table, she pulls out the tiny jewellery box containing her mother's engagement ring – Mum gave this ring to her, her wedding ring to Isla, when her fingers swelled with arthritis. Inside the box, folded small, is a torn scrap of paper, his address and phone number scrawled on the back.

It was after four in the morning when they finally parted that night. The only ones left up, ensconced in two armchairs by the hearth, empty brandy glasses on the table in front of them. They'd drunk themselves sober.

'Can I walk you to your room?' he asked, considering her as if working her out.

'I'm sharing with my sister.'

'I know.'

They stood, groaning and laughing at their aching legs. She tried not to notice that she was taller than him. *I can wear flats*, she thought. *I mostly do anyway.*

I am an idiot, she thought then. *An absolute idiot.*

Along the dark corridor they walked in silence. When he took her hand, she pretended not to notice. Outside her room, she leant her back against the wall and stared down at her shoes, but she could sense he'd placed one hand against the wall above her left shoulder, that he was very close and that he was looking at her. When she finally managed to raise her face to his, he kissed her, immediately, on the mouth. She was glad he'd saved them both from the awkwardness of wondering whether or not it would happen. He'd made it happen.

'I'd like to write to you.' She wasn't expecting him to say something so old-fashioned. 'Would you mind that? Do you have an email address?'

'We don't even have a computer,' she admitted – it was she who was living in the past. 'I can give you my postal address? I have a telephone number too. We have electricity, at least.'

It was a joke but he didn't laugh. Wordlessly, he pulled a tan leather wallet – hand-stitched with red cotton – from the back pocket of his jeans. From it he drew out a receipt, the bill for tonight's meal, which the boys had insisted on paying.

She dug in her bag, found her sister's eyeliner and held it up.

'Eyeliner on a bill,' he said, tearing it in half.

'Classy,' she replied, and they both giggled.

But after a few letters, the kohl crumbled and he had to run and nick a pen from reception.

'My sister'll kill me,' Annie joked. 'I've squashed it.'

'I'll buy her another one.'

He kissed her again, one hand on her waist. He smelt of wine and a cologne she imagined was expensive. Like the wallet. He brushed her cheek with the knuckle of his forefinger.

'Annie Andrews,' he said. 'Thank you for the most wonderful night.'

Now she presses the receipt to her lips, watches herself do this in the dressing-table mirrors, like a child. Like a child, she studies herself, reflected from all sides – her hair in two long braids, her earlobes small, unpierced. By the time she was ready for the rebellion of the beautician's needle, she was already in the grip of a much, much larger one. Sighing, she pushes her hands flat to her cheeks and stares and stares at herself. That night, once inside the hotel room, she stared at herself like this in the mirror in the bathroom, fingers pressed to her mouth. Her eyes were bloodshot. But they were shining.

'Dom,' she says now to her reflection, and laughs.

She could call Isla. But Isla doesn't have a phone in her student digs. Her parents? Lord, no! What would she say? What *would* she say?

'Mum, Dad, I have fallen in love.'

She laughs again, the mental image of their aghast mouths – two big pink Os.

They wouldn't believe her. They'd be scathing. But she has fallen in love, she has. And because of this, she knows for certain that she hasn't before. Still in her mind's eye, she falls to her knees before her parents, palms pressed together:

'Mum, Dad, I finally understand why I always felt suffocated. All the boys I've met were too small for me, don't you see? They were limited and I must have known they would limit me.'

Yes, she thinks, *this has always been the problem.*

Her shoulders slump. The letter falls onto her lap. Mum and Dad won't be interested in anything she has to tell them. They won't have the imagination to conceive that two people can fall in love quite spontaneously; they'll have a fit when they find out he's not from around here, tell her she's a fool, that she's let herself get lost in fantasies yet again, that this is why she got into trouble in the first place. *Trouble...* as if Callum wasn't the apple of their eye, as if they didn't absolutely dote on him when they thought no one was looking. *You are the fools*, she wants to shout at them sometimes. *So concerned with what other people think, you can't live properly yourselves. You are good, yes, you are, but you are joyless.*

An epiphany: they are not butterflies!

She draws herself up tall, straightening her shoulders. *I am a butterfly*, she thinks. A butterfly who landed in a net only because she was aiming for the sky. Dom has seen this in a way no one else has, not even herself.

And in that moment, it occurs to her that she can't tell Isla either. Not because she has no phone – but because she won't understand.

'For God's sake,' she will say. 'Listen to yourself. What, is he going to save you?'

'I don't need saving,' Annie replies, lost in her imagining. 'I've been looking after myself and my son since I was sixteen!'

'Aren't you forgetting you're living rent-free?' Actually, no, that's too cruel; Isla would never say that – though she would bring feminism into it. She's been reading Simone de Beauvoir and Germaine Greer and now it's like she's the first woman ever to discover equal rights.

But this is not about being saved. She can give him his freedom, that's what he said. She is the only person he has ever met who can do this.

She breathes in deeply, exhales, feels a kind of catharsis. And then another, smaller epiphany: this will be the first time she can't say something to her kid sister, the first time she will have to cut out the parts Isla will think are stupid. The butterfly stuff is a case in point. This will have to be for her and Dominic alone... the thought gives her an exquisite pain in her heart, an emotional indigestion. Until this moment, Isla was the one who understood everything about her. Now, the person who will understand, the *only* person who will understand what she's feeling, is him.

Dominic's letter shivering in her hands, she picks up the phone and dials.

CHAPTER 12

Isla

September 2004

Seven thirty. Still misty, still chilly. DI York is standing on the driveway of the cottage, flanked by a man and a woman, both in uniform, with fluorescent yellow rain jackets. York's dark brown eyes, heavy brow and a jawline softening now in middle age give him the sorrowful look of a hound. That look is all I need to tell me they are here to arrest my nephew for Dominic's murder.

'Is Callum here?'

'He's in bed just now. Can I help? Is something wrong?' These are the questions that leave my mouth, even as my guts fold. Incredibly, I let them into the hallway with a courteous sweep of my hand.

The female PC is telling me she's a family liaison officer and to go into the living room. From one moment to the next, I have lost all authority in my sister's house. I am being told where to sit while two men are taking the stairs a few at a time, their low, urgent voices reaching me without the sense. I stumble through towards the back of the cottage. The apple tree is spotted with fruit; fruit has fallen onto the grass. In the sky, the palest blue is breaking through the grey; steam condenses on the windowpanes. Everything happens slowly. Everything happens within seconds.

Shouts come from upstairs, a bang, the thudding of feet. A moment later, my nephew is grabbing at the front door, dressed only in pyjama bottoms, his back a long pale triangle. A police officer clatters down the stairs. Cal is caught by the shoulder, turned roughly and pushed to the wall.

'Get off me,' my nephew roars, but he stays pinioned to the wall.

I know what comes next. I hear the words before DI York says them.

'Callum Rawles,' he says, 'I am arresting you on suspicion of the murder of Annie Rawles. You do not have to say…'

I don't hear the rest. My head thrums, vision blackening. My body fills with white heat. *No*, I think. *No*. York has said it wrong. He said the murder of Annie Rawles. He said Annie instead of Dominic. Cal wouldn't lay a hand on my sister. There is no way on God's earth he would…

'You can't do this,' Callum shouts. 'You can't do this to me.'

The impossible sight of him pressed against the wall. My nephew. My sister's boy.

'No,' I say. 'You've got the wrong—'

'Come on, son.' York's hands are spread, his head inclined to one side. 'Don't make this harder than it already is, all right? Let's get you down to the station and you can tell us the truth this time, OK? Let's go and sort this out.'

Cal bursts into tears. 'I'm sorry,' he sobs. 'I'm so, so sorry.'

'You can't…' I am rooted to the spot. No more words come. I don't know what the words are. I cannot think of them. Cal. So like his mother, my beautiful Annie. My daft big sister. No. No, no, no. This cannot be. It cannot.

The front door opens. A strange calm descends. Cuffed to the other officer, Cal is a hunched shape in the low, brambled doorway. York glances back at me, his lips pressed tight.

'DC Thornett will look after you,' he says, eyes full of apology, and I notice only then that he is clutching a jumble of my nephew's clothes. 'I'll be in touch.'

And then he's gone. The slam of a car door, the growl of an engine, the gargle of tyres on gravel.

The silence rushes, howls around like a storm. The air holds only static. Confusion. Numbness.

'I'll make us a cup of tea, shall I?'

I look at her, this woman who has been sent to look after me. Her hair is short, black.

'No,' I say, bewildered. 'No, thank you.'

'Why don't you sit down?' She leads me through my sister's house, gestures to my sister's soft velvet sofa, takes the armchair by the French windows.

I sit. 'This is all wrong. Callum would never kill anyone, let alone...'

'Well, they've taken him in now. He can tell them what happened properly.'

'He'll need a lawyer.'

'He'll be appointed a legal defence, don't worry.'

'But...'

But what? I don't know. Oh Cal, what have you done? In my darkest moments I have imagined you were hiding something, yes, yes I have. Your strangeness around me since I've been here, your fleeting aggression, the way you appeared to find it difficult to look at me. The silhouette of you on my bed, staring at me, your wet eyes weird and wild. But not this. Not *this*.

Against the crashing waves at Seacombe Cliffs, Daisy's voice comes to me: *His eyes... they were black, you know? Boiling.* Boiling with hate. Yes, I have imagined him waking up to them arguing, fighting, a hammer raised, that black and boiling hate bubbling over after finding his stepfather standing over the body of my sister, the bloodied hammer in his hand... a blind frenzy with a kitchen knife. But it was Dominic he killed, in my mind's eye. Dominic, not his mother. I can forgive him for killing Dominic; I have already begun to make peace with that.

But they are not arresting him for the murder of my brother-in-law. They are arresting him for killing my sister. They have arrested him. I heard it clearly, even if the fact of it is still drifting down. His own mother. My sister. My Annie. Dear God. I have loved this child since the moment he was born. If what they believe about him is true, what the hell am I going to do with all that love? I can forgive him for Dominic, but not for Annie. Not for Annie.

DC Thornett gives a shallow, grim smile. 'I know this must be very shocking for you. You'll need some time to process it. We'll have to wait for forensics and so forth, but unfortunately Callum's statement is at odds with what the evidence is telling us. But he'll have the chance now to explain...' She trails off.

'What about a lawyer?' I realise I've already asked her this.

'He has the right to legal advice and he'll be able to call you once they've processed him. They've taken his fingerprints already, so...'

'What did you say your name was?'

'DC Thornett. Call me Sue, all right? I'm only here to make sure you're OK and explain everything.'

'Where will they take him?'

'They'll process him in Swanage and then, after that, if they charge him, he'll most likely go to Guys Marsh. But we're a long way from that yet. Best thing is to take it one day at a time.'

'Can I call someone?'

'Of course. You're not under arrest. I'll make that tea, eh.'

I call Daisy. It is too early to call, but she answers after a few rings. She sounds sleepy.

'Isla,' she says. 'Everything OK?'

'They've arrested Callum.'

'What? Oh my God, what for?'

'Murder.'

'Right. Stay there. I'm coming over.'

It's only after I've put the phone down that I notice she didn't express much shock. I told her Cal had been arrested for murder. And she didn't ask who.

CHAPTER 13

Annie

June 1991

His laugh is high and short. She hears him take in a gulp of air. 'You actually called me.'

'You did ask me to,' she replies, turning so that the cord of the phone wraps itself around her waist.

'Is that why? Is that the only reason?'

'I got your letter.'

'And?'

'I liked it. And you're not.'

He sounds like he's wheezing – is he laughing? 'Not what?'

'Not wasting your time.'

There is a pause. For a moment she wonders if the line has gone dead, but then, that sound again, the sound of him breathing.

'So,' she adds, emboldened, 'are you going to come here first or am I going to come to you?'

'Seriously?' He laughs properly then, like a dog yelping at a doorbell. 'How about I come to you? We can go walking, if you like. Whatever you want. I just want to be with you. I want to talk to you.'

She smiles, at no one, at herself, at him, even though he can't see. It's a stupid smile, but she doesn't even care. She gives him the name of some B & Bs she knows in town, but he asks her for the name of the nicest hotel in Inveraray.

'The Loch Fyne is very swish,' she says. 'I've waitressed there a few times, but it's awful expensive.'

He says he'll take care of it, not to worry. He'll drive up. No, she says, it's too far. He'll take the train, he says, then hire a car. She cannot imagine ever having the confidence or the freedom to do such a thing; almost asks how he'll find her but stops herself just in time. He is in his thirties. He will find her.

And he does. Two weeks later, he finds her white town and calls her from the finest place in it.

'My room overlooks the loch.' He pronounces loch *lock*, like a typical Englishman – she makes a mental note to teach him to say it properly. 'And I can see… is it the Cowal Hills?'

'Aye, it is.' She fights off the mental image of herself in that room, looking out, him at her shoulder, his arms circling her waist.

That evening, she leaves Callum to stay over with her parents. She has given them a version of the truth. She suspects they know fine well what the real truth is, but they are old now and she is twenty-six and they haven't the strength to argue with her anymore. Through annoying drizzle, she hurries in her trainers to the elegant sandstone manor house, where shiny cars are parked at the end of the wide curve of the drive. Normally she'd be fazed by such opulence, but she worked Friday evenings here for a few months with her best friend Lizzie Macdonald before she got pregnant – something she wishes she hadn't told Dominic. Once inside, she changes into her heels, leaves her rucksack in the cloakroom and totters to the bar.

Dominic is sitting on a high stool, a crystal whisky glass in front of him. He is wearing chino-style trousers, not jeans, brown leather brogues, a pale blue shirt and a dark blue fine-knit V-neck sweater. His hair is longer, pushed back in a way that makes him look European. He looks classy, she thinks, although Isla would say he looks like a dweeb. When he stands to greet her, she curses herself for wearing heels.

'Hey, you.' He holds her by the upper arms and kisses her on the cheek. He smells the same – citrus, something else she can't name, and the peaty scent of single malt. He leans back a little, still with his hands on her arms, and smiles. She tries to decipher his face, whether or not he is disappointed at the sight of her, whether he is already regretting his grand gesture.

'Hey yourself.' Heat climbs up her neck, her mind all but blank.

He asks her what she wants to drink. Gin and tonic, she says, cringing at the question in her intonation, but he replies only *Good choice!* and she feels her ribcage sink with relief. And within moments, they are talking – talking, talking, talking. This place! That view! His journey here, her day at the shop, the brown water he called reception to complain about only to find out it was perfectly normal, *due to the peat deposits, sir*, and how excellent it all is, how she must take him on the whisky tour one day, how lovely her home town is, really how utterly beautiful, she must be so proud…

And then they are sitting in the restaurant on the high-backed upholstered chairs she has never sat in, only walked among across the thick plaid carpet and bowed and nodded and smiled and served new potatoes with tricksy silver tongs and poured gravy from a china gravy boat without spilling a drop. And the shine tarnishing on the loch and the amber-pink sun melting into the hills do make her feel proud to be part of this place, proud to see it through his eyes and feel a new sense of ownership over this immense and stirring landscape.

But it is not, thank God, it is *not* boring or awkward or anything like that. It is unfamiliar and familiar, more formal than she has experienced and yet more relaxed. And at the same time, she feels she does, after all, know how to do this, how to be, with him. *I am brave*, she thinks. *I am a butterfly.*

'I feel so childish next to you,' she says when he pauses to pour the wine, twisting the bottle at the very last second in the way she remembers from a month ago. 'You've done so much.'

'But you're much more accomplished than me. You've raised a child! You've taught yourself to paint. I've done a few courses, that's all.' He waves his hand, dismissing his own achievements. 'A bit of travelling, built up my parents' business and made it moderately successful– nowhere near beats raising an entire human when you were no more than a teenager yourself.'

She giggles. 'You forgot my level-one Spanish.'

'I apologise.' He gives her that ironic smile. 'That was an oversight. And you did that for your sister, right?'

'*Si, señor.*' She grins at him. 'Well, for me as well. We're both nuts for Almodóvar, you know the Spanish director? What with our parents being so strict and his films being a bit, you know, risqué. And *Carmen*, the opera? That's in French. I have the CD. I sing along to it when I'm cleaning the flat.' She picks up her glass, hopes she's surprised him. 'Anyway, yeah, so after the Five Sisters, we promised ourselves another trip, and because I've never been abroad she suggested Spain, but we have to wait till she's finished her degree next year… sorry, I'm talking too much.' She gulps the wine he has chosen. It is a French one, but to be honest, she can't tell the difference between it and the plonk she allows herself on Saturday nights when Callum goes to bed.

He tips his glass towards her. 'Well, here's to Spain.'

She is grinning again. She can't help it. It's like she has no control over her mouth.

They talk about everything and nothing, as they did at the Cluanie Inn. And as on that night, time disappears like dry sand through spread fingers. He makes her laugh with wee stories from his cottage business, things the guests have left behind over the years: a long black wig made of real hair – *Really?* A set of sex toys in a box – *Oh my God, you're joking!* A stash of pills – *As in drugs? In Dorset?*

'You'd be surprised.'

'And do you contact them? The people who leave these things?'

'We do. I didn't with the pills – if anyone had called, I would have said I'd thrown them away.' He raises an eyebrow. She's pretty sure he's insinuating that he took them himself but dares not acknowledge it. The latter stages of teenage life and whatever her peers did narcotics-wise passed her by entirely.

'With the sex toys,' he continues, 'I said I'd discovered a box, did that ring a bell, would she like me to open it?'

'I'm guessing she said no.'

'She said no *really quickly.*' He laughs – they both do. 'The worst one was a dog,' he goes on, and by this time she is wiping away tears of laughter. 'An actual live dog, a little scruffy brown and white thing. They got all the way back to London before we could reach them. They actually got home and put the kettle on before one of the kids must've said, hey, where's Scruftie, or whatever its name was.'

She laughs, genuinely, rocking back in her chair. 'One of the house parties I went to when I was a kid,' she tells him, 'like, fourteen or something, we all got really drunk and at the end of the night no one could find the dog. We looked everywhere, and eventually one of the lassies found him in the chest freezer.'

Dominic almost chokes on his wine; a thrill passes through her.

'He was fine,' she says. 'Poor wee mutt had only been in there a few seconds; one of the lads had put him in there for a laugh. Lads, eh? Idiots.'

Dominic wipes his eyes and leans forward. 'That,' he says, 'is classic.'

After dinner, she wonders if he'll ask her to come to his room, but instead he insists on walking her home.

'That's kind, sir,' she replies, confused. 'But I don't need your protection.'

'I'd be doing it for myself. I need to digest the ridiculous dessert you made me eat on my own.'

She loves the way he does this, turns chivalry – which Isla has told her is in fact an attempt to get women to believe they are weak – into selfishness, which of course it is not. Dominic's approach is not sexist, it is generous. He gives her the power – no, that's not right – he points out that it is she who holds it. Or maybe that neither of them do; yes, that's better. This isn't about power at all, in fact, but about something much purer and kinder, a meeting of minds and, she is beginning to hope, bodies.

He holds her hand all the way, but at the door of the shop, he only lifts her chin and kisses her less deeply than at the hotel all those weeks ago, and she worries that her conversation over dinner has established her as she fears she really is – a naïve girl who knows nothing at all about anything – and that he no longer wants her.

'I'll see you tomorrow,' he says, taking a step back.

'Callum is with my parents,' she says. 'You could come up for a coffee?'

He shakes his head, but a warm smile spreads across his face. 'That's not why I came. I'll see you tomorrow, OK? You owe me a picnic. Ten o'clock?'

It is after midnight. Once inside her flat, Annie sighs against the front door. If she is a butterfly, then her stomach is one great net of them. She changes into her PJs and is about to go to bed when the phone rings.

'I'm at a payphone.' It's Isla. 'So?'

'Oh, Isla.'

'Oh God.' Down the line, puffs on a cigarette – disgusting.

'I know what you're going to say, but this is different.'

'Like Malcolm was different? Like Fergus? Like Duncan?'

'Oh, come on. Malcolm was eleven years ago, I was a child. Fergus was, well, I was still full of the baby hormones, and Duncan, yes, I suppose, but I soon got the measure of him.'

'And you have the measure of Dominic Rawles, I'm guessing? Did he take the silver spoon out of his mouth?'

'He's not posh. I think his parents rented out a few cottages, but he's built what they had into a profitable business, that's all. They have fifteen places now. He basically turned it around.'

'And he told you that, did he? Modest.'

'It wasn't like that, we were just talking… He's travelled all over. He did an MBA in New York, and he does triathlons.'

'Gosh, what a lot he's told you about himself.'

'Please, Isla. I've never felt like this before, like… I feel like I want to run after him and drag him back here just so I can be with him, do you know what I mean? At least I let people in.'

Isla says nothing.

'Are you giving me the silent treatment?' Annie asks, worried now that she's offended her wee sister.

'You're such a daftie, that's all. I worry you're going to get hurt. What do you really know about him anyway?'

'Well, I went out with Duncan for over a year and I had no idea who he was. I knew Malcolm better and I only spent a few hours with him.'

'But you were only a kid – you just said that.'

'I was old enough to get pregnant. And I'm not a kid now. Dom came all this way. And I invited him in and he didn't come up – he just kissed me and walked off. We're going for a picnic on the loch tomorrow with Cal.'

'You're *not* going to let him meet Cal?'

'Keep your wig on. I'll introduce him as a pal, that's all. I won't do anything stupid.'

'What about Mum and Dad?'

'They're not invited.'

'Very funny. Have you told them?'

'I've said we met that weekend and that he was passing through. They'll be fine. They'll be glad I've found someone with a bit of maturity.'

Isla sighs heavily. 'I'm not meaning to be negative, OK? I'm just…' The phone beeps, Isla's money running out.

'I'm fine,' Annie says quickly before the line dies. 'Don't worry about me. I'm happy, actually happy, and I can't remember being this happy since I was a kid. Please. Let me have this.'

'I will. I'm happy for you. Honestly I am.'

CHAPTER 14

Isla

September 2004

Daisy storms into the cottage, her hair pushed flat at the sides by sleep, making her quiff look even taller. 'Cal couldn't murder a fly,' she says. 'It's nonsense! They have no evidence!'

'I know.' I don't know, I don't, but I'm glad of her certainty.

'Hi, Sue,' she says to DC Thornett, as if in afterthought. 'How's things?'

DC Thornett grimaces a little. 'All right.'

'He didn't do it, you know that, don't you?'

Thornett's eyes widen.

'Sorry,' Daisy says. 'Not easy, is it?'

There is a pause. I feel acutely, again, like an outsider. After a moment, I touch Daisy's elbow and gesture towards the garden. 'I could do with some air.'

DC Thornett nods. For how comfortable she looks, she may as well be sitting on a spike.

In the garden, Daisy takes my arm.

'Christ,' she says softly.

We walk towards the apple tree, the black hulk of the studio crouching beyond. The morning air is nippy. Still in my PJs, I pull Annie's cardigan tight around me. I took it from the hook on her bedroom door last night and put it on this morning when

I crept down to make the tea. It smells of her and I push it to my nose at intervals, like lavender.

'Has Cal spoken to you at all?' I ask Daisy once we're clear of the cottage.

She hesitates. Her eyes are puffy from crying and she's wearing yesterday's clothes. 'He was waiting outside my house when I got back from being with you.'

'Did he say anything?'

Another pause, as if she is trying to choose her words. We have reached the back fence, where we stop.

'He said he'd been to the police station, then gone for a drive over to Studland. He'd been for a walk on the beach, he said. Why, did he say anything to you?'

It is my turn to choose my words. Cal is my nephew. But Daisy is my sister's most trusted friend, and now, with Cal in custody, I need her to be my friend too. Without her, I have no one; it's as simple as that.

I check the back door, but Thornett is still in the house.

'I don't know what happened,' I say, keeping my voice low. 'But it looks like he might be more involved than he's letting on. He said he didn't kill her. He said that, those exact words. I thought he was trying to tell me something, almost by omission.'

'That he killed Dom, you mean?'

'That's what I thought, but it's not Dom he's accused of killing.'

'*What?*'

This time I study her as a cop might. She looks suitably incredulous, but I could, of course, be wrong. After all, I've been wrong about everything else.

'I know,' I say. 'It's so shocking.'

Daisy's eyes have filled. 'That's not... it's not...'

'Not what happened?'

'I don't know what happened.'

Don't you? I think, hate myself for thinking it.

'I thought maybe he'd told you something last night,' I say. 'Given you some clue.'

She shakes her head. 'No. I'm as shocked as you are. *Annie?* Oh my God. How? Why?'

'I was beginning to think maybe he'd walked in on them fighting and… The hammer would have been in the studio is what I've been thinking.'

'A *hammer?*' Daisy claps her hand over her mouth. 'Oh my God,' she says through her fingers.

'He said he saw Dominic with a hammer. I thought… I thought maybe Cal took the knife out with him, for protection, but… oh, I don't know, I don't know! He's as good as told me there's more to it, but he won't tell me what, and last night he was quite…' Sitting on my bed, staring at me in the dark – this, I find I cannot say. It is too weird; despite everything, I don't want her to think badly of him.

'Quite what?'

'Nothing I can put my finger on. I just wish he'd talked to me.'

'Hey, don't upset yourself.' Her voice trembles.

'There's no way he could have killed Annie, is there? Not that I think he's capable of killing Dom… I mean, we're all capable of murder, aren't we? That's what they say. Just a question of the stakes being high enough. But Annie? He can't have done that – he just can't.'

'I agree. Hundred per cent.'

I search her face, but she looks as devastated and heartbroken as me, mirroring my expression like a child gauging a parent in precarious mood. 'You said he was intense with her. The way he looked at her. What did you mean by that?'

'He was… he's quite an intense kid. He's always been that way. Annie was like that too. The way she looked at you when she was listening, do you know what I mean?'

I do. Like she was heading for a brain bleed. She would lock eyes and hold on, as if what you were saying was water from the holy font. Cal never looked into my eyes like that, but he was… watchful, like an animal.

'I never paid too much attention to it,' I say. 'With Annie, I mean. I was used to it, I suppose.'

We look out towards the sea, greyer today under the changeable sky.

'Cal told me he used to go to Jan's sometimes when things got a bit… She said Annie stayed with you.'

'She did. He didn't beat her up regularly or anything. They fought, but it was how they were.' She sighs. 'But after Cal came back, yes, it got worse. Up until she miscarried, she wasn't scared of him. It was more…'

'More what?'

'Like not sticking with it would be failing in some way, like she couldn't bear the thought.' She stretches her neck, moves her head from side to side and lets out another heavy sigh. 'Look, can we talk about this another time? I'm sorry, I just feel like I'm betraying her somehow. Do you mind?'

I feel myself blush. 'Of course not. I'm sorry, I didn't mean to—'

'It's OK. You're her sister. I just—'

'If they charge him,' I interrupt, mortified, confused, 'I should get him a lawyer, shouldn't I?'

'I don't know. I've never been through anything like this before. It's all so… it's all so bloody shocking.' She sighs, bites her lip; her chest rises and falls. 'I do know they have twenty-four hours to charge him before they have to let him go. One of Dominic's good friends is a barrister; I'll give him a call, OK?'

'OK.'

'Come on,' she says. 'Let's make some proper coffee and I'll see if anything needs doing in terms of the changeover.'

'Oh God, the changeover is today, isn't it? I completely forgot.'

She checks her watch. 'It's fine, it's barely nine o'clock. I'll give the head cleaner a call. She's been with them for years. I'm sure she'll have heard already – you can't fart at one end of this village without someone smelling it at the other.'

CHAPTER 15

Isla

In the afternoon, a pinched-looking woman appears at the door and introduces herself as DI Hall. After an initial show of concern, she suggests we sit at my sister's old pine kitchen table and fills me in on what's happening. Cal is being processed. She is now in charge of the investigation. I wonder if that's due to a conflict of interest. Perhaps the police feel, as I do, that DI York was looking after Cal more than he should.

'He hasn't called me,' I say. 'I thought he had the right to a phone call?'

'He is permitted a call, yes. But he declined.'

He declined. I breathe this in. 'Can I call him?'

'I'm afraid not.'

'Right.'

'How well do you know Callum?' she asks with affected casualness.

'He's my nephew.' I sound sarcastic even to myself. 'I've known him since he was born.'

'And are you close, would you say?'

'We were very close when he was a child, but my sister moved away when he was nearly twelve. He came to see me last summer. I hadn't seen my sister in over a year, but we spoke once a week, kept tabs, you know? I live in London and we were both busy.

There's a limit to how much…' I make myself stop. Whatever guilt grows inside me by the hour, I don't need to justify myself to this stranger. She hasn't asked me how close I was to my sister.

'We're just trying to build a picture.' DI Hall's dark grey eye-shadow has formed tiny rivulets in the creases of her eyelids, and there is a small black blob in the corner of her right eye. Annie and I had a code for eye bogeys: one would wipe the corner of her eye with her finger, the other would immediately do the same. I suppose this is pretty common. But I don't put my finger to my eye. I don't tell this woman she has an eye bogey, even in code. Unsisterly, I know, but she's not my sister.

'When he came to stay, how did he seem?'

Haunted, low, troubled. But only in retrospect. 'Fine,' I lie. 'Just… normal.'

'Did he mention his stepfather at all? Trouble at home?'

I shake my head, on firmer ground. 'No, he didn't. I asked after everyone, as you do. He said they were fine.'

'So you weren't aware of any tension between him and his stepfather?'

'No more than a normal amount.'

'And what about your sister?'

'What about her?'

'How did she seem?'

Drawn, tired, the lines on her forehead deeper than they should have been in her thirties. She didn't laugh as much – she used to get the giggles so much she'd have to hold on to the back of a chair, a tabletop, work counter. I hadn't seen her laugh like that in a long while.

'She seemed normal,' I say. 'She was tired with the demands of running a home and the business and keeping up with her own career. Spinning plates, you know?'

'Your brother-in-law wasn't very hands-on?'

'I didn't say that.'

'So as far as you're aware, your brother-in-law wasn't a difficult man?'

I shrug. 'Men are more selfish by nature. At least, that's the impression I get, once the charm offensive is over.'

She raises her eyebrows a fraction.

'I know he liked to have parties,' I add. 'Everyone-back-to-our-place type thing. He often stayed for lock-ins at the pub, but Annie didn't complain about that so much as simply tell me – more of an eye roll than a huge marital issue. He got on her nerves sometimes, but I'm sure most couples get on each other's nerves sometimes, don't they? I really wouldn't know.'

'And there was no one else, as far as you're aware?'

'What do you mean?' The penny drops. 'Do you mean an affair?'

She gives an almost imperceptible nod. Jan said Dominic took liberties – was that what she meant?

'Absolutely not,' I say.

'What about your sister?'

'Annie would never have an affair! She was loyal, a loyal person.' It occurs to me that she would, actually, if pushed to it. She would open herself up to someone new; she would not lose faith in love itself. It is me who cannot stand the thought of such self-revelation, the terrifying vulnerability that comes with it. 'Why do you ask? I mean, is that information you have?'

'As I say, we're just trying to build up a picture. Can you confirm that your nephew called you to tell you what had happened?'

'He did.'

'And how did he sound?'

'He'd just discovered his parents had been burnt to death; how do you think he sounded? He was almost incoherent with distress.'

If she picks up on my irritation, she doesn't show it. 'And what time was this?'

My face heats; old gungy eye remains unruffled. 'It was… late. I didn't check my watch. One-ish?'

I can't stand the look of this woman, her attempt at a sympathetic smile or whatever it is she thinks she's going for. I stand, busy myself in the kitchen. There is little to do; Daisy must have washed up. She and Jan are like a SWAT team. They have lowered themselves down on ropes from helicopters.

'How would you describe Callum's relationship with his mother?'

'It was close. I've told you that, haven't I? He was maybe a bit intense.'

'Intense how?'

'Daisy mentioned it, that's all. The way he looked at Annie, all black and boiling, she said, but that's the intensity of youth, isn't it? He's sensitive, that's all she meant, as was my sister. It was just the two of them for years. It's completely normal that he'd be protective of her; he's hardly going to murder her, is he?' I plunge my hands into the soapy water in the kitchen sink, squeeze the cloth, wipe the surfaces even though they are clean.

After a moment, I turn to face the detective. 'Look, I don't mean to be rude, but I can tell you one thing: whatever happened that night, Cal didn't kill anyone, all right? It's just not possible.'

I turn away before she can read in my face that I sound so much surer than I am. I may not believe he killed my sister, no matter what he has and has not said. But as for Dominic, I'm less sure – I just can't figure out why he's lying, or even if he is lying. Maybe it's me who's lying – to myself. If we want something to be untrue, if we want it violently enough, then somewhere in us, somehow, we make it so. It should be no surprise to me that I can do this. Annie and I were raised on denial after all.

CHAPTER 16

Isla

Half an hour after DI Hall leaves, Daisy calls me on my mobile.

'Right,' she says, without saying hello. 'Dominic's friend's going to call you.'

'Oh my goodness, you're a star.'

'Have you got a pen? I'll give you his number too. His name is Thomas Bartlett.'

'I know that name. I met him once. It was when Annie met Dominic, up in Scotland.' Nice eyes. Quiet intelligence. The two of us outside the Cluanie Inn, berating ourselves for smoking when we'd spent a day in such clean air but still enjoying the hit. He was so respectful, didn't make any kind of attempt to move things onto a less platonic footing – so much so, I began to wish he would.

'That's him. The annual boys' yomp.'

I take down Tom's number. 'Thanks, Daisy.'

'He's a good guy anyway,' she adds. 'Not like Dominic.'

I let that go and ring off but make a mental note to ask her what she meant, what she truly thinks about my brother-in-law.

In the late afternoon, restless beyond measure and with no call yet from Thomas or Cal, I decide to get some air and go and see Jan. She's a family friend, and she's older. If anyone knows about

Dominic and his history, it's her. I am like the police, I think. Trying to build up a picture.

I walk along the lane. With my back to the duck pond, I recognise Jan's place, remember Daisy pointing it out along with my sister's rental cottage next door – Annie called it Heartbreak Hotel, I think. Yes, I'm pretty sure it was that one.

Jan is cheerier than yesterday, even manages a smile when she opens the door.

'Isla,' she says. 'Good for you, getting out. Come in, come in.'

Her home is cosy, with low ceilings and dark lintels. The walls and curtains are reds and pinks, an emporium of ornaments populate every surface, an upright piano against one wall, a tiny guitar and what looks like a small harp propped up in the corner. There is a fireplace with three thick cream candles on the grate; a baggy armchair, too big for the room, is a throne for two black cats.

I follow her through an internal set of doors into a small kitchen with an old pine table and four Ercol chairs. She tells me to sit. Without asking if I want tea or coffee, she fills the kettle over the small Belfast sink and places it on the stove to boil.

'They've arrested Cal,' I say.

Jan nods, spooning loose tea into a blue enamel teapot with white edging. Of course. She knows. 'They've not charged him, have they?'

I exhale heavily and shake my head.

'No. I can't believe they'll make it stick. He hasn't called me or told me anything, but weirdly, I feel like I'm sinking under information. Dominic being abusive, her marriage… Daisy told me she'd suffered a miscarriage. I didn't even know they were trying for a baby.'

'Trying.' She huffs, as if *trying*'s a strong word. 'I think he'd agreed, but she didn't exactly announce that she'd stopped with the pill.'

The words hang for a moment, settle, mix in with DI Hall's questions about my sister and Dominic's fidelity, the fact of Annie's miscarriage. I didn't ask how far along she was. I didn't ask if there were any circumstances I should know about. A thought flashes: Dominic's features bunched in fury; Annie, pregnant, cowering, her hand raised in self-defence; him with a hammer raised above his head. The possibility that the baby wasn't Dominic's drifts but does not land. That's not what Jan is saying.

'I thought they were happy,' I say.

'They were, for a time.' Jan puts the teapot on the table with mugs and a cloudy half-full bottle of milk. She sits, crosses her legs, one Doc Marten boot emerging from her long skirt. As she speaks, she clutches a silver bauble pendant on a long chain around her neck, causing it to emit an almost inaudible chime. 'And then they weren't. Annie was very independent.'

Daisy said something similar, though I can't remember exactly what. I meet Jan's eyes. The lids sink at the edges in a way that makes her look wise. There is no judgement in these eyes. Her fingernails are short – musician's fingers, bedecked in handmade rings, one with an amber stone, plain bands of hammered silver around her thumb. She pours two mugs of tea and pushes one towards me. Out of a drawer hidden beneath the tabletop she pulls out a rectangular tin and a small pipe.

'Was my sister seeing someone else?' I ask.

'She was doing what she could to be happy.' Jan pinches a clump of tobacco from the tin and pushes it into the chamber of the pipe. 'But then, when Callum came back from university, things got more… difficult.'

'In what sense?' I think about what Daisy told me, about him returning as a man. Clashing stags. Annie caught in between.

'Dominic thought he'd outstayed his welcome. Callum was still figuring out what he wanted to do, but he was helping out with the cottages – giving them a lick of paint, fixing things, doing quite a bit of gardening. Annie was paying him – not much, I don't think, but it didn't go down too well.' She flicks her lighter and holds it to the bowl, sucking on the long, thin stem. The brown filaments twitch as if alive. I could murder a cigarette.

'Do you think he did it?'

She sucks at her pipe then shakes her head as smoke curls around her. 'Not her, no.'

Meaning: but him, yes. From the living room, a clock chimes the quarter-hour. Considering how quickly news travels in this place, it's amazing how difficult it is to get people to talk. But then, I am an incomer.

'The police asked me if Dominic was having an affair,' I say.

Air escapes her nose in a derisive blast. 'Did Ross ask you that?'

'No. It was a woman detective.'

'Hmph.' She pulls on her pipe. 'Must have brought her in from Bournemouth.'

'So was he?'

'Dominic had many affairs.'

'*What?*' I press my hand flat to my forehead, tears pricking.

'Annie didn't care,' she says with a dismissive wave of her hand. 'Well, she did at first, but the last few years, they didn't bother her so much. As I said, she found her own happiness.'

'Did Cal know?'

'Dominic wasn't exactly discreet.'

I translate: not only did Cal know, everybody did. How utterly humiliating.

'I'm beginning to feel like I didn't even know her.' I brush at my eyes.

'You did know her,' Jan says gently. 'She was still that person. It's just that she spared you things she wanted to protect you from. She was looking after you, in her way. If she'd even imagined she was in danger, she would have told you, I promise. You were on a pedestal for her.'

'Me?'

'My clever sister, she'd say.' Jan's warm grey eyes glitter. In other, happier moments, they would be full of mischief, I'm sure of it. This house, her clothes, the swing of her shiny silver hair tell me she is full of joy and generosity, music and laughter. But now is not the time for any of those things.

'Was Dominic with someone? Now, I mean? When he died?'

She closes her eyes. Yes, then.

'Someone local?'

A snort, an out-breath filled with a kind of dark, humorous disdain – the kind of mirth you reach when all hope, all respect, all affection for a person has gone. She fixes me with a withering gaze. 'There was no one local left.'

CHAPTER 17

Annie

September 1993

'Don't peek.' Out on the lane, Dominic turns her ninety degrees, his fingers greasy and damp over her eyes. Gravel replaces the smooth tarmac, crunches beneath her feet. They take five or six steps before he tells her to stop.

'Ready?' he asks.

'Yes.' Of course she's ready. Over two years of letters, phone calls, snatched kisses, introductions, polite cups of tea with her parents, picnics, long walks, stolen nights before he left at dawn for the pretence of his hotel, a small registry office wedding, a blessing in her parents' church, a long, long car journey and finally, hallelujah, they are here. She wanted to come sooner, oh, she longed to, but it wouldn't have been fair on Cal, and besides, there was so much to arrange, between the shop and Callum's new school and then Dominic saying he wanted to fix the place up for when she got here, and on and on, a list so long she thought she would never reach this day. So yes, she is ready. She is ready to open her eyes. She is ready to start her new life.

He lifts his hands away and she blinks at the hulking shadow in the sun.

'Oh my heavens,' she says.

The shadow coalesces into a thick thatched roof, sand-coloured stone bricks, cute wee windows chequered with lead, a front door the colour of Dijon mustard. An oval gunmetal sign reads *Rainbow Cottage* in looping cursive font. Roses red along the driveway, brambles over the door. A red sports car on the drive.

'Do you like it?' His arms circle her waist from behind, a kiss on her neck.

'Of course I like it. I love it.' She twists out of his embrace and turns to Cal. 'Well? What do you think?'

Her son's eyes are full of fear. He's barely spoken since they left Inveraray, and no wonder. Everything he has known he has lost. She is the only constant and he has only half of her now. Dom is hurrying back down the drive. He tells them to wait while he grabs the car – his parents' glossy jeep, left to him last year along with all the rest.

'It'll be OK.' She squeezes Cal's hand, tries not to be upset when he wriggles out of her grip. 'You'll love it here; it'll just take a bit of getting used to.' She has told him this over and over, held him at night and reassured him that yes, he will make tons of pals, yes, of course, Granny and Grandad will come and see them. They won't. They are far too frail, far too cautious, but hopefully he can accept the idea over time rather than in one great lump. And Auntie Isla will visit. And they can go to the beach every single weekend, and yes, they will get a dog, promise. But looking at him now, she is filled with the uneasy feeling that it won't be enough, that his Scottish accent will make him a target for bullies, that he will never settle, never be happy again, and that this will all be her fault. Has she sacrificed his happiness for her own? Is that what she's done?

'Come on then,' Dom says, slamming the car door shut and striding towards the cottage. 'Let me give you the grand tour!'

He flings open the front door with a ta-da, ushers them immediately right into the new kitchen he has put in. The room is spacious, with a large old pine table and six chairs.

'I went for the range oven,' he says. 'I hope you like ranges. And there's a microwave if you need to warm stuff up. A dishwasher, so no more washing-up at the sink.' His eyebrows shoot up, his hands land on his hips. 'All mod cons!' Before she's had time to reflect on her apparent ownership of the domestic appliances, he leads them up the narrow staircase and throws open the first door on the left.

'This was my room,' he says to Cal. 'I've had it painted. Do you like blue? I'm told you like *Star Wars*.' He gestures towards a *Return of the Jedi* poster in a frame, and she remembers telling him once that she and Cal often watched the old *Star Wars* movies together on video. He has remembered, and this touches her.

'You've gone to so much trouble,' she says, nudging Cal. 'Isn't this fantastic? You love *Star Wars*, don't you?'

'Thank you,' he says, as if to his shoes, and her heart shrinks.

Undeterred, Dominic ushers them along the landing to the master bedroom, which he has also had painted – an off-white. He has replaced his parents' bed and bedroom furniture. He is keen to tell her so.

'It's oak,' he tells her. 'And the bedding is all new too. John Lewis. I went to Poole for it. Do you like it?'

'It's lovely,' she says, smiling, though she wishes they could have chosen furniture together, and she wouldn't have picked a stripy duvet cover. 'It's all lovely. Thank you so much.'

'The curtains are closed because the main surprise is outside.' He throws his arms around her and twirls her round. As soon as her feet touch the ground, she pushes him away gently and holds out her hand to Cal.

'Come on,' she says. 'Shall we go and see the garden?'

But before they are allowed outside, there is a new white bathroom suite to admire, with chrome taps from Germany and a special shower head that can make the water run hard or soft; the new carpet on the winding stairs to notice now that they're descending, with special brass runners, steps left bare at the sides, which cost extra. The living room is yet to be updated: tired cream walls, an old-fashioned brown three-piece suite and a fireplace with broken tiles. A glossy knight in armour stands to one side, which, it turns out, houses the fire accessories.

'Don't worry about any of this,' Dominic says, flapping his hand as if to shoo away this last evidence of his parents' existence. 'My guy had to start on one of the cottages, but he's going to come back and do this room as soon as he's finished.'

'I know how to paint a room,' Annie says. 'My dad taught me. I've painted loads of rooms.'

But he doesn't appear to hear. He is standing at the French windows and grinning like the Cheshire Cat.

'Can you see it?' he asks, beaming.

She steps through and out onto a patio. The garden is huge, an apple tree at its centre, and beyond, a kind of chalet, painted duck-egg blue.

'Is that another house?' she asks, though it is not quite big enough for a house.

'It's not a house.' He giggles in his funny hoarse way. Like a schoolkid who has hidden something unpleasant in the teacher's desk.

She takes in the wide sweep of the land beyond the low, sparse fence. A little further on, a lone tree, branches bare and silhouetted, is host to a dozen or so birds, which sit like notes on a stave; further again, fallow fields stretch away to a distant and barely perceptible smudge of grey across the paler sky.

'Is that the sea?' she half gasps.

'It is.' His fists fly up to his chest. He is a child. A man-child. 'But what do you think of your studio?'

'My what?'

'Your studio! I had it built!'

Her scalp tightens. Her eyes fill. 'You made me a studio?'

'You're going to paint there, my darling. You're going to be famous!' And then he's giggling again, overjoyed, almost skipping over the grass, shouting at her to come on, come on, come on.

She follows, hurrying, caught in disbelief, dizzy with the onslaught of it all. No one has ever spoilt her like this. She is not prepared, has nothing within her she can reach for to help her cope. It is too much. It is all too much.

'Hey.' He pulls her to him, wraps his arms around her. 'Don't cry. I didn't mean to make you cry.'

'I don't know what to say.' She pushes her forehead into his chest. 'Thank you so, so much.'

'You're not in the gift shop now,' he says.

Held in his tight embrace, she doesn't see Cal slink back into the house, up the stairs and into his room. And so when he tells her later that the framed poster fell from the wall and smashed, she has no choice but to believe him.

CHAPTER 18

Isla

September 2004

When I get back to the cottage, there is a new-looking blue BMW on the drive. I cup my hand to the window to see inside, but it's empty. I unlock the front door and call hello, thinking that perhaps the car is an unmarked police vehicle and that DI York has realised Cal is innocent, has dropped him home and is waiting to apologise. But there is no answer.

From the living room, I see immediately that there is a man in the garden. He is standing beyond the apple tree, staring at the wreckage of my sister's studio. A burgundy body warmer over a long-sleeved top, dark jeans, his hands clasped behind his back. When he turns to survey the vast stretch of land on the other side of the fence, I recognise the neat profile of a bald, clean-shaven man: intelligent, erudite-looking.

Thomas Bartlett. Tom.

Something like relief passes through me. I open the patio door and call his name. He turns and raises his hand before dipping his head and walking slowly back to the house.

'Tom,' I say as he draws near.

He gives a solemn smile. 'Isla. I came through the side gate – hope that's OK?'

'Of course.' I manage a smile. 'You look the same.'

He rubs at his head, the hair he has left these days close-shaved at the sides. At the neck of his shirt, a dark tuft – I avert my eyes.

'That's very charitable,' he says. 'You haven't changed either.'

An awkward silence falls.

'I'm so sorry,' he says. 'Such a terrible thing. How are you coping?'

'I'm coping. There's no choice for the moment. Thanks for coming.'

'The least I could do. Dom wasn't a saint, but he was my friend. And Annie, of course. It wouldn't have seemed right to just call.' He pinches his earlobe briefly before steepling his fingers and spreading them at his chest. He has the self-effacing, almost priest-like manner of a man who, I suspect, has always hung back when it came to women. Friends with a man like Dominic, he probably found himself in his shadow. For such a short man, Dominic's shadow was surprising long.

I realise I haven't said anything.

'I don't know what to do.' I blink hard against tears I have no time for.

'There's not a lot you can do. Callum's not a minor. All we can do is support him. They've got until tomorrow morning to charge him, and if they do, I'll represent him of course.'

'He didn't kill Annie. He just didn't. But it's possible he—'

Thomas raises a hand. 'Don't tell me anything. It's Callum I'll be talking to about how best to construct a defence, should it come to that. OK?'

I meet his gaze. His brown eyes are as kind as I remembered, crinkly now at the corners. He must be in his forties, I think.

'Do you still smoke?'

He smiles. 'I try not to.'

'Me too. And you live around here now?'

'I have a place in Studland. Not too far. I work out of Bournemouth.'

Another silence drifts, lands.

'Can I get you something to eat?' I say, keen for him to stay a little while. The feeling that he's someone from my past, someone I've known for years, infuses me, even though that's not really the case. 'I think Daisy bought some wine, if I can find it. Come in for a minute at least.'

He follows me into the cottage. Inside, he looks too tall for the low ceilings. He refuses a drink, saying he has to get going quite soon. We sit on opposite ends of the sofa. Immediately, I wish I'd taken the armchair – we are too close – but he is soon talking me through the process: what will happen if they charge Cal, his rights, mine. I won't be able to call him. If he doesn't call me or agree to see me, then I won't be able to speak to him.

'I'd better get going,' Tom says eventually, and I wonder who he's going home to; if he has someone. 'Here.' He hands me a business card: *The Bench Associates*.

'Thanks. I remember being so impressed all those years ago. I'd never met a barrister before.'

He smiles shyly. 'You were so trendy, I remember thinking. Intimidating. You had that kind of tie thing in your hair and those big shoes.'

'Beetle-crushers. I thought I was the bee's knees in those.'

That shy smile again. 'And you're well?' he says. 'Apart from all this, I mean? I'm sorry, that was… inept.'

'It's OK, I know what you mean. I'm well. I was, I mean. I'm in London now. I work for Habitat. They've been great actually.'

'That's good.' He frowns. 'If they charge Callum, it will take quite a bit of time. You might need to arrange a sabbatical or something if you can. These things can take months. At least.'

'I'd already decided to do that. Whatever happens, there's no one to run the business, and even if they let him go, he'll need support while we figure out what to do. He's only just out of uni and I'm all he's got, you know?'

He nods in agreement, appears to be blushing slightly, though I'm not sure why.

'Good plan,' he says. 'Yes. Right then, I should probably go. Call me if you need to, OK? I might not be there immediately, but I'll call you back when I can.'

'All right,' I say, suddenly desperate for him to stay and keep talking to me, help me negotiate my bewilderment. Surely he can tell me not to worry, that Cal will be home by tomorrow afternoon?

But no. Instead, he says goodbye and I watch him get into his car, start the engine and reverse out of the driveway. When he's gone, the silence weighs heavy. I return indoors, pour a glass of red and take it through the sitting room, out into the back garden. I'm still restless, still identifying my own disappointment at Tom leaving, when the phone rings.

I run into the house and pick up. I recognise DI York's voice immediately.

'Sit down,' he says. 'I'm afraid it's not good news. Callum has confessed.'

CHAPTER 19

Isla

The receiver slides in my hand. From one moment to the next, I am covered in sweat.

'Isla?' DI York says. 'Isla? Are you still there? Look, I'll come and see you. I'm coming now, OK?'

'I can't. This can't…' I hear York tell me to stay there, the rattle of the phone in the cradle, the dead atonal note stretching away. I drop the phone and curl up on my side on the sofa. Push my forehead into the back, focus on the soft cushion, the harder press of the covered buttons – hard, soft, hard, soft. *No*, I think. *No, no, no.*

Cal has confessed. It is impossible. Impossible. But as the words float down, my mind races in loops. If he did it, if, in some bizarre sequence of events, he did it, which he didn't, he absolutely did not, but if he did, if, if, *if…* that means Dominic didn't kill my sister as I have assumed. It must have been an accident, if it even happened. But how can anyone kill a person by accident with a hammer? And what about Dominic? Surely it was him? Is Cal lying for him? But why would he protect him if he hated him so much? And if Dominic didn't kill my sister, and Cal didn't kill Dominic, that leaves only Annie. Annie with a knife. Annie pushing a knife into her husband's belly. My sister, my lovely Annie, a murderer. And Cal killed her – his mother, my sister.

'No, no, no, no, no, no,' I snivel into the sofa cushions, face slick with snot and tears. 'No, no, no, no, no.'

Twenty minutes later, the crunch of tyres on gravel. I unfurl, force myself to stand, to put one foot in front of the other. The bell rings as I reach the front door.

York brushes his large feet on the welcome mat, his head bent.

'I called Daisy,' he says. 'She said she'll be here in an hour. Call me Ross now, OK?'

'Thank you.'

'I'm so sorry,' he says, once we're sitting in the living room.

'You're absolutely sure it's my sister he killed? You're sure it's not…'

Ross flinches. 'Why, has he said something to you?'

'He wouldn't talk to me. He just… closed down. Did he *actually* confess?'

'I'm afraid so.'

'Right. Right.' I close my eyes. Kaleidoscope images flash beneath the lids. I have the impression I'm going to fall forward and so open them again, steady myself with my hand against the arm of the sofa.

'Do you need water?' He stands up and leaves the room, returning a moment later with a glass of water. 'Here.'

I take it and sip. The glass is too heavy; my hand trembles. I just about manage to get it onto the coffee table. 'What happened?'

'That's what we have to find out.'

'What's the evidence? I mean, have they found his fingerprints on the hammer? Are they absolutely sure?'

He sighs, glancing up at me with his sorrowful eyes. 'They have enough.'

'Enough. And that means Annie killed Dominic?'

'We haven't had forensics back yet, but that's what Cal is saying.' He exhales heavily, pats at the pocket of his jacket. It is after six on a Saturday; I know that gesture.

'You can smoke,' I say. 'On condition you offer me one.'

'Annie didn't like smoking in the house.'

Here at last is one thing I know. Annie hated smoking. We step out onto the patio; he offers me a cigarette.

'I don't smoke by the way,' I say, taking one.

'Me neither.' He lights first mine then his.

We stare out at the dilapidated husk of the shack, its details fading now with the oncoming dusk. At the horizon, the sky is pinking. Horror and beauty in one view.

'I don't want to look at it,' I say, nicotine giving me a head rush. 'But I look at it all the time. I'm exhausted, but I can't sit still, can't sleep. I just can't believe it. I can't believe any of it. Cal's a great kid. He's gentle, you know?'

'I've known Callum since he was a lad,' Ross says. 'And I agree: he's no malice in him. But sometimes we go outside of ourselves. Sometimes feelings overwhelm us. I've no doubt he acted on instinct, but it's up to him and his solicitor now.'

'Can I see him?'

'I'll take you in tomorrow. He's still at Swanage, but they'll move him, probably to Guys Marsh.'

'Is that a prison?'

He nods grimly. 'I'll put a word in, make sure someone's looking out for him.'

'Oh God.'

'Try not to think about it.'

'I can't help it. That's not his world. He's a wee boy.'

'Unfortunately not, in the eyes of the law.'

We smoke, in the heavy air.

'When you spoke to Cal here, he said Dominic didn't respect her, and I could tell by your face you knew what he meant. What did he mean?'

Ross sighs heavily, takes a long drag. 'I was at school with Dom,' he says as he exhales. 'My parents knew his parents; they were nice people. Too nice.'

'But what about Dom? I thought he was all right, maybe a bit crass at times, but no one seems to have a good word to say about him.'

He shrugs. 'Dominic Rawles was a very charming man, as they say.'

'I get the impression he was a ladies' man.'

Ross opens his mouth as if to speak, but the words take their time, as if he is sorting through to choose them, like cards for a trick.

'Disarming,' he says. 'That's the term for it, I think. Very sociable, life and soul, one for grand gestures. They threw a lot of parties. Not so many this last couple of years, but when Annie first came. Always invited all and sundry. He'd ask complete strangers back from the pub if there'd been a band on, that sort of thing. Fancied himself as a muso. I came here a few times. That's how I met her. Annie. I remember talking to him out here once, right where we're standing. We were talking about school and having a laugh about the old days, as you do, and I was reminding him he always had a girlfriend, always got the most attractive girls, you know?' He takes a drag. 'Well, he got Annie, didn't he?'

'He did.'

'And I suppose I was teasing him. I said something like "How come a short-arse like you manages to always get the girl?" It was good-natured.'

'And what was his secret?'

'He said his history teacher had told him there were two schools of charm and that Churchill and Disraeli embodied them. Winston Churchill was charming because he made you feel like he was the only person in the room, whereas Disraeli made you feel like *you* were the only person in the room. He said he was fifteen when he realised he'd never get girls to notice him just by walking into a room. And he loved girls. Loved to be in love was how he put it. So he went for the other school of charm. He said if you asked women enough questions about themselves, you could create the impression of intimacy, and that was a great way of getting them into bed. He'd understood girls weren't afraid of short men. They didn't see you as threatening, so you could infiltrate enemy lines – I'm using his terms, by the way. He said being short was like a Trojan horse. Before they knew it, they were waking up next to you wondering how the hell they'd got there.'

'So he was never really interested in them, more in himself through their eyes?'

'I don't know. Maybe. He just knew that appearing fascinated was a way in. But it wasn't real. It was about getting laid. I mean, when you're fifteen, that's fair enough, it's all you think about.' He gives a short laugh. 'But you're supposed to grow out of it, and I'm not sure he did. Maybe he needed the affirmation. Got hooked on it, I don't know. He'd certainly found a way of getting people to do things for him – *because* of him sometimes.'

'Because of him?'

'Things they might not have wanted to do or wouldn't have done under normal circumstances. Even bad things.'

'Do you mean Cal?'

He pulls on his cigarette, exhales a pensive cloud. 'And your sister.'

Annie. All those years ago. A charm offensive, refined over decades. She wouldn't have stood a chance. He lured her here, made her jack in her life, her parents and just… go. But why *her*? There were surely other beautiful women nearer to home. What did he want with a naïve young woman with a kid? And one who came from so far away?

'He was funny too,' Ross adds. 'But again, he was always the one to laugh the loudest at a woman's joke. Not that women aren't funny.'

'No, I know what you mean.'

He holds up his cigarette, casting about for where to put it.

'Just throw it down,' I say. 'I'll sort it out.'

He throws it to the ground and grinds it out. I do the same. He crouches and picks up both butts and puts them in his pocket; I am touched by his manners. Sometimes charm is quiet, small.

'You're on your own,' he says, glancing back to the house. 'I can get someone to come.'

I shake my head. 'Daisy's coming, you said.'

'Ah yes. Good. Good.'

The pause that follows tells us both it's time for him to go. Sure enough, he shifts, half turns towards the cottage.

'Thanks for being honest with me,' I say. 'I feel so in the dark about everything.'

'I won't be heading this up, I'm afraid,' he replies. 'It'll be DI Hall, who you've met. She'll be chatting to Daisy and Jan and anyone we think might tell us anything, but essentially, he's confessed, so he's obviously the main suspect. I'll be able to keep tabs. And you can call me whenever. I'll leave you my home number too.' His gaze wanders, back to the crime scene. 'Terrible business,' he says, as if to himself. 'Your sister was much loved.'

'Yes,' I say. 'People keep telling me that.'

CHAPTER 20

Annie

September 1993

On the Thursday of their first week, Dominic tells her he's invited some friends over on Saturday night.

'Everyone's dying to meet you,' he says. 'I thought we could do a big chilli or something.'

'OK,' she says, unsure how far 'we' extends to him – she has done all the cooking so far and is beginning to wonder how and what he ate before she got here.

But there must have been some hesitation in her voice, because he takes her hands in his and asks if it's a problem.

'No, I… it's just that Cal's only just started at school. I was thinking he might need things calm and quiet, you know? While he settles in? It's a lot for him to cope with.'

'He'll be fine! Get him on the football team – he'll have friends in no time at all.'

'Cal doesn't like football,' she says. Why are they talking about football?

'Rugby then, whatever his sport is. He won't mind if we have a few friends over – it won't be more than fifteen, twenty, tops. It'll do him good. I read somewhere that kids whose parents have a good social life end up being more confident, more outgoing. He can come down and say hello. Tom's coming. Remember Tom?'

She does. He was nice. Even Isla said so. And Dominic's confidence is leaking into her, as it always does.

'All right,' she says and is rewarded with a kiss.

'It'll be great.' He lets go of one of her hands, pulls her towards the stairs. 'I think a celebratory cuddle is in order.'

She laughs, despite his use of the word. It isn't a cuddle; it's sex. They are adults, they are married. It's as if he's trying to play it down, as, she has noticed, he plays down most things – her worry a couple of days ago that she had no pals here was dismissed as 'nonsense', she'd soon have hundreds; her conviction that no one would want to buy paintings from an incomer was 'ridiculous', she'd sell tons. It's as if his grasp on reality is completely different from her own. Cal will be fine, a gathering of twenty people is a few friends not a party, a chilli for twenty folk will get made somehow.

And sure enough, when Friday morning comes and she asks him what's happening about the party, he tells her not to worry, that 'we' – that odd plural again – will 'grab some stuff from Swanage' once he gets back from his 'quick' bike ride, the bike ride he told her about the other day but of which she has no memory, and now she's wondering what quick actually means, here in the real world where she is pretty sure she lives, even if he does not. In his cycling kit, one hand on the back door handle, he tells her the bookings will look after themselves.

'The bookings?' she says.

'It's changeover day,' he explains, except there's no explanation in the words themselves.

'What? You can't leave me to do all that!'

He sighs, hobbles back through the house in his cleats. She follows him into the hallway, where he pulls a ledger from the phone-table drawer.

'There,' he says, opening it where the red cord marks the place and running his finger down the page. 'That's the list. It pretty much manages itself. There'll be no problem.'

Except there is a problem. At quarter to eleven, a woman calls to say she's locked her suitcase inside the cottage along with the keys. Anxious and unable to drive, Annie runs from the edge of the village into the centre, to the row of houses opposite the duck pond, squinting briefly at the map before seeing a young woman waiting at the end of the path of the tiny mid-terrace cottage.

'Hello,' she says, waving the spare key. 'Sorry that took so long. Dominic didn't tell me where the spare keys were, but I found them eventually and I don't… I don't have the car today.'

And although the woman smiles, a look of disappointment or confusion or something passes across her face.

'Is Dominic around?' she asks.

'He's away on his bike.' Annie passes the woman by and unlocks the cottage door, standing back to let her inside.

A moment later, she re-emerges with the suitcase and the key, which she places in Annie's hand before seeming to stall on the wee path.

'Are you one of the managers?' she asks.

'Managers? I suppose so. I'm Dominic's wife.' The word still brings the heat to her face. She's hardly a blushing bride and the whole feeling embarrassed like some butter-wouldn't-melt virgin is getting right on her nerves. But when she looks up, she sees she's not the only one blushing.

'Wife?' The woman is nodding so much Annie fears her head'll fall right off. 'Sorry, I… OK, well, tell him Maria said goodbye. Tell him I hope he has a nice life, will you?'

'I will, aye.' Annie stares after her, this odd woman who can't even get herself out of a house successfully but who is now apparently capable of getting into a car and starting the engine all by herself.

Annie waves, but the woman either doesn't see or doesn't want to wave back, because her focus is fixed firmly on the road ahead. Annie double-checks the cottage is locked before, curious, she decides to go inside and have a look around. Dominic has yet to give her a tour of the properties, so she may as well take the opportunity to get the lie of the land.

The cottage is tiny. It is minuscule! The ground floor is all one room: a kitchen in a corner at the back with a two-stool breakfast bar, giving out onto a courtyard with a wee table and two chairs. Towards the front, a sofa, an armchair, a television and an open fire, the black grate crumbly with burnt-out coal. It is really well done, neutral wheat and cream colours, cosy yet spacious. Upstairs, there is one bedroom – the white bed linen whipped up like a meringue – and a surprisingly generous bathroom, in which a bath stands on claw feet, two dirty wine glasses on the window ledge, towels left on the floor. She would never leave a room like this. Her upbringing would not allow it, though Dominic's would. *For God's sake*, she remembers him saying on the romantic break he took her on last year, *they have staff to do that!*

She remembers him telling her how he modernised after his parents died, how he intends to modernise all the cottages one by one. It's not him of course, it's his builder – that sleight of hand that comes so naturally. She has to admire his vision though, even if vision is obviously easier if you can afford what you envisage. Upstairs he has achieved the same sense of space despite the small dimensions. He hasn't tried to cram in two small bedrooms, creating instead a kind of retreat for one, love nest for two. The woman's manner earlier was a bit strange, she thinks now. Perhaps she was a writer, someone highly strung, oversensitive, socially awkward. Someone who would wish the owner of a holiday rental company a nice life. Weird phrase.

She makes her way down the narrow staircase. A quick glance around to make sure nothing needs her attention – she sees a note propped on the mantel.

Dominic, it reads.

The paper has been folded into three and tucked into itself to make a kind of wallet. It isn't addressed to her. It's none of her business. But at the same time, a woman has left a note for her husband. And the note is not sealed.

Cheeks burning, she thumbs the paper out of its folds. Inside is written: *Maria*. And a phone number.

Tingling with unwelcome suspicion, she refolds the note exactly as it was, slides it into the back pocket of her jeans. On the front path, however, she finds she is panting, her hand at her chest. She tells herself to calm down, for goodness' sake.

'Cooee!' On the other side of the low bay hedge, an older woman with shiny silver hair is kneeling before a flower bed with a trowel, one hand raised in greeting.

'Hello,' Annie says. 'Lovely day.'

The woman leans back and smiles. She has the friendliest smile Annie has seen since she got here.

'You must be Annie,' she says. 'Unless you've come all the way from bonnie Scotland for your holidays?'

'No, I'm Annie right enough. I was just helping one of the guests. She'd locked herself out.'

'Oh dear. Dominic not about?'

'He's away on his bike.'

'Is he now?' She raises her eyebrows and fixes Annie with a stare that looks as if she's peering over reading glasses. 'Got you to take over, has he?' She rocks back and stands before hobbling from foot to foot. 'Ah. Pins and needles. Ah, ah. Bugger!'

Annie laughs. 'I get that when I've been sitting on one of my legs.'

'Murder, isn't it? I'm Jan anyway. I know Dominic, knew his mum and dad. It's quite a move you've made; it must be a lot to take on. Would you like a cup of coffee?'

'I'd love one,' she says, meaning it. 'But Dom will be back soon, so I'd better head.' She smiles, shields her eyes with her hand. 'I'd love to another time though?'

'I'll hold you to it. You've got acquainted with Heartbreak Hotel anyway. That's one down, I suppose.'

'Heartbreak Hotel? Sorry, I don't follow.'

'Sorry. Nickname.' Jan gives her a wry look. 'A lot of single women book that place, if you catch my drift. Come here to *find themselves* and what have you. It's advertised as a creative retreat for artists and writers, but I've never seen much art happening there. Speaking of which, you're an artist, are you not? A real one, I mean.'

'God, no. Is that what Dominic told you?'

'Don't be modest; he said you'd deny it! I'm sure he said artist. Or was it musician?'

'I can ring things up on a till. I do paint a bit, but it's just a hobby. I think Dom's got big plans for me.' Annie laughs, embarrassed.

'Well, don't be running around after him, OK? He has a special talent for getting folk to run around after him, so get wise. Listen, how about coffee next week? Tuesday, eleven o'clock, how are you fixed?'

'I'll have to check my schedule.' She opens her palm and stares into it for a second before looking up. 'Tuesday's great – I'm free all day.'

Jan grins. 'See you then. And if you need anything, my number's in the book, OK? And tell Dominic Jan said she'll be checking up on him and to look sharp.'

Annie returns to the cottage expecting to find Dom, but he's not there. Cal returns from school a little before four, and still Dominic is not back. She helps Cal with some homework, telling him that if he gets it all done, she'll take him to the beach at Swanage tomorrow morning. She's starting to get anxious about the supermarket shop, but when Dominic finally returns at half past four, he goes straight upstairs for a bath. And when Callum tells her he's starving, she gives up and toasts some crumpets.

'Crumpets,' Dominic says when he returns downstairs, plucking one from Cal's plate. 'Excellent.'

She remembers the note but doesn't give it to him, instead waiting until Cal has disappeared into his room, which he does immediately after his snack and without a word.

'Any chance of a coffee?' Dominic says. 'My legs are killing me.'

She makes coffee and takes it through to the living room, where Dominic is reading the local paper in the armchair.

'I had a call from one of the clients this morning,' she says. 'She'd locked herself out. Think she was a wee bit disappointed to get me, to be honest. I think it was you she was wanting.'

He lowers the newspaper and frowns. 'Which cottage?'

'The tiny one next to Jan's. I met her. She's nice.'

'Ah, the old hippy. Yes, she's a character.' He takes the note from her, opens it. Pushes out his bottom lip in apparent memory loss before his face clears. 'Oh yes, she was looking for work. I said I'd pass her number on to a mate of mine.'

'What kind of work?'

'What? Oh, just, you know, clerical.'

She waits. When he says nothing more, she suggests they head to the supermarket together before it closes.

He groans, throws his head back. 'Can we go tomorrow? I'm knackered.'

But she's promised Cal she'll take him to the beach in the morning. And then there'll be the house to clean, the cooking for so many, and if they have to shop for it all as well, they'll be jiggered by the time anyone gets here… is what she doesn't say. Instead, she finds herself saying not only OK but that if she could drive, she would go. To this, he doesn't reply, his face hidden once more in the pages of the *Purbeck Post*.

It is only later that she wonders why she accepted Dominic's wishes like that, why she didn't put up a fight. What kind of pathetic doormat is she? Isla would be horrified at her. She'd say she is just like their mother, who always acquiesces to their father, always cooks his tea, always takes him his coffee into the living room so he can drink it while he reads the paper. It's like it's genetic or something.

And so now it's late on Saturday morning and Dominic is finally suggesting they pick up some 'food and booze' in the MG.

She frowns at him. 'But where's Cal going to sit once we've got the stuff?'

'Callum won't want to come to the supermarket. Hasn't he got… I dunno, homework? Computer games? Masturbation to be getting on with?'

Her cheeks burn. 'I beg your pardon?'

'Oh, come on, I was joking!' He throws out his hands, tries to grab hold of her for a kiss, but she turns her head away. 'Look, I'm sorry. Pretend I didn't say it. It'll never happen again.'

She glares at him. 'He's twelve.'

He pushes her against the wall. His face looms close, his lips almost touching hers. 'You can't possibly be offended by a little joke. Loosen up, will you? Look, we'll have a lot of fun later, OK? I think it'll do you good to have a few drinks and relax a bit, yes? It's all been a bit stressful, I can see that.'

'OK,' she hears herself say.

He kisses her on the lips. 'Cool. Thank God, I thought I'd brought the wrong girl home for a minute there.'

Before she has time to consider what this means, he is shouting up the stairs: 'Callum! Your mum and I are going to the supermarket, OK?'

He half pushes her towards the door. Her legs stiffen.

'Wait a second.' She hurries up the stairs.

'Oh for God's sake,' she hears him say behind her.

She pushes open Cal's bedroom door. He is on his bed, glued to his Game Boy. 'Hey. We're just popping out, OK?'

'I thought we were going to the beach,' he says without looking up.

'Aye, I know I said that, but Dominic's invited a load of folk over. We have to buy some food, and we'll have to cook and get the house ready, so I don't think there's going to be time today.' She is still talking to the top of his head, his crown a tiny pale circle in his black hair. 'I'm sorry. I'll take you tomorrow, OK?'

'OK.' Still he doesn't look at her.

She bends, plants a kiss on that tiny pale circle and heads out to buy food for a party she wasn't asked about, for people she doesn't know, by a man whose behaviour she barely recognises. But, she reasons, he's throwing the party for her so she can meet people and make friends. Besides, she's made her bed now… Her mind doesn't even finish her parents' favourite saying before it is interrupted by Isla's *Och, wheesht, hen, and just get oan with it.* She smiles to herself. Shush, woman, and just get on with it.

CHAPTER 21

Isla

September 2004

Ross picks me up from the cottage and drives me to the old town hall building where Swanage police station is housed. He has persuaded Cal to see me, if only for a few minutes. In the car, he tells me I am like Annie but at the same time completely different, which makes perfect sense to me and I tell him so.

'We're sisters,' I say, then, 'We were sisters.'

'And you were close?'

'I thought so.'

'You thought so, but…'

'I didn't know she and Dominic were so up and down. I didn't know they… fought or that he had affairs.'

'She never spoke to you about… that side of things?'

'No. No, she didn't. And of course, now I'm wondering why that is. What she was afraid of, whether *she* might have had an affair even.'

'I don't think she was afraid of anyone,' he replies, eyes fixed on the road. 'She was feisty. Gentle but feisty.'

'But yesterday, when you said she was much loved…'

'I meant that sincerely. I didn't mean to imply anything. I can't stand gossip – it's dangerous. Your sister was kind and she built good relationships here. She had a lot of friends. Her work is sold all over Purbeck and further afield – Lyme Regis, Bridport, there's a gallery in Dorchester, I believe.' He takes a deep breath, apparently to get him through what is so obviously costing him a great effort to say. 'But Dom was… I'm not saying he got what he deserved, but…'

'He was a bastard,' I finish.

'I think that's the term.' He glances across and smiles sadly.

'But yesterday you said people did bad things because of him.'

'I didn't.'

'You did. You said he had a way of getting folk to do things either for or because of him. Even bad things, you said.'

A slow nod. 'Ah yes. Yes, I did say that.'

'Like what? I know there's Cal and Annie, but might there have been someone else, someone driven by him to… do something bad? In the context of what's happened, I mean?'

He opens his mouth but says nothing.

'I didn't mean anyone in particular,' he says finally, and I have the sense he was going to tell me something but that now he's decided against it. 'As I said, I can't stand gossip.'

We fall into the silence he has effectively imposed. Perhaps to fill it before I can break it again, he puts the radio on. Pop music drifts into the car – a song about 'good times' grating horribly. I picture Annie the last time I saw her, think of all the times I saw her or spoke to her on the phone, right from the very beginning… *How's everything? Yeah, fine.* Callum was settling in, she'd started painting… then later, her work was selling, she was busy with the business. *How's Dominic? Dominic's good, yeah.* Mountain-biking, jet-skiing, another triathlon. Then the last few years, the pub, the bands. *Yeah, yeah, all good, he loves it.*

And I think of the night our lives changed – not that we knew it yet – see her lying in the bath at the Cluanie Inn, hear myself say: *For God's sake Annie, this is our weekend!* Then later, when she'd been on her first date and she was up to high doh with excitement and I just couldn't let her have it, could I, not even for a moment: *What do you really know about him anyway?* And even when it was obvious how delighted she was to be getting married, how thrilled with the idea of escaping the life that had held her down for so long, I was so full of ideas I'd read in books, I couldn't just be pleased for her. *You've never really spent that long with him. And now you're getting married and moving all the way to bloody Dorset?* They were the words I chose when the word – the *only* word – I needed was *Congratulations.*

I should have thrown my arms around her and told her I was delighted for her. I was trying to protect her, but that wasn't my job. She never wanted or asked for my commentary, but I gave it anyway, and it doesn't matter, it doesn't matter one bit, how kindly I meant it. It doesn't matter how much I loved her. To wish her well and be there to pick up the pieces if everything came crashing down – that was what mattered. That was my job.

If she felt judged, it's because I did judge her. What did I know? Theories from books are not the same as real, messy, complicated life. *At least I let people in*, she said, all those years ago. She only said it because she felt she had to defend herself. From me.

And now she's dead.

Callum is brought into a small interview room by a police officer, who unlocks his handcuffs and goes to stand in the corner, trying to be invisible. I feel my face flush. My nephew, in cuffs. My nephew, in sweatpants and sweatshirt, his hair uncombed, shadows under his eyes darker than I have ever seen, baby beard fluffy as a gosling's wing. The sight of him is dreadful. If only I knew what to feel, but all I feel is hot and confused.

'Hey.' I reach for his hands, but he withdraws them under the table. 'Are you OK?'

He nods. *Look at me*, I want to say. *Look at me.*

'You've confessed,' I say instead. 'Did they force you?'

'No.'

'Did you do it?'

He shakes his head; tears roll out of his eyes. 'Don't ask. Please don't ask me.'

I want to grab him by the hair. The desire makes me feel sick, but it persists. If shock is a punch or a kick, rage is a bomb that detonates, mushrooming up and out from the inside, pressing hot against the guts, the ribs, the skull. I want to grab him by the hair and pull his face to mine and say: *If you killed my sister, you can at least tell me the fucking truth.*

'Why won't you tell me?' Voiced, the question is a fraction of itself. I sound plaintive when in reality I am shuddering with fury.

He sniffs, wipes his nose with the back of his hand, but says nothing.

'What about manslaughter?' I have no idea what I'm saying. Vague notions based on television.

He meets my gaze, his eyes rimmed in red. He looks ill – hospital ill, terminal. 'Can you get me a lawyer? I need a decent one.'

'Tom's coming to see you today.' Tom, who called me last night to tell me only this but who stayed on the line for an hour.

'That's good. He's a good bloke.'

The silence that falls feels like the end of something – of wild walks and long days and picnics at the seaside. Of innocence, a relationship that hovered somewhere between aunt and nephew and older sister and baby brother. The longing to turn back time is a weight on my chest. I am breathless with it, suffocating – beneath it, my rage expires.

'Are you sure you can't tell me? Cal? She was my sister.' A last ditch: emotional blackmail.

His mouth distorts. More tears. I wonder if I've ever seen anyone in so much pain, know that I have not. He has told me he didn't kill her, but he has told the police he did. Which is it? The latter, obviously, so why do I cling to the former?

'Look,' I say, one hand tight around my opposite wrist, 'I understand you telling me you didn't kill her in the moment, I do. You were scared. Perhaps you couldn't accept it or it was an accident.' I am desperate for him to interrupt, to correct me. But he does not. All he does is weep into his hands.

My grip tightens; my nails dig in. 'You can't talk about it, I get that. But if… if you didn't do it, love, why would you tell them you did?'

His chair scrapes across the lino floor. 'I'm sorry,' he says, looming above me, wretched. 'I know you must hate me, but I…' His face crumples. He turns away.

CHAPTER 22

Annie

September 1993

It is 8 p.m. Downstairs, the music is turned up so loud Annie can hear it from the shower – thumping, gritty rap music, so at odds with Dominic himself, who is fastidious, clean as a bar of soap, crisp as sheets on a line.

She is aching a little from lifting enormous pots and pans. She has made two chillis – one veggie, one meat – has washed about thirty potatoes and put them in the oven. She has bought two tubs of sour cream, done her best to make eight avocados' worth of guacamole from a recipe in one of Dom's pristine cookery books. She has thrown a cloth over the dining-room table, loaded on twenty plates Dominic showed her in the old mahogany dresser, before adding another ten on his suggestion – *just in case we get a few stragglers*. She has never known anyone with so many plates. Her parents had about six, she thinks, eight tops.

As for Dom, he has made a tour of the grass on his sit-on lawnmower, which doesn't seem to her to be as much work, though she has fought off the thought. Life isn't measured in grams, her dad used to say, mainly to Isla, if they had to share an apple or a bar of chocolate between them and Isla complained about getting a sliver less. Dominic's mowing seemed to take him about the same amount of time and he did tell her she was amazing to have made such a feast, that he knew she'd be up to the job because *nothing fazes you, does it?* In the moment, she responded to his flattery, to his arms around her waist, his lips against her neck, but now she's not sure how she feels about it all.

The hot water runs over her face. She hopes it will wash away her grumbles. What she really wants to do is crawl into bed and have a nap, but Dominic tells her a stiff drink will sort her out.

She wishes Isla were here. If she were, what would she, Annie, say? That she had to do all the cooking? To which Isla would respond with something clever, something from Simone de Beauvoir or Germaine Greer, which would explain to her why she shouldn't have done it if she didn't want to, that she is living in bad faith. It is all so hard to get right.

She dries herself and, still with the towel around her, tiptoes onto the landing. Cal's door is ajar; she can see him hunched over his Game Boy, his bottom teeth hooked over his top lip in concentration.

'Hey,' she says.

He eyes her briefly from under his brow before returning to the screen.

'You OK?'

'Yeah.'

'Do you think you'll come and say hello later?'

He shrugs.

She sits down beside him. He shifts, an inch, away from her.

'I really am sorry about today,' she says.

'S'OK.'

'I promise I'll take you to the beach next weekend. I know this is a lot to get used to, but we'll get there because we're tough, aren't we? Tough and strong?'

A flash of a smile. She strokes his hair, tries to kiss his cheek, but he darts away. Fair enough, he's twelve. She leaves him, pulling his door shut. The party will be noisy. She hopes it doesn't go on too late.

In her and Dominic's room, there is a black dress, arranged as if reclining on the bed. Confused, she frowns at it before lifting it and holding it up in front of her. It is her size. And it is new; there is a tag, though the price has been peeled off. It isn't a brand she recognises. It isn't really her style.

'Present.' Dom's voice comes from behind her. He is standing in the bedroom doorway, a crystal tumbler in each hand. 'For my beautiful wife for her first Purbeck party. Here.' He hands her a glass. 'My best single malt in my best crystal for the best thing that ever happened to me.'

'Thank you.'

He takes a swig. 'Come on, get it down you; the guests'll be here in half an hour.' He moves into the room, pushes the door with his foot, then turns and waggles the handle until it clicks shut.

She sips. The whisky is smoky and warm. Just the smell of it is transportive: peat streams running pinky-brown down the hill, ferns, wet bark, the sun on the loch. Home. She takes a larger sip. Fire flashes down her throat. Isla can't stand whisky.

Dom lifts the glass from her hand and sets it down on the dressing table. His forehead presses against hers and he undoes the towel where she has folded it over at her chest. She lets it fall, cradles his head as he pushes his face to her breasts and breathes her in.

'God, you smell good,' he says, his hands running over her, pushing her softly until she falls backward onto the bed.

She is about to say they shouldn't, that they don't have time, but his head is between her legs, and as the heat from the whisky travels down her, so a thousand electrical currents travel up, and she closes her eyes and reaches up for the oak struts of the bedhead and grips onto them tight, tight, tight, until she has to twist and press her mouth into the soft white pillow, and still this is not the height of it, because now he is trailing his tongue up the length of her belly, his thumbs glancing her nipples, his lips on her neck, now closing over hers, and he's lifting himself to look into her eyes and, knowing him now and what is to come, she scrabbles again for the pillow as he enters her and rolls her on top of him, his hands finding her waist. Once again she grips the bedstead while she moves on him and he in her, both of them staring into each other's eyes until, suppressing cries, they fall into each other's arms only to break apart half laughing, their breath and pulses slowing, their sweat drying.

'Fuck,' he says.

'Is that all it was to you?' She laughs and he turns onto his side, tracing a lazy finger from her neck to her navel.

'We'd better get dressed.' He kisses her, a peck on the lips, and jumps up. 'Guests'll be here any minute.'

She grins at him, all tension melted to liquid and drained from her. 'I need another shower. And then I'll put on the dress.'

'Be quick!' He grins back and she thinks how late he left it to make love to her, wonders momentarily if, actually, he'd be delighted to be caught in the act, if what just happened was in part driven by how imminent the party is, the thought of himself answering the door with a swagger and a knowing blow of his fringe all part of his naughty schoolboy charm. She doesn't much care; he is a better lover by a thousand miles than any of the boy-men in her admittedly small experience, so much so she can barely wipe the stupid smirk from her face.

CHAPTER 23

Annie

Dominic is brilliant. Wherever he is, energy follows, visibly transmitting itself to whoever he is talking to: backs straighten, arms loosen, wave about. He animates his guests as a hand does a glove puppet. She watches him, her own sly pride a surprise. Like so much of what Dom makes her feel, it is unfamiliar. Women particularly enliven in his presence – their eyes round, their mouths open in mock shock or amusement, their heads fall back when they laugh. They are tactile and, yes, flirtatious. She fights against a proprietorial feeling – that pride again – but cannot help herself: he is hers, *hers*. He wanted something different and she was it. She is his exotic flower. She is his butterfly.

She wishes Isla were here. *You've never really spent that long with him. And now you're getting married and moving all the way to bloody Dorset?* Yes, if Isla were here, she would have to admit it: this is not a bad life.

The party passes in a blur of topping up drinks, handing out endless tortilla chips and being introduced to ever more inebriated folk. Dom stops her from bringing out the heavy casserole dishes, insists she carry the lighter stuff: the basket of French bread, the bowl of rather wrinkly jacket potatoes, the sour cream and the 'guac'. He shouts to everyone to help themselves, indicates which is the meat and which the veggie, tells them to dig in, that there's plenty. He doesn't mention that she made it all, but she tells herself that to want praise is vain and peevish, and to grow up.

More topping up. People float out into the garden, light cigarettes. The music is loud and she wonders if Cal has managed to fall asleep or if he's upstairs with his hands over his ears, seething. There are, of course, more than twenty people here, but if she's honest, she knew there would be. She's getting better at translating what Dominic actually means when he says something.

Some of the guests have gathered around a bonfire at the far end of the garden. She slips her aching feet out of her heels and into her clogs and heads across the grass to join them. It is here that a bonnie woman called Daisy introduces herself, her cheeks pink from alcohol and the heat of the fire, her long blonde hair not unlike her own, but where Annie has worn hers loose down her back, Daisy's is tied into plaits, giving her the wholesome look of an archetypal country girl.

'How long have you known Dominic?' It is the same question she has asked all evening.

'We were in the same year at school.'

'Ah, OK. So you'd know Thomas, would you? Thomas Bartlett, is it?'

'I know Tom, yeah. He's in London now.' Daisy meets Annie's eye and smiles. 'You're definitely Dom's type.'

'Really? And what's that then?'

She describes a wavy line in the air with her hand, as if she's wielding a sparkler. 'Blonde, essentially. English rose type. Sexy-looking.'

Annie laughs. What other reaction is there?

'Sorry,' Daisy says. 'That came out wrong. I meant it as a compliment. Sorry. I'll shut up. I think I'm a bit drunk. Shut up, Daisy.'

'Don't worry about it. I'm flattered. And you're not so bad yourself.'

They chink glasses, but Daisy appears to be studying the patio stones now as if she's hoping for a portal, which endears her to Annie even more. They chat for a little while longer. Daisy teaches Spanish at Swanage Secondary School; Annie tells her that her sister Isla studied Spanish at uni but so far hasn't done anything with it. At the discovery of a shared love of Almodóvar, Daisy suggests they have a movie night sometime, and with a tingly feeling, Annie begins to hope that she has made her first friend.

It is only when Daisy excuses herself and goes to the house to make herself a strong black coffee *before I drop any more clangers*, her magnificent Viking tresses fading into the shadows, that it occurs to Annie that if she is Dominic's type, then so is Daisy. She wonders then if Daisy's awkwardness at the outset is perhaps because she and Dom have a history. She will ask him later, although only if the mood is right – whenever she asks about his romantic past, he either tickles her or says something flippant, but he can't hold out on her forever.

Later, the guests have thinned out. Annie has lost track of Dom. He isn't in the living room or the dining room or the kitchen. She heads upstairs, thinking to check on Cal, who is fast asleep and looks peaceful, thank goodness. She is about to go back down when she hears a distinctly female giggle coming from her and Dominic's room. Her heart beats faster – it is astonishing how instantly this happens. In breathless silence, she edges towards the door. Another giggle, low but definitely female, the soft rounded vowels and consonants she is getting used to, a voice she has heard tonight.

'Seriously though, you need to tell her,' the voice says. 'It's not fair for her to hear it via gossip.'

Annie's hand is on the door handle; her legs, she realises, are trembling.

'Annie's a free spirit.' It is Dom's voice; she can't hear it as clearly. 'She's not tied to convention. Honestly, you don't know her like I do. She's not like other women.'

'Not like other women? Bit misogynistic.'

'I don't mean it like that. Don't twist my words. She'll understand.'

'Understand what?' Annie finds she has pushed open the door and is staring at her husband, who is sitting close, far too close, to Daisy, one arm draped around her shoulder. That they are fully dressed comes as the most unwelcome relief.

Daisy stands, too quickly, her hands rising to her crimson cheeks. But Dominic remains sitting and only smiles.

'I was just telling Daisy how extraordinary you are,' he says. 'And she called me a misogynist, can you believe that?' He laughs.

'I'm going to head off,' Daisy says, eyes down, hurrying past Annie. 'It was nice to meet you, Annie,' she calls from the stairwell. 'I'll see you soon. We'll do that Almodóvar thing.'

Dominic throws out his arms, his eyelids heavy, his expression silly. 'Come here, you.'

She falters but stays where she is, one hand still clutching the door handle. 'What was that?'

'What was what?'

'That. This. You and Daisy in our bedroom. Debating whether to tell me something. Tell me what? Are you guys… I mean, were you…' She wants to say *snogging*, but it's a child's word, it doesn't carry the weight she needs; but at the same time, if they were, she doesn't know where that leaves her. Flustered, she coughs into her hand and tries to straighten herself up. 'Were you with her just now? Being intimate, I mean?'

'Being intimate?' He laughs, his wheezy old man's laugh, his ears dark pink, the lobes bigger from this angle than she thought they were. 'I've known Daisy for decades. I was *chatting* to her.'

'You could have chatted to her downstairs. There's plenty of room.'

'Seriously? I was coming upstairs to use the loo and she was coming out and we got chatting and we just… we just ended up

in here, that's all. We wanted to sit down. Listen, I never did get
to the loo; I'm dying for a pee.' He jumps up and heads towards
her. She shrinks away as he passes, but he takes hold of her arm.

'The chillis were amazing,' he says and kisses her fast and rough
on the mouth. 'You're a bloody marvel; I knew it the moment I
met you.'

CHAPTER 24

Isla

September 2004

For the entire day, my chest is a cave. I make tea that I don't drink, toast I don't eat. The only person I want to talk to is Annie.

Late in the afternoon, Ross calls round. We sit in the living room, where I have drawn the curtains against the view. I ask about Cal's statement. Whether he was lying, what Ross makes of it. He can't tell me anything is what he's come to tell me. He's here just to check I'm OK.

'Have you got forensics?' I ask. 'I mean, you must have proof.'

'No forensics yet,' he says.

'Is he going to plead manslaughter, do you think?'

'I don't know. I expect his solicitor will advise him. And Tom's been in and had a word. It's out of my hands now.' He stands to go. 'Call me if you need anything at all. I know you're in touch with Jan and Daisy, but still. Keep in touch.'

Once Ross has gone, I make yet more tea and take it into the garden. Outside, the light is falling. The air feels fresh and I close my eyes to it as well as the sight of the burnt-out cabin. I meant to ask Ross when I can get rid of it. I wonder what Cal will do, what he's doing right this moment. The only thing that makes sense now is the thing I least want to accept: the reason he told me he didn't kill her is because he couldn't bear to tell me that he had.

It occurs to me that I have chosen confusion. The truth was clear, but I didn't want it. The *truth* is that my nephew killed my sister, by accident or for reasons I have yet to find out, and tried to get away with it. And once the evidence stacked up against him, he had no choice but to confess. I have no idea what happened; all I know is that I will have to try to understand – to understand and stop this frightening tide of anger from rising into a sea of hate. I will have to do that for Annie's sake.

Later that night, I text Ross to ask if there's any news.

He calls back immediately.

'Hi,' he says. 'I was about to call you.'

'OK. Have you got news?'

'I have. There's been a change. Callum's changed his plea.'

My scalp tightens. 'To what?'

'I'm so sorry,' he says. 'He's pleading not guilty to murder.'

'*What?* But that doesn't make any sense. Either he did it or he didn't. What the hell?' My mouth clamps shut, opens, but nothing comes out. 'Can I call him?'

'I'm sorry, you can't.'

I know this. 'Has he spoken to you?'

'He won't see me. He won't talk to anyone apart from his solicitor. And Tom obviously.'

'Does this mean he'll be out on bail?'

'Not on a murder charge unfortunately.' Ross sighs. 'I'm sorry.'

'It's not your fault. It's just so confusing. Why would he say he killed her if he didn't? Surely it's the other way round? You deny it until you admit it?'

Another long sigh. 'I can't really comment. I just thought you should know.'

It's my turn to sigh. I should feel relieved, I should – he's saying he didn't kill her, thank God – but more than anything, I can't figure out how to feel. *I didn't kill her*, he said – in the heat of the moment, from the heart. He looked right into my eyes when he said that. And I believed him, I did, and I still do. But I also believed he was trying to tell me he killed Dominic – that he was trusting me to pick that up without saying it out loud. And once I've said goodbye to Ross and pulled on my sister's old cardigan and taken a glass of wine to the end of her garden, I am faced with the uncomfortable knowledge that I still believe him on that too. Cal killed Dominic. In some dreadful, horrible eruption of violence I can only assume came from Dominic's treatment of my sister, possibly from Cal walking in on him murdering her, Cal flipped and killed him. Even the idea sends blood thumping into my ears, even the words – murdering, killing. Murder, for Christ's sake. But that must be what happened; it's the only possibility – Cal killed Dom in a fit of rage, tried to cover his tracks and, in some horrible twist of fate, ended up taking the fall for his mother's death instead. What a mess. What a bloody mess.

I know it is monstrous to take a life. Life is the last thing you can ever take from someone. No matter how evil a person, murder is an act that robs us of our humanity and from which there is no return. I know I know I know that. But what's done is done. And if Cal can plead and be found not guilty of killing Annie, he will effectively get away with killing Dominic, my absolute bastard of a brother-in-law. And what shocks me perhaps more than anything, what makes me feel my loneliness all the more keenly, is that despite where I stand or thought I stood morally, despite my upbringing, despite all of it, deep down, where no one else will ever get to see, lies the dark knowledge that I will be OK with that. I am OK with murder.

CHAPTER 25

Annie

September 1993

Saturday morning, a week after the party, Daisy calls to ask Annie if she and Callum fancy coffee or a walk the following day.

Annie's mind goes straight to Daisy's little tryst with Dominic.

'I'm not sure,' she replies.

'I'd say walk then,' Daisy says, misinterpreting. 'The weather's going to be good, so we could go over to Worbarrow Bay. I'll take you to Tyneham village. It's dead spooky; Callum will love it. Pack a swimming cozzie, a towel and some sandwiches, et cetera, OK? Oh, and trainers or walking shoes – it's quite a trek down. Pick you up at ten-ish?'

'OK.' Annie supposes she can at least find out if her suspicions are true. Besides which, she deserves a break. Yesterday Dominic left her to attend to the changeover once again – she supposes this is what will happen every week now.

'I'll make a fruit loaf,' she adds 'We can have a shivery bite.'

'A what?' Daisy laughs, making Annie laugh too.

'Sorry. It's a snack you have after you've been swimming. When you're shivering, you know? A bite to eat.'

'Gotcha! A shivery bite! Love it. In that case, I'll bring a flask of tea and we can have a shivery drink – oh, that doesn't work at all, does it? Just ignore me, ha ha ha.'

Possibly for the first time since she's got here, Annie feels herself break into a wide grin. It is only when she puts the phone down that she reminds herself that no matter how lovely Daisy seems, it is only a week since she found her in some dodgy private bedroom conference with her husband.

The next morning, at the beep of a horn out on the driveway, Annie calls up the stairs to Cal to get a move on. Dominic is still in bed after getting in late last night. He'd been taciturn with her before he left because she'd refused to come with him, saying it wasn't fair on Cal, it was way too soon.

'Why can't you just come for a few drinks?' he grumbled. 'Callum is twelve, for God's sake. It's only along the road.'

'I've just moved him away from all his friends, his grandparents and everyone he knows, and last week we had the party. He needs some quiet time with his mum.'

'He'll only be watching the TV or on that stupid Game Boy thing he's never got out of his hands.'

'Oh, so what? You're giving me parenting tips now?'

'No. I just think you could come for an hour, especially as you're off without me tomorrow morning.'

'Off without you? You were off all day, leaving me to sort the cottages again, which I can't remember ever agreeing to, by the way.'

'Oh, come on, there's barely anything to do.'

On it went, back and forth until…

'For God's sake,' she said in the end, raising her voice. 'You're the adult here, remember? So wheesht and just get oan with it.'

'What are you saying? Is that Gaelic?' His bottom lip stuck out – it actually stuck out. And his flabby earlobes were ridiculous – she couldn't believe she hadn't noticed before – and his nose was too long. 'I didn't get married to go out alone. I don't see why you can't just come for one.'

'Aye, and I don't see why you can't see why, so I suppose you'll have to lump it.' She stared him down, hard, until she burst into laughter at the sight of him. 'You're nothing more than a spoilt wee kid, aren't you? On you go, away and play with your pals. Mummy'll tuck you into bed later.'

He stared at her, shocked. But after a moment, he shrugged on his coat and kissed her on the cheek. 'I won't be long.'

It was 10 p.m. before he phoned her from the pub, slurring down the line that there was a band on, that he was sorry for being grumpy earlier and that he loved her – she knew that, didn't she? Two in the morning before he stumbled through the front door; three before, after much clomping about and the stink of burnt toast, he crawled into bed and fell asleep with his arm around her waist.

I thought I was marrying a man, she thought, listening to the soft rumbling of his snores. *But he's as pathetic and silly as a child.*

Cal appears on the stairwell with the fishing net and bucket she bought him yesterday in Swanage. She wonders if he's too old for the seaside, but he hasn't said as much, so she's kept shtum.

Daisy is waiting on the driveway in her red VW Beetle. She waves madly and Annie feels that same rush of happiness before the sight of Daisy and her husband on the bed flashes again in her mind's eye. She hopes that whatever was going on can be explained. It isn't easy knowing no one at all, and it would be great to trust someone as well as like them. Once she'd had Cal, her best friend Lizzie kind of faded away. The other mothers in town were at least ten years older, and of course she had to earn her keep. Friendship is a habit she's fallen out of, she realises. She'd like to get the hang of it again.

'Jump in,' Daisy calls out from the car.

Wordlessly, Cal clambers into the back. Annie tries not to watch him, not to analyse his every expression. He looks neither happy nor sad. Resigned, maybe. A pit hardens in her belly. *Och, wheesht and just get oan with it.* They're here now, they've made this move and there is no bloody way this will not work out – she will make sure of that.

She climbs into the front and is surprised by a one-armed hug from Daisy, a kiss on the cheek.

'All set?' she says. 'You've got trainers on, good. It's a couple of miles down to the bay and the path's quite rocky. Lovely day though.'

She is wearing shocking-pink-framed sunglasses and her hair looks so cool in its long plaits done up today on her head and revealing piercings at the top of her ears. She doesn't look like a Spanish teacher; more like an art teacher.

'How's it going, Cal?' She starts the engine, pulls out onto the lane. 'I saw you the other day; you looked like you were making friends?'

'Um, yeah.'

'I didn't say hi obviously. Don't want to ruin your street cred.'

'Is that right, Cal?' Annie says, turning round. 'Have you found a couple of pals?'

He looks out of the window. Music drifts into the space: 'Holiday' by Madonna.

She continues to watch her son in the rear-view mirror. The hint of a grin has lifted one corner of his mouth. The joy she feels at this is, she knows, out of proportion, and in that moment the aim of the day becomes about getting the other corner to lift, maybe even see some teeth.

Daisy points out all the sights as they pass: the tiny village of Kingston at the top of the hill, the Scott Arms pub on the corner where, she tells Annie, you can have a drink overlooking Corfe Castle, which lies ahead now in the sharp dip of the valley.

'Looks like an eighties pop video, doesn't it?' she says. 'Like Ultravox or one of those bands. Oh, Vienna.'

'Or U2 – what's that album cover?'

'I know the one you mean… oh God, it's on the tip of my tongue.' She bangs the steering wheel. '*Unforgettable Fire*!'

'Aye, that's it. The valley looks like it's been cut out of the hill.'

'That's the Purbeck Ridge. You can walk right along, over to Studland, see all the millionaires' houses.'

They park and walk down the long track to the beach. It is sunny and bright, but the wind is strong enough to blow your eyebrows off, a remark Annie makes to Daisy, who laughs easily, as it seems she does often.

By the time they plonk themselves on the pebbles of the bay, Annie is starving. But Daisy won't let anyone eat anything until they've all been in the water.

'Last one in has to pay for ice creams on the way home,' she says, dropping her loose cotton dungarees to her feet. She pulls her T-shirt over her head to reveal a red Speedo swimming costume and hobbles squealing down to the water's edge. She is strong-looking and compact. There are tan lines on her arms and legs, and the back of her neck is red with sunburn. Another few seconds and she's in, head under and back up again, shrieking and laughing like a madwoman, her golden plaits darkened to wheat. 'It's so lovely! You have to run in! Come on, run!'

Annie pulls off her trainers, jeans and T-shirt. Underneath, she has on her black one-piece from Markies.

'Ach, my legs are blue,' she mutters. Her thighs are dimpled, and chubbier than she'd like. But Daisy clearly doesn't care about any of that stuff, so in that moment, Annie decides that neither does she. *Ouch, ouch, ouch* – the pebbles are murder on the soles of her feet.

'Come on, Cal!' she calls. 'I dare you!'

But he has sat himself down against the white cliff and pulled up the hood of his sweatshirt. She can't even tell if he's watching.

The sea is liquid ice on her toes.

'No way,' she shouts, laughing, backing up a little.

'What kind of Scottish person are you?' Daisy shouts back, by now swimming doggy-paddle in a circle. 'I thought you Jocks could stand the cold?'

There is nothing for it but to run in like she used to run into the loch as a kid. Yes, she thinks, I did used to do that, before the pregnancy, before Cal, before everything. I used to inhabit my body with less thought. She glances back at Cal, who gives her a double thumbs-up and – joy – a grin. That's it. That's all she needs. And for that moment it seems his happiness, and with it her future, depends on this: her ability to throw herself into the freezing sea. With a scream, she wades one, two, three paces before stumbling on a rock and falling, arms flailing, head going under. She comes up swimming, yelping and laughing, laughing, laughing, salt on her lips, on her tongue. Daisy is laughing too, and when Annie looks towards the beach, she sees to her great joy that Cal's arms are folded across his stomach, his head thrown back.

I have made him laugh, she thinks. *And if I can still make him laugh, we will be OK.*

After lunch, Cal takes his net to the rock pools at the far-left side of the bay while Annie and Daisy pour themselves the last of the tea. With the angel's pause of silence, the ease she has felt all day drops away, replaced by a stone-like feeling in her gut. But if she's going to leave Inveraray behind, she must also leave behind this ability to never talk about anything, ever.

'I need to ask you something.' Like that, the words are out.

Daisy sips her tea, her eyes fixed on the sea.

Annie steels herself and asks: 'Did I walk in on something?'

Daisy glances at her, her expression perplexed. 'Walk in on what?'

'At the party. You and Dom together. In our bedroom. You looked very close. I wondered if you'd been… intimate.'

Daisy's eyes round. 'As in sexually? Ha!' She shakes her head. 'No,' she says, still shaking her head. 'Just no.'

'Have you ever…?'

'No.' She opens her mouth, as if to add something, but closes it again and presses her lips tight.

For no reason she can put her finger on, Annie believes her. Without another word, they return their gazes to the sea stretched out before them, constant and shifting and greyer now that clouds have moved over the sun.

'I remember my sister showing me a Spanish poem about the sea,' Annie says. 'It was about a woman looking out and thinking about how wide it was, how vast. I had just enough Spanish to make out those few lines. I think the title meant "The Unhappily Married Woman". Isla translated it for me, but I've forgotten the title in Spanish.'

'Can you remember the poet?'

'No.'

'"La Malcasada"? Was it that?'

'Yes! "La Malcasada". I'm pretty sure that was it – clever you! That title made the lines so sad. Like, without it, it was just a description of how big the sea is, but because you knew this woman was unhappy, the description had this sense of… longing, you know? Loneliness. Sadness. Just a woman looking out over the wide, vast sea.'

Daisy gulps. 'That sounds beautiful,' she says after a moment, her eyes glossy.

'It was.'

As they continue to stare at the sea, Annie feels a familiar creeping loneliness. She didn't expect to feel it, not with Dominic and a new life opening out before her. She knows she can bear it, just as she knows the sight of water has the power to give the feeling poignancy, the kind that hovers over the edges of pleasure, the kind that has a beauty all of its own – like that poem. She never tired of Loch Fyne, the yellow slick of evening sun on the water, the clear air, the light.

'Are you OK?' Daisy asks.

Annie keeps her eyes on the horizon. 'I need to ask you what Dominic isn't telling me. If it's not about you and him, then what?'

'It should be him that tells you.'

'I'm asking you.'

Daisy groans, picks up a stone and throws it into the water.

'He was with someone,' she begins. 'They went out for years. Sonia. She was from over in Studland, but they met in London and realised they were both from here and went out through their late twenties, and when he had to come back because he ran out of money—'

'Hang on. He told me his parents needed him to take over the business.'

'Did he?' Daisy blushes. 'Well, maybe I've got that wrong. Anyway, Sonia followed him back here and got a job in Swanage. They didn't move in together, but we all thought they'd get married. I mean, he was still mucking about, but we thought he'd settle once they tied the knot, you know?'

'Mucking about?'

She closes her eyes, as if she's put her foot in it; opens them again. 'He cheated on her a fair bit.'

'*What?*'

'Don't worry, he's nuts about you.' She picks up another pebble and lobs it into the sea. 'Anyway, they got engaged, but I think every time she tried to set a date, he didn't take her on.'

'So you knew her?'

'Only as part of a group, but yeah. She was nice.'

'Was?'

'When he turned thirty, he finished with her. By fax. He sent her a fax at work.'

'Oh my God, that's terrible.'

'It was bad. I told him he was a dick. He felt bad about it, and I think he did ring her to apologise, but by then she'd…' Daisy sucks air through her teeth, grimacing. 'By then she'd thrown herself off the cliff at Kimmeridge.'

PART TWO

CHAPTER 26

Isla

September 2004

They take Cal to Guys Marsh, a grim red-brick jail near Shaftesbury. It is with a heavy feeling that I walk into that stale space, a sense of disbelief, as if I have come to the wrong place. I give my name to the woman at reception and go and sit on the hard plastic chair she indicates for me. But minutes later, she calls me back to the little window and tells me that Mr Callum Rawles is not seeing visitors.

'But I'm his aunt,' I explain – not yet understanding that who I am has no relevance at all. 'Isla Andrews? I'm his next of kin.'

'I'm afraid he's not seeing anyone at all, Ms Andrews. The message I have here is for you not to come again. I'm sorry.'

My breath hitches. 'Not to come? What, ever?'

The woman looks at her screen, then back at me. 'That's what it says. I'm sorry.'

Outside, the day is too bright after the gloom of the interior. I stagger to my sister's car, get in and weep fat rolling tears into my lap.

'Annie.' My voice is as small as a child's. 'He won't see me.'

It takes me half an hour to compose myself enough to drive back to Rainbow Cottage and, when I get there, another forty-five minutes to find a screwdriver and remove the stupid, twee, bullshit chocolate-box name plate from the cottage door.

I visit Guys Marsh a further three times, filled each time with a strong cocktail of denial and optimism, before it sinks in that when he says he doesn't want to see me, he means it. He does not want to see me, not even for five minutes, not even for a few seconds, not at all. Doesn't want to talk to me, doesn't want to look at me, doesn't want me to look at him. Perhaps he realises I've worked it out and is afraid of me saying something that will give him away. Perhaps he is ashamed – he will feel as I do that to take a life is the ultimate heinous act. Perhaps he did kill An— No. No. No, he did not. That's not what's happened. I cannot even let myself think it – even if that thought invades my conscious mind, it is fear, that is all, a bogeyman thought, to be pushed wilfully aside. I must keep my faith in Cal, for his sake, for Annie's and for mine. He has pleaded not guilty, and not guilty is what I must believe absolutely.

But still, the pain of his rejection is sharp. If I can trust him, why can't he trust me?

Despite nips of whisky at The Square and Compass, the first breath of oncoming autumn has us shivering around the graves of my sister and her husband – he is no brother of mine, not even in law. St Nicholas's church is full. That Cal does not attend pierces me, but Jan tells me not to think about it, and to try and understand the anguish he must be feeling, the impossibility for him of facing the village in such traumatic circumstances, accompanied by prison security. I nod and say yes, of course, but it's a performance for the sake of giving my sister a peaceful send-off. Privately, I cannot believe Cal hasn't come to say a last goodbye to his mother.

Jan and Daisy pretty much take care of the wake back at the cottage: there are pasties and sandwiches from Haymans Bakery in Swanage, and three kegs of copper ale donated by the pub. I get the impression folk are there more for Annie than Dominic, even though he was the local. She would have loved seeing everyone, I think – that she was loved is of some comfort.

There are winter jobs to do on the cottages, a fact that helps to cut short any conversations about that night, about how Cal might be doing. We are in the dark. At least, I am. If Jan and Daisy know more than I do, they don't admit it. It's not like I can tie them to a chair and shine a light in their faces; I have to keep them on side. And more than this, I have to believe most humans are good – it is the feeble torch by which I light my way through this darkness.

I quit my job; they tell me to get in touch when it's all over. There is too much to do here in Purbeck – I want to keep things ticking over for if and when Cal is released. If he is found guilty, I will have to cross that bridge then – I simply can't think about it now. Besides, if I stay and get to know Daisy and Jan, there might be more to bring to light – there might be things they're not ready to tell me now but might in time.

I write to Cal every week, neutral letters relaying inane incidents at the cottages: one kid who drew a full metre square of Picasso-style artwork on the wall of Seacliff View and his parents never said a word; a dog that chewed a foot off the kitchen table at Rose Cottage over in Langton – nothing controversial, nothing incriminating. I hope he is bearing up, ask him to write or call if he needs anything.

He doesn't write. He doesn't call. Jan and Daisy tell me they also write to him and do not hear back. I have no reason not to believe them, tell myself to stop being so suspicious when doubts creeps out in the night.

Tom calls often, as a friend. One evening, we end up watching an entire movie together, quipping down the line, making each other laugh. He is as modest and kind as my first impression of him gave me to believe all those years ago – as unassuming, as thoughtful. He tells me Cal is holding up, and that he will do his best for him. Since I have not been allowed to see my nephew, what has passed between him and his counsel is a mystery to me. I have no idea what to make of anything, wish I could call him and ask: look, did you or didn't you? But I can't. All I know is life can turn in an instant and all the caution in the world cannot protect you from its whims. Caution cannot save you. It has not saved me.

'Hurry back, babe,' Patrick says on the phone. 'There's no one to help me smoke my Consulates.'

'I'll be back soon. Don't have any parties without me or do anything interesting. Love you.'

'Love you. Good luck.'

Despite my promises to Patrick, London is draining from me. My veins are filling with the fresh-air smell of my childhood, the cold kiss of wild water on my toes, the mulchy aroma of wet auburn leaves underfoot. Sitting in places I know Annie once sat, walking the paths she walked, I imagine the connection between us, between this world and the next, and she comes to me as she does in my dreams often, walking towards me along the shore of Loch Fyne, stretching out her arms and telling me she's sorry, always that she's sorry. I try to tell her it's OK. I don't like the thought of her worrying. It is ironic, frankly, that Annie would visit me from beyond. As the cautious one, it is perhaps obvious that I would be the agnostic. Hedging my bets, planning for a variety of outcomes. That I will see her again is a possibility only if I allow myself to believe. And so I allow myself to believe, in her – her ghost.

The tourists are all but gone now until spring brings them back again. Once the work of the business is done – bookings, phone calls, running repairs all the way up to one ongoing renovation of a steading – I walk, sometimes alone, sometimes with Daisy.

Sometimes we take the coastal path from Seacombe, through Winspit and on to where the coastline throws itself open in the wide embrace of Chapman's Pool. Carefully we stagger and stumble over the slick black ledges of shale, where Jurassic creatures have scrawled their white messages across the millennia, ammonites like tiny tyre tracks, like cartwheels. In late September, Daisy swam here a few times before the weather turned too cold. She is in possession of her body in a way that I am not. She throws it into the sea like a much-loved old friend while I, refusing to join her in the water, wait on the stones, towel at the ready, soup in a flask. The Isle of Purbeck is pretty in what to me seems a peculiarly English way; smaller in scale than the mountainous Highlands, but it still helps put things into perspective the way my homeland always used to do.

The year turns. It is no longer the year my sister and her husband died horribly. The ruin of Annie's studio has been cleared away. A gardener friend of Daisy's laid fresh turf over the blackened land. It is a relief not to have it in my eyeline anymore, although the sight is indelible, of course. January brings new resolutions, a new dawn. Will it bring a new start for my haunted nephew? If he didn't kill my sister, then it must. The rest, all that I am sure he is hiding, he can tell me in time, and we can make our peace with it together. I hope.

And at last the day comes: the Crown versus Callum Rawles. The outfit I have chosen is a cheap black shirt dress from H&M and the cowboy boots I bought in New York last year with Patrick. Casual enough so I don't feel like I'm going to a funeral all over again, smart enough without looking like I'm going for a job interview. I find my father's wallet in my bag; inside it, the black-and-white photo of Annie and I as little girls, standing in our parents' garden in dresses made by our mother from old bits of fabric. It knocks the breath from me, even though I look at it often. I sit down a moment, rub Annie's wedding ring, now circling the ring finger of my right hand; the half-heart bracelet I bought her nowhere to be found – lost in the fire or perhaps mislaid years ago.

In the mirror, my reflection is a variation on what I saw yesterday and the day before – a slow, incremental change. When I see Cal, it will be different. I have not seen him since September. I hope his appearance is not too much of a shock, my own feelings of powerlessness during the trial not too overwhelming. He has denied murder, confessed to murder, and denied it all over again. With so many changes and without any contact, his innocence is the fine thread by which I have to find my way back to him. His guilt is the knife that will sever that thread. Mum always told us to take three deep breaths. And that is what I do. The moment has come.

I call Daisy, let it ring three times: I'm on my way.

CHAPTER 27

Isla

On the way to pick up Daisy, I call to say a quick hello to Jan, hoping that the sight of her will calm me down. And it does, a little. She is wearing a long skirt as usual, blue Doc Martens, a brown ribbed polo-neck sweater with a sheepskin gilet I haven't seen before over the top.

'Just thought I'd say bye before I go,' I say, hovering on her doorstep.

'You did right.' Seeming to understand, she opens her arms, pulls me into a skinny but fulsome hug.

'I'm scared,' I say, my words muffled in sheepskin.

'I know. But soonest begun, soonest ended, eh.'

A movement next door catches my eye. A woman crossing the front window, no more than a shadow. These days Jan takes care of the meet-and-greets for this cottage; she says she doesn't mind. Heartbreak Hotel, booked almost all year round. My throat still blocks when regulars calling to book assume from my accent that I'm Annie; my chest still tightens at the painful questions that sometimes arise – *Well, could I speak to Dominic or Annie Rawles please?* Gah. I break apart from Jan and ask her, with the low-key irony we have established between us, if the current occupant of Heartbreak Hotel is a writer or an artist.

'Poet,' she replies, eyes fixed on mine. 'Keen to access the Jurassic.' Her gaze flickers; she quickly corrects her expression to a smile, looking over my shoulder and bringing her hand up in a wave. 'Hello there.'

I follow her gaze to where the woman is standing on next door's path. She is very pretty, I think, as she and Jan exchange pleasantries, with fair hair and blue eyes.

'Hope you find inspiration,' Jan calls out. 'Watch you don't get caught in the storm.'

'Thank you.' The woman waves and heads off towards the footpath.

'You're far too early, you know,' Jan says. 'You'll make yourself even more nervous if you have to wait around.'

'Don't worry. Daisy'll keep me right.'

'Did you pack snacks and plenty of water? There can be a lot of waiting around – I remember that from jury service.'

'Yes. Not that I'm particularly hungry.'

'You'll be fine.' She shivers. 'Rather you than me though.'

Jan has already apologised for not coming. She hates court-rooms, for reasons she hasn't said and I haven't wished to pry into, so I take my leave and drive to Daisy's Purbeck-stone bungalow at the far edge of the village. She is waiting at the front window and waves when she sees me. Another minute and she's jumping into the car with a rush of cold air. Gone are the jeans and loose shirts, the trainers. Today she is wearing a midnight-blue wrap-over dress, a generous dark grey scarf, an elegant black wool coat and black high-heeled ankle boots. She has even painted her short square nails black, which looks super funky.

'I almost didn't recognise you,' I tease, trying not to stare at her impressive cleavage as she throws her scarf in the footwell and buckles herself in.

'I do dress as a woman sometimes.' She winks – the lick of blue eye pencil and a brush of black mascara has made her eyes even bigger, even bluer than usual.

'I just popped in to see Jan.'

'Aw, shame she's not coming.'

'Aye.' I start the engine. 'Off we go then.'

And like that, after all these months of anticipation, we are living a moment I almost believed would never come, a moment whose imminence has weighed on all of us – myself, Daisy and Jan – Tom too. We have coped, because there has been no choice. We have forced our focus onto the practicalities – organising Cal's defence, the finances, the cottage, the business, my house in London, the winter work required to get the cottages ready for the busier season to come. But strangely, after months of all that brisk pragmatism, now in the car the air is thick. And sure enough:

'I need to tell you something,' Daisy says, her discomfort palpable.

'OK.' I keep my eyes on the road.

'I've been called as a witness.'

'*What?* For the defence?'

'Yes.' She sighs. 'Tom wants me as a character witness.'

'OK.'

'Only, I'm not allowed in court until I've given evidence. I'm sorry.' She must feel me looking at her but she doesn't look back. When I return my eyes to the road, I sense she's turned towards me. I am, frankly, too gutted to speak.

'How are you feeling?' she asks – an attempt to move past what she's just told me. I'm still digesting the fact that I'm going to have to sit on my own for a great deal of the trial, and if I'd known, I could have asked Jan. But then, no, I couldn't. And Ross is a witness for the prosecution. There is no one else.

'How was Jan?' Daisy asks, and I realise I still haven't replied, which will be killing her.

'Fine,' I reply, trying to keep it light. 'We waved to the latest inhabitant of Heartbreak Hotel.'

'Oh yes? Not quite the honey trap it once was.'

The hairs on my arms lift. 'A honey trap? What do you mean?' I am remembering something Jan said. A conversation I had with her in the first days – a lifetime ago – a conversation lost in the trauma of all that followed. *Was Dominic with someone when he died?* I asked her. And she closed her eyes and I knew she meant yes. And when I asked her if it was someone local, she replied with a cynical edge that there was no one local left. I know from Daisy that Dominic had had many lovers before Annie and many after they were married. But I never pushed Jan on what she said that particular day. Now I think about it though, if he had already slept with everyone in the area, who were these new lovers, this fresh meat? I never followed it up – never thought to.

Daisy is looking out of the window, pretending she hasn't heard me.

'Daisy,' I say. 'What do you mean, a honey trap?'

'What?' She turns, as if hearing me only now, and pretends to try and find a music station on the car radio.

'Daisy.' My arms straighten against the steering wheel. 'My nephew might be about to go down for the murder of my sister. I know you don't want to gossip and I respect that, but you've known me long enough now. I'm not an outsider anymore, not really, and if you don't trust me now, you never will. Please. Just tell me. What did you mean?'

Still she tries to fiddle with the radio dial.

I bat her hand away. 'For Christ's sake!' My voice is louder than I mean it to be. 'Stop,' I say, more quietly. 'Why did you say that? Not quite the honey trap it once was, you said. Was it Dominic's? Dominic's honey trap? Is that what you meant?'

She sighs. 'It doesn't matter anymore. It's over.'

A passing place appears at the side of the road. I swerve in and stop the car, turn off the engine and look at her. 'It matters. To me.'

She closes her eyes. 'All right.'

I start the engine and pull back onto the road, wait for the silence to browbeat her into talking.

'A lot of the women who stayed there,' she begins after a moment, 'were in a… specific place. The cottage description makes a romance of how bloody small it is. Call it the Hermitage, sell it as a retreat, and in they flock. Dom always did the bookings for that one. I think… I mean, I know he had a fling with some of the women who rented it over the years.' Her lips bulge as she blows out her discomfort. She shakes her head.

'And?'

'Jan reckons he was with a woman the day he moved Annie down here,' Daisy replies, as if she's answering a different question. 'He'd left Annie in charge of the changeover. That was Dominic all over – if he could palm off a responsibility, he would. And he just took off, knowing that on Friday morning this woman would be leaving, too much of a coward to face her. I don't know how it went, but she eventually rang the cottage and of course poor Annie ended up answering.'

'This was in her first *week*?'

'Yeah. I remember because they had a party the next night. She told me later that this woman concocted an excuse to get Dominic to come to the cottage by locking herself out.'

'That's impossible.'

'I know. She must have posted the keys back through the letter box – it was pathetic. And then she called Dominic, except she got Annie.'

'Did Annie realise?'

'Not then. She said she had a horrible feeling about it because the woman actually left her number, but Dom had a reasonable explanation so she took him at face value. But later, once she began to realise what she'd got herself into, she put two and two together. I thought he'd stop when he married her. I told him to. But… he didn't. He didn't stop.'

'So... he continued to sleep with women who rented Heartbreak Hotel, women he himself booked in? It was like a *supply* for him?'

'I'm sure it wasn't every single woman, but I would imagine there were a fair few over the years. All I know is, he was precious little help with the coal face of the business – the tradespeople, the plumbers and decorators, the cleaners and the laundry company and whatnot – but he always took care of that cottage. Personally, if you know what I mean. And then when he started his little midlife crisis booking the bands at the pub, well, I don't know exactly how it went, but there were a fair few attractive musicians stayed at that place. Female musicians, if you follow.'

'So he booked musicians at the pub and then, lo and behold, he had the perfect accommodation for a lead singer or a sexy guitarist? Oh my God, you couldn't make it up. Poor Annie.'

'She was all right. She just got on with it.'

Did she? Until this moment, I've assumed Cal's return from uni destabilised my sister's already fragile relationship with Dom, culminating in whatever the hell happened in her workshop in the dead of night. But maybe she was always heading towards that face-off. Maybe she withstood and withstood and withstood until one night she could withstand no more. The police tell me she stabbed him, but I cannot believe it. If it's true, any hope of easing the fact lies in the circumstances that drove her to it, circumstances I am hoping the trial will bring to light. But then again, if it *is* true, where does that leave Cal and what I believe about what he did? Another circle, and round and round I go. Unless there was a third party...

'Daisy?'

'Mm-hm?'

'Was Dom seeing someone else the night he died? Do you think that might have been the reason for the fight? A last straw?'

She reaches for the radio; for the second time, I slap her hand away. 'Daisy! For God's sake!'

'Stop interrogating me,' she says miserably.

'I'm thinking maybe Annie just… cracked? Maybe after the miscarriage? Maybe she was sick to death of it – him, his stupid affairs, the whole lot. I imagine everyone would have known?'

'Well, yes, but villages are a bit like huge dysfunctional families. We gossip and bitch, but when it comes down to it, if something like this happens, we're as tight-lipped as it gets, even about a shit like Dominic. He's a shit, but he's *our* shit.'

Ain't that the truth, I think. And if there's one thing Annie knew, it was that. She was the scandal of our village by the time she was sixteen. But she was their scandal, and they would have fought any incomer to the death if they'd dared say or do anything to harm her.

'So,' I push, 'do you think something tipped her? Maybe a last affair that was one too many? Maybe she found out that day? I'm sure Jan told me he was seeing someone when he died.'

'Anything's possible. I didn't keep a file on him, OK?' Her cheeks pink. She's lying.

'But… don't you think we should have told the police?' *Don't you think* you *should have?* is what I mean. *You or Jan.*

She throws herself back into her seat and looks out of the window. 'It's got nothing to do with anyone. It had been going on so long it wasn't even gossip anymore. It was boring. I mean, do you want those details in the press? In court? The only thing that matters is did Cal kill her? And he says he didn't, so we have to hope that's true.'

'I don't know what he says. He said he didn't, then he said he did, then he didn't.'

'Well, pretty soon we'll hear what he's got to say once and for all, eh?'

'I suppose.'

Daisy wins her fight to put the radio on. I resolve to pursue the matter with Jan. We drive the rest of the way silent save for the odd inane observation: the temperature in the car, the nothing quality of the white winter sky, bad driving on the road. It is only when we get to the courthouse and Daisy climbs out that I find myself watching her walk in her dress and heels, her hair a shock of blonde, her voluptuous figure and rosy skin like a plump ripe apple. It's got nothing to do with anyone, she said. The way she clammed up. The way she *lied*. Annie didn't care about Dominic having anonymous affairs; she was used to it. OK. Maybe.

But what if he'd been sleeping with her best friend?

CHAPTER 28

Annie

October 1993

Annie decides to let Dominic tell her about Sonia when he's ready. Daisy reckoned he probably meant to tell her but couldn't find the words. He is mad for her, Daisy said. Couldn't have married her fast enough. Don't worry. Honestly. But Annie can't get it out of her mind. That poor girl. Such an extreme thing to happen. The information builds a head of pressure. The more she bites her lip, the more the need to hear him say it in his own words swells in her chest, blocks her airways, leaves her responses curt, her eyes falling short of his, her hands clumsy when she places his dinner in front of him, the bang of china on tabletop. And when the question finally bursts from her, it is all the more explosive for being suppressed.

It is the following weekend. Dom has persuaded her to leave Cal at home and come to the pub to see a folk band he thinks are the next big thing. She doesn't really want to go, but, feeling browbeaten, as is often the case, she has agreed. Cal thinks he's old enough to be left in the house. He is adamant. But the problem is, the cottage is set well away from the other houses. There are no reassuring noises from the flat next door, no street lamp outside his window like there was in Inveraray. Here, the darkness at night is darker. The shapes night makes in the rooms won't be familiar to him yet, not in a sleepy state. He might be too scared to venture upstairs, might fall asleep on the couch and get cold… too scared even to call the pub.

She tries to forget about Cal, but that only makes her think about Sonia. She and Dom are almost at the centre of the village when the head of pressure bursts, releasing a chaotic outpouring of tearful questions:

'Why didn't you tell me about Sonia?'

'Didn't you think your wife – your *wife*, for God's sake – had a right to know?'

'Do you think I'm so weak I can't cope?'

'Is it because you feel responsible?'

'Or' – and this is the one she really wishes she hadn't said – 'are you ashamed?'

'Whoa,' he says, throwing up the palms of his hands. They have reached the village green, where he halts next to the duck pond. 'Stop! Just stop!'

'I'm sorry,' she says, though she is still fizzing. 'I wasn't going to ask at all, but we're married and I don't think there should be things we can't talk about. There was so much I wasn't allowed to talk about growing up. I thought I'd left that behind.'

'All right, all right.' Dominic sits on the stone bench and pulls her down to sit beside him. The smell of guano and stagnant water is strong, the seat cold beneath her bottom. He looks at his watch.

'Don't let me keep you,' she says bitterly, quashing the strong urge to slap him across the face. 'Wouldn't want to miss five minutes of the band, would we?'

'Annie.'

'Were you ever going to tell me?'

'Of course I was.' He pushes his hand through his hair and sighs. 'Or maybe not. I don't know. I didn't want to tell you. It's a horrible thing to have to talk about. It was horrible, a horrible thing that happened, and I didn't want it in this part of my life…

in us, do you know what I mean? In this beautiful, happy thing. When I met you, you were so… outside all of that. You were like clear water, there to wash it all away, do you know what I mean? You didn't know anything about Sonia and that made me feel… clean, I suppose. Pure. Light. I can't explain it.'

'But you finished with her by fax. By fax!'

He shakes his head. 'Thanks, Daisy.'

'Don't blame Daisy. I made her tell me. It isn't Daisy who caused a woman to jump to her death.'

'Oh, that's not fair!' He stands, paces away, paces back, his eyebrows low and dark. 'That's not fair.'

'I'm sorry.' Her heart slows. A dull, creeping embarrassment begins to fill her.

'Look,' he says, standing above her now, his hands spread. Negotiation, she reads in the gesture. Appeasement. Management.

She hardens, flashes him a hate-filled glance. 'What? Are you going to explain it away?'

'Not at all! What I did was completely out of order – don't you think I know that? It was cowardly and wrong and I wish I'd told her face to face. But I didn't *cause* her to… do it. And to be fair, on the… on the fax, I said I'd come over to talk about it later and that it wasn't her fault. But when I went round, her flatmate said she thought she'd gone to meet me and then we couldn't find her and then the next morning they… found her.' He rubs at his forehead and lets out a groan.

'I'm sorry,' she says, chastened, unsure what to think.

'I should have told you. I should have told you before I asked you to marry me. Not that this defines me. It doesn't – it does *not* define me, all right? But I wasn't honest with you – I can see that.' He gets up, kneels in front of her and takes her hands in his. 'That's why you were so wonderful for me. You were from somewhere far away, so different, so free. My butterfly. Sonia was… she was…

conventional. She'd never have got pregnant by mistake, God no! She'd never have been capable of that amount of spontaneity.'

Stop, she thinks. *Stop criticising her to get to me.*

But he does not stop. 'She would never have agreed to marry me and take off to the other end of the country the way you did,' he says. 'She wasn't brave like you. She didn't have your wild edge. And she would never have been able to put up with my... needs.'

'Needs?' She shifts, uncomfortable on the cold stone slab.

'Freedoms,' he says, taking her hands now in his as he did when they said their vows. 'You're an artist. And in a way, I am too. I'm not a businessman, not really, not in my *heart*. I only did business to please my parents, you know that, but my true love is music. That's where my real passion lies. You and me, we don't live in the world like others do. We need our freedoms. You know what I'm talking about, don't you?'

She thinks she does. She feels what he's saying in her guts, has always felt it, since she was a wee girl. It is Dominic who made sense of her, retrospectively, made her understand why she was the one always getting into trouble, always on the wrong end of a judgemental gaze, always questioning what others seemed to accept. That night when she met Malcolm, the boy who would unknowingly become Cal's father, her friend Lizzie shook her head when she told her she was going for a walk in the woods with an outsider, here on a lads' weekend from Glasgow, as if she had already decided at fifteen not to live life in the moment but to follow some code that prevented her from danger whilst at the same time stopping her from ever having any fun. Even Isla, whom Annie loves, has looked at her as if she's a lost cause, a disaster waiting to happen. *Oh, Annie, what now?*

It was Dominic, Dominic who gave her the words to express who she was. Because he sees her and understands who she is, what she is: a butterfly. Butterflies need freedom.

'Of course I know what you're talking about.' She squeezes his hands as she stands up. Kisses him on the mouth. 'Not another word about Sonia, unless you need to talk, in which case I'm here, always, OK? Come on. Let's go and see this crazy band.'

CHAPTER 29

Isla

January 2005

Salisbury Crown Court is neither the High Court of Justiciary nor the Old Bailey, but despite the contemporary glass and pale brick of the architecture, it is still intimidating for someone like me, brought up as I was on a fear of authority – God's, specifically – and for a moment I could be eight years old, walking into church, the anticipation of quaking in my pew an old muscle memory. There is a small clutch of reporters outside, but by the time they've twigged who we are, we are all but inside.

Our bags are searched. We are asked to sip from our respective plastic water bottles, to declare any sharp objects. Daisy leaves me to go and wait with the other witnesses; I make my way to the courtroom and sit in the public gallery at the back, along with curious onlookers and members of the press. I don't look at them. I don't want to catch them looking at me. The layout of the courtroom is familiar to me only from glimpses of score-settling afternoon TV shows: beech-wood veneer, black leather benches, the discreet buds of microphones. With a twinge of self-pity, I wish Daisy were here. I just wish she'd given me fair warning – I would have felt her absence less.

Cal is brought in. Nothing could have prepared me for the sight of him, accompanied by two security guards. He takes his seat in the clear Perspex dock. My eyes prick; a hard ball of sadness swells in my throat. Bowed as if already condemned, he wears the dark grey suit, white shirt and sober paisley tie I sent in for him via Ross. He has turned twenty-three whilst in custody, but today he looks no older than eighteen – a child. At the same time, he looks ancient – hunched with osteoporosis, a thousand aches and pains. His shoulders are high around his thin neck, the shoulder pads half collapsed where he no longer fills the jacket. That suit is from his graduation. I remembered it when I found it in his wardrobe last week. Annie sent me a picture of him in it, in a letter. *Look at my handsome boy*, she had written. *All grown up!* But he was not grown up then and he is not grown up now. He is little more than a prematurely aged boy.

But boy or man, he is accused of killing my sister. I have speculated and speculated but all I have now are the facts. I am his guardian. I am his aunt. I am his next of kin. Whether he is found guilty or innocent, those things still apply. The image of him with the hammer raised above his head has been with me since they arrested him; the idea that to charge him with murder, they must have a decent case, that for him to have confessed in the first instance he is deeply involved somehow. Ross says the burden of proof is on the prosecution, that they will bombard us with facts. I know what I think, what thoughts I have pushed away, but I wonder what these new facts will turn out to be.

I'm about to hear them, I suppose, first in the cold light of the prosecution, then in the softer glow of the defence. It occurs to me that what I think is irrelevant, and at the same moment, I wonder what I even think anymore. It's as if this courtroom has whited out my mind of all I have tried to write there these last months. Do I want Cal to be found not guilty? I think so. But more than that, I want him to *be* not guilty. I want him to stand at the box and tell us all what actually happened and for everything to become clear. And if there are things he is determined to hide, if there is a different truth, I want him to tell me once I get him home. Without the truth, our relationship will wither away. It cannot stand on lies, not about my sister's death.

I press my feet to the hard floor to stop my legs from jackhammering.

The judge, a woman in her late fifties, early sixties, has the air of a headteacher, although that's probably my own association. Just the sight of her when the usher bids us rise for her grand entrance makes my stomach drop to my shoes. The swearing-in of the jury takes an eternity – various problems and setbacks – but eventually we get there and the judge tells them in the strictest terms not to speak about the trial to anyone outside this courtroom. *What?* I think. A murder trial? Is that even possible? It will be all over the news. And what are they supposed to do when they return home to their spouses? *How was your day? Oh, fine, same old, same old…*

Now, as the court clerk reads out the counts on the indictment – count one, murder; count two, manslaughter – I glance around, one hand on my stomach to calm the waves of nausea rolling through. The witness box and jury panel are positioned to the left and right of the judge respectively. The senior barristers for the prosecution and the defence sit beside their juniors with their backs to us, facing the judge. Tom is recognisable only by the wide coat-hanger set of his shoulders, his bald pate covered today by his wig.

But counsel for the prosecution, Mrs Peterson, is greeting the jury now. I must have tuned out, because she is already on her feet, face etched with the kind of sorrowful expression that I assume is meant to imply that the tragedy here is not the death of two innocent people but the death of innocence itself in the form of Callum Rawles, a young man who threw away his life in an act of pure evil. Callum Rawles: murderer. A swell of hate rolls through me. Innocent or guilty, this boy is still my blood.

Beneath her tight off-white curls, Mrs Peterson's face is pink, a little pudgy, her nose too short somehow, the philtrum running long down to thin mauve lips. Behind round tortoiseshell glasses, her eyes are small – shrunk, possibly, by a strong lens prescription. I wonder if she's had trouble getting her contacts in today, whether she lay awake last night worrying about the case, woke up with those sore, mean little eyes. She blinks often – an affectation? Behold my blinking state of disbelief, ladies and gentlemen of the jury, at the atrocity of these events I am obliged to relay.

'… that on the eighth of September of last year, the defendant, Callum Rawles, then aged twenty-two, was living at home with his mother, Annie Rawles, and his stepfather, Dominic Rawles. The relationship between the mother and stepfather was by all accounts tempestuous. The relationship between the defendant and his stepfather was strained.

'At a little before midnight that same evening, the bodies of Annie and Dominic Rawles were discovered initially by the emergency services in the mother's cabin-style art studio in the rear garden of their home. Both were dead. Both bodies were very badly burnt. The prosecution case is that earlier that evening there had been a massive row between the couple, culminating in Annie Rawles killing her partner by stabbing him through the abdomen and penetrating his intestines with a large kitchen knife, leaving him to bleed to death. The prosecution say that the defendant stumbled upon this event but too late to prevent its tragic conclusion. His contribution was to pick up a hammer and strike his mother to the head, inflicting a blunt-force trauma that led to her death. His next actions were an attempt to conceal the identity of his mother's killer by dousing the bodies in white spirit and setting both on fire.'

She proceeds to list the witnesses, but my mind is still in the cabin, still with Cal sloshing turps over my sister's body, striking a match, his face half in shadow, half in orange light.

I force my attention back to Mrs Peterson, who is still in full flow.

'… prosecution say that it is not without significance that the defendant changed his account as to what he said occurred in his mother's studio.'

I close my eyes. Lies. He told so many lies. Oh, what a tangled web.

'Murder is heinous,' Mrs Peterson goes on, 'in whatever circumstances. Matricide is… unpalatable. The bludgeoning of one's own mother with a hammer to the back of her head is almost beyond imagining.' She pauses, no more than a second, the slightest momentary dip of her head before pulling herself tall once again. 'But make no mistake, ladies and gentlemen, it did happen. That night, it *happened*: a violent and terrible crime made all the more wicked by the defendant's callous actions immediately following the event that caused her death: placing the murder weapon into the hands of a dead man, a man who had taken the defendant into his home and raised him as his own son but who could not now speak in his own defence.

'Ladies and gentlemen, I urge you to listen with care and to focus on the evidence, and on the events of that night alone. You will hear about a boy's love for his mother, but I would urge you to understand that love can become jealous and strange. It can become angry, out of control. And I would ask you to consider that love, jealous love, can turn to obsession, and yes, to fatal violence. Because the prosecution case, ladies and gentlemen, is that on the night in question, high on a heady mix of marijuana and alcohol, the defendant did slaughter his mother in a crazed attack, the motives for which are at best unclear, at worst troubling. We submit that the evidence will clearly demonstrate that at the very least, the defendant intended to and did cause his mother serious injury, as a direct result of which she died, and is therefore guilty of the first count on the indictment, namely the murder of Annie Rawles.'

She goes on, but I don't take it in. To have heard almost nothing of the events of that night, to then hear them pour out in one long piece of dramatic narrative rhetoric is…

For a moment, I cannot hear or see. I fear I might be sick.
The court adjourns for lunch, which I cannot eat.

After lunch, the prosecution calls the first witness, DS Lewis,
who was the first at the scene. She looks so young, I wonder
how on earth she isn't still at school. Referring to her notebook,
her voice trembling a little, she paints a picture of my nephew's
extreme distress, his agitation. Yes, he seemed like he was panicking. Yes, it could well have been extreme feelings of remorse. No,
she did not see any blood on his clothing, she tells the court,
but yes, the laundry load found in the dryer included the defendant's clothes, which could mean that he had already laundered
his clothes by the time the emergency services arrived.

Tom stands to cross-examine. He moves slowly, his self-
effacing manner transformed by his barrister's robes into quiet
self-confidence.

'DS Lewis,' he begins politely, 'you described my client, Callum
Rawles, as distressed and agitated. You asserted that he acted as
if he were panicking or remorseful. Can I ask, do you have a
qualification in psychology?'

'No.'

'So your assessment of his state of mind is merely your opinion?'

'Well, yes, but we deal with—'

'If you could answer the question, thank you. In your *opinion*,
could his state of extreme distress have been exactly that? Distress.'

Mrs Peterson is on her feet. 'Your Honour, if I may – DS Lewis
is not an expert witness.'

The judge raises her chin. 'Mrs Peterson, your witness has
offered an opinion unchallenged; she can now be cross-examined
on that opinion.' She turns to Tom. 'Mr Bartlett, please continue.'

'Thank you, Your Honour.' Tom appears to study a mark on
the floor briefly before looking up at DS Lewis, whose head has

shrunk into her neck. 'DS Lewis, if you would answer the question please. Could Callum Rawles have been distressed simply because he had witnessed something utterly traumatic?'

She nods. 'Yes.'

'So it wasn't necessarily remorse?'

'Not necessarily, no.'

'Thank you. No further questions, Your Honour.'

What? I think. Is that *it*? No further questions? What about the laundry? Clean laundry isn't *evidence*. Family houses always have laundry around the place; why didn't he call attention to that? But my anxiety is swept away by the usher's call for us to rise.

The judge exits. It takes me a few seconds to realise that, though we have barely begun, the court has been adjourned until tomorrow.

CHAPTER 30

Annie

March 1996

Callum is spotty, too tall for himself, teeth too big, blazer sleeves too short. His hair never sits right – it grows out instead of down. Right now, it is slicked with hair gel, ready for school, but Annie knows rogue spikes will stick up at the back over the course of the day. Embarrassment comes off him in waves, a palpable self-consciousness that makes her want to pull him into her arms and plant a thousand kisses on his cheek, tell him he's gorgeous and that she loves the bones of him. But she doesn't obviously. That would be World War Three.

'Bye, Mum,' he calls out. The cottage door slams shut. A moment later, she hears the faint shush of bike wheel on gravel and counts the slow seconds of angst she always feels at the thought of him riding out into the lane, not looking, not concentrating, the blind bend, the idiot tourist in a sports car. And then it's gone. Until 4 p.m. she will almost forget him and he her, his world now his friends, computer games, football, maybe even girls. She makes a second cup of tea and takes it with her to the studio.

She has five galleries selling her work now. It is enough to keep her busy while Cal is at school, and not too much to prevent her from taking care of him and the house and attending to the business. Over these first years together, she and Dominic have slid into a routine made, if she's honest, by her acquiescence to his needs. It is something she would never admit to Isla, but it's easier this way and the thing is, her life here – with friends and a job she loves and a beautiful house – is still so much better than it was five years ago. She knows fine well Dom is not the man she thought he was, but she has told herself that this is what marriage is, for most people: a slow peeling-away of layers, the management of inevitable disappointment at the truth beneath.

We are all only human, after all.

Besides, she disappoints him too, all the time. She is not the social animal he thought she was, although she cannot remember ever promising to be such. She is not sporty, but then she only ever said she enjoyed swimming in the loch and walking in the hills – and swimming and walking are what she has continued to do, with Daisy. Sometimes he jokes he wants to take her back to Inveraray and ask for his money back, as if she were faulty goods. The first time he said that, she laughed. The second, she told him to get lost and he punched her to the ground. A mistake, he said, apologising. He didn't mean to catch her so hard. Now when he says it, she ignores him.

As for Dominic's *needs*, they are many. He *needs* to go mountain-biking for his stress levels. He *needs* fifteen-minute showers that leave the bathroom walls running with condensation. He *needs* lunch made for him since he never has time to make it for himself, let alone her, though presumably he must have managed before. He *needs* to be at his laptop all afternoon, though what he does there she cannot fathom, since she takes care of most of the bookings, the tradespeople and cleaning staff. He *needs* dentist's and doctor's appointments booked for him, haircuts, physiotherapy sessions, bike repairs. She is so much better at these things apparently. He doesn't know what he'd do without her. Evenings, he *needs* to help at the pub with the music scene – looking after the acts, taking the tickets, helping pack away their gear, all on a voluntary basis. At weekends, he *needs* to sleep in late because these nights are always, in reality, early mornings. But the folk in the pub tell her that her husband is a legend. They don't know what they'd do without him.

To his credit, Dom has acquired two more cottages since she arrived here, even if she ended up project-managing their refurbishment. His wealth astounds her – both his ability to spend it and the way it appears in his hands like flowers from a magician's sleeve. In material terms, it is almost meaningless, but she cannot deny loving the freedom it brings, freedom to work and to build her reputation here in this place grown finally familiar. Like everything else, money has been an adjustment. Growing up, it was to be kept safe, eked out, stored. For Dom, it is to be scattered like seeds, grown like crops.

'You can't take it with you,' he says sometimes when he has made a particularly extravagant purchase.

To keep him cheerful, she replies with a phrase from her homeland, if not from her home: 'Ah yes, there's nae pockets in a shroud.'

The difference between her folks and her husband is confidence. Her parents lacked it; she knows that now. It is why their rules were so rigid, their judgement of anyone not sticking to those rules so harsh. Dom's disregard for boundaries used to excite her. Now it makes her uneasy, as does his flexibility when it comes to the truth. He told people she was an artist before she arrived, so that by the time she got here, that is what she was – her new acquaintances were the mirror in which she saw herself not as a shopkeeper with a child out of wedlock but as an artist, a wife, a mother, a businesswoman. For her part, she has simply let her work speak for her. Which, thankfully, it has.

*

At the weekend, they are invited to yet another party. Daisy is going too, so Annie knows she will at least have someone to talk to while Dom performs his customary disappearing act. They leave Cal watching a movie with two pals, stocked up on popcorn and cola, lolling around in their sleeping bags on the living-room floor like hedonistic mermen.

In the lane, Dominic takes her hand, a loving gesture perhaps prompted by the fight they had earlier over instructions for the plumber who is refitting the en suite in Seaview Croft. He did not hit her in the face. The bruise on her hip is from where he pushed her against the table after she asked him why, if he was so keen on micro-managing, he had taken off for the entire day. Before that, she'd slapped him. Before that, he'd shaken her by the shoulders until she thought her head might fall off. Before that, she'd asked him where he'd been. They made their peace an hour ago, when he joined her in the shower. The violence repaired itself in the usual way – another kind of physical communication altogether. And still, of course, she has no idea where he was all afternoon. She wonders sometimes if other people's marriages are like this but has no one to ask. Daisy lives alone and never speaks of anything even approaching a love life; Isla is a lost cause.

They walk, hands swinging a little, their talk of who might be there tonight. In the front windows of Jan's house, candlelight flickers. As they head up the hill towards the pub, from behind them comes the squeal of a gate hinge. Annie peeps over her shoulder to see a blonde woman with a black trilby emerging from the front garden of Heartbreak Hotel. Dominic too glances before quickening his pace a little.

'Slow down,' she says after a moment – she's almost having to run to keep up with him. 'No rush, is there?'

'Sorry, didn't realise I was walking quickly.' He is still walking quickly. He has not slowed down at all.

'I'm getting out of breath. Slow down, will you? I don't want to arrive all sweaty.'

'You need to exercise more – you're unfit.'

'What? What the hell are you on about? I'm as fit as a fiddle, I just don't want to sprint when I'm in my glad rags, that's all.'

He slows his pace but only a fraction. Her confusion clears. *Ah*, she thinks.

'Do you know that woman?'

'What woman?'

'The lassie that came out of our cottage.'

'Which cottage?'

'You know fine well which cottage. The Hermitage.'

'Did she? Sorry, I wasn't paying attention.'

They have reached the house. He rings the doorbell and raps the knocker, puts his hands on his hips and blows at his fringe. 'Did you remember the wine?'

She holds up the bottle she has bought and wrapped in pale pink tissue, since Dominic, even though these are his friends, never concerns himself with such trivial details. She watches him, sees the effort it takes him not to look behind.

'You do know that lassie, don't you?'

His eyes screw up, as if she's said something mad. 'What are you on about?' He hammers on the door with his fist, as if trapped inside a room. And yet they are outside.

'Stop being weird,' she insists. 'You knew which cottage she came out of as well.'

He stares at her, his eyes black. For a moment, she fears there will be a repeat of this afternoon – if not now then later.

But the door opens. From inside comes a blast of heat, of music. Dominic steps forward, all handshakes and good humour. She follows, her mood dark now where it was light. When she turns to shut the door, to her surprise, the woman in the trilby is walking up the path. Strange. If the woman is an incomer, how come she's been invited to a party in the village?

'Wait up,' she says, raising her hand in a wave.

As she hurries towards the door, her coat billows out to reveal a waistcoat with a watch chain, and a long black skirt. Her style reminds Annie of Stevie Nicks.

'Thanks,' the woman says, grabbing the edge of the door. She is pretty, with an attractive gap-toothed smile. Her eye make-up is heavy and black, her fingernails short and square and, like her eyes, painted black.

But it is not the black-painted eyes, rather the black fingernails that Annie sees later, much later, when Daisy has pleaded drunkenness and told her she's off home, when everyone else is equally drunk but nowhere near ready to leave; these same nails Annie sees in a room upstairs, half hidden beneath the pile of coats on the double bed in the master bedroom: eight short, square black fingernails, she counts, gleaming like buttons, four on each side, running up the back of her husband's white T-shirt, almost distracting her from the nakedness of his hairy white arse.

Dominic comes staggering through the door. Annie is waiting for him in the living room in the dark, her entire being alive with a fury the likes of which she has never known. She has been sitting here like this for one and a half hours. The light in the hallway goes on. He sniffs, clears his throat. Attempts to hang up his coat – once, twice, before dropping it on the floor. He pats the back pockets of his jeans, as if to check for cigarettes or keys, and turns to peer into the living room.

'Annie?'

She opens her mouth to answer, but no sound comes. The room dims.

'Annie?' The shape of him at the door, blocking the light. 'Where did you go? What are you doing?'

'I'm sitting in the dark,' she says, finding her voice and relishing its sarcasm.

'I can see that, but what are you doing here? How come you left?'

She takes a large breath. How to phrase it?

'I couldn't find you,' she begins, matter-of-fact. 'So I went upstairs to get my coat and saw you shagging the woman you claimed not to know out on the road and who I now realise you do know. You know her really well. In the Biblical sense apparently. That's how come I left.'

In the silence that follows, part of her is thrilled. She wonders if this means that part of her love for him has died. And now he will grovel and say he was drunk, that it meant nothing, that *she* came on to *him*, she *seduced* him… one of those cowardly little excuses people make when they get caught.

But he doesn't. Instead, he sighs heavily.

'I thought you understood.' His voice is soft, quietly disappointed.

'Understood what? That you'd be shagging our clients in our friends' house? I can't remember having that conversation.'

'And yet it's a conversation we've had more than once.' His words are clear; he is not as drunk as she thought he was, which is more terrifying, not less. Any thrill she felt vanishes. Her stomach hurts; her mouth fills with a sour taste.

'When did I agree to you shagging other women?'

He raises a hand: stop. 'Please. Don't say shagging. I hate it when you use that word. You and your sister. It's vulgar.'

For the second time, she opens her mouth to speak without success. He's been rutting like a dog on their friends' bed and she – *she* – is the vulgar one?

Slowly he comes into the room. The hairs on her neck rise; her body braces. But he doesn't raise his hand. Instead, he goes and sits in the armchair. She wishes he'd turn on the light, but at the same time she is happy to stay like this, in the semi-darkness. She's not sure she wants to see clearly, not anymore.

'When we got together,' he says, with the air of someone who is about to tell a story. 'When I wrote to you, remember?'

'Of course I remember.'

'What we talked about, what we *established*... I thought you understood. Freedom. You said you understood. We agreed on it. We're equal partners. Butterflies.'

'Butterflies.'

'Butterflies.' He says it kindly. 'Free to fly.'

'But I thought...' She stops, remembers a few years ago, when she asked him about Sonia. Sitting on the stone bench amid the stagnant stink of pond and goose droppings, he told her why she, Annie, was special, why she was not like Sonia. He criticised that poor woman, but now, horribly, she sees that right from the start, by telling her his other girlfriends were nets compared to the butterfly that she was, he was effectively flattering her by criticising other women – all other women. Her vanity has made her traitorous to her sex – she has wanted to be other. She has wanted to be better. And with a feeling of falling, she understands what he has always meant by needs and freedoms. It is clear, so clear, that what he was talking about then, at the duck pond, and before, at the Loch Fyne Hotel, and before that, way before, the first time they met, was an open marriage, and that she has agreed to it without realising. And all this time, he has been flying freely without her knowledge either of his actions or of her own consent. If she's not been a net, it's because she's had no idea what that meant.

'You're free too,' he says, with an air of polite suggestion. 'You've always been free.'

'So there have been others?' She has started to cry. Hates herself for it. Tears run from her eyes and nose down to her mouth, but she will not wipe them, she will not sniff, she will not let him know that she is crying. *Bastard*, she thinks. *Bastard*.

'Don't do that. You must have had someone? It's been years. In fact, don't answer that. I don't want to know, because that's your private business.'

'My private business? So, what, you think I'm taking lovers on the side? Who the hell would I be sleeping with? When? I don't have time – I'm too busy doing stuff for you. For us.' She sobs, loudly, and a wave of anger at herself almost flings her from her chair. He is not worth this. She has believed him to be so much better than anything and anyone she left behind, but he's not. He's not fit to lick her father's boots.

'Don't upset yourself. Please don't cry. I'm so sorry you didn't understand. Now you do, it'll take some time, but you can handle it, I knew that the moment we met, Annie; why do you think I chased you all the way up to Inver-bloody-aray? I literally travelled the length of the UK to find you. That's how special you are – don't you see that?'

'I'm not special! Everyone is special to someone. How the hell have you even—'

'I'm discreet! I'm not a monster! I'm sorry you saw us; I'll be more careful in future, OK? And I never sleep with anyone from the village.'

'Well, aren't you gallant?'

'Annie.' He shakes his head, as if she has let him down.

She wants to pack all her belongings into a bag and leave, but she won't, she knows fine well, because she has nowhere to go. She's made her bed. It's as bald and as real as that. There is no way in hell she'd turn up at Isla's door with a kid in tow, and she'd rather die than return home to the creaking swivel necks of the village; good God, she'd rather throw herself off a fucking cliff. She gasps into her hand. Sonia. Poor, poor Sonia. 'Oh God.'

He crosses the room and sits beside her, pulls her into his arms. 'Come on. Don't be upset. It's an adjustment of the mind, that's all. Think of the Bloomsbury set, think great actors, painters, intellectuals the world over.'

'But everyone must know.'

'You don't care about that.'

It's true, she doesn't. Caring what other people think was battered out of her long ago; she is inured, bulletproof. Just not enough to return home.

'Don't we have a nice life?' he is saying. 'You love your walks, your swims with Daisy. And look how successful you are – work in every gallery as far as Lyme Regis. Callum's doing well at school, he's made friends. We live in such a beautiful place and you' – he takes her hand, rubs her knuckles with his thumb – 'you've made this house into a home. And I can be quite amusing sometimes, can't I? I'm not that bad, am I?'

Every thought and feeling has been displaced by confusion. She should be furious. But she is not. She is floating above him, numb, a gas.

'Shall we go up? Come on. We can talk about this in the morning, OK?'

She lets him usher her to bed. Lets him wrap his arms around her, nuzzle her neck. She is in the bed and outside it, with him and watching them. They don't make love. But she knows for reasons lost to herself that if he wanted to, they would. And that his arms around her would make no difference to what she knows: that inside her, there in the dark, is a deep pit of loneliness. But loneliness is like shame, she thinks. If you hold your head high, no one can see it. No one can know it is there.

CHAPTER 31

Annie

Dominic is snoring; his breath sour, his guts gaseous, noxious. She lifts his arm from around her and gets up, pulls on her cardie and buttons it over her pyjamas. Downstairs, she makes a cup of tea and takes it into the living room. Outside: the ever-changing view of her workshop, the apple tree, the land, the sea. If she could fly, she would, over the cliffs, away, away, and be free.

Her tea goes cold. It's after one in the morning. The need to walk seizes her. If she can't fly, well, she has her feet.

She is halfway along the lane when she starts to cry. By the time she gets to the duck pond, she is in full flow – hot, stinging tears of frustration. She came here to be free. Instead, she has swapped one trap for another. She sits on the stone bench and lets herself weep. It feels like she could weep for hours, weeks, years, lose herself in this near ecstasy of misery. Down at Heartbreak Hotel, the lights are all out. She should go and batter on the door. She wouldn't need words; a quick Glasgow kiss to the forehead would do: *Take that, ya wee tramp.* She would have the element of surprise in her favour.

Someone is calling her name. A little way up the lane, Ross York is jogging towards her. She brushes her tears away with her fingers, composes herself. She likes Ross. She has spoken to him many times now at various parties, and twice at New Year's Eve celebrations at the pub then back at the cottage. His personality is never going to set the heather alight, but he is kind – kind and decent – and she considers him a friend.

'Hey.' He makes a show of exhaling even though she knows he's a keen runner.

'Hey.'

'Are you OK? Can I sit down?'

'Sure, yeah.' She pats the bench. 'Runny nose, that's all. Cold air.'

'I saw you leave the party. I came out to find you, but you'd gone. I should have gone home right then, but I didn't have my coat, so I went back in. Fatal mistake – I'll pay for it in the morning. Are you sure you're OK?'

She glances up, but the way he's looking at her is too concerned, and she drops her eyes to his shoes, which are brown lace-ups. His trousers are dark cotton. His coat is open, his shirt unbuttoned at the collar, no tie. He looks like he's at work, as he always does. Ross can't do casual. It moves her, though she has no idea why.

'You've got your pyjamas on,' he says.

'No flies on you – I can see why you're a detective.' She smiles. 'I just fancied a walk.'

'Well, it's a lovely night. Chilly though. Shall I walk my lady home?'

She returns his shy grin. 'Why, thank you, kind sir.'

The night is starry, the moon no more than a white paring, the air fresh. Back down the lane, they pass blacked-out terraces and houses, the community hall.

'Listen,' he says. 'It's none of my business, but I saw him go upstairs with someone – I didn't see who, but when I saw you leave like that, I put two and two together.'

Someone, she thinks. *I wonder who.*

'I'm sorry you have to put up with that,' he says – have to, not had to, but she lets it go. 'You deserve better.'

The backs of his fingers touch against the backs of hers. All she can think about is that he knows – about tonight, and given what she now understands, more than tonight. Everyone knows, of this she has no doubt. She wonders what it would be like to be held by Ross, imagines she'd feel safe. He is taller than Dominic and broader. An image flashes: the two of them in an embrace, out here on the road, Dominic running, looking for her, seeing them, feeling what she felt. That would show him. But Ross is too dear. She's not a user.

'It's not as bad as all that.' She hears the lack of conviction in her own voice.

'But it's not... it's not respectful.'

She glances away, towards the coast, the sea lost in the darkness. 'I'd still be stuck in a gift shop in Inveraray without him. I'd never have escaped. He was my lifeboat.'

'But you've escaped now. You don't have to stay in the lifeboat forever. Just because the waters are rough doesn't mean you can't swim to shore, especially if someone can throw you a float.'

She smiles, catches him smiling back out of the corner of her eye.

He laughs softly. 'I overstretched that, didn't I? Seriously though. You have rights. And you have a friend. All you need is a friend in this life.' He stops walking, making her stop too, and takes her hand. 'I meant I'm your friend.'

'I knew what you meant.' Her heart melts. Men are boys, and some are still adorable.

'I know what it's like to be lonely in a marriage, that's all. Since my divorce there's no one at home to support me or keep me company, but it's better than someone being there and doing neither.'

She squeezes his hand and drops it before carrying on. Beyond the main village now, they take the left turn that runs down the hill towards the bigger houses with views over the sea. Now that he is no longer holding her hand, she wishes he were. He is as lonely as she is, and he has seen her loneliness even if she hasn't admitted to it. Her fury has abated, she realises, just by walking a little way with him, just by hearing him talk.

They have reached her front gate.

'Thanks for walking me home,' she says, turning to face him. 'You're a good man, Ross York. See you soon. And don't worry about me.'

'You can't ask me to do that, I'm afraid. I will. I do.'

She meets his gaze, reaches a hand to his face.

He pulls her into his arms and kisses her – deeply. She was right. It feels good, and yes, she feels safe.

'I'm sorry,' he says. 'I shouldn't have done that.'

'Neither should I.' She takes hold of his hand. 'We need to go home.'

'We do.' He lets her hand drop, runs his knuckle down her cheek and smiles – so kindly her eyes fill. 'If you ever want to go for a coffee or something, let me know, OK? As a friend. I'd never—'

'Thanks. You're so lovely. Goodnight.'

Once inside, she closes the door and leans against it. He is still there, she knows, his hand half raised in a wave. There are women who would give anything for a man like him. Someone who would love them and respect them and be grateful and faithful and want nothing more than to grow old and stay as loyal as a pair of swans.

And there are women like her.

CHAPTER 32

Isla

January 2005

At the sight of the bleak, cheerless windows of Daisy's home, it occurs to me, not for the first time, that she has no one to greet her after such a day, no one to have put the heating on or cooked a hot meal, no one to pour her a drink and say, *Hey, how was it?* Not that I have that here, but I had it in London. Patrick was not my lover, but he was my friend, and I'm beginning to think that's more important than anything – to have a friend who is, quite simply, there, in a low-key, mundane way. But Patrick will find love, of course. He will move on.

What did Annie have? I wonder. No friend in Dominic, that's for sure. She had Daisy – or did she? How true a friend was this woman sitting next to me? Would Annie have preferred to live alone, in control of herself and her environment? A successful job, tons of friends, peace and quiet at the end of a packed day, watch exactly what you want on TV, eat what you want, when you want, read when you want, go to bed when you want. Is that what Daisy prefers? I've never asked her about her romantic life. For some reason, it has felt intrusive. Is that because she's so private or because she's hiding something? Does she live on the edge of the village so she can take lovers without everyone knowing, or so she can take one particular lover, whose discovery would mean disaster?

'Sorry again about today,' she says. 'About not telling you before. At least we can travel together. And I'll be with you when Cal takes the stand.'

'That's American, isn't it? Stand?'

She pulls a face. 'I don't know, is it?'

'I think we have a witness box. Tom must've told me. Anyway, don't worry about today. It is what it is.'

She opens the car door but doesn't get out. Instead, she turns to face me, her expression pained. 'There's something else I haven't told you.'

My chest tightens. I find I can't speak.

'Annie was…' She sighs. 'She was at my house earlier. That evening. It was after she got back from mine that… it all happened.'

'Oh, Daisy.' I close my eyes, open them, meet her gaze. 'Why on earth didn't you tell me? Don't you trust me?'

'It's not that. I… I don't know anything about that night, all right? She came to my house in the late afternoon. We… talked. And then she went home. But she went home decided. She was going to ask Dom for a divorce. The next I knew of it, Cal called me in a state and I went straight round, but they were already…'

'Oh my God. This is so late to be telling me this. Why didn't you tell me before, *why*?'

'I don't know.' She looks away.

Cold air leaks in from the open door of the car. It snakes around my neck where I have taken off my scarf, runs like water down my back. When someone you care for has lied to you or is evading you, it is, above all else, awkward. I am thinking of Daisy getting into the car this morning, my sudden awareness of the voluptuous figure she keeps hidden in loose clothing, plays down with her practical swimsuit, her punky hair. I am thinking that Dominic, the Dominic I now know about, must have noticed her. He must have. I am thinking of the flashing thought I had this morning that Daisy might have been the catalyst for what happened, the thought I had about her private nature just a few seconds ago.

'You said you talked,' I say. 'Did you have anything you needed to tell her? Anything important, anything that might have upset her?' I can't put it any clearer without accusing her directly.

She throws one leg out of the car. Her head is still turned away from me. *Textbook lying body language*, I think, anger rising.

'Not that I can think of.' She is out of the car, head chopped off by the roof. I can't see her face, can't read it, and she knows it. She's closed up like a Venus flytrap again, the truth suffocating in her jaws.

You said something to my sister, I want to say. *I know you're lying to me.*

But instead, I say OK and goodbye, that I'll see her in the morning. Her heeled boots click on her driveway; the elegant coat I didn't know she possessed swishes as she walks towards her low wee house. I watch her stop and dig her keys out of her bag, open the door, go inside. I watch the light go on in the hallway, another light blooming a few seconds later, further inside – her kitchen, where I have sat at her table and drunk tea or wine and got to know her these last months. Where whenever I've started theorising about what happened, she has asked me to change the subject, told me she finds it too upsetting.

'We know nothing,' she would say. 'It's pointless to pontificate.'

Is it pointless – or dangerous?

Preoccupied and alone inside my sister's car, I imagine Daisy now, reaching into the fridge for the bottle of Chardonnay she always keeps there, pouring herself a drink with shaking hands, the bottle tinkling against the lip of the glass. I imagine her taking a long gulp, guilt dampening her hairline. She is a good person, I think. That's why she finds it so difficult to lie. It's also why it's so difficult to think of her betraying Annie. But she *is* hiding something, she has always been hiding something, and right now it feels like I have always known it.

I restart the engine, head back into the village. Jan's one front window glows orange through the chink in the curtains. Next door, the lights are on too. Another attractive female is staying there – a poet, did Jan say? She'll be one of the last clients booked by Annie – by Dominic, I correct myself. Handled personally… or not, as it's turned out.

I continue through the thinning lamplit houses, take a left towards the sea. Heartbreak Hotel, Jan said once, in that wry, seen-it-all way of hers, the bowl of her pipe glowing orange, fading to grey. It was the first time I'd heard the nickname, and it was then, or maybe later, that Jan admitted that yes, on the night they died, Dominic was sleeping with its occupant. I didn't press her on it. And in the hazy days that followed, I never followed it up, too bamboozled by events, overtaken by Cal's strangeness, his withdrawal, his arrest. I have always known or suspected that the police's version of events, while skirting close to the truth, is not the whole truth. I have believed or chosen to believe that it was Dominic Cal killed, not my sister, and part of me still believes that. But there is even more going on here, I'm sure of it, and now that the trial has started, the sense that Jan or Daisy or both know more than they're admitting to has flared up once again. And much as I try to push these thoughts away, for fear of driving myself crazy, still they persist.

This morning, Daisy called Heartbreak Hotel the honey trap, letting slip that the place was a shag pad for Dominic's extramarital affairs, shutting me down when I asked about that night in particular, telling me that my sister's private life was not to be paraded in front of everyone. I agree with her, I do, but whatever Jan didn't tell me months ago, whatever that thing is, I suspect Daisy knows it too or is even the thing itself: the woman, the catalyst. Maybe that's what she told Annie that afternoon, sending her to a furious confrontation that ended in death.

'Aargh,' I shout, punching the steering wheel. 'Aargh.'

I park up outside my sister's cottage. Tiredness and grief are rocks in my pockets. The more I think it through, the more I realise that yes, Daisy lives alone; yes, the charming Dominic, who was an old friend, might have seduced her in a vulnerable moment; yes, it would have killed her to keep such a thing from Annie, killed her all over again to tell her; and yes, such a revelation might have been the spark for the tragedy that ensued; and yes, yes, of course she wouldn't want to tell me, Annie's sister.

But the thing is, Daisy can't lie – she's *rubbish* at it. There's no way she would have been able to keep an affair with her best friend's husband a secret and still look her in the eye. Even if Dom would have had no problem whatsoever betraying my sister like that, there's no way Daisy would have been able to do it even once, let alone keep an affair going. And now I'm wondering if it's got more to do with the honey trap. If Dominic was involved with a tenant, is it possible Daisy heard it from Jan and felt bound by loyalty to my sister to tell her? And that the blatant insult of it, after years of acceptance, drove Annie to confront Dominic? Which would doubtless render someone as sensitive as Daisy sick with guilt – the idea that what she told her best friend that day drove her, albeit indirectly, to her death. It would be something she could not tell me.

As they say in court: it's possible.

One thing Daisy is right about is that my sister, who survived shame for so much of her early life, was blinded by love and hope for her future and walked directly into shame of another kind entirely. Dominic *found a way of getting people to do things for him… even bad things.* Bear humiliation, abuse, shame. In life, my sister had more than enough shame, shame not even her own. She should not be made to bear any more in death. I get that, I really do, and I respect it. If Daisy and Jan said nothing, not even to me, it was from the desire of two people who loved her to leave her some dignity.

But that doesn't mean I don't want to know the truth. God knows, I deserve it. I'm her sister.

I restart the car, head back – to Jan's.

CHAPTER 33

Annie

October 1999

Annie continues to wave to Cal even as he turns away and heads into his halls of residence. She waves after the door has closed, after Dominic has pulled the car into reverse, back into first, and coaxed her to get in. It is only when they turn out onto the road to head back to the home that no longer has her son in it that she bursts into tears. She is thirty-four. Eighteen years have vanished, the fact of it more astonishing than a car crash. And already – too soon, too soon – her beloved boy, her sounding board, her cheerleader and trusted companion since she was no more than a girl, is gone.

Whole seconds later, it occurs to her that Dominic, not Cal, should be these things – another second for it to sink in that he is not and never has been.

She pulls a tissue from her bag and presses it flat to her face. Dominic's silence makes her aware of any noise she makes, so she weeps silently. Dominic. He is all she has now. He is her husband, but he has never been hers, not really, not even in those first heady months when she thought he was, and certainly not in the way Cal has been – her boy, her wee man. Dom is and always has been absent – either mysteriously busy, or drunk, or, she has come to accept, with other, unknown women. And so, over the years, she was left with Cal, who had his own friends, of course, but who always seemed happy to spend time with her – just being, with no more to it than that. Cal, who let her talk about her work, who walked with her and sat while she sketched, who read the same books, who let her critique his A-level essays, valuing her input even though she had no degree, who told her she was insightful, that she'd made a good point. Who was kind in a thousand small ways. Who loved her with so much affection, so much presence, so much loyalty.

Her boy is gone. In his place, a great chasm of loneliness has opened up. She can almost see it, almost peer over its edge: black and fathomless, a void she will never fill. The emptiness is stark and tangible and physical. It takes her breath away. And all she can do is weep silently, swallow the tears that now fill her throat, with no hope of a gentle hand on her shoulder, no *there, there, there*. Her emotions are inconvenient, she knows, to the man sitting beside her. She is a pain in the neck. And now Cal is gone, she has no one to tell that she has never felt so sad. Never in all of her life. Dominic will take offence. He will make it about him. Cal has been her life. Cal, not Dominic. Dominic is all that's left, and he is not enough. He is nowhere near enough.

'Come on,' he says, an edge of impatience in his tone. 'He's only away for twelve weeks.'

Hate fills her. He is denying her feelings, as he always does, sweeping them to one side as if they are not important, as if she does not even feel them at all. She is alone: alone, alone, alone, with this man she no longer loves, no longer even likes.

'Come on,' he says again. 'It's normal for them to leave home, you know. It'll do him good. He needs to grow up a bit.'

'Please don't tell me what my son needs.' Her voice trembles with a rage that has come as swiftly as a wrecking ball. 'Don't you dare.'

'All right! No need to get *quite* so angry. I just don't see why you're so upset, that's all. He's not dying. Exeter is a great uni. This is a great thing. You should be happy!'

'Just… just shut up, OK? For once in your life, just shut up.'

She doesn't feel the pain immediately. She doesn't feel anything, not in the moment, except perhaps heat. She hears the click of his seat belt; the knowledge that he has undone it is something that also comes later, along with the hot throb in her nose where, she realises as the blood drips diluted by tears onto her hands, onto her jeans, he has hit her with his elbow.

'What the hell?' She turns and punches him, hard, in the side of the head.

'Get off,' he yells. 'I'm driving, for Christ's sake.'

She punches him again in the upper arm, making him swerve, screams at him that he's elbowed her in the face, that he's broken her nose.

'I hate you,' she shouts, batting off his hand as he tries to grab her hair, one hand still on the steering wheel. 'You're a bastard. You think you're so brilliant, but you're not. You're not kind and you're not even nice and you don't care about anyone but yourself.'

'Don't be such a drama queen,' he shouts back, both hands back on the steering wheel.

'Let me out of the car.'

'Don't be ridiculous.'

'Let me out. I can't stand another second with you. Let me out.' She opens the door.

'What the hell?' The car screeches to a halt. 'Stop being a lunatic. Calm down, for God's sake.' He tries to stop her from unbuckling her seat belt, her fingers clumsy, scrabbling. She undoes the clasp, but both his hands are around both of hers, holding them fast. He is telling her to stop, to calm down, to stop being crazy.

'Fuck off,' she shouts, shocking herself, and him, shocking the trembling ghosts of her parents. She has never spoken to him like that before, never come anywhere close. 'You don't know anything about me. You don't know anything about Cal. You've never been a husband to me or a father to him. You've never shown him any affection, any love.'

'You never let me anywhere near him!'

'That's not true! You weren't interested! You were always cycling or water-skiing or whatever the hell you find to do instead of being at home. With us.'

'Is it any wonder when you wouldn't leave him alone for five seconds? It's not my fault he always came first.'

'Yes! Yes, he did! He's my son. You should have thought about that when you asked me to marry you. You claimed to respect me for being a mum – God knows, you were halfway to canonising me – but when I wouldn't drop everything and spend one hundred per cent of my attention on you, you sulked like the spoilt child you are. You could have got to know him! But no, you were off having your pathetic midlife crisis. Shagging anything with a pulse. Sorry for saying shagging by the way – I know how vulgar you find it.'

He is still holding her hands. Blood is all over her chin; she can feel the viscous slick of it, see the red stain getting bigger on her pale grey T-shirt. Bizarrely, it comes to her that she must look a mess. The thought has come because her temper is leaving. She can feel it ebbing away down the length of her, the vague hint of embarrassment she knows will follow. She knows she won't get out of the car. The moment has gone. It's always like this. It isn't always him that starts it.

'I'm sorry I made your nose bleed,' he says.

'I'm sorry I punched you in the head.'

He laughs. 'You nearly made me crash the car, you crazy bitch.'

'Aye well, don't elbow me in the face then.'

He lets go of her hands, digs in his pocket for a clean tissue and hands it to her. 'I don't think it's broken. I didn't hit you that hard; I must have just caught it.'

She finds her bottle of water in her bag, pours some onto the tissue and cleans herself up in the vanity mirror. Her nose is a wee bit sore, but it's not broken, no – she can wiggle it.

'OK?' Dominic says, starting the car. 'You're not going to jump out?'

She shakes her head, looks about her. They have pulled into a track where some disused farm buildings loom on a desolate patch of concrete. Further up is a scrappy copse of trees. The light is falling – grainy dusk, pink on the horizon. She is expecting Dominic to reverse out onto the main road, but he drives forward, towards the trees, and stops the car.

'Get into the back seat,' he says.

And she does, as does he, both of them pulling off the bottom halves of their clothing with the perfunctory focus of athletes stripping off sports kit.

'I hate you,' she says and bites his ear, astride him and watching out of the back window for cars.

'What can I do to make you love me? I want you to love me.'

'You can stop being such a slut. That'd be a start.'

'I'm not sure I can.'

She moves, feels him getting near. She waits. Another second; he gasps into her ear, and she grabs the back of his hair and pulls his head back.

'Give me a child,' she says. 'I want another child.'

'All right,' he says, stupid with the rush. 'All right.'

'I'm serious,' she says, as he shrinks inside her. 'No more women.'

'All right,' he whispers into her neck.

'You're a shit.'

'I know. I know I am. I'll stop. I'm sorry. I love you. Don't leave me.'

CHAPTER 34

Isla

January 2005

'Isla,' Jan says, evidently surprised to see me.

From within drifts the tantalising aroma of something savoury and delicious. My mouth actually waters.

'Are you all right?' She frowns. 'Of course you're not. Come in, come in – let's get you out of the cold.'

The dark walls and amber lights are a cocoon. It is so warm inside it almost makes me cry. We go through to where the wood-burning stove is aglow. Soft throws in burgundies, warm browns and deep greens sprawl across the sofa and the armchair, which she takes. I sit on the end of the sofa nearest her, so she can hear me if I talk quietly. Even if there's only the two of us here, what I have to ask, what she has to tell me, needs to be hushed.

'How did it go?'

'Awful,' I reply. 'By the time they'd finished with the swearing-in of the jury, we only really got the opening statement. But it sounded bad. No wonder they're pressing for murder. He's going to end up going down for life.'

She presses her lips into a thin line and shakes her head. 'Let's hope not.'

'You told me once that Cal was very attached to Annie, do you remember? The prosecution seemed to be trying to make something of that, like he was weird or something. I don't know who they've spoken to, but they're hinting that he was jealous of her and Dominic and that it led to a flare-up of rage. I'm guessing that's the Freudian angle.'

'I didn't mean like that, for God's sake! He was just a bit of a mummy's boy, that's all. Understandable if you think it was just the two of them when he was growing up. He was a late developer too. At fifteen, sixteen, you see them round about and they've got full beards, shoulders wide as ploughs, but Cal barely had a shadow on his top lip, you know? He only filled out after he left for uni.'

I nod. It's true. Even today, he looked like a boy.

'Men are twenty-five before they hit maturity,' Jan goes on. 'Did you know that? Their brains are still growing, even at Cal's age. And for the record, I don't think you need to have inappropriate feelings to be jealous of a parent. I think he probably was jealous of his mother's relationship with Dominic – well, not jealous exactly so much as he guarded her jealously, I think is what I'm trying to say. And no wonder. Dominic was a bad lot. Sorry, I shouldn't speak ill of the dead, but he was spoilt. Spoilt rotten. His parents were lovely, but they waited a long time for him, and when he finally came, they ruined him. They never said no to him. Ever.'

'Daisy said Cal hated the fact that Annie stayed with him.'

'He did. Dominic wasn't fit to lick her boots, he said, which is true, of course. He hated the way she washed Dom's clothes and made his dinner and all of that. More so after he got back from Exeter.'

'Enough to be so resentful he'd…'

She shakes her head. 'Who knows? But he wasn't in love with her, that's ridiculous. If you're looking for someone who was in love with her, you're barking up the wrong tree.'

'Meaning?'

She raises both eyebrows. 'A certain doe-eyed detective.'

'*Ross?*' His name leaves me instinctively. But yes, I think now, catching up with myself. Ross. His reticence in the car when he took me to see Cal. Annie was *gentle but feisty.* Gentle – a particular word, an intimate word now I think about it properly. *She never talked to you about… that side of things?* Something from that conversation must have lodged in me – why else would I feel like I knew?

'I can't believe we haven't talked about this.'

'Not at all. You weren't here to drag up muck on your family, love. If you'd asked me this when you first got here, I wouldn't have said a word anyway. Back then, you were trying to get your head around what'd happened. It was only a few days before they arrested poor Cal, wasn't it? And of course, you've not seen him to talk to. Don't beat yourself up; you've been doing everything you can, keeping everything going. And now, of course, it's all coming out.'

'And Ross was in love with Annie.'

'Like a puppy. I never understood why she didn't leave Dominic for him. But we don't always make the best choices, especially in matters of the heart.'

'So they had a… thing?'

'A few years ago now, but he held a candle – a big fat church candle.' She smiles.

Ross was in love with my sister. It must have been hard, watching her from a distance, knowing Dom mistreated her so badly. He must have longed to do something about it. How deep was that longing? How far might he have gone to save her from her pig of a husband, knowing that he, Ross, could love her and take care of her? In all of this, haven't I been shocked to discover that the north of my own moral compass was not quite as true as I thought it was? In making peace with the possibility that Cal might have killed Dominic, in still wanting him to walk free, haven't I let love for my nephew trump what is right? Everyone likes to think they would do or say or think the right thing, but the fact is, we don't, not always, not when love is involved.

I wipe at my eyes. I'm so tired, I almost can't sit up straight. I long for a hot meal, a large glass of red. But there's more I need to ask.

'Jan?'

'Yes, love.'

'Daisy said Dom had several lovers who stayed next door. Do you remember I asked you one time if he was involved with someone the night he died? I was thinking… Do you remember? Was he sleeping with a woman in Heartbreak Hotel that night?'

I'm expecting her to avoid my question. But she nods gravely.

'Bloody idiot,' she says. 'He promised Annie he'd stop after Cal went to uni. It was supposed to be a new start. Like a baby was going to repair things, not that it worked out that way.'

'Did he?'

'Stop?'

'Promise.'

'Promise, yes. Stop, no. Leopards, spots. It wasn't the first time with that one either. Eva Robertson. Came here a few times over the years to play at The Square and Compass, the restaurants round about, Swanage, the Pig over in Studland. We had the odd jam session up at the pub. Before arthritis put a stop to my world-famous ukulele career.' She shakes her head, a rueful smile. 'She was a good enough guitarist, but she wasn't as good as she thought she was. Dressed like we did in the seventies: little waistcoats, watch on a chain, and a black trilby, which she would take off halfway through the set, you know? Shake out her lovely mane, all very sexy in an affected sort of way. Once told me that wherever she laid her hat, that was her home, and I nearly threw up on her feet. I didn't take to her, as you might have picked up.'

'Do you think Annie found out about her? I know she was at Daisy's just before she went home that night. I'm wondering if Daisy told her and she went home raging, ready for a fight.'

Jan looks at me, her eyes like stones in the evening gloom. 'It's possible.'

'So that makes sense, except I can't imagine her attacking Dom. But you said she gave as good as she got.'

She leans over to the leather ottoman for her wee tin, her other hand digging into the pocket of her fleece. As she talks, she stuffs woolly tobacco into her long-stemmed pipe without once having to look at her hands. 'I have thought it might have had something to do with that strumpet, more than once. But gossip's a dangerous thing. It can be life and death – literally, in this case. When I heard they'd arrested Callum, I assumed it was the other way round. Who killed who, I mean.'

We sit in silence for a moment.

'Could she have anything to do with it?' I'm grasping at straws – I know it even as I say it. 'The musician woman, I mean. Could she have stormed into the cabin and killed Annie in a fit of jealousy?'

'Not unless she could fly.' Jan gives a hollow laugh. 'She was here.'

'You saw her?'

'I'd had an early night. I could hear her stomping about, music on too loud. Next thing, there was cigarette smoke coming through my bedroom window, so I got up to shut it and I saw her in the garden, smoking and drinking – looked like whisky. Fancied herself as a troubled soul, would pour her heart out to whoever would listen. Poor-me rock chick, you know? Twit.'

'So no then.' I feel my back curve in disappointment, my head drop.

Jan lights her pipe, her mouth puckering around the black mouthpiece. 'I saw her again on the Friday morning. Changeover. She was getting into a taxi, guitar case and carpet bag, Janis bloody Joplin. I would have waved, given her the time of day, but by then everything was too terrible.' A pensive suck; she angles her head away so as not to blow smoke over me, before brushing a strand of tobacco from her lap and looking at me once again. 'But just because she didn't do it' – the stem of the pipe wags at me like a stern finger – 'doesn't mean she didn't *cause* it. Good riddance, I thought. Find someone else's husband to fuck, excuse my French. Or better still, find your own.'

I gasp, almost laugh, her language shocking me and providing much-needed relief in equal measure. I consider her a moment, her silver hair falling forward in a shining sheet. *She is a wizard*, I think. *She is timeless*. I have no idea how old she is. Know almost nothing about her.

'Were you ever married?'

She relights her pipe, puff, puff, puff. I long for a cigarette, a boozy Consulate night with Patrick. For everything to be as it once was. For a second chance at being the sister I have not been.

'I was.'

'But not now.'

'Not for a long time. I married a… I married a Dominic, let's say. Only the fights were less… even.'

'I'm so sorry.' *We don't always make the best choices, especially in matters of the heart.*

'Don't be. It ended up in court, which was horrid, but I escaped. My daughters helped me get a restraining order. It was a bit fraught, but I've got two kids and five grandchildren and I do as I please. My girls don't speak to him. As far as I'm concerned, I'm the lucky one.' She smiles as if to say: *Simple!*

'Good.' It is all I can think to say. My head is light. I should go but am not sure I can stand up.

'Listen,' Jan says. 'I've got a chicken casserole in the Aga. I've made far too much and I'll never get through it on my own. Don't suppose you can help me with it, can you?'

CHAPTER 35

Isla

'The prosecution calls pathologist Dr Elizabeth Rowlands.'

Day two. The usher disappears behind the door at the back left-hand corner. A risked glance at Cal and I see his jaw clenched, his spine still bent, his head low on his neck like a vulture's. I look away.

A woman in her late forties, hair cut in a neat French-style bob and expensively highlighted blonde, enters the witness box, declines to take a religious oath and instead affirms. She is wearing a wine-coloured trouser suit and a cream silk blouse, the lanyard around her neck either spoiling the effect or enhancing it, it's hard to tell: elegance, seriousness, responsibility.

Mrs Peterson establishes Dr Rowlands' name and her credentials – the message beneath that her opinion is one that matters – before instructing both her and the jury panel to examine the first photograph in their bundles. At this, she makes a slow turn on her heel and informs the court at large that the image being considered is one of the first victim, Dominic Rawles, it being necessary to put the crime in the context of the night in question. That my sister killed him is not up for discussion. Turning back, she asks Dr Rowlands to describe what she sees 'in layman's terms, if you can'.

'The fire damage to the first victim was less severe due to a lesser quantity of flammable agents on the body. The victim sustained third- to sixth-degree burns to the skin, internal organ shrinkage, the flexing of the limbs due to muscle contraction. We were able to ascertain a deep knife wound to the abdomen penetrating through to the small intestine.' She speaks flatly. 'Allowing for tissue shrinkage, we calculated that the original entry wound would have measured approximately four centimetres in length.'

'And can you tell the ladies and gentlemen of the jury how such an injury could have come about?'

'Yes. This is a deep stab wound and consistent with being made by an instrument such as a knife with a wide blade. There is one entry point. The burns are consistent with severe fire damage.'

'Let us focus on the wound. How would you describe the degree of force used to make a cut of this kind?'

'Considerable. The depth of the wound means that the knife was pushed in hard. The fact that there was a single entry point would suggest that this wasn't a frenzied attack. This is a deep, penetrating abdominal trauma resulting in perforation of the small intestine.'

'Fatal?'

'If not immediately treated, yes. In this case, loss of blood was the cause of death.'

Mrs Peterson asks the jury and Dr Rowlands to turn to the next photograph, which, she informs us, is a picture of the knife. Through the series of questions, she establishes that, in the expert professional opinion of the pathologist, the fatal wound was caused by a violent attack using my sister's kitchen knife, found in my sister's hands at the scene, my sister being the likely perpetrator.

'Would you please turn to the third photograph in your bundles. Again, apologies for the distressing content. This is a photograph of part of the skull of the second victim, Mrs Annie Rawles. Dr Rowlands, could you describe the picture for the court?'

I close my eyes, but it only makes the images in my head starker. I open them again but keep them lowered.

'The hole you can see is a blunt-force trauma of approximately two centimetres in diameter located in the occipital bone of the skull.'

There is a collective intake of breath. When I open my eyes, I catch some members of the public gallery looking away from me. Some of them are press; I recognise them from yesterday, from here, and from outside, questions called out from behind microphones, camera bulbs flashing, my picture no doubt bound for the front page of the *Purbeck Post*. I haven't gone near a paper, haven't dared watch the news. I bow my head once again.

'That's the back of the skull, is that correct?'

'That's correct.'

'And in your opinion, what type of weapon would cause this kind of injury?'

'It's consistent with a common or garden domestic claw hammer.'

'If we can turn to photograph four in your bundles.' The shush of paper, a long beat. 'You can see the victim's hammer, which she used for nailing her canvases to their frames. The hammer was found at the scene in the hand of Mr Dominic Rawles. Dr Rowlands, is this the hammer?'

'The hammer found at the scene matches the injury, yes.'

'So in your professional opinion, this is most likely the weapon used to cause the severe injuries to the skull leading to Annie Rawles' death?'

'Most likely, yes.'

'Given the evidence, how much force would you say was used in the wielding of the murder weapon?'

'Considerable. To make an impact of this kind, there was no hesitation. It was a full-force blow most likely resulting in instant blackout followed by death by bleeding out.'

Nausea rises. I fight a constant battle not to weep audibly. I want this to be over. Just over.

Mrs Peterson pushes her spread fingertips together, appearing to kiss the ends of her forefingers several times.

'Dr Rowlands, could the victim's husband, Dominic Rawles, have driven the hammer into Annie Rawles' skull in a violent fight?'

'That's highly unlikely.'

'And why is that?'

'Because if Dominic Rawles received a stab wound to the abdomen at the hands of Mrs Rawles, which is my opinion, he would have to have been facing her. In order to have hit Mrs Rawles in the back of the skull, he would have to have been behind her.'

Mrs Peterson nods so slowly I want to scream at her for being such a bloody cliché.

'I see,' she says. *We buy into this*, I think. *Like television. We all know she is not actively processing this information. We all know she has read it, studied it, worked out every question and answer… She sees, she really does, nodding slowly, kissing her fingertips in thought.* I hate her.

'But,' she continues after her big pause, 'having been stabbed by Mrs Rawles, could Mr Rawles have grabbed the hammer, which was kept in the studio, and smashed it into her head as she tried to flee the scene?'

Dr Rowlands shakes her head. 'No. When a person is stabbed, their hands go to the site of the wound. It's instinctive. A survival instinct, if you like. He wouldn't have grabbed a weapon after such an event.'

Mrs Peterson frowns, as if she is only just able to grasp the facts. Disingenuity. Cheap magic. My belly heats. Irritation. Rage.

'So, let's see.' She pretends to run the events over in her mind. I imagine her pacing in front of a mirror, practising. 'Indulge me, if you will, but… is it possible that it was entirely the other way around? That Annie Rawles, having been bludgeoned on the back of the head by her husband, then grabbed the knife, turned and stabbed him in retaliation?'

'No, for the same reasons.' Dr Rowland's tone is one of patience summoned, not felt. 'Once Mrs Rawles had submitted to that kind of trauma to the head, her hands would have travelled to the site in the same way. She would most probably have fallen and collapsed to the floor.' She shakes her head a fraction. 'She would not have been capable of attacking anyone.'

Mrs Peterson pinches her chin, a gesture both humble and arrogant at the same time. 'So, it having already been established that Annie Rawles killed her husband and that her husband could not have killed her, are you saying that there must have been a *third party* present?' Oh dear God.

'Yes.'

'And the role of this third party?'

'The person who killed Mrs Rawles.'

'Is that your firm opinion?'

'Yes. It is.'

Another group inhalation from the courtroom. Any more and this will be shaping up like a yoga class. I cannot look up, I cannot. And I must tune out with the stress of it, because when my senses return, Mrs Peterson is describing the murder scene as found by the emergency services, and once again, glad as I am not to have to look at the photograph, my mind does not spare me.

'… charred remains locked in a strange embrace. Remains so deteriorated as to be identifiable only by personal effects, dental records and DNA, bodies known by, indeed *loved* by, the defendant, callously set on fire in an attempt to disguise the true cause of their deaths…'

Blackened bodies, locked in an embrace. Annie's head on Dominic's chest, his hand around the handle of the hammer. My Annie, her hair almost white against the sticky blackness. So my mind by turns sanitises, drenches in horror. My sister's hair would not have been white. A memory of my dad flashes, listening to a play on his wee wireless in the kitchen, telling me pictures were always better on the radio. I miss him so acutely then it hurts.

'Dr Rowlands, can you explain the positioning of the bodies in relation to their respective deaths – if, in your opinion, they fell as a result of their injuries?'

'The victims are collapsed almost into each other's arms, as you can see. It's unlikely they would have fallen in such a… perfect pose, for want of a better word.'

'So they have been *arranged*?'

'Your Honour.' Finally, an intervention from Tom, who is on his feet. 'Leading the witness.'

'I agree.' The judge glowers.

'Let me put it another way,' Mrs Peterson says with what is almost a leer. 'If they did not fall where they were slain, is it possible, in your professional opinion, that they were moved post-mortem?'

'That's possible. But the limbs are bent due to the contraction of the muscles, giving what's known as a pugilistic or boxer's pose, in this case making them look a little like they are embracing. Embracing and fighting manifest in a similar way.'

Love and hate. Embracing and fighting. A thin line.

'And can you share with the court the time of death in both cases?'

'The time of death for both victims is estimated at between 8 and 10 p.m.'

'And finally, just to be clear, in your professional opinion, could their deaths have been caused by the fire?'

'No. The blood samples taken from the victims showed low carboxyhaemoglobin levels in both samples – below ten per cent. There were no sooty deposits in the mouth and nose of either victim. Put simply, the victims had not inhaled any carbon monoxide. In other words, when the fire started, they were not breathing.'

Stomach folding, I glance at Cal, who is resting his cheeks on his hands, his bottom lip protruding. The time of death was between 8 and 10 p.m. He didn't call me until one in the morning. A possible five hours later.

'Dr Rowlands, thank you.' Mrs Peterson shifts, looking now at the judge. 'No further questions, Your Honour.'

The court adjourns for lunch. The usher bids us rise, which we do, watching the judge leave by the back left door. Cal is led away by security, his head dipped.

I follow the stream out into the foyer and head outside for some air. Ross was right to warn me the prosecution would bombard us, but still – there is *so much* evidence. All I have to go on is Cal's insistence that he didn't kill my sister, his later admission that he did, his final plea of not guilty, but I'm almost one hundred per cent sure he's hiding something. And the thing is, despite his shutting me out, I *know* him. I know him of old.

That's when it hits me – why he has refused to see me all this time. Of course. It wasn't because he feared I would say something incriminating. It is precisely because he feared *he* would – because I know him, have known him since he was born. He cannot hide from me. He must have realised that, had he faced me across a visiting table, he would not have been able to stop himself from telling me the truth, and even if he could have kept his lips sealed, he must have feared that I would read it in his eyes. And now, whatever happened that night, whatever his reasons for hiding, for pleading not guilty, this is a murder trial, and if he goes down, he will go down for life.

CHAPTER 36

Isla

We have been back for a little over five minutes, and Tom is on his feet for the cross-examination. It is still strange to see him up there in his robes and wig, his head high, his shoulders back; almost impossible to marry it with his low-key country-boy style, his shyness.

'Dr Rowlands,' he says. 'Can you tell us, in your examination of Annie Rawles, whether you detected any markings or bruising to her neck?'

Dr Rowlands performs that same fractional shake of her head. 'The tissue damage was too severe to ascertain that kind of information. With sixth-degree burns, there is an extensive level of charring. The examination focused on the skeletal damage.'

'Does that mean there were no bruises?'

'No. The temperature of a fire of this sort will rise to around six hundred degrees Celsius within a few minutes. Mrs Rawles had been doused in flammable agents. Even on the skeletal level, the damage was severe – fracturing et cetera.'

'So there may have been bruises?'

'There was no skeletal evidence of strangulation, but that doesn't rule out bruising to the neck tissue.'

'You said it was possible that the victims had been posed, but you also stated that their lovers' embrace was in fact caused by muscle contraction, causing the limbs to bend. Which is it?'

'Either or both are possible.'

'Is it possible then that the deceased were not posed but in fact adopted their positions post-mortem?'

'It's possible.'

'So there's no reason to think their embrace was staged?'

'There's reason, but... no, there's no proof it was staged.'

'Thank you. And in terms of the time of death of both victims, the window you gave was between 8 and 10 p.m. Are you able to make any distinction between the time of death of each victim?'

'No, it's an approximation. Both victims died within that window.'

'There's nothing to say that one died before the other?'

'No.'

'So they could not have died by each other's hand but they *could* have died simultaneously? At the exact same moment?'

'It's possible.'

'Thank you.' He gives a brief nod. 'No further questions, Your Honour.' And sits down.

A wave of nausea rolls into my stomach. Tom has done his thing, and again, all I want to do is shout: is that *it*?

After taking one look at me and telling me I wasn't fit to take the wheel, Daisy is driving. The day I've just had feels like a month, a long and gruelling month. And despite taking paracetamol on my way to the car, I have an absolute boulder of a headache. Mrs Peterson, a woman who in my mind is now firmly a pig – snout for a nose, trotters for hands, wig the funny tuft pigs sometimes have on the top of their head – is to blame for this headache. Her sneering theatre, her ill-concealed joy at driving home this cinch of a case is to blame for my stumbling out at recess, the flask of tea drunk alone in the foyer, silent and shell-shocked on the bench, sandwiches untouched, the trailing gabble of reporters...

all her fault. The fact that Daisy and I forgot where we'd parked and it took us twenty minutes to find the car is her fault too. If we'd got a ticket? If we now crash on the way home? All her fault.

'Did you call Jan?' Daisy asks.

'Yes. While you were in the loo. I said I'd keep her in the loop.'

'OK. Dark, isn't it?'

'Five o'clock. Feels like ten.'

We drive in silence, headlights fuzzy in the mizzle, the intermittent slide of the windscreen wiper. Daisy makes no attempt to put music on, as she usually does. I am glad of the peace.

'I don't know what's worse,' I say after half an hour or so. 'The thought that he did it, or that he'll go to prison. I don't know what I want for him.'

'I know what you mean. I don't want him to go to prison, but if he did do it then…' She sighs; her hands tighten on the steering wheel. 'Please God, let him not have done it.' Her voice catches. I pretend not to notice, try not to examine it for sincerity.

'I just wish I knew why he's pleading not guilty. If he did it in anger, OK, he should go to prison, but surely if he did it in panic, by mistake, that's manslaughter, isn't it? Why would he plead not guilty to something he's so obviously done? Sorry, I know we've had this conversation, but I just don't know how to feel or what to think. But at the same time… Tom isn't exactly making mincemeat of the prosecution, and let's face it, it's looking like he must have… and if he has, I'll never… how can I forgive him? But I have to, don't I? For Annie. Does that make sense?'

'It does.' Oncoming headlights catch the sheen on her eyes. 'I loved her.'

'I know.' Do I? I think I do.

Daisy shakes her head. When she blinks, a tear trails down each of her cheeks. 'Cal loved her too. He loved her so much. It just doesn't make sense.'

'But he was angry with her.'

'Yes, but it was Dominic he hated. That's what's so confusing.'

'Do you think he could have got so frustrated with her that he'd – lash out?'

'I don't think so. If he'd been drinking spirits and smoking hash… maybe he meant to scare her, or both of them. Maybe he'd got to the end of his tether with all the fighting.'

Cal at the end of his tether, Annie at the end of hers. Dominic drove Annie to violence. He had a way of getting people to do things for him, Ross said. *Because* of him.

'Ross told me Dominic caused people to do bad things,' I say, unsure if I have the brass neck to follow through with what I'm thinking. 'What do you think he meant?'

'Cal, I suppose. Maybe Annie? Causing her to commit murder?'

I hesitate. Gossip is dangerous, this is not my town and Ross is not my friend. But Annie was my sister, Cal is my nephew and I want the truth.

'I got the impression he meant someone else, someone outside the family. I don't think he meant that Dom made people do things by, say, blackmail or something; more like he got under their skin, drove them to… bad things. Like Annie and Cal weren't the first, almost. I take it you know Ross had an affair with Annie?'

She nods. 'Yeah.'

'So do you think he might have been referring to himself?'

For a long moment, Daisy says nothing. Gossip is terrible, yes, but surely she's not prepared to protect Ross if he had something to do with Annie's death.

'He might have meant Sonia,' she says.

'Who's Sonia?'

'Dominic's serious girlfriend before Annie. He was pretty heartless towards her and she… well, she took her own life. Ross wouldn't have wanted to gossip about that, but she's maybe who he was thinking of. I always thought she must have been fragile – mentally, you know? But Annie wasn't fragile and Dominic drove her to murder, didn't he? Which is something she would never do, not to mention the way he made her live. I think now he probably did drive Sonia to… What I mean is, without him, she would still be alive.'

'How did she…?' I whisper.

'She threw herself off a cliff.'

My breath staggers. 'Oh my God. How awful. That poor, poor woman.' But even as the words leave me, I still think Ross meant himself, because it was during that conversation that he asked if my sister had ever told me about *that side of things*. And I know now he was talking about himself, his affair with my sister.

'When Ross said it,' I begin carefully, 'I got the impression he was about to admit to something but that he decided against it. Jan said he was still in love with her when she died. It must have been hard watching her suffer like that. He must have hated Dominic. Today they kept talking about a third party. Do you think it's possible that Ross…?' I glance at her, but she shakes her head emphatically.

'God, no. He's police.'

Not my friend. Not my town. Gossip is dangerous. Drop it.

But, I think, pressing my mouth tight shut, *if he's police, he would know how to cover his tracks.*

CHAPTER 37

Annie

April 2002

It is 3 p.m. In the studio, the light is superb, perfect for finishing her painting of Old Harry Rocks as seen from the grounds of the Pig Hotel at Studland, a private commission for one of the hotel guests. She is breathing more easily now, her work calming her as it has the power to do. On the trestle table, a pregnancy test, two lines blue and parallel. She cannot take her eyes off them, cannot stop smiling.

As well as her work, the peace of the empty house soothes her too. Dom is meeting someone about a chalet that's come up over in Uplyme. Cal, home on his Easter break, is on shift at Santori's and is taking pizzas to Jan's later for a movie night catch-up, bless him. He will stay over. Neither of them will acknowledge that this is because he can't stand being in the house. He is saving madly, working three jobs, so that he can buy an old car and do it up. Dominic is grumbling about having a wreck on the driveway, but Annie's told him to shut up about it. Most kids Cal's age are stuck on computer games or getting stoned in the park. Besides, Dom's just jealous, barely knows one end of a spanner from the other.

When she hears his car on the drive, she makes herself take three deep breaths, a childhood habit that has never left her, something her mum always told her to do in times of stress.

Wondering if he has really been where he said he was going is another habit. Dominic's promises to be faithful have proved as reliable as dust in the wind. It's fine. Depressing, predictable, but fine. She didn't believe he would be, not for one second. She wonders if the baby will change things. Probably not. At the sound of the back door closing, his footsteps on the back path, she wonders how he'll react to the one promise he did keep, how he'll feel about being a dad.

And now here he is, at the door, the heat of irritation radiating from him.

'You're back,' she says evenly, pushing a lick of daffodil-yellow paint onto the edge of a blue branch. She eyes him carefully over the top of the easel while with one hand she slips the pregnancy test into the loose, deep pocket of her jeans. He is glowering – there's no other word for it. Now might not be the time; best wait until he's in receptive mood. 'Chalet not great?'

'Chalet was fine.' The emphatic way he says *fine* makes her scalp tingle. She stops painting and looks at him just in time to catch an expression of such disgust that for a moment she thinks she must have done something terrible. She corrects the thought, as Daisy has helped her to practise doing. She has not done anything terrible. The way Dom looks at her has little or nothing to do with her.

'Are you OK?' she asks lightly, almost with concern. 'You seem a bit stressed.' This trick she has learnt from him: the art of mini-mising. He does not seem *a bit stressed*. What he seems is furious.

'Surprised to find you here, to be honest.' He walks slowly further into the cabin, glancing briefly at her work before continuing towards the beanbags at the back. He doesn't sit down.

Her chest tightens. It's not quite fear, not quite dread. But still. 'I said I was working this afternoon.'

'Thought you might be out with Ross.'

Something within her shifts. She feels for the test in her pocket. She can no longer hit him back, not now. She has no idea how to answer.

Dominic has crossed back to where she is still standing by the easel. 'Well?'

Avoiding his gaze, she pretends to push the tip of her brush to the canvas, but he is near, too near, his heavy breaths carrying the sour tang of wine drunk earlier in the day, possibly at lunch with some woman or other, alcohol half metabolised, the rank notes of dehydration.

'I thought we'd agreed not to sleep with other people anymore,' she says. 'Didn't realise we weren't allowed coffee.'

She is on the floor, a shooting pain in her spine. He has pushed her, so suddenly she didn't see him move, did not have time to protect herself. She's landed on her coccyx, she thinks. The pain has travelled down between her buttocks. He is standing over her, as if daring her to pick her lousy body up off the floor.

'I'm sorry,' she says quietly, feeling herself shrink, this shrinking a direct result of what must be allowed to grow within her. 'I won't see him again, I promise.'

'Good. I know you fucked him, by the way.'

Ah. She has always wondered. Well, that answers that. Heat flashes up the length of her. 'But that was back when we'd agreed—'

His hand comes up, clenches into a fist. Shoulders rising, she closes her eyes and waits. Nothing. She opens them to find him bending over her, reaching for her. He grips her forearms, tightly, forcing her to stand. His fingers push into her flesh, hard as wooden blocks.

'Sorry,' she says, over and over, hating herself. 'I'm sorry, I'm sorry, I'm sorry.'

'Look at the state of you.' He grabs her upper arm. The brush drops from her hand. He drags her out of the studio, towards the back of the house. She has to run to keep up, fears he will pull her over. The movement is awkward. Pain shoots up her spine, down her backside to her legs. 'Lovely Annie. Everyone loves Annie, oh Annie, she's so special, such a talent, such a nice person, oh Annie, with your cute Scottish accent that everyone loves, and your lovely life, and your ridiculous hobby subsidised by me, me who provides all of it, me who gets to be slagged off, oh yes, Dominic, what a bastard, he doesn't deserve her.'

He is half dragging her across the garden. She tries to wriggle out of his hold, but it is too tight. She bites down against crying out at the pain. He is making her walk too fast, ranting all the while, striding across the grass.

'Dominic the fuck-up, Dominic who had to come back from London with his tail between his legs, Dominic who got everything handed to him on a plate, Dominic who made a girl throw herself off a fucking cliff, yes, that's what everyone says about me, thanks to you – don't think I don't know that. I mean, do you even tell people how hard I work? Do you? How much I help out at the pub, for nothing? How I've built this business practically from scratch? How you're quite happy to share the profits and pay for your sponging bastard of a son? Eh? Do you?' He stops, seems to consider the house a second. 'Actually,' he says, turning her around roughly, almost yanking her arm out of its socket, 'since you love your workshop so much…'

He marches her back towards the studio, saying nothing now, breathing heavily, almost panting. Pain sears her lower back, shoots down her legs; her arm feels like it's going to pop out of its socket. At the cabin door, he pushes her inside so hard she staggers, falls, crashes into the shelving, sending tins and jars flying. Red paint upends, glugs slowly down between the floorboards; turps leaks from a lid not screwed on properly.

'Dominic.' She tries to get up, but he pushes her forehead, hard, with the flat of his palm.

'If your studio is so precious to you, why don't you live here? Go on, live here!' He slams the door, locks it. She listens, hears him raving like a madman as he storms back towards the house.

Half crying, half panting, she scans the mess in her beloved workshop. That's when it dawns on her. Dominic's rage has nothing to do with Ross. It is anger backdated from a week ago, when she challenged him about using her workspace to drink and smoke with his friends, leaving it for her to clear up, something he's started doing lately, more whenever Cal is home. When she asked him politely to stop, he told her he'd paid for it all, saw no reason why he shouldn't use it too. But he didn't hit her.

But now he has. Now he's locked her inside the source of the anger, as punishment.

She cleans up the mess, her back and backside solid with agony. Hopefully by the time she finishes, Dominic will have seen sense and will let her out. But an hour passes and still there is no sign. The sky turns to dusk. In the house, no lights go on. Dominic has gone out.

Or not. He is calling her name, though she can't see him. A moment later, not Dominic but Ross appears at the side of the house. She bangs on the window.

'Ross,' she calls out. 'Ross!'

He sees her, thank God, and with a perplexed expression heads towards the cabin. The key must be in the door, because he unlocks it and lets it swing open.

'Annie?'

'Cheers,' she says lightly, though she cannot look at him. 'Stupid me, I locked myself in.'

'From the outside?'

'I mean, Dom locked the door but he didn't realise I was in here. I must have fallen asleep.'

He is looking at her, confusion turned to concern. 'Annie.' How tenderly he says her name.

'I have to go,' she says. 'I'm supposed to be at Daisy's half an hour ago.' She pushes past him, out into the garden. It hurts to walk – badly. She must have popped a disc.

Ross is following her. 'Are you all right? You're limping.'

'Am I? I'm just stiff.' She laughs merrily. 'Getting old.'

'Annie, wait.' He catches up with her, takes hold of her arm.

'Get off!' The words come out much louder than she meant. She has shouted at him, at Ross, who recoils as if burnt. 'Sorry. Oh my God, Ross. I'm so sorry.'

'No, I'm sorry, I…'

She shakes her head, horrified. 'I'm… I'm in a rush, that's all. Look. OK, I'm just a wee bit embarrassed. We had a fight. He locked me in and I know how that looks, but he must have forgotten, that's all. Cal's due home anyway, so… and then you came. It's not like I would have been there all night.'

The way he is looking at her is too much; she turns away and tries not to hobble to the side gate.

'Can I give you a lift?' he calls, his voice helpless. 'Let me help you, please. Annie!'

'I'm fine, thanks. And thanks again for rescuing me.' She is out on the lane, wiping at her face with her hands, furious.

Daisy opens the door and beams in surprise. 'What the hell do you want?'

'Wondering if you want any knives sharpening.'

Their eyes meet. Daisy frowns, picking up instantly, though not the half of it. 'Trouble at mill? Come in then. You staying over?'

'Is that OK?'

'No, I've changed my mind. Piss off home.' Laughing, she walks ahead into the kitchen and pulls out a bottle of Chardonnay. 'One large white wine coming up.'

But Annie's back is throbbing and a creeping dread is growing at the warm, sticky dampness between her legs. She hangs back in the hallway, presses her hand to her back, wincing.

'Just popping to the loo,' she calls brightly, the knowledge of what has happened beginning to land.

And at the sight of blood in the toilet bowl, she stifles a sob with the back of her hand.

'I hate you,' she whimpers. 'I fucking hate you, Dominic Rawles.'

A knock on the bathroom door.

'Everything OK?' Daisy's voice is low, her mouth close to the door. 'Don't cry on your own, honey, come on. You know me – I'll cry with you. I've got a gold medal in crying.'

Annie squeezes her eyes tight, swallowing sobs like solid things. How can she possibly tell Daisy what has just happened? How can she tell anyone?

'Annie?' comes Daisy's sweet voice, wobbling now with concern. 'Talk to me.'

'I've hurt my back,' she manages, hopes Daisy will attribute the smallness of her voice to this. 'Is it OK if I have a bath? I think I've twinged it moving my easel. Is that OK?'

'Of course it is. Shall I pass your wine in?'

'That'd be brilliant, thanks.'

A moment later, Daisy knocks again. Annie slides the bolt across and, hiding behind the door, opens it a crack.

'Sorry, I'm not decent,' she manages, as if they haven't stripped a thousand times, shivered and hooted with laughter at the madness of themselves on many a beach since that first swim all those years ago.

A glass of wine appears in the grip of a disembodied hand. 'Here.'

'You're an actual angel.' She takes the wine and pushes the door closed, composing herself now, almost there when Daisy calls from the other side.

'I've put some PJs and a bathrobe outside, OK? I'm ordering a curry. Chicken jalfrezi and a side of those spinachy potatoes, am I right?

And at that, she pushes her face into a bath sheet and weeps.

CHAPTER 38

Isla

January 2005

The next day, Ross is called first. He makes his way to the witness box with a now familiar lugubrious tread. He is carrying a sheaf of paper, and when he is sworn in on the New Testament, his voice is a little croaky, as if he has a cold. I wonder who in this room knows how intimate he once was with my sister, how much he still loved her when she died. I think of Annie, driven to murder by Dominic. Dominic's girlfriend, driven to suicide. *He'd certainly found a way of getting people to do things for him – because of him sometimes. Bad things.*

Mrs Peterson establishes Ross's name and official title before launching in.

'On the afternoon of Thursday the ninth of September 2004, you formally interviewed the defendant at Swanage police station, is that correct?'

'That is correct, yes.'

'Can you tell us what he said?'

Ross takes out a pair of glasses from his inside pocket, puts them on and reads out the beginning of an account that pretty much matches what Cal said on that terrible day in my sister's stuffy dining room.

'Thank you, Detective. And is it possible the defendant was under the influence of strong alcohol and marijuana on the evening in question? Over half a bottle of vodka, to be precise.'

'Your Honour.' Tom is on his feet. 'No blood tests were conducted on my client on the night. There is no proof that my client had drunk any amount of vodka. Just because over half the bottle had been drunk doesn't prove my client drank it, or that he drank it on the night in question.' He does not say *night of the murder*, I notice, even though Dominic's murder has been established.

The judge peers at Mrs Peterson. 'Agreed. Detective York is not here to give his opinion.'

Mrs Peterson nods, barely perceptibly. 'Let me put it another way, Detective. You retrieved several reefer butts, a significant quantity of hashish resin and a half-empty bottle of vodka from the defendant's room, is that correct?'

'It is, but that doesn't mean—'

'Thank you, Detective. If you can just answer the question. It's possible the defendant was under the influence of drugs and alcohol on the night in question?'

'It's possible.'

Peterson pauses before getting Ross to take us through the rest of Cal's version of events. We are even subjected to a tape of his 999 call.

'Come quickly,' he sobs, his private anguish loud and raw for all to hear. 'Please come quickly. They're inside. I can't get them out. Please.'

I close my eyes. Funny how it's our eyes we close to somehow *hear* less, when in fact it concentrates the sense even further.

'Very distressed, as you can hear,' Mrs Peterson says. 'And yet we know now that the defendant cannot possibly have seen what he claimed in that call. And that if the victims were already dead at the hands of a third party several hours earlier, the fire could not possibly have been accidentally started by them but most likely by that same third party—'

'Mrs Peterson,' the judge interrupts. 'Where is the question?'

Mrs Peterson nods, raises a hand briefly. 'When he made this call, Detective, was the defendant in fact *acting*?' She raises her eyebrows, waits for confirmation.

Ross sighs. 'That's correct.'

Is *Ross* acting? I wonder. If he was involved, he would want to get away with it, naturally. I don't for one moment believe he was motivated by malice, but instinct or impulse are less subject to control. Maybe I'm fixating, but I can't stop thinking about Ross telling me that Dom caused folk to do bad things. *Things they might not have wanted to do or wouldn't have done under normal circumstances.*

Why would he say that and then not tell me who or what he meant? If he loved Annie, he might have acted in a way he wouldn't under normal circumstances and known how to get away with it. But he wouldn't want her son to go to prison for something he himself had done, would he? Yet if Ross is involved, if Ross is guilty, why would Cal have confessed to killing Annie in the first instance, and why, later, when he pleaded not guilty, didn't he implicate Ross? Or someone else, even if he had no idea who? If he knew it was Ross, there's no reason as far as I can see for Cal to protect him, even if he was a good family friend. Who would he be doing that for? What did he owe? Is blackmail in here somewhere? But then who—

'Can you tell me why you began to suspect the defendant's version of events to be false?' Mrs Peterson cuts through my spiralling thoughts.

Ross coughs into his hand. When he speaks, his voice is a little clearer. 'We found several sets of footprints matching the defendant's on the rear lawn, which went all the way to the entrance of the studio.'

I know this.

'Anything else?'

'There were traces of the victim's blood on the lawn and on the defendant's shoes, which had been cleaned but not thoroughly enough.'

Oh God.

'And can you tell us why this disproved the defendant's claim to have been unable to drag his parents from the blaze?'

'If the fire had been raging, as he initially claimed, he would not have been able to get so close to the entrance. It would have been too hot. If his footsteps reached the studio, it means the fire had not yet established itself or had not yet started when he got there. The blood on the lawn and the traces on the defendant's shoes indicate either that he was in the studio during the violence or that he entered after the victims' deaths but before the fire occurred or took hold.'

'And it was after his arrest, when the police put all this to him, that he changed his story, is that correct?'

'Yes.'

'So it wasn't remorse that made him change his story, it was the knowledge that he had been caught in the lie.'

'I… I don't know.'

'And once he'd been formally charged, after consulting with his solicitor, he changed his plea to not guilty.'

'That's correct.'

My stomach lurches. I have no idea how Tom can argue against any of this. It is hopeless, just hopeless, and with every minute that passes, my optimistic belief that my nephew might be innocent of my sister's murder fades. And with it my desire to see him walk free begins to falter.

'Thank you, Detective,' Mrs Peterson says with a toothless smile. 'Your witness.'

Tom is on his feet. 'Detective York, you know the Rawles family well, is that correct?'

'Yes.'

'So well, in fact, that you were replaced on the case after Callum was arrested due to a conflict of interest?'

'That's correct. I'm a family friend.'

'How well do you know Callum?'

'Pretty well, I'd say. I met him when he was about twelve, when he first came here with his mum.'

'And how would you describe him as a person?'

Ross raises his eyebrows briefly. 'He's a nice lad, perhaps a little young for his age. Artistic, like his mum. He's good at fixing things. Fixed my car once. He's polite, works hard. He got a good degree, I believe, and had plans. He's not a deadhead is what I'm saying. He's got a bit about him, a future. He's a good kid.'

'What about his relationship with his mother?'

'They were close.' He clears his throat once again.

'And his relationship with Mr Dominic Rawles?'

'Dom… Mr Rawles hadn't really been much of a father to him. He wanted Annie but I think he was less keen on being a parent.'

'Was Dominic Rawles abusive?'

Ross lowers his head a fraction. 'He hit her once or twice that I know about, enough to bruise. And he was… unfaithful many times over, unhelpful around the home… domineering, I'd say. He was a bully.' Again he clears his throat, perhaps to stop himself from saying more – risk creating a motive for himself.

'Did Callum know about the abuse?'

'Yes. But I can't believe he'd kill his mother over it. I can't believe Cal would kill anyone.'

'Mr York, it's been established that in the immediate aftermath of the night in question, Callum Rawles lied comprehensively. How would you describe his state of mind at that time?'

'Oh, he wasn't himself at all. Traumatised, I'd say. Couldn't stop crying, hadn't slept. He'd had to ID the personal effects. It was tough on him; he was only twenty-two, let's not forget. And he was scared too, obviously, though I didn't know that at the time.'

'But knowing now that events were not as straightforward as they first appeared, if there had been some terrible set of circumstances that had left him traumatised but that he felt might incriminate him unjustly, might he have felt there was no other choice but to lie?'

'It's possible. Yes.'

'So it's possible that he changed his story not because he felt the game was up but rather because once he'd had time to recover from the trauma, he was able to see more clearly, by which time he had been arrested and confessed?'

'It's possible.'

It is all so flimsy. I can barely stand to listen.

'Thank you, Detective. No further questions, Your Honour.'

It is a relief when the judge adjourns us until tomorrow. I glance at Cal, but he is being led away and does not search me out.

CHAPTER 39

Annie

September 2004: the day of the fire

It is 4 p.m. Daisy has invited her over for a drink at half past, so she is grabbing a quick shower and changing from her paint-splashed overalls into her jeans. If she leaves soon, she will be back by the time Cal returns from his shift. She no longer leaves her son alone with Dominic, though if anyone were to ask her why not, she wouldn't be able to say whether it was because she worries what Dom might do to Cal or the reverse. Cal has become a man this last year. He is taller than Dom, quicker, stronger and, she suspects, brighter. And she has seen the way her son looks at her husband.

What is certain is that Cal is saving not for a car, as he has claimed, but to get out of here. As soon as he has a deposit and enough to get him started, he will be off to London and will never come back. He has not said this to her; he has not needed to. They both know there is no way he can stand to live much longer under the same roof as Dominic, but then Annie is not sure she can either. Since the miscarriage, her life, so idyllic on the surface, has become a poison she fears will kill her – a mundane and constant danger that leaves her nerves shredded, her energy in tatters. It is exhausting to live on high alert. As Ross would say, it is no longer worth staying in the lifeboat – time to take her chance in the rough water.

She steps out of the shower, pulls a towel from the heated rail and wraps it around herself. On her arms, a faint leopard print of bruises from yesterday evening, when Dom trapped her in the hall and grabbed her by the wrists.

'I'm going out,' he said, as if she'd told him not to.

'Fine.' *Let go of me.*

'I might bring some friends back later for a jam.'

Her eyes were fixed on his hands, the knuckles whitening steadily with the increasing force. She felt his eyes on her, willing her to complain, to wince in pain. She did not.

'I just thought you'd probably want to be with Little Lord Fauntleroy,' he went on, a new and unamusing nickname for Cal. She said nothing.

'I suppose I have to find some fun somewhere,' he tried then, his fingers pressing so hard now she had to push her lips tight to stop herself from crying out.

'All right,' she managed. 'Have a great time.'

He left her in the dark hall, her heart beating fat in her chest. She should have left then, she thinks now as she pulls on her clean jeans and T-shirt, her cotton cardie. Should have packed up and just… left. Called Daisy from a Travelodge on the M4 – *What the hell do I do next?*

Daisy opens a bottle of Chardonnay and pours them both a drink. Here for all of three minutes, Annie already feels calmer – she wishes she could stay and never go home.

Out in Daisy's garden, the mellow September sun has fallen on the patio to the west of the house, where they sit at the tiny round table on two ornate wrought-iron chairs. The set was a gift from Annie, a steal from a house clearance over in Studland. Daisy will still sit here even when winter comes, cup of coffee, hat and coat and scarf on. She would live outside if she could.

'It's still so warm,' Annie says, pulling off her little cotton cardie and arranging it on the back of her chair.

She turns back, sees Daisy's face fall.

'Your arms.' In Daisy's eyes, tears well instantly.

Too late to put the cardigan back on. Annie opens her mouth to speak but closes it. She is too tired – of all of it. She slumps against the chair back.

'Annie.' Daisy's voice is full of tenderness.

Annie expects to be pulled into her friend's arms – Daisy is the queen of hugs – but when she opens her eyes, Daisy is still sitting in her own chair. The expression on her face is not like any Annie has seen before: her grave blue gaze is fixed on Annie's. It occurs to her that Daisy gives hugs for life's low-key, shitty moments, the bad days when nothing has gone right, or good news, or hello or goodbye, but that none of these things are happening now. Now is too big. Distance is what Daisy is giving her. A space into which she, Annie, must step. But if she does, what then? What happens then?

'I used to hit him back,' she says.

Daisy waits. She doesn't say *you can tell me*. Doesn't need to.

'We used to fight all the time… well, you know that.'

'I know you had your fall-outs. I knew they were bad, but…'

'And then afterwards, we'd… well, you know… make up.'

Daisy says nothing. More space opens. A wide plain. A vessel.

'But since,' Annie gasps, unsure if she can go on, 'since I lost the baby…'

'*What?* When?'

'Do you remember that time I did my back in?'

'The time you came over and got straight in the bath?'

Annie nods.

'Oh God, Annie. Why on earth didn't you say something?'

'It's a big weight to offload. I didn't want to upset you. It's not always been this bad.'

'Wait. Did he *cause* it? The miscarriage?'

'I don't know. Maybe. Thing is, he's got angrier over the years. He doesn't know about the baby. But since he agreed to try for one, or since Cal went to uni maybe, he's become meaner. He started using the studio for his mates and it felt... mean, you know? Purposeful. I think he takes women in there too sometimes, to taunt me or goad me into saying something, I don't know.'

'He takes *women* there?'

Annie expects to feel the familiar creeping burn of shame. But it doesn't come. Here, with Daisy, it doesn't come. It is like that first swim – Daisy in the water, shouting at her to come in, her own embarrassment falling away in front of someone she understood instinctively didn't care about anything beyond wanting her to enjoy the water, enjoy *herself*. Stumbling into the sea, she felt herself return to a time before that dark terror, that frightened pregnant child, weeping and alone in her parents' cold bathroom, dressed in her school uniform. In the pure, joyous surprise of the cold water, there she was, all along: Annie, a child again, new. Daisy did that without even knowing.

I love her, she thinks. *I have loved her since that day.*

'Annie?' Her friend's eyes are pools. She is water. She is the sea.

Dominic. Dominic is shame. He is a constant competition she never wanted to enter, a poisoned apple she never wanted to eat.

'I think for him it's about winning,' she says into the space, with no real idea what she means. 'Before, he always won, you know? We would have a fight, and he would get his way or at least believe he'd got his way, and then we'd go to bed and make up and that'd be it. I agreed to him seeing other women – you know that, don't you? I agreed to it.'

'I didn't, no.'

'I saw him with someone else.'

'Saw him? As in actually... oh Annie, I'm so sorry.'

'It's fine. Really. It was ages ago. That's how I found out I'd agreed to it, even though I didn't know that's what I'd done. And the weird thing was, I… I didn't care. I didn't care enough. I've tried to understand it, but all I can think is that the sight of him like that – the baseness, you know? Not that sex is base, just… I don't know what I'm saying really, but I think I lost every ounce of respect I had for him in that moment. But I never let on. I just got on with it. *I've faced worse*, I thought. I've faced a whole town before now. It wasn't as bad as that. Nothing could be as bad. And I always hit him back.' This last she repeats, for pride, as if it's a good thing.

A silence falls, so deep Annie thinks she can hear the ocean, the heavy exhalation sound it makes. Daisy is looking out over the fields towards the cliffs. Perhaps she can hear the sea too. How adorable is the familiar dappled flush of her cheeks, the perfect roundness of her shoulders, her small expressive hands, the half-moons on her nails. Everything about her looks so lovely.

'But you stopped hitting back?' Daisy says, still looking out to the horizon.

'Yes. After the baby.'

Daisy shifts her chair closer and reaches for her hand. *Whatever this is*, Annie thinks, *whatever happens next, Daisy will be with me, no matter what.*

'I think what's changed,' she explains to herself as she explains it to her friend, 'is he feels like he stopped winning.' She looks up. *Yes*, she thinks. *That's it. Or somewhere near it.*

'Like he lost the upper hand or something?'

'Maybe. He was scared of losing me. When we dropped Cal off at uni, he admitted it. He knows he's a shit and he knows I know it too. Actually, he knows everyone knows it. I think, in his mind, I hold the power now and something in him finds that humiliating. Except I don't want power; I'm not interested in it – it's him that sees the world that way. He brought me here like some sort of exotic prize – of course, we never think of ourselves that way, do we? When we're young. We poke at our thighs and our boobs and whatever we don't like and we think, *Yuck*. We think, *I wish I had long legs, thin arms, whatever*. It's only when you look back, you think, *God, I was gorgeous*.' She laughs, but it is a sad sound even to her own ears. 'His young bride with the long golden hair, his princess. It's taken me until right now, right this second, to realise it was never about me.' She curses the tears that come, tears of self-pity, which she has refused to feel all these years. *You've made your bed, hen, wheesht and just get oan with it.* She has got on with it, God knows she has, but she can't get on with it anymore. It is too hard. It is too horrible.

'You don't have to stay with him. There's always a home for you here.'

'Thank you.' Annie sips her wine, feels the alcohol warm her. 'He told me I was a butterfly. What a load of bullshit, eh? That's how he got me to go along with everything – leaving my folks and moving here, running the business, keeping house while he did what he wanted, the commitments that were all about what a great guy he was. It was only and always about him, his status, his vanity.'

'Oh, Annie.'

'Don't feel sorry for me! I was vain too. I fell for the flattery. And I've done what I wanted over the years. I could never have become a painter without him. I'd never have had the means or the contacts – or the confidence.'

'You don't know that.'

'OK, well, maybe I would have eventually. But I'd never have met you.'

Daisy's eyes fill – water, leaking from its source.

'And something else.' The thought occurs to Annie only now in this busting of the dam, this colossal rush. 'I've just realised this second what made our marriage such a bloody war. I was never supposed to be *me*. I was supposed to be his *idea* of me. I was never supposed to shout or be sarcastic or say no or hit back. I wasn't supposed to reflect back to him how stupid and childish he was. I held up the wrong mirror.'

'You were only sticking up for yourself.'

'I know. I do know that. The thing is, he didn't want a butterfly, but he knew I aspired to be one. I as good as told him the first night I met him. I let him into my dreams and he used those dreams against me. But he didn't want a butterfly at all. He wanted a… well, a canvas, I suppose, a blank canvas – mixing my metaphors now – but whatever I've given in to, it's been my choice. I shut part of myself off and I made a go of it. For Cal, for myself.' She sniffs and smiles at her friend. 'I'm going to leave him. I'm going to go back now to ask for a divorce.'

'OK. I'll stand by. You and Cal can both come here. Cal will have to take the couch, mind you.'

They share a brief, exhausted laugh.

'Thank you,' Annie says. 'I just need to believe I can find real love, not fireworks and fancy tricks that end in cruelty. I want kindness. I'm never going to settle for anything less than kindness.'

When Daisy says nothing, Annie looks up to see that she's crying.

'Annie,' she says. 'I need to tell you something.'

CHAPTER 40

Isla

January 2005

The following morning, Daisy remarks that we are in a groove. We glide, heads down, shades on, past the reporters, cruise through security. I have brought lunch and have plenty of tissues packed. I walk to the courtroom as if I work here. Take the same seat as yesterday. Try not to notice the large television on a wheeled stand in front of the bench.

The prosecution calls DI Hall to the witness box. There is a faint sheen on her black pencil skirt suit, her complexion grey, her wrists thin. Once her oath is sworn, Mrs Peterson gets on with the Mrs Peterson show.

'Let us focus firstly on the fire. Can you shed any light on when it started?'

'The fire was found to have commenced at around 11.45 p.m.'

'And as we've heard, the defendant called the emergency services at a little before midnight.'

'That's correct, yes.'

I glance at Tom, who is utterly still, face forward, shoulders straight. I return my gaze to Mrs Peterson, who runs through the circumstances of Dominic's death, DI Hall explaining the working theory that my sister grabbed a knife from the kitchen on her way out to confront him, an altercation that resulted in her stabbing him in the abdomen.

'... and that the defendant disturbed the scene and reached for the hammer, which was kept in the workshop.'

Mrs Peterson affects earnest attention. 'And yet the hammer was found in Dominic Rawles' hands?'

'That's correct. However, the handle had deteriorated too badly for fingerprints to be taken. The fire damage was severe.'

'So... for the sake of argument, Detective, what's to say the defendant placed the knife in his mother's hands, not the hammer in his stepfather's? That he killed not his mother, but his stepfather after his stepfather had killed his mother, in an act of rage? A crime of passion, if you will?'

'Because his prints weren't on the knife.'

'Not on the knife... Are you saying that the defendant's prints *were* on the hammer?'

God, I hate her. I hate this woman. Not because she is signing my nephew's prison sentence, but because she is making my belief in his innocence – at least of Annie's death – more and more difficult to sustain. And she is enjoying it far too much.

'Not around the handle,' DI Hall replies. 'As I said, the handle had deteriorated too badly in the fire for us to take prints. But at the top of the stem, immediately below the metal head or claw, we were able to recover partial prints matching the defendant's.'

Mrs Peterson points a remote control at the television. A picture of a hammer appears. On Peterson's instruction, Hall approaches the screen, indicates where the fingerprints were found and explains to the rapt courtroom the indication that 'the defendant grabbed the hammer at the top before transferring it into his hand so he could wield it'.

Mrs Peterson nods. 'I see. And that fits with the more... impromptu nature of the crime. It was to hand, lying on a shelf, perhaps.'

'It was kept in the studio, it being one of Mrs Rawles' tools.'

'The defendant came upon his mother standing over her husband's body. The hammer was *right there*. He grabbed it and took a swing.'

'It looks that way.'

Of course his prints were on it, I think. *He was always using the tools. It proves nothing, nothing at all!* But Mrs Peterson is already quizzing DI Hall on the blood traces and DNA samples, the footprints and the blood analysis. Dominic and Annie's blood samples were high in alcohol, it transpires. Like the circumstances of her marriage, this surprises me. Annie was never much of a drinker. But then she had grown up in ways I had not witnessed at first hand. The same goes for me. If she were alive still, I wonder if part of her conception of me would be based not on who I am now but on who I was in childhood. But then Annie was always wild. Wild in life, wild in death.

Mrs Peterson is thanking DI Hall and the judge is handing her over to the defence. My heart tightens. Come on, Tom. Stitch her up.

Tom stands and waits a beat for the silence he knows will fall. And it does. He tips his chin, grips his robes at the chest, and I realise that he has his own act, his own dance. But what he says next shocks me to the core.

'No questions, Your Honour.'

'*What?*' I whisper, reeling. What about the fingerprints on the hammer? For God's sake, Tom, why aren't you arguing against this stuff?

A moment later, the prosecution closes its case and the court adjourns for lunch.

CHAPTER 41

Isla

After lunch, the defence calls Daisy Miller.

My breath is a ball in my chest. Daisy appears at the back of the court, glamorous in another soft, chic dress, her skull ring, near-white quiff and short black-painted nails the only indication of her more edgy everyday style. She looks, I think, like a teenager who has been told to dress smartly for an aged relative's birthday party. Waiving the Bible, she promises to tell the truth, the whole truth and nothing but the truth.

I can tell from Tom's side profile that he is smiling. I know from seeing that smile how warm it is, how reassuring.

'Ms Miller, would you describe your relationship with the deceased, Mrs Annie Rawles, as close?'

Daisy straightens her back. Her neck flushes; the pink climbs up into her cheeks. 'Yes. I loved her very much. She was my best friend.' Her eyes are already wet with tears. She blinks.

'And you knew her son, Callum, not only as a family friend but also from the secondary school in Swanage where you teach Spanish. Is that correct?'

I smile to myself. He is arranging the words for her.

'Yes,' she says, leaning forward a little into the microphone.

'And how would you describe Callum?'

'He was studious, never got into fights at school or had detention or anything. The other teachers all liked him. And at home, he was quite sensitive but funny too, polite, kind, a lovely son. Just a really great kid.'

'And what was his relationship like with his mother?'

'Close. They got on really well, made each other laugh. He loved her very much.'

'So in your opinion, would he purposely strike his mother with a hammer in order to cause injury?'

She shakes her head. 'Never. Under no circumstances. He loved her.'

'Thank you, Ms Miller.' He nods to the prosecution. 'Your witness.'

'Ms Miller,' Mrs Peterson begins, 'you've described your relationship with the Rawles family as close. You were frequently with them at home, often had days out with the defendant and his mother to the sea and so forth, is that correct?'

'That's correct.'

My chest tightens. Daisy's eyes dart about. She looks stressed.

'How long have you known the defendant?'

'Since he first came here. So that'll be ten years, give or take. A long time.'

'You described the defendant's relationship with his mother as close, yes?'

Daisy frowns. 'They were. They loved each other very much.'

Mrs Peterson checks her notes, though I doubt she needs to. '*Intense*. Did you or did you not describe their relationship to Mrs Rawles' sister, Isla Andrews, as intense?'

I close my eyes. A moment of weakness in a time of stress, forgotten. Oh God.

Daisy's eyes flit around the room. I bow my head; heat blazes in my face.

'I may have done,' I hear her say. 'I didn't mean anything by it.'

I look up. Daisy's brow is furrowed, her face as red as mine feels. For the second time, Peterson checks her notes. 'You described the way Cal looked at his mother as "black and boiling"; what did you mean by that?'

'I… nothing. I said that in the immediate aftermath of… what happened. I only meant he was sensitive. He's not weird or anything, if that's what you're getting at.'

Shut up, Daisy, I think. And thankfully, she does.

'But it had been just him and his mum for twelve years, hadn't it? The two of them against the world after Mrs Rawles became pregnant at fifteen. Until Dominic Rawles came along and *snatched* her away? After he *stole* her?'

'Your Honour,' Tom says, thank God. 'This is hardly fair. Conjecture and leading the witness.'

'Mrs Peterson,' the judge says, 'may I remind you that the time and place for comment is in your closing speech.' A telling-off. Too late. It has been said aloud.

'Thank you, Ms Miller,' the prosecuting counsel says. 'That's all I need to ask.' She sits back down.

Tom stands to re-examine. 'Ms Miller, in the immediate aftermath of the trauma, you described Callum to his mother's sister as a little intense in the way he looked at her sometimes. Can you recall any moments when you might have noticed him looking at her in that particular way?'

'Dominic wasn't always nice to her. He'd put her down then pretend he was joking. She stood up for herself, but I remember a couple of times Cal looking at her like that… like he was wondering whether to wade in or not.'

'Would you describe the look as protective?'

'Absolutely. That's what I meant. Dominic didn't just put her down, he hit her, enough to leave bruises.' Her eyes flicker, her face flushes. 'He cheated on her – constantly – with many different women. Cal knew that. Everyone knew. As I said, Annie could stick up for herself, but it's obvious her son would have wanted to protect her.'

S.E. Lynes

Why has she mentioned Cal knowing about Dom's affairs? What does she mean by that? *Obvious her son would have wanted to protect her.* Is she hinting that despite appearances, Cal was capable of stepping in physically? That he had long held back the desire to do just that? Surely that's incriminating? Why would Daisy do that?

'Ms Miller—'

'Sorry, just to say, everyone knew all that but only a few of us knew Dominic pushed her so hard she lost a baby.' Daisy is crying, her hands closed into fists. 'He was a bastard – that's what you need to understand. An absolute bastard.'

'Thank you, Ms Miller. Please don't upset yourself. No further questions, Your Honour.'

CHAPTER 42

Annie

September 2004

Head and heart still throbbing with what Daisy has just told her, Annie returns to the cottage. Everything has changed. Today is the last day of this shitty life. Tomorrow will be a new start.

It is after 8 p.m. Her hands shake as she unlocks the front door. The decision she has taken, what she knows she must do, all of it is too much. But it has to be done. She has to find a way to leave Dom and somehow stay in one piece. She pushes open the door. The cottage is in darkness. Her skin prickles, an adrenaline rush she realises has been part of her life for far too long.

Home should not feel like this.

She tiptoes upstairs and along the landing, an instinctive response to the silence and the dark. In his room, Cal is crashed out on his bed, fully clothed. That makes sense; he is working crazy shifts, not to mention the half-burnt-out joint in a saucer by the bed. But oh, just to look at him. His dark hair, his neck thickened out this last year, his jaw squared, his T-shirt hitched up a little to reveal a belly with not a pick of fat, his legs muscular and long, his stripy socks half coming off like one of the Dr Seuss cartoons she used to read to him when he was wee. She has let him down, this beautiful boy. This is all her fault; she is the one to blame for this shitty, shitty life. They don't need Dominic; they never did. She should have left him years ago.

'I will make this right,' she whispers before closing his door and creeping downstairs.

From the fridge, she pulls a third-full bottle of Sancerre and drains it into a glass. She takes a large slug, another, hand pressed to her chest, taking deep breaths. A third gulp and the glass is empty. A moment later, she creeps into the living room. Light from the cabin leaks across the grass and in through the window, extinguishing all hope that Dominic is out, out with the lover he thinks she doesn't know about. Annie doesn't hate her, not really. It's her husband she hates. She has known it for so long she wonders how she could have lied about it to herself for all these years. But now she cannot stand to, she won't, live another minute like this.

A slamming sound comes from outside – the cabin door. Her heart beats faster. Footsteps, Dominic's, approach the house. Her breath staggers, her mouth dries. She has drunk down Dutch courage to tell him her decision, but now it occurs to her with startling clarity that it is impossible. She was mad to even think it. She is his possession. While he might not want her, like the spoilt kid he is, he won't want anyone else to have her. And if he can lash out at her for refusing to be a doormat, there's no telling what he will do if she tells him she's leaving. There can be no announcement; it is too dangerous. She will have to pack some things and leave a note. Neither she nor Cal can afford to be here when the storm hits.

She hears him pee, the run of the taps, a clearing of his throat. A moment later, he is draped on the door jamb, his shirt untucked, his bottom lip shining.

'Look what the cat dragged in,' he says, as if he's some great wit.

She says nothing. Even sarcasm he has beaten out of her. She doesn't want him to hit her, that's the bottom line. This is all there is now.

'What's the matter?' he says. 'Cat got your tongue?'

'What do you want me to say?'

'Hello might be nice.'

A wave of disgust rolls over her, emboldens her. 'Not seeing your girlfriend tonight?'

He shrugs, though she can tell he is surprised. 'Not like you show me any love, is it?' Instant victim. Not his fault but hers. This is what he does.

'No, it's weird, because I'm not even allowed to have a coffee with a man. I thought we'd agreed to be faithful.'

'Faithful.' He laughs. 'You sound like something off *Little House on the Prairie*.' He laughs again, though without mirth. '*Faithful*,' he says, mimicking her accent. '*I thought we'd agreed to be faithful*.' The accent drifts; he gives up. 'Honestly, you're so small it's a wonder you're even visible. Now, be a good girl and bring us up some snacks, would you? And there's a bottle of that Bulgarian red in the rack. Bring that too – I'm running low.'

He leaves her. A moment later, she watches him stumbling towards the studio, her studio, her place of work. He is chuckling away to himself, chuckling so much that as he steps up onto the raised decking at the door, he almost falls over. Prick.

In the kitchen, she opens up the cutlery drawer. As she closes her fingers around the handle of the large chopping knife, her stomach gripes. She reaches the loo just in time, sweat pricking at her hairline, trickling from her armpits, breath shallow and quick. She had decided not to confront him, but it is not a choice she can make, not anymore. Her body has made a different choice; it has told her no, it will not take another second of him and his monstrous, humiliating ways. Her body has taken over.

In the back garden, darkness is falling. The grass is cold, soft on the soles of her bare feet; the handle of the knife warms, quivers, slides in the damp palm of her hand. She steps up onto the decking and throws open the studio door.

'Bring you a snack,' she whispers, peering in. 'I'll bring you a fucking snack.'

CHAPTER 43

Isla

January 2005

The next day, Daisy is finally able to come into the courtroom with me and we sit close. A moment later, she takes my hand and it feels natural, sisterly. We are silent, both in a kind of pre-shock. Once the jury has filed in, the barristers and their juniors have taken their places and the judge has sat down, the defence calls Callum Rawles. His name causes a tightening in my chest now so familiar I am beginning to feel strange when it is not there.

Callum rises from his chair. My eyes are fixed on his face. I will him to turn, to look at me, and as he passes, he throws me a glance so profoundly sad, so full of apology, that my stomach hurts.

At the witness box, he begins the secular oath. The microphone fluffs. He hesitates, backs away and starts again. His voice is quiet, higher than a man's. He is only almost a man.

Tom establishes his name. When he asks what his occupation is, Cal replies that he works as a pizza maker, barman and handyman. I wonder what on earth this has to do with anything – his expertise in this case does not reside in his professional status.

'And these are the jobs you got upon finishing university the summer before last?' Tom asks.

'Yes.'

'Are you planning on entering the restaurant business, or maybe a trade?'

'No, it's just a temporary thing. I was applying for jobs in London. I was saving for a deposit for a flat. To rent.'

'So they were student-type jobs, would you say? Something to help you get on your feet?'

'Yes. And I was paying Mum a bit of rent.'

Tom nods slowly while my mind works frantically on why he's going into all this. To establish Cal as what he is, perhaps – a man not quite a man, not independent yet, but working his way towards it, starting out. A boy. Ah. Of course. An innocent.

Tom turns now towards the court.

'Ladies and gentlemen,' he says, 'we've heard various testimonies from the prosecution, various theories on what happened that night. I think it's time we heard from the only person in this court who knows.' He grips his robes and turns back to Callum.

'Mr Rawles, I'd like you to talk us through what happened, starting with the moment you woke up – can you do that?'

Callum dips his head to the microphone and begins the account I heard in my sister's dining room months ago. I wonder at what point that account will change.

'And were you drunk?' Tom interrupts. 'Stoned?'

Cal shakes his head. 'The vodka was from a week ago. I'd taken it out with me when I went to a mate's and brought it home because there was half left. I'd smoked a bit, but I wasn't stoned. I was just, you know, chilled.'

'So you weren't out of it? You're not claiming that as an excuse?'

'Not at all. No.'

'OK,' Tom says, slowly and calmly. 'You heard them fighting. This was at what time?'

'It was about nine.'

'And what happened then?'

'I ran downstairs and out of the back door and I ran to the studio.'

'So there was no fire?'

Cal shakes his head. My hair follicles lift. *Here*, I think. *Here is where the road forks.*

'There was no fire,' he says. 'I ran to the cabin. I opened the door.'

He pauses; his chest rises and falls. My own chest swells with a lungful of air. Here it comes, finally. Some freak event, some random action that makes sense of it all. He will identify the third party in one explosive revelation, the court will gasp, and I will know, at long last, that my nephew did not kill my sister. And I will know who did.

'I opened the door,' he repeats, his voice thin with stress. 'And he had his hands round her neck. She was choking. He was strangling her.'

'Who was strangling whom?'

'My stepdad. He was strangling my mum. She was making a choking sound. I grabbed the hammer. But not like they said. I just grabbed it by the handle from the shelf. My fingerprints round the top were there from a few days before, when Mum asked me to bring it from the house so she could hang a picture. She'd left it on the sideboard. She taught me to carry it like that, with my fingers round the neck. She taught me to carry scissors by holding the blades closed in my hand.' He looks up, his eyes full of tears. My heart constricts. Daisy squeezes my hand.

'Callum.' Tom's voice is kind as he coaxes him back on track. And once again I think, *Here it comes, here comes the truth – Dominic grabbed the hammer from Cal, my sister turned, Dominic—*

'You took the hammer from the shelf,' Tom goes on. 'Can you tell us what happened then?'

'He was choking her.' Callum's voice cracks. 'He was *killing* her. I… I just panicked. I grabbed the hammer and I… I swung it at him. Except he moved her. He pushed her round. He *used* her.

He used her as a shield… a human shield.' His mouth contorts; tears run down his face. He is there, I think. He is there in the cabin that night and he is seeing it all again, and I am seeing it too – in the lines on his face, in his eyes, his mouth. He is back there, that night, in pain, desperate. We are moving inexorably towards disaster, and yet here I sit, still hoping for a miracle. I am still hoping that he did not kill her.

'And the hammer landed in her head,' he says. 'It went right in.' He gasps, throws the flat of his hand to his forehead.

I come up, as if for air. The hammer is still in my nephew's hand. It is in my sister's head. There has been no miracle. No last-second switch. I am aware of myself processing what Cal has just admitted to whilst still hoping it is not true. For a second, both possibilities exist. He did not kill her. He did.

'At first I didn't understand. He was holding his stomach. She collapsed on top of him. I thought she'd knocked him over, but then I saw the knife sticking out of his stomach. She was on top of him and she was just… still. There was blood everywhere. There was blood just… everywhere.' He sniffs, pushes his mouth closed tight. His eyes roll back; his jaw clenches.

'Thank you, Callum. I know this is very difficult. When you swung the hammer, were you aiming to kill someone?'

'No! Oh my God, no! I didn't think about… I didn't think anything. I just swung it, you know? I was just trying to save her. I was trying to save her from him.' He presses his fingertips to his eyes.

'Callum,' Tom says gently. 'Do you need to take a break?'

He takes his hands from his face and shakes his head. From his pocket, he brings out a tissue and wipes his eyes. 'No. No, I'm OK. I'm OK.'

'All right.' Tom pauses, letting the effect of this full and frank confession sink in, leaving the courtroom to sit in silence thick as soup. 'Can you tell us what happened after that?'

Callum blinks, the slight but constant shake of his head more like a nervous disorder than any conscious act, a kind of sustained disbelief that has become muscular. It happened, he knows it did, and yet... Perhaps he is like me, suspended between two truths, only one of which he wants to believe.

'Nothing,' he says. 'Nothing happened. I didn't know what to do. They were both so still, but it took me a while to understand. I was still trying to understand, you know? And then my stepdad, he did this big breath and his chest sank and then he went really still all over again. And then I knew they were... I knew they were both dead. I knew there was no way back.' He looks up. I see Tom nod to him in encouragement.

'And then,' he continues, 'I'm not sure how long after, it was like someone else was moving my arms and legs. I took the hammer and cleaned the handle with my T-shirt and I put it into Dominic's hand. But I didn't pose them. I didn't do that.'

'But you're admitting you tried to cover your tracks?'

'Yes. I did. I knew I couldn't bring them back. I knew what I'd done was wrong and that I'd go to prison. I got showered and changed and washed my clothes and stuff, but again it was like someone else was doing it. Then I went back to the studio and I poured white spirit on them and threw a match on it. And it went up fast, really fast. I waited for a bit, and then I called 999.' He bows his head.

There is a kind of wondrous pause, as if we have all stopped to watch snowflakes drift down from the ceiling.

'Callum,' Tom says. 'Why did you lie?'

'Because I panicked. Because even though I didn't do it on purpose, I knew I'd done something terrible. And because it was too late to make it right.'

'And why did you tell the truth only later?'

'Because when I calmed down, I realised...'

'Realised what?'

'That it wasn't murder. What I did.' His voice is so quiet, even with the microphone. 'I know it was terrible, but I wasn't trying to kill him or anyone. But he was killing her and I had to save her. I had to save her from him, but I didn't. I didn't.' His face falls into his hands. I think I hear him sob: 'I fucked it up.'

The room appears to breathe.

'Thank you, Callum.' Tom tips his chin. 'No further questions, Your Honour.'

The cross-examination makes much of Callum's lies and of his actions after the fire. Peterson tries to tie him up in knots, but there is not much you can say to someone who has admitted to everything, whose motive rang truer, at least to my ears, than those insinuations of Freudian murderous intent, and whose testimony matches all the evidence. Even her attempts to make him seem weird fall flat. We have heard that he was well liked, that he held down jobs; we can see that he's a regular kind of kid.

I hope I've got that right. I hope my own hope hasn't skewed my judgement.

We are dismissed until tomorrow, when we will hear the summing-up and – it's possible – the verdict. When I stand to leave, my entire body aches.

CHAPTER 44

Isla

I don't sleep. When I pick up Daisy the next day, she too has dark circles under her eyes. When we reach the court and hurry inside, journalists push against us; I hear my name called out over and over. Cameras flash. The courtroom is fuller than at any other point during the trial. Daisy and I sit close. We don't speak. We are stunned, insides knotted with anxiety.

At the start of this trial, I hoped against my every instinct to discover my nephew was innocent of murdering my sister. I believed he'd killed Dominic, perhaps, because that was the easier truth, the one that allowed me to carry on. Now I know he is guilty of taking Annie's life, but I believe it wasn't murder and understand why he couldn't face me. I have run the endless loop of suspicion – Ross, Daisy, even Jan – grasping at theories and speculation when, actually, the truth was just as Cal said it was. He did and didn't kill her – Dominic pushed her into the path of the hammer he, Cal, was bringing down in defence of her. It was a truth he needed help to understand, and I'm guessing he will need help to move on from it too.

Now, if he walks free, he will not be expected to return downstairs but will instead cross this room to where Daisy and I are sitting. He will come home with us in the tight space of the car. He will be sitting in the living room of the cottage, possibly as soon as this evening, possibly on the armchair while I watch him from the sofa. He will wake tomorrow in his own bed and we will face each other in the daylight. Or he will be sent down, for life, and I will inherit my sister's life, my sister's house and wonder what the hell happens next. It is as simple and complicated as that.

And here we are, impossibly and possibly, for the summing-up. Mrs Peterson urges the jury to consider the evidence, which she lists exhaustively before outlining the burden and standard of proof, the legal ingredients of the offence of murder. It is not enough to *not mean to* kill someone, she tells us. If you intend to inflict grievous bodily harm, as anyone would expect to do when swinging a claw hammer, and if the victim dies as a consequence, that is still murder. Even if the defendant only intended to cause lesser actual bodily harm, if the result is death, it is still, at the very least, manslaughter.

'As for motive,' she says with relish, 'the story that he witnessed his father in the act of strangling his mother? We only have the defendant's word, and as we know, the word of a liar is worth nothing, nothing at all.'

She asks the jury if they really believe that two people can die at exactly the same moment, as if she is asking them to believe in fairies. She begs us not to be lured by the innocent aspect of youth. This is a man who struck his mother with a hammer in a fit of rage. There is no question of accident or defence of another, since the other was already dead. He then, in an act of supreme callousness, soaked his own mother and stepfather in flammable liquid and set them both on fire.

Mrs Peterson pauses for what I suspect is the last time. 'I urge you, ladies and gentlemen of the jury, to find the defendant guilty as charged, of murder.' With a curt nod, she returns to her place and, with a billowing of black gown, sits.

Tom Bartlett stands, his face placid, unassuming. In his movements, he is caution itself, courteous towards the judge and jury. Slow.

'Ladies and gentlemen,' he begins. 'Over the past week, you have heard two stories: one bent around circumstantial evidence in order to secure a conviction for a murder with no motive, the other matching the evidence exactly, told by the only person in this room who knows what happened that terrible September night.' He continues his long speech to the jury, reiterating the facts of the case. When he pauses momentarily, I sense he is nearing the end.

'My client has no argument with the evidence. He has no argument with the witness statements. He has made no claim to put himself elsewhere on the night in question, nor to lay the blame on an altered state due to drugs or alcohol. In the early days of the investigation, yes, he lied. He lied to protect himself. He lied because he is young and he was terrified. He confessed because he was so utterly filled with guilt and horror at what had come to pass; believed, like any good person would, that it was his fault. But once he realised he had acted only in defence of another in mortal danger, he told the truth, the whole truth, from which he has not wavered. And it was a difficult, terrible truth, a burden no young person should ever be expected to bear. He killed his mother in defence of her life, a tragedy from which he will *never* recover. His punishment is already upon him, as your eyes and your guts will have told you.

'The defence does not try to suggest Callum Rawles did not kill Annie Rawles. But *murder*? Intent to hurt her? *Kill* her? No.' He shakes his head, lips pressing tightly together momentarily. 'No. If there was intent, it was to hurt the man who was murdering her, a man who had psychologically and emotionally, physically and violently abused her for *years*. What happened was a fatal combination of defence of another and accident. Are you seriously going to find that it wasn't necessary for my client to act in his mother's defence? Of course he grabbed the nearest weapon to hand! Of course this was a proportionate response! Callum Rawles did not instigate this horrific violence. As we have heard, he is not a violent man. It was Dominic Rawles who was the violent man here.

'Ladies and gentlemen of the jury, the truth – the *truth* –is that my client is a gentle, sensitive boy who loved his mother, the mother who had raised him to be kind and good whilst still but a child herself. The *truth* is that my client had nothing even approaching a violent disposition, not a malicious bone in his body, as you have heard. But none of us knows how we will react when faced with terrifying and life-threatening violence. None of us. My client acted instinctively and in reasonable defence of another. He acted in the firm belief that his mother's life was in imminent danger. All the evidence supports it. All the witness statements support it. My client's evident suffering supports it. In order to find my client guilty on the first count of murder, you have to believe that there is sufficient proof that he intended to grievously harm or kill his beloved mother out of some long-held ill-defined rage that somehow no one close to him knew about or suspected. In order to convict him of manslaughter, you have to believe he was intending to harm his mother or kill her because she was attacking him or because he was not in his right mind. Neither of these stories makes sense. The only version of events that makes sense is my client's account of that night, and the reason it makes sense is because it is the truth.

'Ladies and gentlemen, I ask you to find my client not guilty on both counts.'

There is a pause before the judge speaks. She addresses the jury at some length, identifying succinctly the legal ingredients that the prosecution has to prove, going on to summarise the evidence that we have heard over the past week.

'Members of the jury,' she says in conclusion, 'I would remind you that before you can convict the defendant of murder or, in the alternative, manslaughter, you must be sure beyond all reasonable doubt of his guilt. Nothing less will do. Now please retire to consider your verdict.'

Once the jury have left, the judge adjourns and leaves the bench. Cal is led away by the security guards. I stare hard at his back, hoping that he will feel my gaze and turn, but he does not.

From the cafeteria, Daisy and I get tea and a piece of carrot cake between us. We pull away small chunks with our hands, get cream cheese icing all over our fingers.

'I can't bear it,' I say.

'You can. I guess it makes sense now why he wouldn't see you.'

'I suppose so. I wouldn't have wanted to face me either.'

'And I suppose he wouldn't let Tom speak to you because he wanted to be the one to explain when the time came.'

'Maybe.'

Later, a woman nudges me on the arm. She is a journalist, I think.

'We're back,' she says.

I glance at my watch. An hour and a half, that is all. I have taken longer over choosing a coat.

In the courtroom, there is a murmur of excitement. I feel it only as dread. This is it. The jury are already in their seats, the judge on her throne, Cal in the dock. I cannot imagine what he is feeling. I have no idea what I feel myself. My guts are lead. They are water. I am thinking of rituals, of the rituals of law. The pomp and ceremony of the law. We need these rituals, these costumes. They hold everything in place. They are the gravity of gravity. I reach for Daisy's hand.

The court clerk rises.

'Will the foreman please stand,' she says.

One man stands up. He is fair-haired and short, with square wire-framed glasses.

I haven't really noticed him before, but I do now.

'Members of the jury,' the judge says, 'have you reached a verdict with which you all agree?'

'We have, Your Honour.'

The judge's jaw flexes; her eyebrows rise. I wonder if she has a preference, what she believes.

'Members of the jury,' the clerk continues, 'on count one of murder, do you find the defendant guilty or not guilty?'

'Not guilty, Your Honour.'

I close my eyes, open them. The courtroom is still there. I am still holding Daisy's hand. I am staring at Cal, whose head is tipped back, as if to the sun. His eyes are closed.

'And is that the verdict of you all.'

'Yes.'

'And on count two, do you find the defendant guilty or not guilty of manslaughter?'

'Not guilty.'

'And is that the verdict of you all.'

'Yes.'

Cal drops his face into his hands. His shoulders shudder.

The judge is thanking the jury.

'Mr Rawles,' she says, 'you are free to go.'

'Oh my God,' I say to Daisy, tears running down my face: of relief, of thankfulness. He is innocent. I knew it, despite all the evidence against him, I knew it. My nephew. My sister's wee boy. His strangeness since that terrible night is so clear to me now – it was strain, trauma, confusion, fear. That night when he sat on my bed, he just wanted to tell me what had really happened but must have realised he would burden me with it, and could not. Poor kid. He has been so brave – brave and selfless.

And there he is, stepping down from the dock. He gives a fragile smile, apparently to himself, before crossing the courtroom towards Tom, who pulls him into an embrace. I turn to Daisy and put my arms around her; we sway from side to side. When I look up, Cal is walking towards us, his eyes bright and scared as an animal's. He is getting nearer. Another moment and he's there, his face stained and crumpled, his neck too thin in his shirt collar. I have no idea what to feel or what to do. He is my nephew, my sister's son. He killed and didn't kill her. He needs me.

He shakes his head slowly, his eyes closing.

'I'm so sorry,' he says. 'I'm so, so sorry.'

I know I need to take him in my arms and hold him tight. I know that this is what he needs: my forgiveness, my love, a home. I throw out my arms and pull him to me, but despite knowing he is innocent, despite loving him as I know I do, it is still the performance of what I want, what I should want, to do, and I know I cannot share this with another soul. After a moment, I hold out my hand to Daisy, who joins us in the hug. And this is all I can do, I think: act it until I feel it, for Annie's sake.

PART THREE

CHAPTER 45

Isla

The atmosphere in the car is subdued. We are dazed. The pieces have fallen. It will take us a while, I think, to pick them up.

We drop Daisy at home. She tells us she'll see us in a few days. From the car, I call Jan, who has already heard the news from Ross. She does not say *thank God*. She does not ask me to pass on my congratulations.

'It's over,' is what she says. 'Tell Cal to come tomorrow and I'll talk to him then.'

I ring off and relay the message to Cal.

'OK,' he says, getting out of the back seat of the car and into the front. When he closes the door, the tension of the two of us alone is almost unbearable. I can't believe he doesn't feel it. He is so quiet, his back still curved, his head low, as if under a heavy load. It is freedom, I think, this load. Guilty or not guilty in law is one thing; another entirely in one's own mind. His mother is still dead by his hand.

And later, as we readjust to the two of us in the cottage, a situation unfamiliar even before, if I had to use one word for him, I would say *preoccupied*. When I ask if he's hungry, he doesn't appear to know. We hover like ghosts. We communicate like robots. The grief that hangs in the air feels new, other. The pieces lie about.

I put the television on, find a film that has already started. It's a Bond movie with Pierce Brosnan. We stare at the screen, neither of us really watching it but both needing the benign company it provides.

'Do you want a glass of wine?' I ask him.

He shakes his head.

'I didn't get champagne, I'm sorry. Maybe I should have.'

'Nah. That would have been tempting fate.'

True. And given the reality of what happened, the mood is far from celebratory even with a not guilty verdict.

'They took your vodka,' I say. 'And your hash, I'm afraid.'

His smile is a trembling line.

'I don't suppose you'll get it back,' I try.

'They'll probably smoke it,' he jokes. He is trying too.

But whenever I attempt to meet his eye, he looks away. I realise he hasn't looked directly at me since we left Salisbury, maybe even since the day I came here. I wonder what he plans to do now. It is too soon to ask or even think about. His life has been taken away and returned to him just when he thought he'd lost it forever. His mother is dead at his hands. I am trying to prioritise his loss, but it is, frankly, hard. And now, down in the dark corner of all of it, I have a feeling that despite how truthful he sounded in court, there is *still* something he hasn't said. Why else would he be unable to look at me? Me, his auntie, his only blood?

He stands up so suddenly it makes me jump. 'I'm going to go up.' He looms over me like a shadow. I can't make out the detail of his face. 'Sorry I'm not much company.'

'Don't be silly. It's fine. I won't be long myself.' I wait, wondering if he'll bend down to hug me or something. Take my hands – kneel, even – tell me that, at last, I know everything there is to know and that we'll figure out a way to go forward. But he doesn't.

'Thanks for everything,' he says. But he is already turning away.

'Don't mention it.'

His shoeless feet tread soft and slow along the hall, up the winding stairs. The TV is too loud; I lower the volume and sit, spine rigid as steel, head cocked, ear trained. The bathroom door hinge squeaks. The shower rumbles through the pipes. I haven't even laid out a clean towel for him. I have not dared. I keep remembering the silhouette of him sitting on my bed in the dead of night, the sense that he wanted to tell me something. That he had, after all, killed Annie is what it must have been. It is the reason he couldn't face me in the run-up to the trial.

So why do I feel like he can't face me now?

Above, his feet pad along the landing into his room. In the days after his arrest, when the police left us, I cleaned and tidied it, washed his bedding – it was a kind of therapy. I even wondered if I should buy a new duvet cover but didn't. I wasn't confident he would return, nor, if he did, that he would want me to choose something so personal. I remember lifting his mattress, wedging it with my knee to get the fitted sheet back on. And remembering this now, something else comes, something I haven't thought of before. He was saving for a car – it came up in the trial. When I heard that, it rang a bell, because someone, maybe Daisy, maybe Jan, maybe even Annie, must have told me. It was Daisy who told me he kept his tips under the mattress. Annie told me this too. I can hear her as if she were here.

'A fat roll of notes,' she said – a phone call, a year or two ago. 'He'll be paying for that car like a Mafia boss.'

I imagine him licking his fingers, counting out the bills, like a gangster.

But there was no roll of cash under Cal's mattress. I have no idea why this matters, only that it does.

CHAPTER 46

Isla

My sister is walking along the shore of the loch, her sandals dangling from her hand. I am sitting on the ground. I am waiting for her. As she comes nearer, I look up. Her face is a shadow in the halo of the sun.

'Annie,' I say.

But when she sees me, she begins to cry.

'I'm sorry,' she says. 'I'm so, so sorry.'

I'm under the water, under the loch.

'Isla.' It's my mother's voice, muted. She's in one element, I'm in another. 'Isla, darling, come out of the water.'

The rush of water breaking around my head. The popping of my ears.

'Isla.' My mother's voice, clearer now. 'Out you come.'

My eyes open to cold moonlight leaking between the curtains. I haul myself upright, pull the pillow up behind my back. My face is wet. I wipe my cheeks with the heels of my hands, and in that moment I feel my sister's presence so strongly, I look around, expecting her to be sitting on the bed. She is not.

No, she is not. She is with my parents now and will never sit on the end of my bed, never fuss me when I come to stay, never make me feel like I am someone she wishes to savour like a treat. And somehow her not being here now is worse than when she died, as if she's been taken from me a second time. There is no shock to numb the pain. There is no anxiety over Cal's verdict. The pieces have fallen and there is only grief and heartbreak and a new, lingering certainty: I will never see her again.

'Annie,' I whisper into the lonely dark. 'I'm sorry too. I'm sorry I didn't stay closer to you, I'm sorry I didn't see you this last year, I'm sorry I judged you and I'm so sorry you felt you couldn't tell me what you were going through. If I'd known, I would have come. I would have killed him myself.'

Wiping tears from my face, I get up and creep along the landing, dry my face with loo roll and dip my head to the bathroom tap. Cold water soothes my throat. On the way back, I push Cal's door open and peer in, deciphering the jumble of his bedclothes. Something about them is weird. I tiptoe in, reach out to pat the amorphous form. It collapses. Cal is not in his bed. He is not in his room.

Downstairs, there is no sign of him. Already my breath is shallow and quick. I look out into the back garden. There is no one there. I pull on my coat and Annie's wellies and step out. It is freezing; my teeth chatter. I should go back for a hat, gloves, but already an uneasy feeling is taking form inside me. The fields are as still as stone, the smudge of the horizon whispers. Sonia flashes in my mind, a faceless woman, a shadow, the edge of a cliff. My heart thuds. Where the hell is my nephew?

On the far side of the cottage, a small square of yellow light shines from the garage. I have never been inside, had all but forgotten about it.

The clank of tools reaches me before I get as far as the door. Inside, stark grey breeze block, harsh white strip light. Three bikes hang from the ceiling. At the far end, a collapsible workbench. On it, a green metal toolbox. Cal has his back to me. He is wearing his pyjamas and dressing gown, his slippers. He is rifling through the tools, his head bent to the task. He must be freezing.

As if in sympathy, I shiver. 'Cal?'

He startles, visibly, and turns. His eyes are bloodshot. He is holding a hammer.

My throat blocks; my legs almost give way from under me. 'Cal?' I don't have my mobile phone with me. I have nothing. If I ran, he would catch me. I would not make it to the lane. 'Cal?'

He shudders, blinks. Stares at me, his expression bewildered, as if he's wondering what I'm doing here. Then down at his hand, then around himself, taking in his surroundings. He is wondering what *he* is doing here.

'What the hell?' he says, and my breath returns in a rush.

'Were you sleepwalking?' My chest rises and falls, rises and falls. I see the black silhouette of him on my bed. Did he sleepwalk that time too? Is this what he does?

He looks at the hammer, at me. 'I must have been. I'd been thinking about doing some jobs. I was going to ask you about it.' He raises the hammer a fraction before throwing it onto the bench as if repulsed. He makes a quiet *aargh* sound. My fright subsides – a jagged line, descending.

'Come on.' I stretch one arm out towards him. I cannot, cannot think about going further into the garage. 'You're in shock, darling. It's all… well, it's all so overwhelming, isn't it? Come on. Let's get you back to bed, eh?'

As meek as a lamb, he lets me guide him back into the cottage, up the stairs, even into bed. I talk to him all the while – low tones, near-nonsense gabble – the day we've had, we're all going to need time to heal, good food, fresh air, early nights…

'Like when you were wee,' I say, tucking the duvet around him. 'Try and sleep now, OK? Night.'

'Night.'

It might be like when he was wee, but I do not kiss him on the forehead. Instead, I steal out of his room, heart thudding, chest tight.

*

It is after midday when Cal comes downstairs. He looks even more tired than he did yesterday, and no wonder. His hair sticks up at the back of his head. Without his dressing gown, I can see his pyjamas are hanging off him as off a skeleton.

I make him bacon and eggs. I do this for myself, to try and manufacture some shred of maternal feeling. But he is not my son. And he is not my nephew, at least not the same nephew as before: the Cal I made fudge with in my mother's kitchen, walked with in the hills and woods and along the streams around Inveraray. That Cal is gone. Gone is the brooding young man who came to visit last summer, even though I know now this was not a phase but a troubled boy living in a troubled household, saving hard to get out. He could have come to live with me. The idea is so obvious as to be absurd. If I'd kept closer contact with my sister, she would have known she could ask. Surely she knew? I could have offered. I could have helicoptered him out of here, and if I had, my sister would still be alive.

As it is, she is gone and, at least for the moment, the Cal I used to know is lost to me. And yet even after the near terror of last night, I am glad to see him eat, to clean his plate with the heel of the bread and tell me thanks, that it was delicious. He doesn't mention sleepwalking, the garage, the hammer. And because I dare not mention these things either, I have no idea if he remembers or not.

'I'm going to pop and see Jan.' Rising, he addresses his words to his empty plate.

'She'll be glad to see you.' *Look at me. Why can't you look at me?*

'I'll see you later.' He plants a kiss on my cheek, the first contact since I hugged him in the courtroom.

'Do you need a piece to take with you?'

He frowns.

I smile. 'A sandwich. You've been away from Scotland too long.'

He shakes his head, claps his hand to his belly and tells me he's stuffed.

'What do you fancy for tea?'

He is already in the hall, pulling on his lace-up boots. 'Anything's better than what I've been eating these last few months.'

'I'll take that as a compliment.'

'I didn't mean it like that, sorry.'

'I know. I was joking.' God, this is hard work. We used to joke without laughing, Annie too. We were *beyond* jokes – we fired back, kept our faces straight. Laughter was for wimps; not getting it was simply not on the table.

'Sorry,' he says.

'Can't imagine it was great craic where you were.' I can hear the fake jollity in my voice. 'Not exactly been a barrel of laughs round here, to be honest. We're probably a wee bit rusty. Soon knock that off you, eh?'

'I'll see you later.' His sad smile, aimed at no one, opens a chasm neither of us can hope to cross.

'Do you need the car?' I ask. *Can we talk about last night?*

'No, it's OK. I could do with the walk.'

'I'll be here if you need me.'

The catch clicks. A moment later, I'm in the garage, looking through the toolbox. I grab the hammer, hold it up, retrace my steps until I'm directly below the strip light. I bring the claw up to my nose, turn it this way and that, smell it. What am I doing? What am I looking for? This isn't even the murder weapon, which is still with the police. So why was Cal looking for it? Why did he have it in his hand? What was he going to do?

I put the hammer back in the toolbox, unable to identify anything in myself beyond vague dejection.

Back in the cottage, I make coffee, try not to think about last night. Cal with the hammer, eyes red under the white light. Don't think of an elephant. An elephant, an elephant, an elephant. Don't think about a hammer. A hammer, a hammer, a hammer. What the hell was Cal doing in the dead of night with a hammer in his hand? Don't think about the roll of cash. Roll of cash, roll of cash. Where the hell is that cash?

And then I'm in his room, looking under his mattress. The police would have returned the money. Ross was still in charge then; he wouldn't have pilfered Cal's savings. On my hands and knees, I look under the bed, but even as I search, I know there is so much that is more important than this: where we go from here, who we are now. The business. Counselling for Cal – I think he needs it. Maybe we both do, if I'm to trust him again. It's what people do – more enlightened, emotionally literate people with backgrounds different to mine. But right now, all I want is to find the cash. I search in his drawers, his wardrobe, in his sports bag, his record stack, in shoeboxes I find under the bed.

It isn't there.

I have no idea what this means.

Time drags. I clean the cottage, intend to walk to Seacombe, calm myself with the crash of wave on rock. But I'm too antsy to be that kind to myself. All I want is to call Annie and tell her everything. I could call Daisy, but she's done enough and must need a break from all of this. I call Patrick and tell him an airbrushed version of the good news, but he is at work and can't talk beyond telling me how pleased he is, and that he hopes this means I'm coming back soon. In the end, I call Tom, who tells me he can't talk right this second, but now that the trial is over, there's nothing to stop us going for a walk sometime.

'I'd like that,' I say, meaning it so much my heart constricts.

'I'd like it too.'

Daisy texts at around 2 p.m. to tell me she's at Jan's and that she's seen Cal, who is on his way back. My stomach heats with nerves. Jealousy, too, in the mix – the idea of the three of them together; myself, his kin, the outsider. I try to read one of my sister's novels, but the sentences dance about. I flick through her DVDs. I meant to rewatch all the Almodóvars these last months, to try and feel connected to her, but without her here, I didn't have the will.

The key rattles in the door. I pretend I haven't heard. I am hoping he goes up to his room.

'Hey.'

'Hey.' I make myself turn.

He smiles – it is a broad, happy smile; it reaches his eyes. Too soon, I think, far too soon for a smile like that. 'What're you up to?'

'Nothing.'

He sits on the armchair and rubs at the legs of his jeans. 'It's cold out.'

'Cal, where is your cash?'

'What?'

'Daisy mentioned you were saving for a car. Apparently you kept the money rolled up under your mattress. Only it's not there.'

He pales. Looks out onto the garden, his jaw flexing beneath his skin. I can't read his expression. I can't read it at all.

'That was my tips,' he says – not an answer. 'And Mum gave me some cash for a few repair jobs I did.'

'Was it a lot?'

'About £825.'

'And you kept it under the bed?'

'I have more in the bank. That was just my tips.'

My stomach clenches. 'So where is it?'

He shrugs. 'I don't know.' He is still looking out, towards the sea. I want to shake him by his skinny shoulders, make him look at me. 'Maybe Dom took it. He stole from me all the time. Stole my weed, stole cash if I left it about. I didn't think he'd take the whole roll though. He'd steal a twenty out of my coat pocket then tell me I must have mislaid it.'

He is remarkably sanguine for such a huge loss.

'And you know it was definitely him?'

'I didn't realise it had gone. It won't have been Mum.' He smiles.

Did he just joke about his mother? Didn't steal it, why? Because she's dead? No. He didn't mean that. He can't have.

'What do you think happened to it?'

'No idea. Unless the police took it. Dodgy copper.'

'I shouldn't think so. Ross would never. And DI Hall seemed pretty straight. I didn't like her, but… no, I don't think so.'

Again, he shrugs. Still he doesn't look at me. And none of this is major, but none of it is… right. He had been saving for years. Years.

'Cal? Is there something you're not telling me?'

He throws out his palms and manages to cast me the briefest glance, his eyes round, exasperated. 'Maybe Dom took the whole lot into the studio and it got burnt. I really don't know.' He gets up out of his chair and leaves the room, calling over his shoulder, asking if I'd like a cup of tea. He has brought a fruit cake from Jan, he says, and it smells insane and he's going to have some right now, would I like a slice? We are not yet twenty-four hours free from the second-most traumatic experience of our lives, and he's entirely unperturbed by almost a thousand pounds gone missing and is asking me if I'd like a slice of cake as if everything is normal, as if normality didn't end for us that night, as if everything I thought I knew didn't vanish with my beautiful sister and her husband in the flames of her beloved studio. My nephew, her son, is horribly close to cheerful and my skin is aflame with the sheer wrongness of it all.

CHAPTER 47

Isla

Cal and I keep our distance. Or rather, I keep my distance from him. He eats a *lot* – a lot of toast, three or four fried eggs at a time, whole bags of pasta with melted butter and grated cheese. He is helpful, pops to the Co-op in Swanage in his mum's car, cooks dinners for which I have no appetite but which he wolfs. Already, his colour has returned, his face filled out a little since the gaunt near-skeleton he was in court. I try not to let his speedy recovery bother me, try not to think about the missing cash, the notion that he is too happy in his freedom. I see him smile to himself sometimes when he thinks I'm not looking. I say nothing.

But whatever I push aside during the day returns in force at night. I wake up in the wee small hours, sweating, haunted, my sister's arms reaching out, her apology still in my head when I wake. I am under the water, under the loch, my senses muted. I think constantly about Cal sitting on the bed the night before his arrest. I asked him difficult questions that day. Was he intending to talk to me or silence me? How far would he have gone to silence me?

Don't think about a hammer.

A few days after his release, he broaches his sleepwalking episode, though only in the lightest terms. He reminds me he often made repairs to the cottages over the winter months and asks could I give him some jobs?

'It's your business,' I say, fighting the strain I hope he won't hear in my voice. 'You can do what you like. You're my boss now.'

I give him the skeleton key, suggest he start by doing an inspection for me, maybe make a list of any odd jobs.

'No problem,' he says. No problem – like that – and I watch him take a toolbox from the garage, load it into the boot of my sister's car. His car now. Everything is his now. Don't think about a roll of cash.

As far as I'm aware, this is how he busies himself over the next days, which for me merge together, time by turns as thin as a gas, as thick as fog. I do a lot of unnecessary cleaning, sort through my sister's cupboards, though not yet her clothes, walk down to the cliffs, back again. Patrick calls for a chat. Cal is doing well, I tell him.

'Good,' he says. 'That's great news, babe.'

'I'm still trying to figure out what comes next,' I say evenly. 'Too soon to talk about new beginnings in any real way. We're muddling along. I'm still just trying to put one foot in front of the other, to be honest.' Even if, I think bitterly, others are running.

When I put the phone down, the pendulum weight of grief swings into me. I think mainly of the repairs I will never make to my relationship with my sister, all the times I judged her, called her crazy, all the times I didn't visit. Cal remains chipper. He is not tired to his marrow like I am. Gone is the shadow in the dock, the broken boy who met me at Wareham. In his place is the Cal of old: kind, quietly happy. I should want that, I know, but still the sense that he is hiding something persists, festers, metastasises. His demeanour is not wrong, but it is not right. He is acting not like someone who has lost his mother in the most traumatic of circumstances but like someone who did something bad and got away with it.

Dominic caused people to do bad things.

I push the thought from my mind, but it persists at the edge like a bad dream. I am reading too much into everything. I am walking around empty rooms. I am driving myself mad.

I realise I haven't seen Daisy since the trial, over a week ago now. How strange it is to be without her when for so long I saw her every day. Perhaps she's giving me space. Perhaps she's back at work. I text her: *Hey. Haven't seen you. Fancy a walk sometime?*

She doesn't reply, which is even stranger; she usually comes back straight away. She has been my wing woman in all of this. She has hidden things from me, yes, but in the end she came clean. So where is she now? Is she hiding something else?

I groan – loudly. She's probably back at work, Isla! Stop obsessing. She took so much leave, she has to get back sometime.

But what if she's avoiding me? Daisy can't lie – she's as transparent as a window. But what would she have to lie about now? Why would she avoid me?

I check my phone. Still no reply.

This is hopeless. Everything is making me paranoid. Everyone. It's as if I've only just arrived here all over again. I don't belong in this place; I know how communities – all communities – work. The terrible business is over. They've got their local boy back. The ranks have closed and I am left on the outside, trying to see in.

Jan, I think. Jan won't be weird. She is kind and wise and she'll invite me in.

My reflection in the hall mirror almost makes me shriek. I look a bloody fright. My eyes are ringed with lead grey, my hair a greasy mess. The lenses in my glasses are speckled with God only knows what. I look as mad as I feel. I sniff my armpits. Good Lord.

'You stink,' I say to my reflection.

The hot water at least soothes me. Being clean revives me. I put on a little make-up – Annie's, which I've been using since I got here. She doesn't have much: only a concealer stick, which matches my skin tone because it was hers too, black mascara, a green eyeliner pencil and some bright red lipstick, which is barely used and which, now I think about it, may once have been mine from about ten years ago. The lipstick looks bizarre – way too much for this place, like the red plastic lips you find in Christmas crackers. I wipe it off and start again. A little concealer under my eyes, some under my nose, which is dark pink around the nostrils with endless crying; some mascara, a tiny bit of the green on my swollen eyelids. It works. I look a little more like myself, like a human anyway.

It's cold out, snow still threatening but not quite committing, an icy nip in the air. It feels good actually – like it'll freeze bugs, numb feelings, focus the mind. I pull Annie's woolly hat over my ears. I have been wearing her clothes more since the season changed. Not her trousers – they are too short – but her jumpers and scarves and hats. There is no one around, not even kids hanging out on the green. The run of tiny terraced houses is in darkness, save for Jan's. Heartbreak Hotel isn't rented out right now; the other one in the row is a second home to someone, I believe – empty now the winter is here. I push the wee gate and walk up Jan's narrow brick path.

'Isla,' she says with a wide smile. 'Come in, come in.'

The sweet aroma of baking greets me. It's warm inside. As we pass the living-room door, I see the wood-burning stove is fired up. The radiators are warm to the touch. In the kitchen, the Rolling Stones play out from an old portable CD player.

'How the heck are you?' she asks, turning down the music, putting the kettle onto the small stove. She opens cupboards, fetches down mugs. The gas hisses lavender blue; biscuits lie on the round wire rack. She lifts four onto a gold-edged plate. 'Gingerbread,' she says.

'Funny how they call it bread,' I say. 'It's not bread at all, is it?'

'One of life's great mysteries.' She puts her hands to her hips and blinks, and I want to thank her for being so herself, want to tell her how comforting her soft humour has been these last months.

We go through and sit by the fire. A childish urge grips me: to lay my head on her lap and have her stroke my hair. But I am not a child.

'What do you think you'll do now?' she asks, her pipe bowl pulsing orange as she holds the long match to it. The air fills with sweet woody smoke.

'I guess I'll let the dust settle,' I say. 'There's the business. I need to ask Cal what he thinks.'

'A break is what you need, certainly. You should get away, take a holiday. Have you spoken to him? Cal?'

'Not much,' I confess. 'Things are a bit strained, to be honest. He's doing some jobs in some of the cottages. He said he used to do that… before.' I don't tell her about the hammer – or the cash.

'He did. He's got a good eye too, like his mother. I dare say he'll want to get stuck into the business, and he'll be great at it. His handyman skills were one of the many things that irritated Dominic, who couldn't hang a picture, let alone build a shelf unit.'

He'll want to get stuck into the business. So much so that he'd… No. No.

I study Jan a second. 'Do you believe him?'

She meets my gaze. 'Who?'

'Cal.'

'What about?' Her brow knits, her forehead creasing. She can't be confused about what I mean; that's impossible.

'About what happened that night,' I say, trying to keep the impatience out of my voice.

'In what sense?'

'Just that. Do you believe he told the truth about what happened?' I try not to pull a face. Try not to ask if she needs me to spell it out. I wait, watching her smoke her pipe like a wizard, expecting her to tell me that of course she does, why would I ask such a thing, but she does not.

Slowly she draws the pipe from her mouth.

'I think,' she says, head cocked in deep thought, 'that when life presents us with something impossible, we have no idea how we'll react, what we'll do.'

'Is that a yes or a no?'

She sucks on her pipe, her eyes crinkling. 'It's neither.'

'So, what? You're saying that whatever he did, ours is not to question?'

'Something like that. Cal is a good person. Hold on to that. And if I were you, I'd let that dust settle.'

'So you think there's something he's not saying?'

'I'm saying let the dust settle.'

My hands curl into fists. I thought I knew this woman. I thought she was kind. I know it's only been months, and maybe it's her age, but she's just one of those people who make you feel like everything is going to be OK, even when it's not. I thought she was wise, but she's just affected, with her pipe and her shiny silver hair and her cheeky sense of humour and her fucking velvet cushions. It's like she's playing a part – Mrs Gandalf, mystic crone. It's like she's trying to lord her wisdom over me and make me feel small and ignorant and alone. *When life presents us with something impossible, we have no idea how we'll react, what we'll do.* For Christ's sake, why not just cup my face in those bony old hands and say *Shush, child*?

And that smile – like Cal's, just like Cal's. That's not grief, it's latent relief, like she's pleased with herself. *My sister is still dead!* I want to say – to shout. *My nephew still killed her!* I am glad he hasn't gone to prison. I think. But am I the only one who can't settle on what to feel? Am I the only one who isn't trying not to smile all the time, the only one who feels that just because it's been explained doesn't make it less complicated?

*

I stride back to the cottage stewing, irritated. I don't want to feel this way about Jan, who has been so kind to me, but I can't stand folk who talk in riddles. She has always answered my questions carefully but honestly. Until now.

When life presents us with something impossible, we have no idea how we'll react.

'What kind of bullshit is that?' I mutter to my boots. 'What is the *something impossible*?'

I am still fizzing when I open the door. Still burning with confusion when I discover a letter on the welcome mat addressed to me. A foreign stamp. I recognise the handwriting.

In the kitchen, I hold the envelope against the note on the fridge. The note is from Daisy, telling me she's going to pick up some shopping and that she'll be back later. It is from before, September, when we were all at sea. The writing is an exact match for the envelope.

I tear it open.

CHAPTER 48

Isla

Dear Isla,

First off, I'm so sorry not to have seen you since the trial, but the fact is, after everything, I just needed some time to myself. I meant to call in, but there was so much to organise. The long and the short of it is, I'm in Spain. Mad, eh? But I'll explain.

'What?' I read it again but it still says what I thought it said. I flick the heating on, the lights, and head through to the living room, still with my coat and hat on. It is freezing. Cal has cleared and laid the fire – the kindness of this gesture doesn't escape me, makes me feel mean, suspicious, shrivelled. I strike a match and hold it to the newspaper, sit on the armchair to try and absorb some warmth from the embryonic flames. Scanning the letter, I find where I was up to and read on.

I'm sorry not to have told you face to face, but I thought once I got here, I'd write you a proper letter, which is what I'm doing now.

First thing to say though is that I want you to know how wonderful it was having you with me after what happened. You helped me through those dark days and I hope

I helped you too. It's funny, you're not like Annie at all, but in another way, you're exactly like her. You've got the same sense of properness, the same ability to rise to whatever is needed from you. But you're a lot more sensible.

Anyway, I've rented a little flat in Nerja, a small town on the south coast of Spain. Annie and I shared a love of all things Spanish, as I know you do too. And it's by the sea obviously, and she loved the sea as much as I do.

What I want to say is – you need to come. There are things I need to tell you, and it has to be face to face. I can't say any more than that, I'm sorry, but seriously, please come. If you call me on the number below, that's the local café. It's called Bar La Playa and it's on the beach. I'm there most days. You don't even need to call me. In fact, don't – just come.

Love, Daisy
XXX

At the bottom of the page there is a long number scrawled in apparent haste. I read the letter three times. I am so furious, my limbs feel like they belong to someone else. I want to run into the garden and scream expletives to the wind.

'What is wrong with people?' This I do shout, then I screw up the letter and burst into tears.

Everyone has gone mad. Jan is playing some wise old mysterious crone, Cal is acting like a smiling psychopath, and now Daisy has written me this… this coded message. I remember the glance she shared with Cal, that first day. I remember when I asked her about what happened, at Seacombe Cliffs, how her theory was so identical to his. My faith in my own nephew beginning to waver, I was desperate to trust her, to trust someone. I have been blind. And now she's bribing me with my frantic need for the truth. She knows I'll be on the first plane out. She knows I will move heaven and earth to find out what is so secret she cannot even commit it to a letter or a phone call. Why the hell would she do something so… cruel? And why has she left the country? From one moment to the next, everything feels wrong, false. Cal's confession feels incomplete. Daisy was involved somehow; the two of them colluded definitely. What is Cal hiding? Is he protecting Daisy? If so, what did Daisy do? Is it possible everything Cal said was a lie?

I need a drink.

I am halfway down my second glass of cheap Cabernet Sauvignon when Cal gets home. I drain my glass.

He throws open the door and grins with all his teeth. 'You've lit the fire, yay!'

I can't speak. I don't say hello. Instead, I watch him from the armchair, where all light has fallen away, leaving only the fire's glow. I watch him take off his coat and hat, his scarf, his shoes.

He has been doing repairs. He fetches all the grocery shopping. He laid a fire for me while I was out. He is kind. He was a great son. He is a great nephew. I am a witch, a hag. He can't stop smiling, so what? Four months in prison, of course he's had time to think about nothing but what happened, to make his peace with it, or at least to get to a place where he can move forward. He has known what it means to have his liberty taken away – of course he's going to make every moment count now that he's free. To survive, he will have had to consciously decide to be OK. This is what Annie would have wanted. What she wouldn't have wanted is what I'm doing – brooding and mistrusting and making what is already tragic into something worse. Tears spill. My hands are chapped from constant cleaning; the skin is rough against my face.

Cal peers into the room. 'Oh! You're in there! Sorry, I thought you were upstairs or out. Shall I make the dinner?'

This, finally, is what breaks me. His unfailing kindness, his faith. I weep suddenly and noisily into my hands – great gasping sobs, the most I have cried since this whole endurance test began. My heart hurts. I push my fist to my chest to ease it. A strange howl leaves me – like a hoot after a long, hard laugh. A moment later and Cal is there, staring down at me with my sister's green eyes, my eyes, the Andrews eyes. Green like leaves, like the loch, hair dark like his father, a man I never met.

He sits beside me and takes my hand.

'It'll be OK,' he says.

'Will it?'

'I hope so.'

'How? How can you hope so?'

He doesn't reply.

'Daisy's gone to Spain,' I say. 'She wrote to me. She's saying I have to go out there and that there's something she has to tell me. It's about Annie, I know it is.'

'Then you should go. There's nothing happening here. Any phone bookings will go to the answering machine.'

'Couldn't you hold the fort?'

He lets go of my hand. 'I'm going away too. I just… I have to get away for a few days. A few weeks maybe. I just need to be on my own. Thought I might go home.'

'To Scotland, you mean?'

He nods. 'I think it would be good to remember, you know?'

'OK. I can understand that.'

The evening is the best we've had since he was released. Cal makes spaghetti bolognese and we share the rest of the wine, plus a further half bottle. We even manage to reminisce about Inveraray, his childhood memories of me, Annie and his grandparents. We are skirting around conversations we need to have, but I don't care. Not tonight. I am too damn tired. Talking and laughing about the old days feels like a break we both need, and when he goes to bed, he hugs me and tells me he loves me.

'Me too,' I say, meaning it.

It is only the next morning, finding his bed empty and a note on the kitchen table telling me he's gone, that I run the conversation over in my mind. When I told him Daisy was in Spain, he expressed no surprise; no surprise either about her having information about Annie's death. And then he said he too was going away. When I call him on his mobile, it rings out from the living room and something tells me he has left it behind on purpose. With a pain in my chest, I wonder then if when he said he loved me last night, what he meant was: goodbye.

CHAPTER 49

Isla

I drive to London early the next day to pick up my passport, the timing coinciding with Patrick's day off. This small but lucky break feels like everything. That I will see my friend, someone from my life before, from a time when I used to laugh a lot, drink because I was out having a good time, when the occasional cigarette was my biggest source of guilt. Alone in the car, music loud, I find myself singing at the top of my voice to songs I know, filled with a sense that they too come from a time before, and that by singing, I am visiting myself in that time, and finding the person I used to be.

But the music only needs to stop for me to take the equally familiar kick of reality to the solar plexus. My head is mince, my heart in tatters. Mince and tatters, ha. The only truth that is left now is what Daisy has not told me – what, potentially, Cal cannot. He left before I could push him for more, avoiding me, leaving it, perhaps, to Daisy. I don't even know if I'll see him again, only that, as I suspected, he has not told me everything. At a service station, I call Ross and tell him Cal has gone to Scotland but that I'm worried. He tells me not to worry, that it sounds perfectly reasonable under the circumstances, but to call him if Cal doesn't get in touch within the next few days.

Alone in the car once again, I am at a loss. One thing is clear: my nephew has done something so bad he is afraid even to utter it, and Daisy is in on it. *Dominic caused people to do bad things.*

Daisy has had to leave the country and is making me leave the country too so she can tell me the bad thing she has done, or helped Cal to do. And given that whatever it is resulted in the death of my sister and her husband, I'm guessing it amounts to murder. A third person. The hammer. Why else would Daisy flee if not because she fears some new evidence, the eye of the law, like Sauron's, turning its gaze to her? And my nephew has put himself in hiding until it's safe to come out.

Patrick opens the door and grins, scooping me up in his arms and holding me tight.

'Babe,' he says.

We settle with coffee in the living room we used to share. I try not to notice the changes. Patrick has moved the furniture around, and there's a new picture above the fireplace – a framed black-and-white photograph of a male nude he tells me is a Robert Mapplethorpe print. I pretend I've heard of him. 'Wow,' I say. 'Nice bum.'

'So, what's with the passport?' he asks.

And I tell him everything. He holds my hand when I start to cry.

'So tomorrow I'm going to Spain,' I say. 'I feel like I'm going to an execution.'

He frowns. 'Have you spoken to her?'

'Daisy? No. I was so angry, I can't face it. I'm just gonna go and look into the whites of her eyes. I won't let her fob me off again.'

'Come on, that's not you talking. There's bound to be some explanation.'

I meet his eye, fix him. 'I'm going to a place called Nerja. The bar is called Bar La Playa and it's on the beach, that's all I know. *Playa* means beach anyway. I'll write it down before I leave. She hasn't even given me an address. Don't you think that's suspicious?'

'A bit, yeah, actually,' he says, visibly chastened. 'So why go?'

'Because my sister is dead and I have to know what happened to her.'

*

I sleep badly in my old bed, rise before dawn with a very stiff neck and leave without waking Patrick. At Heathrow, I call Jan, who doesn't pick up. An uneasy feeling creeps through me, but I tell myself to stop spiralling over nothing. The whole flight to Malaga, I think of her, Daisy and Cal, on a loop. I decide Jan is either out for an early walk or gone to see one of her daughters – that this is the most reasonable explanation. But I no longer have any idea what my feelings are about her or Daisy or my nephew. Right now, I just want to know how my sister died and for the whole thing to be over, and when it is, I'll be on the first train back to London. I will return to my life. There is no place for me in Purbeck – there never was.

The plane touches down a little after midday. It takes me another hour to hire a car. *Me gustaría alquilar un coche, por favor.* Thank God my Spanish hasn't rusted over completely, and that it's winter. No tourists. There's hardly anyone travelling.

The air in Spain smells thicker, heavier. It is cold enough for coats and boots but not scarves and hats. Focusing on the practicalities helps. I buy a map from a kiosk with the euros I picked up at Heathrow and figure out the route: a straightforward coastal road. Usually, I would be fazed by driving abroad, but it is as if every minor anxiety has been wiped from me, leaving only my need for this final showdown. If I don't get to the heart of it by the end of today, I will walk into the sea and keep going.

The coastal road should be breathtaking, but I drive it with eyes blurred with tears. I know I should stop and compose myself, but I press on, fixated. The last leg is always the longest. I can't stop thinking about when Cal was little, the day he and Annie left, his demeanour when he came to see me in London, his terrified voice on that call, his haunted appearance up until the end of the trial. The manic sight of him with the hammer in the garage.

His sudden switch less than twenty-four hours after the trial to an apparently uncomplicated, inappropriate happiness. A rush of guilt washes over me. I am his auntie. He is obviously wrestling with something, otherwise why would he go back to his homeland? I'm not supposed to suspect him or begrudge him his happiness. But I have not switched to happiness. I am topped up with guilt enough to last me the rest of my life. I am sadder than I have ever been. And *I* didn't kill my sister.

I put my foot down, take the winding road faster than I should.

On a side street on a hill, I park up and study the map. All I need to do is head to the seafront, and if all else fails, I can ask.

I head down the hill, and after about ten minutes or so, emerge into shops and bars.

'Calle Filipinas,' I say, reading the street name aloud. There's a sign for Playa Burriana. I assume that must be the main beach. It is all so vague; I should probably have called Daisy.

Another ten, fifteen minutes and I come out onto a larger, wider street. The beach lies beyond, visible between the restaurants and bars. On the corner is a gallery. In the window are two paintings – seascapes – on clear plastic stands. The style is like Annie's, and like an idiot I scan for a signature, my heart quickening with hope, only to slow when I see the initials E.R. I wonder if this is my life now: always looking for Annie.

I reach Calle Burriana. The town is not as desolate as I imagined it would be. People mill about – well dressed, in smart clothes that fit properly. Typical Europeans, I think. They look like they have good diets, moderate exercise, plenty of sun.

And there it is, on the other side of a wide avenue: Bar La Playa.

I catch my breath, for a moment frozen on the pavement. After about a minute, I see a woman with white-blonde hair and a tray of drinks. It is Daisy. Even at this distance, I can tell her by the way she moves. She places the tray on a table at which two people are seated, appears to exchange a few words before heading back towards the door. Is she working at the bar? It certainly looks that way. Despite my fury with her, my heart fills with fondness. I can't suspect her of something bad – it's impossible. I suspect her of having something to do with it, yes, but what?

She disappears inside. I unglue my feet from the pavement, manage to cross the road and walk towards the bar. My throat aches with the need to cry. As I get nearer, I see her re-emerge. Her blonde hair is quiffed up high. She wears a white T-shirt, loose black cotton tunic dress and Converse boots. A sense of dread fills me. I want to like her, so much, and I do, but if the reason she has kept the truth from me isn't spectacular, I'm not sure where that leaves me.

A thump to my guts. I stop dead. A young man has stepped out of the interior. It's… I'm almost certain it's Cal, a little behind her. It is. It's Cal. He is not in Scotland.

What?

Daisy looks up. When she spots me, her body straightens and she gives a huge wave. My insides flip. I don't wave back.

'Isla!' Her hand falls.

I step up onto the decking that surrounds the bar. She holds out her arms for a hug. Half a metre away from her, I stop, take a step back.

'Daisy,' I say, no chance of a smile, turn from her to Cal. 'What the hell is going on?'

Cal smiles, his face flushing. 'Sorry. I lied about Scotland.'

'So you did.'

'Isla.' Daisy's brow creases and her eyes fill. *Save it*, I want to say, anger rising. *So I haven't hugged you, so what? You should be grateful I haven't kicked up merry hell, and even this is only because I am still my parents' daughter, unwilling to make a scene. I am here against my will, my sister's death teasing me onwards like a rotten carrot, making a fucking donkey of me.* I am so damn furious, furious with them both.

'Let's sit down.' Daisy ushers me round to the beachside, where the sand stretches out before us and the water glitters in the late-afternoon sun. There are only a few people here, drinking small glasses of lager, olives and crisps in little white dishes. The day has evaporated in a puff of sheer adrenaline. The air smells so different. Of the sea and garlic and dark tobacco. 'What can I get for you?' she says. 'It's half four. Beer?'

'Sure,' I say, sitting at a free table, eyes drawn to the flat ocean. How wide the sea, how vast. *La Malcasada.* The Unhappily Married Woman. My sister.

'You sit down too,' Daisy tells Cal. 'You're making me nervous.'

Cal sits. Daisy disappears back into the bar.

'This better be good,' I say to my nephew.

'Just let's wait for Daisy. Everything will become clear, I promise. I'm sorry it had to go down like this, I really am.'

Unable to look at him, I glance away. Here we are on the beach, at the end of the land. The most important moments of my life have happened near water. I know what they are about to tell me is big. I know it's possible I'm going to be shocked. I am glad of the water.

I hear my name. Isla. I hear my name as if from under the loch, my mother calling to me. My mother would call to me from the shore, my head still under the water, my name a muted echo of itself: *Isla. Isla.* Me in one element, her in another.

Come out of the water, Isla. Out you come, darling. Isla. Isla.

I break the surface of the water, shake my head to clear the drops.

'Isla.'

My name. I hear it clearly, but I can't figure it out.

'Isla.'

It is my sister's voice. My sister is walking towards me, spreading out her arms, coming closer. She is crying.

'I'm sorry,' she says. 'I'm so, so sorry.'

My chair scrapes across the wooden boards.

'No,' I say, scrabbling backward. 'No.'

She stops. Her hands spring back. I am on my feet.

'What?' I am shouting. The people at the other tables turn to look. 'What the hell did you do?' And I am running away, running onto the sand.

CHAPTER 50

Isla

'Isla.'

'Leave me alone.'

'Isla, please.'

'I said leave me alone. On you go. Go away.'

The sand is cold and wet under my backside. I can't run any further, can't see for tears. My shoulders ache from the last twenty-four hours of travelling. My heart. My heart is a rock.

'Isla.' She is quiet, near.

'I don't understand what you've done,' I say. 'I don't understand anything. Why? Why couldn't someone have told me? Just… told me. I don't… I can't…'

'No one knew,' she says. 'Only me and Cal. Well, at first. Please, Isla. Please.' She sits next to me. I can't look at her. Instead, I look at the sea.

'Have you any idea what I've been through?'

'No. Yes. No. I'm so sorry. If there'd been a choice. If there'd been a safe choice… If you'll give me a chance, I'll explain, I promise.' She reaches for my hand. I withdraw it.

'You don't get to hold my hand. You don't get to be *alive*. You're a fucking idiot.'

'All right. But at least get up off the wet sand. Just… walk with me. I wouldn't have done it if I thought there'd been any other way to keep everyone safe. There was no time to think. Please. Please, Isla.' She stands and holds out her hand. I don't take it. I don't look at her.

But I do get up.

'You'd better start talking,' I say, brushing the sand from my backside.

'All right.' She gestures ahead. 'Let's walk towards Tarzan's rock. We can walk up and down until we get there.'

'To Tarzan's rock?'

'No, to the end of the story.'

'I thought I'd heard the story.'

'Aye, well, you're about to hear another one.' She tries to link her arm through mine, but again I shake her off.

'Speak.'

And she does. She starts at the beginning, from when she first moved away, fills in the gaps between the snippets I've heard these last months. She tells me how the scales fell one by one from her eyes. How by the time she realised what she'd got herself into, it was too late. Our parents were elderly, fading; I was in London living an exciting life and she had made her bed. She tells me how she made her career and made friends and made her life bearable, more than bearable, the humiliations she shook off like water. The shame she'd already learnt to bear back home. The dread and danger she ended up facing every single day.

We walk up to the end of the beach, turn to head back. The low sun is in our faces. She threads her arm through mine. I don't shake her off. She squeezes my arm in hers. She is filling me slowly from my feet upwards. I try to resist her, but I cannot. I never could. By the time we reach the café again, we are up to Cal going to university, a terrible fight on the way home, her ultimatum that Dom give her a baby.

'The beginning of the end,' she says.

Again we turn, and walk back. Behind us, the light is falling. The story will end with the setting of this sun, I think. It is the stuff of fiction. Truth is stranger, they say, and today it is.

'But I'm made of tough stuff,' she says, dipping her blonde head towards mine. 'Daisy helped. You only need one good friend, and she was always there. And Jan. And Ross. But then… then it all blew up.'

She sits on an abandoned deckchair. I sit beside her.

'Are you cold?' she asks me.

I am, but I'm not moving. 'Just tell me what happened that night.'

CHAPTER 51

Annie

September 2004

From the cabin door, the first thing she sees are her canvases – ripped or knifed, she's not sure, paint slashed across them, across the landscape she was working on, all thrown to the ground. Her easel lies on the floor, jars and brushes overturned, the smell of turps, the greasy slick of vegetable oil. The smell of wine, the thick, sweet smell of weed.

On the leather pouffes, Dominic is lying bare-chested next to a woman with blonde hair, naked except for her pants and Dominic's shirt loose over her shoulders. The musician. The one from that night, from the cottage. Eva Robertson. She is asleep or passed out, it's hard to tell. Her fingernails are short, square, painted black.

Bring us some snacks. *Us*. Of course.

'No snacks?' Dominic stands laboriously, zips up his fly and lurches towards her. He grins. 'Whoa. A knife. Scary.'

She keeps the knife out in front of her. 'I actually feel sorry for you.'

His mouth closes. She supposes he's trying to look stern. She's not afraid. She is not afraid of this pathetic man. But from the trestle table he grabs her hammer, and fear flushes through her, hot and liquid.

'You're an idiot,' she shouts, as loud as she can, hoping to alert Cal. The knife trembles in her hand. 'Don't come any closer!' She jabs at him. 'I hate you. You ruined my life.'

'Oh, come on! I *gave* you your life. You'd be growing old at the till of a gift shop in the Scottish hills if it weren't for me, and you know it. I fucking well made you.'

Behind him, the woman stirs, groans. Her heels come up off the floor, land, her torso rising like a seesaw. She blinks, coughs, pats at the floor around her.

A movement brings Annie back to Dominic, who has taken a step towards her. He is holding the hammer above his head.

'What're you going to do, murder me?' Her laugh betrays her.

'Maybe I will.' He shouts the words into her face. His spit lands on her chin. 'Maybe I just will.'

How she hates him. How she hates herself for staying, her hand for shaking now in front of him. Outside this house, she is loved. Why did she ever think she needed a man like him, or any man for that matter? She can't believe she ever did, can't believe that once she understood who he was, she didn't walk out and never come back. She could have stayed with Daisy. Even back at the beginning, Daisy would have helped her build something new. All we need is one friend in this life, just one. And now here she is: Annie Rawles, terror soaking her trousers, a kitchen knife in her hand, her husband's lover staggering around half-naked, drunk, invited here by him to prove something she, Annie, cannot begin to fathom. How can someone like him have reduced her to this, this wretch?

'Stay back.' She hates herself for crying, the pitch of her voice high with shame and fear. 'You don't respect anyone. You don't even respect yourself. You must know – surely you know you're a fraud?'

'A fraud?' He laughs. 'I think you'll find I'm the only one around here brave enough to live an authentic life.'

She tips her chin, feels herself calming. He won't kill her; he's too much of a coward. But to argue with him is pointless. What does she think is going to happen? That he'll have some big epiphany? That he'll *change*? It was vanity to ever think he would, pure vanity.

'Dominic,' she manages, 'I want a divorce. I'm leaving you. Tonight.'

He frowns, the hammer lowered but still in his hand. He takes a step closer. He is almost touching her now. He throws out his free hand. 'All this fuss just because I asked for a few snacks?' He pulls a face. 'Bit dramatic.'

She roars. 'You are not human! You're not a human being.'

He roars back, louder, raises the hammer again, high, high, his elbow bent. He is going to strike her. She was wrong. He is going to kill her. 'You've driven me to this. You're not the woman I married; you're something else. You're… I don't know what you are. Controlling. Manipulative. A self-righteous prig. A bore. It's you who's ruined my life, you…' His eyes blaze. He lifts the hammer, brings it down; she ducks, lunges, hard, feels the knife resist, then plunge… into softness.

'Oh my God.' She topples forward, onto him. Her face lands on his neck. She feels around her head. She's been struck, but the pain has not reached her. The blood has yet to flow. She is dead. Is she dead?

'What have you done?' He is shouting at her, both hands at his belly, clasped around the handle of the knife. Jesus. She's—

'You've stabbed me.' His voice rasps. 'You crazy bitch. You've stabbed me…'

Panting hard, she pushes against him, raises herself up. Feels her head again, all over. It is dry. Where is the blood? Where is the hammer? Her eyes dart about. She turns. Where is the…

Cal is standing at the door. His eyes are round, his mouth open in shock and horror.

'Mum!'

His eyes flick to the ground. She follows them with her own. On the floor, sprawled and lifeless, the near-naked woman, her blonde hair dark with blood, her limbs splayed strangely.

'Call an ambulance.' Dominic's breath is shallow, fast. 'Call an ambulance, for Christ's sake.' His chest rises and falls, faster, faster. In his eyes, she sees terror. She crawls back to him, pushes down on the wound to try and stop the blood.

'Cal,' she shouts. 'Call an ambulance.' She returns her gaze to her husband, looks deep into his frightened eyes. 'You've killed Eva,' she says. 'She's dead. Do you get that? Do you get what you've done?'

'You've killed me,' he whispers, his head lolling back. His eyes flutter, close.

'I think I might have,' she says. 'I'm sorry.'

His chest stills. She is aware of Callum behind her, immobilised by shock. The moment-by-moment of what has just happened is falling, settling. The woman made a dash for it. She got as far as the door. Dominic brought the hammer down.

'I heard voices,' Cal says. 'I saw him with the hammer. I thought he was going to kill you.'

'He was.'

'I only opened the door – that's all I did.' He starts to cry.

The woman must have staggered backward when Cal opened the door. Annie lunged, ducked. Dominic brought the hammer down. He brought the hammer down into Eva's head.

She is dead.

And Dominic. Dominic is dead.

Annie is standing up. She is covered, covered in blood.

'What the hell are we going to do?' Cal is sobbing, his hands up at his chest.

'I don't know,' she says. 'Let me… just let me think.'

CHAPTER 52

Isla

I am watching my sister, listening. What she is telling me explains everything. It makes no sense at all.

'So the body was his girlfriend?'

She nods. 'On and off. One of many. Her name was Eva Robertson. She was a musician at the pub. I walked in on them at a party once, her and Dominic.'

'Jesus.'

'I feel terrible. She didn't deserve to die. And the fact that neither of us killed her doesn't make it right to bury her in the wrong grave. But the thing is, I'd killed Dominic. And there wasn't a scratch on me. A few pale bruises from the night before, but nothing else. I knew I'd go to prison. I mean, I didn't know I wouldn't. It looked like I'd stabbed him after finding him with his lover. I thought they'd pin her death on me too. I was terrified, just… terrified.' She stops, lets out a long breath. After a moment, she gives a pained and doubtful smile. My Annie. My crazy sister.

The sun has dropped, strawberry ice cream melting into the horizon. My sister's eyes bore into mine, craving forgiveness. My big sister. Who is not dead.

'Didn't you worry about evidence? Footprints, dental records and stuff?'

'Och, I didn't think of any of that. We were out of our wits. We're not exactly master criminals.'

'You think?'

She smiles, tells me the rest. How once they'd composed themselves, they came up with a plan. She changed out of her bloody clothes. Between them, she and Cal wrestled her jeans and T-shirt onto the dead woman. The gruesomeness of it makes my throat thicken.

'Are you OK?' she asks me. 'Do you want me to stop?'

'No. I want it all, every scrap.'

Annie's wedding ring went onto Eva's ring finger, her necklace around her neck. From the house, they brought Annie's trainers to put on her feet. Size five.

I glance at Annie's wrist. On it, half a heart dangles from a white gold chain.

'You didn't give her your bracelet,' I say, choked.

'There was no way she was getting the bracelet.'

We exchange the briefest smile before she goes on, tells me how, bedraggled and stunned, she washed the blood from her hands and face in the wee sink she used for her pots and brushes. Eva's clothes lay scattered about: her trilby, her blouse and waistcoat, her high-heeled ankle boots. Annie put them on.

'That must have been so weird,' I say.

'I know. I never wear heels.'

A laugh escapes from me, involuntary as a belch.

Annie lifted Eva Robertson's patchwork leather bag and put it over her shoulder.

'Dom has a type,' she says, her head twitching with disdain. 'We weren't so dissimilar. Both blonde. Short. Curvy. I couldn't have pulled that trick off with you. You're way too tall. Your legs are too long.'

I can't speak. Shock hits me. Anger. Love.

Cal took care of it, she tells me. Poured turps over them, most of it over Eva. He was crying as he did it, he told her later. Annie herself didn't shed a tear. She knows now this was a dissociated state, though she tells me it's the most focused she's ever been. The memories she has pieced together in the months after the fire.

'Survival,' she says. And then, 'I left my son. I left a woman to be buried with the wrong headstone.' She begins to cry. 'I nearly didn't go through with it, but Cal was stronger than me. I'd lost my nerve. He told me it was the only way. I think we both thought if I stayed much longer, we'd both go to prison for life. He told me the police would see a fight. They'd see me and they'd see Dominic, an open-and-shut case. He told me to take his money from under his mattress, bless him. Over £800. He'd been saving for years, and he gave it without a thought.'

She tells me how Cal held her hands and briefed her.

'Like a sergeant major,' she says. 'Told me I couldn't use my bank account or my passport. "You're dead, OK?" he said. "You can't call me or come back here or be seen. You can't tell Daisy or Jan or anyone. You can't check out of the cottage until Eva would have done, or do anything to raise suspicion. You'll have to hide at Heartbreak Hotel for two nights. Keep the curtains closed, light cigarettes, play music, OK? I'll find out where she's playing and cancel, tell them she's sick. Take a cab to the airport on Friday and get the first flight you can. You can't contact me, Mum, do you get that? Don't contact me. It might have to be a year or two, but it's sooner than twenty-five."

'He made me repeat it,' she tells me. 'Made me say *I can't contact anyone*, like that. *I am dead*, like I was the child. He promised we'd figure it out. "If you can get out of the country on Eva's passport," he said, "everything will be OK. I know what to do. Go." And that was it. It sounds like it took ages, but it was all so fast. So, so fast.'

They embraced, she tells me, whispered their parting words: *I love you. I love you too. Go. Now.*

She ran around the side of the house, into the lane. Darkness covered her. A silent village night, nothing doing. She ran the back way, over the fields, up the little lane, eyes peeled, heart battering, all the way to Heartbreak Hotel.

'I thought I'd die of the pain,' she says, crying now. 'And the guilt, oh God! To leave my boy. To not know. But neither of us ever thought they'd pin it on Cal. I know that sounds ridiculous now, but I guess if you know someone's innocent, you think there's no way they could ever be charged.'

We are sitting in darkness now. Behind the ghost of my sister, I can see Daisy and Callum in the café, and someone else, an older woman, smoking a pipe.

'Jan,' I say.

'Yes,' my sister replies. 'We'll get to that.'

I can't take my eyes off them. Their heads are close together. They wave their hands. Jan is half turned away from me; Daisy's face is red, tear-stained; Cal looks on, intense, watchful. Annie and I are both shivering – cold or nerves or both. My sister is still traumatised. I realise I am too, though what I have been through is already paling next to what she has told me. I should let her go to her son, who has endured unimaginable torment and who I have misjudged horribly. But I can't move. She tells me Cal and Daisy called her from Jan's house the day after the trial. I remember his uncomplicated happiness after he returned. His mother was alive, and she was safe. He had saved her.

'Jan called me,' Annie is telling me, 'moments after Ross rang from the court to say Cal had been found not guilty, that he was free.'

'Does Ross know?'

'God, no.'

'Did Jan know all along?'

'If Jan hadn't known, there's no way I would have stayed out here. It was Jan who convinced me to stay put when Cal was arrested. I was desperate to come back. I was out of my mind. But she said I could always come back if he was found guilty, and to give the plan a chance. If I came back, he'd definitely go to prison. If I stayed away, he had a chance.'

If I were you I'd let that dust settle.

I think of Jan telling me she'd seen Eva Robertson that night, smoking and drinking whisky. I tell Annie this.

'She wasn't lying,' she says. 'Well, not about that.'

'How come?'

She stands up, offers me her hand. I let her pull me up, but I don't hug her. Too much. I fear I might dissolve. I am outside myself, looking on. My sister is dead. She is alive. I am not ready to hug this spirit.

'Come on,' she says. 'Let's go and get warm, eh?'

Jan stands to greet me. She holds me in her arms for a long time and whispers apologies into my hair before letting me go, raising her hands to my face.

'We are all so sorry you had to go through that,' she says.

I cannot speak.

Daisy has put the outdoor heater on. When I sit down, she throws a blanket over my shoulders and kisses me on the cheek. I reach up, take her hand and squeeze it. Cal and Annie hold each other tight for the time it takes Daisy to fetch a bottle of Carlos III brandy and five bowl glasses from behind the bar. Cal sits down and rolls a cigarette. I pluck it from his fingers and tell him to roll himself another.

'I thought you gave up,' my sister says, frowning.

I fix her with a look. 'Well I thought you were dead, but here we are.'

'Are you OK?' Cal asks me.

'I'll tell you in a week.' I let him light my cigarette. Once we're settled, I say, 'We're up to the bit where you set fire to your stepfather and his lover.'

'Right,' he says, looking between me, my sister and her friends – an urchin caught by a coven.

He tells us he waited for the fire to rage before calling the fire brigade. He wanted to be sure all evidence would be destroyed but was shocked by how quickly it went up; feared a spark might set fire to the thatch.

'When I rang you, I wasn't faking it,' he says. 'I was petrified and I felt so guilty about Eva.'

'Ach,' Jan chips in, grimacing. 'She was bad news.'

'It's still not right though,' Annie says.

'No,' Jan says, 'but like I told you, she had no kids and no family as far as I know. That was her thing, a lone wolf, which might explain why she didn't give a toss about anyone but herself.' She cocks her head. 'I mean, I know it's not right. But no one knows what they'd do in such an extreme situation.'

Annie glances at me. I see in her eyes that what happened that night, everything that happened, is going to weigh on her conscience, probably forever. I reach over and take her hand in mine.

After a moment, Cal takes up the story once again. He and Annie were convinced it would work, he tells us. Madness, I think, listening to this kid, but then I think: but it did work. They wondered if the police would even find the injuries, unsure as they were about fire damage, forensics – everything. If the injuries came to light, Cal had to hope they'd frame it as a fight. The village would support it. Everyone knew what a stormy marriage it was, what Dominic was, what an arsehole. Everyone would back them up.

'If I'd known I was leaving Cal to get arrested, I never would have gone,' Annie says. 'I didn't think further than survival; neither of us did. I never thought for one second they'd arrest him. I didn't know how I'd do the rest, just that I had to. I'm so sorry.'

'What about forensics though? They said in court they did DNA tests?'

'That was Cal,' Annie says. 'Just as I was leaving, he grabbed Eva's bag and took her hairbrush. Hair the same colour as mine, to the untrained eye.'

'And when Ross asked for something personal,' I fill in, 'you told him to grab her hairbrush from her dressing table.'

'Yep.' Cal pulls on his cigarette. He looks drained.

'You were very convincing.'

'I didn't have to act being traumatised.'

'I guess. What about dental records? Hospital?'

'I didn't think of that,' Cal says.

'I haven't been to the dentist since I moved south,' Annie adds. 'And the baby I lost, I lost at Daisy's.'

I glance at Daisy, manage a smile. Her eyes fill. This woman is at least seventy-five per cent mush.

'I went back to Heartbreak,' my sister continues. 'Let myself in with Eva's key obviously. There was half a bottle of Scotch on the side. I drank some of that to calm my nerves. I was hoping Jan would be aware of me in the cottage – well, Eva, I mean. This will have been ten-ish. I put music on. Lit another cigarette, went outside to let it burn down in my hand. You know me, can't stand smoking. I had on the black trilby. I was trying to make an alibi for myself.'

'And she did,' Jan says with a low chuckle. 'I thought, *That woman is a pain in the arse.*' Her eyelids are heavy, but she looks mellow. She puffs on her pipe, this magical wizard lady.

'How did you know?' I ask her. 'Or rather, when?'

'The Friday morning,' Jan replies. 'The day she left. Saw her getting into the cab, didn't I?' Through the smoke, she grins at Annie.

Annie smiles. 'Our eyes met and Jan just nodded, that's all she did, and I knew she'd understood and that she wouldn't say a word. God knows, I know how a secret spreads through a town, and if it had been anyone other than Jan...'

She glances up at me. 'I called her the moment I got to Spain. She's been keeping me up to date all this time.'

I glance at Daisy. 'But what about you?'

'I didn't know a thing.' Daisy throws up her hands. 'Not till after the trial.'

'So you've had to go through all the grief too.' I turn to Annie. 'Surely Jan could have told her?'

'Have you even seen Daisy try and lie?' Annie is laughing.

True.

'Thank God they didn't,' Daisy adds. 'I'd have blown the whole thing in seconds.'

'And we didn't tell you,' my sister says, her eyes filling for the umpteenth time. 'I'm so, so sorry. But everyone had to react in a way that was completely natural if we were ever going to pull it off. Knowledge was danger, for all of us.'

I think about the last few days, about people not behaving weirdly exactly but acting... off. It has made me half crazy with suspicion.

'I thought you'd had an affair with Dominic,' I tell Daisy. 'I thought maybe that was what you'd told Annie that day and it had made her so cross she went to confront him.'

'Ah, no.' Daisy glances at my sister. 'That's not what I told her.'

My sister blushes. Across the table, their hands find each other. The truth hits me before anyone says it. Of course.

'It's all Daisy's fault really,' Annie says.

'I would have taken it to my grave,' Daisy says. 'But she had bruises all up her arms and I just wanted to convince her that she could leave and be loved unconditionally, even if she didn't want me. That she had somewhere to go. So I told her I loved her, and that I always had. When she died, I thought it was all my fault. I thought I'd given her the courage she needed and unwittingly sent her to her death.' She squeezes my sister's hand; my sister squeezes back.

'It was like a light going on,' Annie says. 'I realised I'd loved Daisy since the moment I met her. So I went home to tell Dom it was over. And as you now know, it went really well.'

We laugh, all of us. I am happy for her, I realise, in a way I never was when she chose Dominic. The tension is falling away, a fragile calm descending. I have questions, so many, but for the moment, they're not as important as this: my sister is alive and she is safe. I lost her and now I have found her and I will never leave it so long, never again let myself drift from her, never fail to look into her heart and make sure she's all right.

'What happens now?' I ask.

'I don't know,' Annie says. 'We're thinking Daisy and I will live here. I've already sold a couple of paintings.'

'So that *was* your work I saw?' My mouth drops open – frankly, I'm shocked I have any capacity for surprise left. 'But hang on, no. E.R.'

Annie fixes me with her green eyes.

'Eva Robertson,' I say then. 'Of course. Bloody hell.'

Annie smiles sadly and nods her head. 'Emily Robinson actually. I couldn't quite cope with stealing her name as well. But that's who I have to be now. I can never go home obviously. I guess Cal might take over the business, if he wants to.'

'Actually,' Cal says, 'I want to go to London, at least for a few years.'

I think of how Annie never got to eat crisps for tea, drink white wine with her feet on the table. I think of Tom, the walk on the beach he promised me.

'I could take over for a few years,' I say. 'I love it there. And Jan and I can come and visit. Who knows, I might even upgrade from incomer to settler.'

'We don't need to decide anything now,' Annie says. 'We just had to get you here and tell you. As for the rest, we'll figure it out.'

Over the dark sea, the moon hangs in the black sky. Here we are, at the end of the land, at the end of this surreal story. My sister is right. We'll figure it out. To go any further right now is to enter another story altogether.

And that will have to wait until tomorrow.

EPILOGUE

Ross slumps back in his seat and glances across the courtroom to where Callum is shaking Tom Bartlett's hand. Grinning, Tom pulls him into a half-hug and claps him on the back. They part, both a little flushed with relief. Cal gives him a thumbs-up before turning away and crossing the courtroom towards his aunt, whose hands are clenched into fists. Isla is a taller, thinner, brown-haired version of Annie, like her and not like her all at once; something about her mannerisms, her voice, the expressions she uses. Cal is hugging her now, his eyes closed, his cheeks damp. Daisy Miller hovers nearby, crying buckets. They are overjoyed of course. It's a good result, the best. Ross would love to go and shake their hands, but it can wait. His eyes find Tom's and they nod their mutual acknowledgement: a job well done. Tom turns to watch the happy reunion, but he too is keeping his distance. For now, the moment belongs to the family.

Ross reaches Swanage after 6 p.m. A quick stop at the nick before going home. He might call in at The Square and Compass, he thinks, drink his own personal toast to the woman he has loved for over a decade. Annie Rawles – Annie, whose kiss he can still feel, whose skin he can still smell. She ran in his veins; she always will.

In the office, nothing that can't wait. It is over two months since the large brown envelope arrived on his desk, a little longer since his conversation with DI Hall, taking care to keep his tone supportive, conversational, and in no way interfering: a catch-up between coppers, anything she needed, don't hesitate, et cetera, et cetera. She needed nothing of course, though the ID of Annie Rawles' body was a ball-ache.

'No fingertips, and the dental records are a nightmare,' she went on. 'None in Swanage. Some long-gone practice up in Scotland, probably at the bottom of a loch.'

He bit down his offence on Annie's behalf, let her carry on. She'd sent to London for DNA. She was a big shot, using the latest methods.

'Pricey,' he'd said, good-humoured.

'At this stage it's cheaper and quicker than a wild goose chase for some dead dentist. Besides, the teeth were so fragmented I'm not sure they'd be much use anyway.'

'I suppose so.' He'd wished her luck, repeated his offer of help. 'Fax them over,' he added at the last second. 'I'll see what I can dig up.'

He was surprised when she did. Sure enough, there wasn't much to go on.

Conflict of interest. Vested interest. Love interest. Why get involved? Because he knew the lad. Wouldn't hurt a fly, as the saying goes. A phone call, a lap or two round the houses, a retired dentist long in the ground, an incredibly helpful dental assistant in Inveraray happy to check the archives, sir, no problem at all. A few weeks later, the large brown envelope addressed to DI York.

He waited till he was alone. Pulled out the records, compared them to the victim's. And smiled. A tough comparison but for the two front teeth. Annie's were close together. Despite the fracturing, the two front teeth on the deceased woman had a clear gap.

'Well, well,' he muttered to himself. 'Well, well, well.'

He'd known something was off, right from the start. Already he had a strong hunch as to who the body was. Dominic had been on and off with that musician, hadn't he? The woman with all the black eye make-up, the one from that party, the night he'd found Annie in her pyjamas in the dead of night, pretending not to cry by the duck pond. Ross had seen the woman a few nights before the murders, in Swanage, at the Black Swan. Eva something. Trouble, that was all he knew. So what happened? Was it Eva Dom used as a human shield? But who was he protecting himself from – Annie or Cal? Unless Dom himself killed her – violent towards his wife, no reason he wouldn't have been violent towards his lover; claimed to love women when in fact he hated them. Annie killed him, that much Ross knew – so did she kill him in a fight involving Eva? Rushed in to protect the other woman, only to find it was too late? And then Cal, hearing the commotion, finding his mum in an almighty mess, told her to go and took care of it, out of love?

He could ring the airport, he thought. Almost did. He'd know the name if he saw it on a flight record, could easily ask at the pub. He could track Annie down right now, bring her to justice and find out the truth once and for all.

But why would he do that? The one truth he knew above all others was that Annie and her boy were good people. Whatever happened, it would have been beyond their control.

A memory flashed: Annie, limping out onto the lane, clearly in terrible pain and distress but too proud to admit it. Dominic had beaten her and locked her in her studio like a dog. In all his life, Ross had never felt so helpless as he did in that moment. No matter how much he'd wanted to, he hadn't been able to save Annie Rawles from that bastard. God knows, he'd tried, but she wouldn't let him, never asked him for help, never told him the extent of it. And here he was, he thought as he slid the documents through the shredder, doing something he would never normally do, and it all came back, as it always did, to bloody Dominic Rawles pushing good people to do bad things – even in death.

Later, alone in the garden of The Square and Compass, Ross looks out over the fields to the sea and raises his glass in a private ceremony.

'To Annie,' he says. 'Rest in peace, my friend.'

A LETTER FROM S.E. LYNES

Thank you so much for reading *The One to Blame*; I really am over the moon that you did. If this is your first book by me, thank you for giving me a try and I hope you liked it enough to check out my others! If you've been with me since the beginning or have read my books before, thank you for coming back, thank you for sticking with me. I really do appreciate it and I love seeing my readership grow with each story. If you'd like to be the first to hear about my new releases, you can sign up using the link below. Your email address will never be shared and you can unsubscribe at any time.

www.bookouture.com/se-lynes

Those of you who have read my debut, *Valentina*, will have noticed that for *The One to Blame*, I have returned to Scotland and to fire! I lived in Scotland for many years, cannot wait to go back and visit my pals there once lockdown eases up, and I'm sure this beautiful country will feature again in my work. Once a place gets under your skin, it stays there.

My last book, *The Housewarming*, was written over the course of the first lockdown and was built on themes of community, personal responsibility and the interconnectedness of society – why how we behave matters. In this book, lockdown was there as the bedrock once again, this time in themes of painful separation, the loss of those we love and the longing to be reunited. Many of us have lost family and friends and perhaps even felt guilty and powerless to help family far away. I suppose Isla embodies that pain of separation, that guilt and that longing. You will know by now that she is reunited with her sister: a happy if imperfect ending, which I felt we all needed at this time!

The story was inspired by a true case history in which a woman who was abused for years by her husband both physically and emotionally one day cracked when he came home and demanded she make him a sandwich. Finding her hand around the knife handle, she returned to the living room and stabbed him several times. The story affected me because of the smallness of what made her break in the end, and how her body overtook her conscious mind, and with it all her fear.

There are several court scenes in this book. They are obviously an abridged version of how such a trial would go and subject to artistic licence due to the demands of having a fictional story to tell. I apologise for any details I didn't get one hundred per cent right.

I try to write my psychological suspense novels with as much psychological, emotional and physical authenticity as I can. I try to make my characters into people you feel you might know. I want you, the reader, to believe in these people and their messy hearts, their zigzag journeys towards fragile resolution. The ending of *The One to Blame* is not perfect, but then neither is life. I wanted to let you decide what happens next according to how you feel about the characters and the way things turned out. I'd love to know if you thought what they did was wrong; how far you believe you know how you would react if faced with something so traumatic. Would you break the law to protect someone you loved, if you knew they had been treated horribly for years? The pandemic has tested many of us – perhaps you have behaved in ways you never thought you would, or found strength you didn't know you had. I am always happy to hear readers' reactions and stories, and delighted to know that my work has transported you or moved you or even made you think, so do get in touch if you'd like, via my social-media links below.

Anyway, enough from me. My next book is well under way, and I so hope you will want to read that one too.

Best wishes and see you soon for another dark tale,
Susie

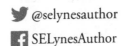

@selynesauthor
SELynesAuthor
@SELynesAuthor

ACKNOWLEDGEMENTS

First thanks go to my editor, Ruth Tross, the finest eraser to my pencil – you are so right so much of the time, it is really quite annoying but also great. To my agent, Veronique Baxter at David Higham Associates, thank you for your continued support and enthusiasm for my work, which shores me up in times of doubt.

Big love and thanks to Kim Nash, Noelle Holten and Sarah Hardy, the amazing publicity team at Bookouture, who do so much more than shout about us authors from the rooftops. Thank you to Jane Selley for another eagle-eyed copy-edit and to all the team at Bookouture – a diligent, committed and dynamic team I am proud to be a part of.

Huge thanks to Lizzie Cooper, an Inveraray lass, who talked to me about life growing up there, gave me some pithy phrases and sent me some stunning photos of the landscape in that beautiful part of Scotland.

Massive thanks to H.H. Phillip Matthews for reading through my court scenes, sighing, and maybe swearing a little under his breath before setting me on the right path. I could not have written it without you and I'm sorry for any mistakes left – they are mine alone.

Thanks so much to Dr Gavin Stark, who talked me through the route of the Five Sisters of Kintail. I gave you the further job of bandaging Annie's ankle, as you will see.

Thanks as ever to the amazing community of bloggers who review books for no fee whatsoever and shout about the stories they love. You know who you are. I salute each and every one of you and owe you all a pint.

Thanks to the Facebook Book Clubs – TBC, The Fiction Café, Motherload Book Club, Book Connectors, Bookmark, Crime Fiction Addict, and UK Crime Book Club.

Big, big thank you to the writing community – readers and authors alike. These friendships have been the biggest and most wonderful surprise on this whole crazy journey.

Thanks as ever to my first reader, my mum, Catherine Ball. I fixed the tobacco strand by the way – good spot. Tell Jan, yes, I nicked her beautiful hair but hey, she got a name check.

Thanks and big love to my husband, Paul, and my girls, Maddie and Franci, for getting me through a second lockdown with humour and grace, and for help with the laundry, the cooking and Saturday night dress-up dinners! And to my son, Ali, for bravely sticking it out over in Italy, living alone and far from home, working hard and staying bright on FaceTime with ever-increasing hair. All this has kept me cheerful and energised enough to write this, my second lockdown book.

CPSIA information can be obtained
at www.ICGtesting.com
Printed in the USA
BVHW031632080721
611454BV00003B/29